WHEN DUTY CALLS

Praise for these bestselling authors…

JOANNA WAYNE

"Joanna Wayne pens…nail-biting suspense
against a steamy backdrop…"
—*Romantic Times*

"…*Lone Star Lawman*
will keep the reader turning the pages…"
—Under the Covers Book Reviews

and

B.J. DANIELS

"B.J. Daniels spins a tight story full of suspects
and danger sure to keep you guessing."
—*Romantic Times* on *Hotshot P.I.*

"Interesting twists abound… *Hotshot P.I.*
is extremely satisfying romantic suspense."
—*Classic Journal*

JOANNA WAYNE

lives with her husband just a few miles from steamy, exciting New Orleans, but her home is the perfect writer's hideaway. A lazy bayou, complete with graceful herons, colorful wood ducks and an occasional alligator, winds just below her back garden. When not creating tales of spine-tingling suspense and heartwarming romance, she enjoys reading, traveling, playing golf and spending time with family and friends. Joanna believes that one of the special joys of writing is knowing her stories have brought enjoyment to or somehow touched the lives of her readers. You can write Joanna at P.O. Box 2851, Harvey, LA 70059-2851.

B.J. DANIELS

is a former award-winning journalist and the author of countless novels and short stories. Most of her books are set in Montana, where she lives with her husband, Parker; two springer spaniels, Zoey and Scout; and a temperamental tomcat named Jeff. Her first novel, *Odd Man Out*, was nominated for the *Romantic Times* Reviewer's Choice Award for best first book and best Harlequin Intrigue. Her book, *The Agent's Secret Child,* took second place in the National Reader's Choice Awards. When not writing, B.J. enjoys reading, camping and fishing, and snowboarding. Write to her at: P.O. Box 183, Bozeman, MT 59771.

JOANNA WAYNE

B.J. DANIELS

WHEN DUTY CALLS

HARLEQUIN®

TORONTO • NEW YORK • LONDON
AMSTERDAM • PARIS • SYDNEY • HAMBURG
STOCKHOLM • ATHENS • TOKYO • MILAN • MADRID
PRAGUE • WARSAW • BUDAPEST • AUCKLAND

HARLEQUIN BOOKS

by Request—WHEN DUTY CALLS

Copyright © 2003 by Harlequin Books S.A.

ISBN 0-373-23013-3

The publisher acknowledges the copyright holders
of the individual works as follows:

LONE STAR LAWMAN
Copyright © 1999 by Jo Ann Vest
HOTSHOT P.I.
Copyright © 1997 by Barbara Johnson Smith

This edition published by arrangement with Harlequin Books S.A.

Visit us at www.eHarlequin.com

Printed in U.S.A.

CONTENTS

LONE STAR LAWMAN
Joanna Wayne

Chapter One

Heather Lombardi jerked upright and gulped a breath of stale air. For a second, she didn't recognize her surroundings, but slowly her sense of place came back to her. She was in a dingy motel room in Dry Creek, Texas, hundreds of miles from her cozy apartment in Atlanta, Georgia.

She blinked, rubbed her eyes, then circled the room with her gaze. Pale moonlight filtered through the window, highlighting the shadowy images that crept across her walls. But in spite of the moonlight, the room was darker than usual. Evidently, the harsh outside light that had glared into her room for the last few nights had burned out.

A square of white caught her eye. She stumbled sleepily to the door and picked it up. Her mind still groggy, she tore open the sealed envelope and hurried back to the bed, flicking on the lamp so she could read the note.

Forget Kathy Warren and get out of town. Now. Leave before your welcome wears out and you find yourself wishing you'd never heard of her or Dry Creek.

It took a minute for the meaning to sink in. When it did, the words were still bewildering. There was no earthly reason why anyone should care if she stayed or left this town. She'd come here on a quest, in search of information about her real mother, the woman who'd given her up for adoption mere days after her birth twenty-five years ago. But so far no one she'd talked to admitted to having ever heard of Kathy Warren.

Heather reread the note, her mind struggling to make sense of the warning. She walked back to the window pushing hard to force it open. She needed fresh air to clear the last dregs of sleep and help her think rationally. The note was probably some teenaged prank, kids out of school for the summer and bored.

Minutes later, she closed and locked the window and went back to bed, jumping at the sound of the squeaky bedsprings beneath the impact of her hundred and twenty pounds. The truth was she'd like to heed the note. She was tired and more than a little homesick. She missed her apartment, missed her own soft bed, missed chatting with her friends.

But she couldn't give up and go running home. Not yet. Questions that had haunted her for a lifetime were still unanswered.

MATT MCQUAID shoved the white Stetson back on his head and let his booted foot grow heavy on the accelerator. A straight yellow line, miles of smooth Texas highway and two weeks of well-deserved vacation stretched out before him. Fence-mending, windmills to check, and some quality time getting to know his own small spread. At least small by South Texas standards.

He'd saved and bought the place while he was assigned to this area, but he'd been promoted last year, uprooted from his land and plopped down in a city apartment a hundred and thirty miles away.

San Antonio never quite felt like home, but he liked the job. So, he was left to commute every chance he got and scuff his boots on cement streets when he couldn't.

The Lone M, a plot of mesquite-dotted, drought-hardened dirt that beckoned to him like a pot of spicy chili on a cold Texas night. Not that anyone but him ever called it the Lone M. The other ranchers referred to it simply as ''McQuaid's country,'' an old South Texas usage, defining the land by the man who owned it. Matt didn't mind. Any name you called it, the wind blew free across wide-open spaces, and it was his.

Damn, but life was good.

No bloody crime scenes to be dissected. No district attorneys demanding evidence that didn't exist. Best of all, there would be no reporters in his face ragging him for information for the news media to twist and enlarge to suit their own purposes.

After the hellacious case he'd just wrapped up in San Antonio, nothing could be nicer than two weeks of conversing with nature and cud-chewing critters. Not that he'd ever willingly give up all the aggravation and challenge of being a Texas Ranger. Being a lawman was in his blood, as necessary as air or food.

Fingering the dial of his radio, he worked until a country song blared from the contraption. He rolled down the window of his pickup truck and sang along, enjoying the sting of the dry wind in his face and the sound of his own voice blending with the whining twang of the female singer. Another ballad of love gone bad. Woman trouble, one problem he didn't have now and had no intention of acquiring.

Matt slowed as he entered the town limits of Dry Creek. The sun hovered low on the horizon, making it difficult to see the road, but painting the shabby town in shades of gold and red that glistened off tin roofs and sparkled on iron cattle gaps. A fitting homecoming, he decided.

Matt turned into the drive of Ridgely's Feed and Hardware Store and parked between a tractor and John Billinger's new truck. He'd already stopped for groceries, but he needed to pick up some supplies so he could start work in the morning with the sun. He might as well let the locals know he was home for a couple of weeks while he was at it.

His boots clattered against the wooden boards of the porch and heralded his arrival even before he walked through the open door.

"Well, look who's back, the Texas Ranger who just stuck it to Clemson Creighton like a June bug to a screen door." Billinger's voice boomed across the store as Matt stepped into sight.

"Just doing my job, Billinger. Trying to make sure you Texans get what you pay for."

"Yep." Paul Ridgely spit a long stream of brown goop into a tin can and then stepped from behind the counter. He extended a hand. "Of course, it took a McQuaid to nail him. Those pretty boys up in San Antonio let the man walk around right under their noses for ten years. You done your pa proud, Matt."

Matt took Ridgely's callused hand and shook it firmly. "I'm sure Jake could have done it better and faster." The men laughed but nodded in agreement without guessing at the sarcasm that rode beneath the surface of Matt's words.

It had been almost a quarter of a century since Jake McQuaid had been sheriff around here, but his legend lived on. Who was Matt to disturb the image with suggestions of imperfection in their hero?

"Didn't much get by old Jake McQuaid," Billinger added. "So, you here for Logan Trenton's big shindig next weekend, or do you even aim to stay long enough to do a little honest labor?"

"Two weeks. Plenty of time to get my boots dirty." Matt hadn't known Logan Trenton was throwing a party. Now hat he did, he hoped he could escape an invitation. "I'm going to spend my time catching up at the ranch."

"Well, I hope you make enough time to come by the house," Billinger said. "I'm smoking some brisket tomorrow, and the wife would love to have you over. Might even bake up one of those apple pies for you and I'd get a piece of it. She's read another of those tomfool articles on cholesterol and heart attacks and has me eating my apples from around the core now."

"I don't know about your cholesterol, Billinger," Ridgely joked, "but that roll of fat around your middle ain't too appealing. She's probably tired of trying to reach around it."

"Don't you be worrying about my middle. I can handle my woman." He leaned over for a better look out the door. "Of course I don't know if I could handle one like that." He nodded his head in the direction of the door and a view of a compact rental car that had just pulled up in front of the greasy-spoon joint across the parking lot.

All three of the men watched as a shapely young woman climbed out. Her short, straight skirt inched up, revealing just enough thigh to assure the onlookers that her legs were as fine as the rest of her.

"Forget the apple pie," Billinger said, rocking back on his heels. "Just watching that woman walk has my blood pressure soaring. She's too much for me, but I bet the Ranger here could handle a woman like that."

"Don't count on it." Matt studied the woman with the practiced eye of a man who had built a reputation of never missing a detail. Her hair was sandy blond, bouncing about her shoulders as she walked. The blue suit fit her to perfection, simple, but probably expensive, and the shoes on her feet would never make it in a cow pasture. Her skin

was creamy smooth and not bronzed by the South Texas
sun.

To sum it up, she was as much out of place in Dry Creek
as quiche at a Texas barbecue.

"What do you say, Matt? Is that a looker or what?"

"She's not my style," Matt said, pulling his eyes away
from her with a severe expression.

"Maybe not, but my guess is you're going to get a
chance to get up close and personal before you leave
town," Billinger said. "Then you can find out for yourself
if she's your style."

"How's that?" Matt asked, hating to admit even to himself that the woman had aroused his curiosity.

"She's been questioning everyone in town. Seems her
momma ran out on her when she was just a baby, and now
she's looking for her."

"Who was her mother?" Matt asked, in spite of himself.

"A woman by the name of Kathy Warren. Ever heard of
her?"

"Nope." Matt turned his attention to a notice of an upcoming auction.

"No one else in town has either," Ridgely said, still
standing and staring even though the woman under discussion had already disappeared behind the doors of the café.
He scratched a bald spot on the back of his round head. "I
think she's barking up the wrong tree. I've lived in Dry
Creek all my life, and if a woman good-looking enough to
birth a young'un like that had come around even for a little
while, I'd dang sure remember her."

"Someone would anyway," Billinger agreed. "This
town is short on pretty women and long on memory. All
the same, I can't help but feel sorry for Miss Lombardi. It's
got to be tough knowing your mom just walked off and
never came back. I can see why she'd want to find her."

Matt let the subject lie. Life was tough, and Miss Lombardi should have learned that by now. Mothers *did* just walk away, and maybe they had their reasons. Or maybe they didn't. Either way the kids they left behind didn't get a vote in the matter. "Do you still run a store here, Ridgely, or is this just gossip central?" he asked, pulling his list from his pocket.

"I'll take your money," Ridgely said, his deep laughter rumbling through the store as he stole a peek at Matt's list.

"Yeah," Billinger threw in, "but if you were half smart, you'd be next door about now offering to help out a damsel in distress. You might just get lucky and wind up with a real looker like your dad did. They don't make many like Miss Susan, but that Heather Lombardi might run her a close second."

"You're right. They don't make many like Susan Hathaway." Matt gave one last look out the door. "But I'll leave luck alone tonight and settle for supplies."

"Yeah, well, I'd say you'll be spending your luck tonight on a full moon with nothing but the wailing of coyotes to keep you company." Billinger fingered a can of mosquito repellent someone had left on the counter. "Personally, if I were in your boots, single, available and some hotshot Texas Ranger, I'd be finding a way to share that moon with Miss Lombardi."

"Chasing down a long-lost mother? No, thanks. I'm on vacation. I'll stick with rounding up cows. They're a lot less trouble."

"I agree with Matt," Ridgely said, already walking toward the back of the store to get the first item on Matt's list. "He don't need to go messing around with the likes of Miss Lombardi. Women like that are nothing but trouble."

The door swung open and a couple of hands from a

neighboring spread walked in. Billinger started a new conversation, and Matt caught up with Paul Ridgely. A few minutes later, Matt was loading supplies and some sacks of feed onto the back of his truck. Delicious odors drifted from the café, and his stomach gnawed at his backbone, fussing about the fact that he'd missed lunch.

He glanced at his watch. It was already seven-thirty. If he ate in town, he wouldn't have to bother with cooking tonight. He knew just what he wanted: a big, juicy hamburger, smothered in sautéed onions and dripping with mustard and mayo.

Ridgely and Billinger would notice him walking into the café and make a few salty comments about his chasing after the slick city woman, but he could take their good-natured ribbing.

Heather Lombardi, or whoever the heck she was, held no fascination for him beyond the fact that she was a gorgeous woman. He could look and enjoy without the need to own or even to rent. After all, he knew his limitations and his strengths. And right now, he had life in the palm of his hand, just the way he liked it. He didn't need a thing.

HEATHER NURSED HER CUP of after-dinner coffee and watched as the young señorita poured a tall glass of iced tea for the newest cowboy to enter the café. The girl lingered to flirt and he rewarded her efforts with a crooked smile guaranteed to set a young heart fluttering.

The effect on Heather was somewhat milder, but she had to admit the man was attractive. His face was a mixture of rugged planes and distinct angles, but the overall impression was both masculine and distinctly Texan, that indefinable quality that separated him and his cronies in town from the few urban cowboys she'd met growing up in the big city.

Heather stared at the man, struck by a sudden impulse. Joining strangers at their table wasn't her usual style, but at this point she didn't have much to lose. Another wasted day was coming to a close. She picked up her coffee cup and headed his way before she had a chance to change her mind.

"Mind if I join you for a few minutes?" she asked, sliding into the seat on the opposite side of the table.

"Looks like you already have."

"I can leave again."

"Why would you? I figure you have a reason for being here or you wouldn't have bothered coming over."

He caught her off guard, had her fumbling in her mind for something to say. "Are you always so direct?"

"Pretty much. It saves a lot of trouble." He stuck out a hand. "Matt McQuaid," he said, wrapping his palm around hers and shaking it firmly. "And you must be the famous Ms. Lombardi."

She grimaced. "So, my reputation precedes me. I'm afraid I've made a pest of myself around Dry Creek the last few days."

"I don't think pest is the right word, but you've gotten a little attention."

And not all of it good. Heather slid her fingers into her pocket and touched the note that rested there.

"Is this business or pleasure?" The man's tone bordered on intimidation, but he followed the question with the same easy smile he'd flashed the waitress.

Heather plunged in. "Business."

"Too bad. I thought I was about to be picked up."

A blush burned her cheeks. "Not tonight, cowboy. At least, not by me, but I would like to ask you a few questions."

"That would have been my second guess."

His gaze bit into her, a penetrating stare that left her feeling exposed. She took a breath and continued. "I'm trying to find out about a woman named Kathy Warren. I don't know much about her except that she was last seen in Dry Creek twenty-five years ago. She would have probably been in her early twenties at the time."

"I would have been a young kid then. What makes you think *I* might know something?"

"Desperation," she finally answered. "So far I've hit nothing but dead ends in my search, and I noticed that everyone in the café knows you."

His eyes narrowed. "So you just came right over to my table with your questions?"

"I didn't think it would hurt to ask you. Apparently I was wrong." She scooted to the outside edge of the booth.

"No, wait." He took her hand and tugged, keeping her from standing. "I didn't mean to offend you. I'm just not good at small talk."

"So I noticed."

The waitress interrupted, setting a plate of food in front of Matt. He caught Heather's gaze. "Would you like something?" he asked.

She took the offer as an invitation to stay. The sandwich she'd eaten was more than enough to fill her, but dessert would buy her more time with the cowboy. His attitude needed adjustment, but, after all, she wasn't interested in friendship, just facts.

"I'll have a piece of the cherry pie," she said, "with a cup of decaf."

Matt bit into his hamburger as the waitress moved on to the next table. "Tell me about Kathy Warren," he said, when he'd finished the bite of burger and taken a long drag on his iced tea.

"She was my birth mother. She left me at an orphanage in Dimmit County when I was just a few days old."

He ate and chewed, taking his time before continuing the conversation. "And you think your mother ended up around here?"

"A woman from the orphanage said she gave Kathy a ride into Dry Creek and let her off at the bus station. I've searched and searched, but there's no record of her after that night."

"So Kathy Warren rode into the sunset and disappeared, probably just the way she'd planned." He looked her square in the eye. "She gave you up. It happens. So why go against her wishes to have you out of her life at this late date?"

The chill in the cowboy's tone caught Heather off guard. Despite his casual demeanor, he'd seemed friendly enough. But now the temperature at the table seemed to have suddenly changed. "You don't waste a lot of effort on sympathy, do you?"

"I didn't know you were looking for sympathy. I thought you were chasing around Texas looking for your mother. I can think of better ways to waste your time."

"Wrong. I'm not looking for my birth mother. She died years ago. I just thought it would be nice to have some closure, to make contact with members of my biological family. But I shouldn't have bothered you with my problems." She jumped to her feet.

"What about your pie?"

"You eat it. My treat for wasting your precious time." She took a few bills from her purse and threw them onto the table. "Have a pleasant night, Mr. McQuaid, if you're capable of that."

Matt watched her march out of the café, her head high, her back straighter than a fence post. She was angry with him. The fact didn't make him feel particularly good. Actually, it ground in his stomach and stole his appetite away.

But if his unsympathetic comments got Heather Lombardi off her mission of recreating the past, he'd probably done her a favor. Fairy-tale endings were the stuff children's books were made of, not real life.

Still, he had to admit, Billinger might have been right. Heather Lombardi in the moonlight would have made for some interesting memories.

MATT SLOWED HIS TRUCK as a couple of deer stepped from the bushes into the glow of his headlights. Experience had taught him the animals could bolt without warning, dashing into the highway and causing havoc for themselves and the vehicle that hit them. But this time the animals played it smart. They turned and loped back into the gathering darkness.

Matt looked in the direction they'd fled as he passed the spot. No sign of movement, but he caught sight of a car, pulled off into the tangle of brush a few yards from the road. Probably young lovers looking for a bit of privacy.

But maybe not.

Matt cursed the lawman instincts that kept him from driving by without investigating. He slowed and guided the truck into a U-turn. Minutes later, he'd located the spot, or at least close to it. He brought his truck to a stop on the hard dirt shoulder of the road.

The gate the car had probably used was at least fifty yards down the road. Undaunted, Matt grabbed a flashlight, ducked between the rows of barbed wire and tramped through the brush. His beam of light roamed the area in search of the car he'd spotted earlier.

He was about to call out when a loud male voice shattered the quiet. ''Somebody's coming. We gotta get out of here.''

Someone was clearly up to no good. Of all times for him to be without his gun. Matt had just about convinced himself to go back for it when the beam of illumination from his flashlight found the car he'd seen originally. Proximity and a brighter light added dimension and color to the vehicle. Small, white, identical to the one Heather Lombardi had driven away from the café in only a few minutes before he had.

Adrenaline pumped into Matt's bloodstream, and he took off at a run. An engine roared to life in the distance just as he reached the white car. He looked up, but all he saw was the glow of headlights darting through the brush to the west of him. Cautiously, he turned back to the car, swung the door open and peered inside.

His stomach turned at the sight.

Chapter Two

Heather Lombardi was slumped over the steering wheel. Her jacket was torn and Matt could see blood on one of her hands. He reached inside the car and gripped her upper arm.

"Leave me alone, you ape!" She kicked at him and jerked away from his grasp.

Her voice shook with pain and a fighting spirit that pulled at Matt's control. He ached to pound his fists into whoever had done this to her. He was far more adept at that than tending the wounded.

"Settle down. I'm not going to hurt you."

Her eyes widened in recognition. "Oh, it's you, cowboy." She rubbed a jaw that was already swelling into an ugly mass. "How did you get here?"

"Pure luck. The real question is how did you get here?"

"I had help." She shuddered. "Two nasty men." She looked around nervously.

"Take it easy. You're safe for the time being, and you can fill me in on the details later. Right now, I want to get you out of this car and into my truck."

"No, I'm not going off with you. I don't know you any better than I knew those guys. Just call the cops, or the sheriff, or whatever it is you have out here."

"If that's the way you want it." He backed away from the car. It took her about two seconds and one brief glance into the darkness to change her mind.

"Okay, I'll go with you." She scooted across the seat, groaning all the way.

"Here, let me help you." He tucked an arm under hers and tugged.

Her groans dissolved into a string of mild curses, mostly aimed at the cowards who'd attacked her. Matt helped her out of the car, and she leaned against him, her bruised body weak and shaky.

"Where to?" she managed.

"It's just a few yards to my truck, but I don't think you're going to make it on foot." He swept her into his arms and was amazed at how light she was. He started off through the brush, frightening a jackrabbit and sending it hopping out of his path.

"You don't have to carry me," she protested, though with little conviction.

"I know. I could let you crawl, but I don't have all night."

"Wait! Go back."

"Don't tell me you changed your mind again."

"No, I need my purse."

"Do you think it's still there?"

"Why not? This wasn't a robbery. It was a scare tactic by some of your friendly townsfolk who don't like strangers." She groaned again. "So much for Texas hospitality."

Matt turned and headed back to the truck. "You must be real special," he said, possibilities bucking around in his head like a spooked pony. "I don't remember hearing about any welcoming parties like this around here since…" Memories rushed his mind. He pushed them back. "Not since I was a kid," he finished.

"Yeah, I'm special, all right."

Matt propped her against the fender of her car while he dug in the back seat for her purse. Sure enough, it was there, and didn't appear to have been touched. The plot definitely thickened. He slung the handbag across his shoulder and started to pick Heather up again.

She straightened on her own. "No, thanks, cowboy. My head's all but quit spinning. I can walk, if you'll just share an arm for support."

"Whatever you want." He led her through the brush, guiding her around a prickly cactus. He had a thousand questions, but he'd let her regain her equilibrium before he bombarded her with them. He opened the door of the truck and gave her a boost as she climbed inside. "The nearest hospital is forty-five miles from here. I'll call for an ambulance to meet us in town."

"No, I just need a lift back to my motel room in Dry Creek. Actually, I'm feeling stronger every minute. I think I could drive my own car and not put you to any more trouble."

She leaned her head against the back of the seat and closed her eyes. "Or maybe not. The stupid jerk with the taco breath slapped me so hard I saw double for a minute or two. And one of him was more than enough."

Matt turned the key and started the engine. It purred to perfection, and he pulled onto the road. "Can you identify the men?"

"I don't think so. They wore masks. One of them should have my nail prints imbedded in his stomach, though, and he won't be walking too straight after where my knee caught him."

Matt smiled in spite of himself. Miss Lombardi was clearly tough as well as gorgeous. But he was starting to have his doubts about her story of a search for a long, lost mother. Her appeal to men who beat up women and didn't bother taking their cash suggested that Miss Lombardi might have a few secrets of her own.

"How did you happen to be on this deserted stretch of highway?" he asked, after they'd driven in silence for a few minutes.

"Not by choice. I was kidnapped back in Dry Creek by one of the men. He was waiting in the back seat floor of my car when I left the café."

"You better start locking your doors."

"The drivers of half of the cars in the parking lot had left their windows down to combat the heat. I stupidly followed the example of the natives, especially since there were plenty of people around." She pushed a tangle of hair back from her bruised face. "The man drove me here in my car and then another goon jumped out of the bushes. I thought it was my car they wanted. My second major mistake of the night."

"The second man must have been driving the vehicle they got away in. I heard it start up just before I got to you, but I only caught a quick glimpse. I don't suppose you got a look at it."

"I didn't even hear the engine. My ears were ringing from being slapped around."

Matt beat an irritated fist against the steering wheel. "A simple carjacking turned ugly. Only we don't have carjackings in Dry Creek." He was thinking out loud, but Heather jumped on his statement.

"Do you think I'm lying about this?"

"No. I'm just saying there's a lot more to this than is floating on the surface of the water barrel."

"Yeah, like someone in your town doesn't like visitors."

He drove in silence for the next few minutes, his mind buzzing and coming up with nothing. Finally, he turned off at a dirt road. Grinding to a stop, he swung open his truck door so he could get out and unlatch the gate.

Heather opened her eyes. "Where in the hell are we now?"

"My place."

"Now, wait a minute. I'm thankful for the rescue, but not so thankful I'm planning on giving up any of my virtue."

"Good. I'd hate to have to settle for entertainment from someone in the shape you're in. But since you're not willing to go to the hospital, you'll have to withstand my first aid. A little liniment and some peroxide for that nasty cut over your eye."

Heather feathered the cut with her fingers. With the rest of her body aching like crazy, she hadn't noticed the bloody cut. "You're not planning on using cow liniment, are you?"

"No, that stuff's too expensive to waste on women."

"Very funny."

Matt took care of the gate duties, and they headed down the road toward the small cabin that had come with the land. "What do you do when you're not searching for long-lost relatives?" he asked.

"I work in the public relations department for a television station."

"So who relates to the public while you roam around Texas?"

"Probably someone vying for my job. I'm on vacation."

She turned to face him, this time without groaning, but her face was more than slightly misshapen, and her right eye was practically swollen shut.

"Are you sure you don't want to see a doctor?" he asked, grimacing at the sight. "You look like a rodeo clown who didn't escape the bull."

"Thank you. And, yes, I'm sure. Ice and aspirin will be fine. They just slapped me around a little." She squirmed and peeked under a stack of papers that occupied the seat space between them.

"Looking for something?"

"A phone. I'd like to report this incident to the authorities."

"You've already done that."

"I beg your pardon."

"You're talking to the law, not a local authority, but the law all the same. I'm with the Texas Rangers. My office is in San Antonio."

"Oh, jeeez. Rescued by a Texas Ranger. They'll love this story back at home." She stretched her neck, rubbing the back of it with agitated strokes. "You're a long way from the office."

"It's a small world. I'm on vacation, too."

"I don't know about you, but this wasn't part of my itinerary." She shifted and moaned again. "I'll rest at your place for a few minutes, but then we have to go back for my car. It's a rental. The insurance company would frown on my leaving it parked it the middle of nowhere overnight."

"It won't be. I plan to have it picked up by the sheriff and dusted and checked for prints, and I want the crime scene checked for any available evidence."

"Didn't I mention that my attackers wore gloves?"

"No. What kind of gloves?"

"Leather. Not the dressy kind, the kind you might work in. They didn't look new. What do you expect to find, other than prints?"

"I'll take what we can get. A piece of clothing would be nice or some unusual tire prints from the other car. That, with any information you can give us, might help identify at least one of the perps.''

''I'll help all I can. I want these men caught and prosecuted, although I'm sure they meant for me to be too afraid to report the attack. They said as much.''

''I'm glad you're not. The sheriff and I will both want to hear all the details and the truth about why you're *really* in Dry Creek. Then maybe we can figure out why someone around here, or a couple of someones, wants to get rid of you.''

Heather tracked a spot over her left temple where another pain was throbbing to life. ''Do you want the story about how I'm a Mafia princess on the run or the one where I'm wanted for spying in twelve countries?''

''I want the truth.''

''You've already heard it. Sorry, Matt McQuaid, Texas Ranger, but I'm just a woman tracing her roots. But I'd still like to take you up on that liniment and the strongest pain reliever you've got. I have a feeling things are going to get worse before they get better.''

''Funny. I have that same feeling.''

Matt pulled the truck to a stop in the carport and climbed out. He hadn't been at the ranch house in over a month. He couldn't remember how he'd left it, though he doubted it was ready for company. But it couldn't be any worse than the one dilapidated motel in Dry Creek, and besides, as long as Heather was with him, she wouldn't have to worry about a repeat visit from her wrecking crew.

The thought of any man dirty enough to use a woman for a punching bag ground in his gut. He expected her to be all right except for some nasty bruises and sore muscles, but if he hadn't arrived the story might have been tragically different. What they'd told her about not wanting to kill her wouldn't have mattered. He'd seen it happen too many times before. Attacks, fueled by anger and power, that escalated into murder.

Two big men against one petite woman. Dirty cowards any way you looked at it. Now all he had to do was find the scum who were responsible and make sure they paid their full dues. That, and keep Miss Heather Lombardi safe.

The woman would be nothing but trouble. He'd suspected it from the moment he'd watched her sashay into the café. Now he was sure of it. He could kiss his peaceful vacation goodbye.

A BRIEF STRUGGLE with the key and the back door squeaked open. "It's not much, but it's home," Matt said, ushering his guest inside, "at least when I'm lucky enough to get back here."

Heather leaned against the door frame and gave the place a cursory once-over. She'd seen worse. They'd entered the back door, passing through the laundry area and into a small kitchen. Nothing fancy, but cozy, with a wooden table and several chairs. Not all of them matched, but they were sturdy and seemed to fit the ranch house's sparse but functional decor.

There were clean dishes in a drainer at the side of the sink, and some glass canning jars filled with preserves on the counter. Somehow she doubted Ranger Matt had put up the preserves himself. She didn't have him figured out yet, but he was a far cry from the Martha Stewart image.

Manhandling criminals probably fit his persona better. She hoped to get a chance to find out by watching him arrest the hoodlums who had worked her over.

"We'll get you fixed up in no time," he said, guiding her through the kitchen and into a den that reeked of masculinity. Dark leather covered the well-worn chairs and couch, and heads of animals glared at her from their positions on the walls. A pair of boots rested on the hearth, and one lamp and a supply of newspapers and magazines covered the end table.

"Sit here," he said, motioning toward the couch. "I'll get the ice and then tend that cut on your forehead."

She eased to a sitting position, tugging her skirt down as best she could and pulling her blouse together. The top two buttons were missing, and a jagged tear revealed more than a scrap of her bra.

"Do you live alone?" she called over the serenade of cracking ice in the kitchen.

"What gave me away, the dust or the curtainless windows?"

"Neither, but I don't see a wife appearing to check out the injured stray you brought home."

"There's no wife."

He returned a second later with a contraption that resembled a sling, a couple of tubes of antiseptic and a brown bottle of something that probably burned like the jalapeños she'd eaten in her enchiladas at lunch.

He eased to the couch beside her and tilted her face upwards. His hands were big, strong and weathered by the sun, but he surprised her with the gentleness of his touch.

"You must have taken a couple of power punches to this cheek."

"I did. The man who drove my car slapped me across the face. I tried to fight back. I poked a finger in the other man's eyes, and that's when he landed the first blow with his fist."

"What about the rest of your body? Did they hit you in the stomach or chest? If there are internal injuries..." His eyes fell to the tear in her blouse. "They didn't..."

She read the new fury, hot and dark in his eyes. "No, they didn't rape me. My blouse must have gotten torn in the skirmish." She bent down and rubbed her legs. "I did get kicked in the shins, but I think I got in a pretty good kick myself. You must have shown up about then. One guy was dragging me out of the car. I glimpsed lights in the distance, and they took off running."

"Don't worry. They won't be able to run fast enough or far enough to get away permanently."

"Sure of yourself, aren't you. Do you always get your man?"

"Sooner or later." Matt took the sling and tied it around her head as if she had a toothache. "I made a pouch for the ice. It should slow the swelling in the jaw. I have another one for the eye, but you'll have to hold it in place. Before you do, I need to doctor the cut." He propped a pillow behind her head. "Lean back and try to relax. This will probably burn a little."

"I knew you'd say that. And men use the term *a little* so loosely when the pain doesn't apply to them."

"Okay, it will probably burn a lot." He dabbed the spot with liquid from the bottle.

She flinched, but didn't complain. "Does it need stitches?"

"No, it's not deep, just jagged. I don't know what caused the cut, so we have to make sure it's sterilized."

"A belt buckle, I think. I caught the edge of it against my head when I was clawing and trying to get away."

"I'd say you're a pretty spunky woman to keep fighting when the odds were two to one."

"I didn't know the cavalry was on the way."

"You should have. This *is* Texas, after all."

"Yeah, right." She grimaced as he smoothed some salve across the cut. Her whole face was a mass of tender, painful flesh, but the burning had stopped. "I'll owe you one for this, cowboy."

"No, you don't owe me anything, except enough answers to help us find and arrest the guilty. I called Gabby from the kitchen. He should be here any minute, so I'll hold my questions until then rather than make you do double duty."

"Gabby?"

"The sheriff, and you'll find out soon enough that his nickname is well-earned."

His gaze fell to the torn blouse again, and her hand flew up to hide the exposed cleavage.

"I can get you one of my shirts," he offered.

"I'd appreciate that. And then you can point me to the bathroom."

"Sure."

He disappeared down the hall and returned a few minutes later with a blue broadcloth shirt, Western-style, with snaps instead of buttons.

"The bathroom is the second door on the left. If you need anything, let me know. There are washcloths in the cabinet under the sink."

Heather stood up. Her legs wobbled, and she grabbed the wooden arm of the couch for support. Matt was beside her in an instant, steadying her with a strong arm. She let herself lean against him for a few seconds, absorbing his strength.

"We can still go to the hospital," he said, his gaze scrutinizing her closely, no doubt searching for clues she was in worse shape than she'd admitted.

"Thanks, but no thanks. I'm in no mood to be jabbed, poked and prodded by an emergency room intern, not after what I've been through tonight." She straightened and took a step that was less wobbly. Feeling more secure, she started down the hall, aware of the concern in Matt's eyes as he watched her every move.

He puzzled her. At the restaurant, he'd been distant and

cool, but here at his house, he was warm and nurturing. Maybe he performed best in the role of hero. Or maybe, she thought wryly, it was her charm that was winning him over.

She stepped into the bathroom and flicked on the light. Leaning across the sink, she glimpsed her image in the mirror and then recoiled in misery. No wonder the Ranger thought she needed a doctor. She might have suggested an undertaker herself. Gingerly, she guided her fingers to the purple-rimmed eye and the pulpy flesh around it.

It had to be that Matt was at home in the hero role, she decided. She had about as much sexual appeal as the Bride of Frankenstein. She readjusted her icy sling so that she could check out the bruises to her jaw. The sight was equally grotesque.

And all of this just because she'd asked a few questions about Kathy Warren, a woman who'd passed through town twenty-five years ago.

Forget Kathy Warren and get out of town.

She'd been ordered to do that twice now. The second warning had been brutal. But Kathy Warren must have been a very hardheaded woman, because Heather had definitely inherited that trait from someone. She didn't like threats, and she didn't scare easily. Left alone, she might have eventually given up and left town when no one remembered her mother. Now, she'd be staying.

She didn't understand it, but the longing she had lived with for as long as she could remember, the need to know who she really was and where she'd come from, had never been stronger than it was tonight.

HEATHER SAT AT THE kitchen table and focused her one open eye on Gabby as he studied the note she'd handed him. ''It was delivered to me at the motel, stuffed under my door while I was sleeping," she explained. "The manager said he hadn't seen anyone around there, but security at that place is nonexistent."

The sheriff refolded the note. "We don't usually have trouble down at the motel. Old Rube don't even have paying guests too often anymore."

"No trouble at the motel. No attacks on women. This town was a regular haven before I came along." She didn't try to hide the sarcasm. She was tired, physically and emotionally, from the events of the night *and* the last half hour of redundant interrogation.

Besides, she didn't like the way the sheriff had been phrasing his questions. She was the victim, not the criminal, but she wasn't at all sure he saw it that way.

"Now don't get all riled, Miss Lombardi. I plan to check everything out. It's just that we don't go fixing fences down here till we know what broke 'em in the first place."

He stood, grabbing his hat from the chair beside him as he did and setting it on his head. "You're a nice woman, and all the talk I've heard around here since you drove into town is how everyone wishes they could help you out. Now all of a sudden, you got someone gunning for you, so to speak. It just don't add up."

"So it must be my fault?"

"I didn't say that."

Matt leaned into the table. "We're not suggesting it's your fault, Heather. We're just trying to make sense of this." He spread his hands as if making a point. "You've come to town looking for a woman who you said passed through here twenty-five years ago. It appears that no one in the area's ever heard of her, and yet you received a note mentioning her by name and warning you to leave town. Now you've been attacked, apparently to put teeth in the warning."

She shook her head in frustration, and pain shot up her neck, settling in under her swollen eye. "I know it sounds bizarre, but I'm telling the truth."

"And you're sure this Kathy Warren you're asking about is dead?"

"It was reported to the authorities at the orphanage, my birth mother died a few months after I was abandoned. Shortly after that, I was adopted." Frustration was threatening to push her over the edge. She'd said all this before.

Matt scribbled more notes in a small black notebook. "Who reported the death?" he asked, turning his face toward her.

"I'm not sure. The woman I talked to thought he might have been my mother's brother."

"Seems like your uncle would've just taken you with him," the sheriff said, his eyebrows raised. "Him being family and all."

"I don't know any of the circumstances. The woman who left me at the orphanage said I was her child but that she couldn't take care of me. She signed away all rights of parenthood."

Gabby stopped at the door. "Looks like you shoulda left well alone, little lady. I'd think seriously about just clearing out of Dry Creek and letting this die down if I were you."

"All I'm trying to do is track down my family, discover my roots. That's not unusual."

"I suppose not. I saw a TV show about that one time," Gabby admitted. "Some girl looked for years and then found her mother living two blocks away. But just looking for your mom's family shouldn't cause you to get beat up."

"Thank you," she said. "When you find the men who did it, I suggest you ask them their reasons."

He squared his shoulders. "Oh, I plan to find out exactly

what's going on. And if this Kathy Warren was around here, I'll find that out, too.''

"I think we've questioned Heather enough for tonight," Matt broke in, moving over to stand behind her chair. "Why don't you call me as soon as you get a fingerprint report off the car?''

Gabby stood and ambled toward the door. "Yeah, I'll do that, though I doubt we find anything, them wearing gloves and all.''

"Check it anyway. One of the gloves might have slipped off in the fray.''

Gabby scratched his whiskered chin. "I can give you a ride back into town, Miss Lombardi. I'm going that way.''

"Miss Lombardi's staying here tonight.''

Heather spun around to face Matt. "That won't be necessary. I'm fine now.''

"It's necessary. I wouldn't have said it if it weren't.''

She stared at him. He was neither smiling nor frowning. He just made the statement and expected her to go along with it. The man was clearly far too used to having the final say, but she wasn't under his control.

She stood and faced him. "What makes it necessary? The attack is over and done with. Surely the men wouldn't dare show up again. Besides, they said they were only supposed to rough me up, and they've already done that.''

"Criminals have been known to lie.''

As far as Matt was concerned, that was the end of the discussion. She could read the finality in his tone and his eyes. She was tempted to insist that she was capable of making her own decisions about where she spent the night, but the truth of Matt's statement held her back.

She had been no match for the two men, especially the older one. It was as if she could feel the evil inside him when he'd slapped her, and it had been his hand that had ripped her blouse. She trembled, remembering the fear, a black cloud of sickening smoke that had rolled in her stomach and filled her lungs as she tried to fight them off.

She struggled for a calming breath and forced the fear to subside. She needed a clear head. Besides, she was safe here with Matt McQuaid. The Ranger was handsome, strong, and apparently as hardheaded as she was. What more could a woman want?

"How's that jaw?" he asked, closing the door behind the sheriff.

"Sore, like the rest of me. You should have asked me about spending the night before you announced that I would."

"I don't like to offer choices when none exist. You need watching over tonight. I'm available, though it wasn't the way I'd planned to spend my first night home."

And that was it. Matter-of-fact. Cut and dried. No "I'm glad to be of service." No wonderful, witty, heroic phrases. Just "I'm available." Matt McQuaid was the epitome of a Texas lawman. All action, few words.

For some reason, she didn't find his manner as offensive as she should have. It was almost comforting on one hand, and more than a little seductive on the other. Oh, well, when in Rome...

"Since I'm here for the night, I think I'll turn in. Which bedroom do you want me to use?"

"That's easy," he said, finally smiling. "There's only one."

Chapter Three

Matt hesitated and then knocked on the door. In spite of claiming she was too tired to talk, Heather hadn't turned off the bedroom light.

"Come in."

He did and then stared at the waif of a woman propped up on his pillows. His T-shirt, bleached to a snowy white, fell loosely off one slender shoulder, revealing silky, ivory-colored flesh. He fought the surprising twinges of arousal that crept through his muddled mind and weary body.

Just fatigue, he told himself, from weeks spent working night and day, falling into bed only after he'd become so tired he could no longer function intelligently. Weeks of doing what he did best, digging through a cavern of lies and cover-up to discover the ugly truths hidden there.

Now, he would be at it again. The sheriff had just called, and what he'd had to say added more fuel to Matt's suspicions. Heather Lombardi, if that was in fact her name, was beautiful and intriguing, but his hunch was she was only skirting the truth with her story about looking for her mother.

"That was the sheriff on the phone," he said, crossing the room and standing over her bed.

"Does he have my car?"

"Yeah. And a little surprise."

"What kind of surprise?" Her eyebrows rose questioningly, pulling the swollen face into a shape that resembled lumpy oatmeal. Even that didn't diminish her appeal. It was her eyes, Matt decided, that pulled so determinedly at his resolve.

"There was an explosive device attached to the engine of your car."

She jerked to a sitting position. "What are you saying, Matt?"

"When the sheriff and his deputy were checking out your car, they found a device that was set to explode when you keyed the ignition. Fortunately, the bomb didn't detonate. If it had, you would have missed the pleasure of being kidnapped and beaten."

"I don't understand."

"It's simple. Someone tried to blow up your car with you in it."

"I understand that part." Her gray eyes were clouded, her voice shaky. "It's the who and why I can't comprehend. When was the bomb planted? Surely not at the restaurant. There were people around. And the men that kidnapped me didn't mess with the engine."

"Where else did you go today?"

She ran her fingers through her tousled hair. "I was at the motel, at the bank, the library." A sigh escaped her lips. "And I drove out to St. Michael's this afternoon."

"What were you doing out there?"

"I wanted to talk to the priest about Kathy Warren, but he wasn't there."

"How long was the car unattended?"

"About half an hour. I left the car and walked to the cemetery behind the chapel. Maybe that was long enough, though I didn't see or hear anyone." Heather squeezed her eyes shut, but not so tight that a lone tear didn't escape and slide down her cheek.

Matt dabbed at it with a tissue from the box on the bedside table. She opened her eyes and stared at him, shock and fear stripping away the air of independence she usually wore so well.

The room seemed to grow warm, and Matt backed away, suddenly aware of her nearness. Aware of the need to take her in his arms and comfort her. His muscles tightened in response to the unfamiliar urges, and he shoved clenched fists deep into his pockets. "I'm sorry, Heather."

"Me, too." She shook her head. "When the bomb didn't explode, the goons must have decided to come after me themselves. But it doesn't add up. They said they weren't supposed to kill me."

"You'll have to help me find the men. That's the only way we'll get answers."

"Then we're in big trouble. I already told you I can't identify them. They were muscular and dressed in jeans, Western shirts and black boots. That description would fit ninety percent of the men I've met in Dry Creek."

"If witness identification is impossible, we have to look for motive and opportunity," he said, easing down to perch on the edge of the bed.

She scooted over to make room for him. "Someone wants me to leave town. That appears to be motive enough in Dry Creek. As I said before, it's a real friendly town you have here, Ranger McQuaid."

He rubbed the stubble on his chin, making a mental note to shave in the morning, a chore he frequently omitted when he was on vacation at the ranch. But then, he didn't usually have house guests.

"For the most part the people around here are extremely friendly to strangers," he said. "Especially ones who look like you. The men around here are strutting like stud horses at the sight of you. The last thing they want is for you to hightail it out of here.''

"That may be true for most of the people, but someone is ready to kill to get rid of me, and all because I asked a few questions about a woman no one claims to remember.''

Matt stood and walked to the window. "Someone remembers her. It's what they remember about her that concerns me. I'll find out, one way or another, but you could simplify matters by telling me the whole truth.''

"Do you have a hearing problem or just a mental block? I *have* told you the truth.''

She spit the words at him, obviously upset by his implication that she hadn't been totally honest. Or maybe she was simply a good actress. Either way, he had no choice but to push for the truth.

"Someone is willing to kill to see that Kathy Warren's past isn't uncovered. That leads me to think your story has a few holes.''

"The holes aren't my making.'' Heather's eyes blazed, and her bruised chin jutted defiantly. "I don't like your insinuations, Ranger McQuaid, and I don't like the idea of spending the night with a man who's accusing me of lying.''

"I'm not accusing, just asking. And it's a long walk back to town.''

She threw her legs over the side of the bed. "Then I'll sleep in the brush with the coyotes and snakes, in friendlier territory.''

She grabbed her skirt and started to wriggle into it. Matt sidled past her. "Just settle down, Heather. You can't blame me for being suspicious. It's my job.''

"I thought your job was catching criminals, not pretending to be a Good Samaritan just so you can harass the victim in the privacy of your bedroom.''

Her words hit Matt solidly, like a good right to the gut. He put up his hands in surrender. ''You're right. I promise, no more questions tonight.''

''It's not the questions I mind. It's that I'm wasting time telling you the truth when you're going to believe what you want anyway. A cop by any other name is obviously still a cop.''

''I apologize for offending you,'' he said, taking her admonishing finger and gingerly moving it down to her side. ''But not for being a Ranger. Now, go back to bed. Give the coyotes and snakes a break.''

She narrowed her eyes. ''Okay, but one more accusation and I'm out of here.''

Her words were more of a growl, but Matt heard the bedsprings squeak as he headed for the door. He'd have to watch his step with this one. Her temper was clearly as spectacular as her body, and he had no desire to tangle with either. Well, that wasn't exactly true, but he knew his limits. And he damn sure knew his priorities.

Walking to the kitchen, he stopped at the sink and rummaged for a clean glass and the bottle of whiskey he kept stashed in the corner of the kitchen counter. He poured a couple of fingers of the amber liquid, just enough to settle his mind and not enough to dull his senses.

Vacation was over. Two men were celebrating a victory tonight, and he planned to make sure the victory cost them a few years of freedom. He never gave a case less than a hundred percent. It was a matter of pride. And the legacy of Jake McQuaid.

Old resentment jabbed him in the gut. The first time he'd seen Susan Hathaway, she'd been battered just as Heather had tonight. But the beating Susan had suffered had left her near dead. His dad had taken her in and nursed her back to health. She could have walked away then, but she had stayed.

She had been the only mother Matt had ever known, always there for him during his youth. The one who had told him wonderful stories, dried the tears he'd never dared shed in front of his tough-as-nails father, understood how much a child could long for the mother he'd lost.

Susan had been there for Jake McQuaid, too. And how had the town legend thanked her? By taking her to his bed, but not the marriage altar.

"Here's to you, dear old Dad," he said, lifting his glass into the air in a sarcastic toast. To a man who never admitted needing anyone. A man who'd buried one wife, run off another, and cheated the only woman who'd stayed with him out of his name.

He downed the whiskey and set the empty glass on the table. Heather Lombardi wanted to connect with a family she'd never known. How ironic she'd ended up coming to him for help. He couldn't even connect with the family he knew.

HEATHER ROLLED OVER in bed. Her head ached, her toes tingled and every body part in between reacted in some similar, irritating fashion. Stretching, she wiggled her arms and legs. No stabbing, breath-stealing pains shot through her, only the aches and pangs she'd already noted, a good sign that nothing was broken or dislocated. Flinging back the covers, she forced her feet to the floor.

Bright sunlight streamed through a small window, painting streaks of light across the bare planks of a wooden floor, reminding Heather of her whereabouts. The ranch house of Matt McQuaid, the host she didn't begin to understand and wasn't sure she completely trusted. Still, he had saved her last night from who knew what, and he was certainly masculine enough for anyone's taste.

Her gaze scanned the beamed ceilings and wide windows of the room. Like Matt, the place had promise, but the house's promises hadn't been kept for a long time. The walls begged for a coat of paint, and the coverlet on the bed had probably been shiny and new when John Wayne saved Texas from the Mexicans, the version of the Alamo battle non-Texans like Heather knew best.

The scent of bacon hit her nostrils just as she reached the oak dresser and caught a glimpse of her face in the mirror. The sight overpowered the smell, killing any chance of a healthy appetite. Her right cheek was purple and blue, the eye above it open now, but circled by puffy mounds of black.

A knock sounded at the door, swift and hard, no doubt the no-nonsense Ranger. "Come in if you dare," she called.

The door creaked open, and Matt stepped inside. "How do you feel?"

"Better than I look."

"Good." A smile lit up the ebony of his eyes and drew the hard lines of his face into more approachable lines. "Are you hungry?"

"I was, until I made the mistake of looking in the mirror."

"It could have been a lot worse. Besides, there are no mirrors in the kitchen, and the bacon's almost done. How do you like your eggs?"

"Last time I had them, I liked them over easy."

"You sound like that was a long time ago."

"A few years. I'm a bagel-and-cream-cheese fan. I can eat those on the way to the office."

"Yeah, I'm a doughnut man myself, when I have to go

into headquarters, that is. Out here, I like the works, especially since I've already put in a half-day's labor.''

She felt on her arm for her watch. It was missing. "What time is it?"

"Eight o'clock. Days start early in South Texas. Gabby's already called, but I told him to let you sleep. He'll be here soon though. The bomb find has him fired up and ready to stick somebody in his jail.'' Matt backed out the door. "Two eggs over easy coming up.''

Heather took quick stock of the rest of her appearance. The borrowed T-shirt hung loose, skimming her breasts and skirting her knees in an uneven drape. All the necessary parts were covered, but she'd have to wash her face and brush her teeth and hair before she could think of facing Matt across the breakfast table.

As for the image of Frankenstein staring back at him, he'd just have to live with it. After all, he'd insisted she stay and then insulted her integrity.

Still, she had to admit that none of the happenings of the last few days made sense. Given only the facts, she might have drawn the same conclusions he had, figuring anyone telling a story like hers had to know more than she was letting on.

But all she knew was that Kathy Warren had been in this town, and someone here knew something about her they didn't want Heather to find out.

But what, and why? To find out, she might need Matt McQuaid's help. That was reason enough to cooperate with him as much as she could. But under no circumstances would she be taken in by his rough, tough Texas charm. She was the victim. He was the law. With that reminder firmly in mind, she left the mirror of horrors and headed down the hall.

BREAKFAST WAS to die for, Tex-Mex at its finest. Eggs peeking from under a smattering of salsa and perched atop a flour tortilla that slid like heaven across the tongue. The bacon was thick and honey-cured and so crisp it broke in her fingers and crackled between her teeth.

"How about another cup of coffee?"

Heather nodded, her mouth too full to talk. Matt refilled both their mugs with the dark brew and set the pot back on the counter before taking the chair opposite hers. Quiet settled over the kitchen, and Heather pushed all troubling thoughts away as she let the satisfying aromas and taste of the meal provide a temporary calm.

Matt watched as Heather chewed the last bite of food.

"Okay, I'm impressed," she said, smiling at him from across the table. "Where did you learn to cook like that?"

"From the woman who raised me and my brothers. She thought all boys should know how to take care of themselves."

"She was a good teacher."

"She was good at a lot of things. Still is, I'm sure, though I haven't seen her in a while."

Heather wiped her mouth and hands on the plain cotton napkin and took a long sip of the coffee. "It sounds like you miss her. Who is she?"

"Susan Hathaway." Matt got up from the table and carried their plates to the sink. "She was a friend of my dad's who lived with us."

"What happened to your mother?"

"It's a long story." He sat back down, this time with a pencil in hand and a black notebook in front of him. "And we have more relevant things to discuss."

"From breakfast to business in a matter of seconds. You don't waste any time, do you?"

"I try not to. Leads, like coffee, are always best hot."

Around headquarters, "sex" took the place of "coffee" in that simile, but Matt decided the tamer version was safer when talking to Heather. He tapped his pencil against the notebook. "I want you to tell me everything that happened last night, beginning with the second you saw the attackers."

"I told you all of that last night."

"You'd just been through a traumatic experience then. This time you might remember more, some scrap of information you failed to mention. It's usually the little things that trip up a criminal. A careless move. A slip of the tongue."

"Do Texas Rangers typically investigate simple cases of battery?"

"You were kidnapped and a homemade bomb was found in your car. That's not a simple battery." He drummed his fingers against his coffee cup. "But this isn't my case, if that's what you're asking, not officially anyway. Even so, if the sheriff requests my assistance, I can get involved."

"Do you think he will request your assistance?"

"After I ask him to."

"Why would you do that? You said yourself, you're on vacation."

Matt's mind staggered under the weight of her question. He'd asked himself the same thing a dozen times since last night. Heather Lombardi was sexy and desirable, even in her bruised and swollen state. Maybe more so. Now there was a certain vulnerability about her that hadn't been there before.

But she wasn't his responsibility, and he didn't usually let his libido do his thinking for him. Heather was not the only reason this case had his attention. "I can't resist a good mystery," he said, when nothing better came to mind.

And that was as close to the truth as anything else he could think of.

"Then you'll help me find out what happened to my birth mother?"

"I didn't say that, but I will find the men who attacked you and tried to blow up your car. They made the mistake of doing their dirty work practically under my nose. I take that personally." Matt swirled the last dregs of his coffee, staring into it as if it had some power to reveal the truth. Finally, he pushed the cup away. "Did anyone use a name during the attack?"

"No. I'd remember if they had. They did refer to someone who wasn't there as 'the boss,' but they never used a name." She propped her elbows on the table and leaned in. "What could have happened twenty-five years ago that would make people this desperate to keep it hidden? Isn't there a time limit on crimes?"

"There's no statute of limitations on murder."

"Murder? Kathy Warren wasn't murdered. She died in a car wreck."

"That wouldn't have prevented her from being involved in a murder. I warned that you might be opening a can of worms that won't be to your liking."

"I can assure you my birth mother took no part in a murder. She wasn't like that."

Matt watched Heather's eyes darken and her swollen lips purse. No doubt she'd created a fantasy about her mother in her mind that she chose to accept as fact. Unfortunately, as an investigating officer, he couldn't afford to play that game. "How do you know what she was like? All you can be sure of is she deserted a helpless baby."

"She was extremely upset that she had to leave me. Cass Purdy told me that much."

"Cass Purdy?" Matt thumbed through his notes. "I don't think you mentioned her before."

"I did, but maybe not by name. She worked at the orphanage when I was there, though she's been gone from there for twenty years. Cass is the one who dropped my mother off at Dry Creek."

"How did you find her?"

"I made phone calls and wrote letters until I located the woman who managed the orphanage fifteen years ago. That's when it closed. She gave me the name of Mrs. Purdy."

"And this Cass Purdy remembers that twenty-five years ago someone named Kathy Warren brought a baby to the orphanage and that she dropped the woman off at the bus stop in Dry Creek. That's quite a memory. How old is this woman now?"

"She's in her seventies, but I believe her."

"Yeah, you're a trusting sort."

"There's nothing wrong with that."

"Not if you can afford to be mistaken. In my line of work, it can cost you your life. Is Mrs. Purdy certain she dropped Kathy Warren off at the bus stop and not at someone's house?"

"Yes. She said my mother was going to New Orleans to meet a friend. It struck her as odd that my mother ended up in Texas with a new baby when she claimed she knew no one in the whole state." Heather pressed the folded edge of the napkin with her finger, ironing away the wrinkles.

"I want to talk to this Cass Purdy myself. Do you have a number where she can be reached?"

"Yes, but there's no need to bother her. I've told you everything she told me."

"Call her, Heather. Tell her we'd like to drive over this afternoon."

"Her number's back in my room at the motel."

"Then we'll get it right after Gabby finishes his questions."

Heather pushed away from the table. "No more questions. I answered at least a hundred last night."

"I know, but I need something more. This won't be fun, but I still need you to relive last night for me. Tell me everything, every word of conversation you can remember, every action. We just need a scrap of a clue to get us started."

"If I had a clue I would have told you already."

HEATHER LEANED BACK in her chair and closed her eyes. Trembling inside, she forced her mind to replay last night's events. The images rumbled and raged, tearing at her control, straining her muscles and sending jabs of pain through her already aching body.

Matt's voice, unexpectedly gentle, broke the silence. "Don't think first, Heather. Share the images with me. Say everything that comes to mind."

"I'll try." She took a deep breath and started talking, letting the memories inside her break through the protective wall she'd unconsciously erected. Her voice grew distant, as if someone else was inside her, ripping out each statement, forcing her to recall the pain, to remember details her mind had refused to accept last night.

"The men were cruel. One of them spoke with a Texas accent, but the other one didn't sound like he was from this area. They were coarse, rough. Every other word was a filthy curse or some vile derogatory term."

"Were both of them like that?"

She nodded, the memories so alive she could smell the men, feel their hands on her. "Yes, but one was worse."

"Go on."

"They were following the 'boss's' orders. Only the older man wasn't afraid of the boss like the other one. He was all over me, ripping my blouse, squeezing my thighs." She could feel him now, groping, trying to pull her from the car. She was going to be sick.

"That's enough, Heather. That's enough for now."

Matt's words shook Heather back to the present. He was behind her, though she hadn't realized he'd left his chair. His fingers dug into her shoulders as his thumbs massaged the corded muscles that ran the length of her neck and knotted at the base of her brain. Opening her eyes, she trembled, leaning against him.

"If you hadn't shown up when you did…" The words died in her throat. "I want those men caught," she whispered. "And I *will* find out about Kathy Warren. If they think they can scare me away, they're wrong."

Matt pulled her to her feet and turned her around to face him. His dark eyes stared into hers, the intensity of his gaze searing clear to her soul. "You are not dealing with these monsters again. The sheriff and I will handle this our way, without your interference."

"I'm sorry, Ranger McQuaid. You may be heading up the investigation, and I appreciate your concern, but you are *not* running me. I will not leave Dry Creek until I know why someone is willing to hurt me rather than have me question my birth mother's presence in this town."

Matt tightened his grip on her, pulling her closer. "I don't know what we've stumbled into, but it's not for the likes of you. Go home. Leave the dirty work to the people who get paid to handle it. We'll contact you when we need you to testify."

"No, I have a right to be here."

"And that right could get you killed. Is that what you want? Would that prove you're a good daughter to a woman who gave you away years ago? Is that what you think you owe her?''

Tears scalded the backs of her eyes. She held them back. Matt had no right to challenge her determination, no right to question loyalty she couldn't defend. ''Can't you protect the citizens of your state, Ranger? Is that why you want me to run and hide while you and the sheriff play lawmen?''

She tried to pull away. He held her all the closer.

''Will you let me protect you, Heather?'' His voice was husky and dry. ''Will you stay here at the ranch so that I can keep you safe?''

She tilted her head and met his gaze. The fire that had colored his eyes seconds ago had dimmed to a smoky haze. She struggled to keep her temper hot, but the burning inside her switched from anger to something warmer, softer, something that caught in her breast and tugged at her heart.

Matt traced the swollen lines of her face with his finger. ''I can't let you stay in town alone and risk this happening again. I don't have the manpower to have you watched there every second.'' His finger lingered on the bruise beneath her eye, his lips so close, she could almost feel them on hers.

She swayed against him. Did she dare stay here, deal with the kind of crazy attraction she was feeling at this minute for a man she barely knew? Did she have a choice? ''I'll stay here if you think it's necessary, but I won't leave town until this thing is settled.''

''You drive a hard bargain.'' Brushing a wisp of hair from her cheek, he tucked it behind her ear. ''Looks like I'll have to work fast or get used to sleeping on the couch. Unless of course...''

''No way, cowboy.'' She pulled away, still struggling for breath and a break in the tension that crackled between them like heat lightning on a summer night. Her attempts were aided by a loud banging on the back door.

The sheriff had arrived.

Chapter Four

Heather quickly pulled on her skirt and the shirt Matt had lent her last night. She might have had breakfast with Matt in a loose-fitting cotton knit, but she wasn't entertaining Gabby and the man Matt had introduced as John Billinger in that getup. Besides, if she was going to be staying at the ranch with Matt, she needed to try to keep gossipy tongues from wagging, for both their sakes.

The three men were standing in front of the hearth when she rejoined them. They stopped talking and turned to gaze at her.

Gabby fingered the soiled brim of the hat he held in his hand, over the round of his protruding belly. "I'm real sorry for all the trouble you've run into, Miss Lombardi. The attack was bad enough, then we find that bomb. I'm just glad the dadburn thing didn't explode with you in the car."

"So am I. Do you have any suspects?"

"Not yet. I've checked the whereabouts of some local teenage boys who've run into trouble with the law before. So far they all have reliable alibis."

Heather moved into the circle of intimidating Texans. Running a finger over her bruised face, she stared from beneath her blackened eyes. "The men who did this weren't teenagers. And attempting to blow up a car with the passenger inside isn't your run-of-the-mill act of vandalism.''

John Billinger rolled back on his heels, his thumbs tucked into his front pockets. He was a tall, thin man, whose face wore the battle scars of long days in the outdoors under a hot sun. ''I wouldn't go jumping to conclusions, Miss Lombardi.'' His thick drawl gave her name a dozen syllables. ''They may not have been teenagers, but they could have been young men out of control. There's some pretty rowdy wranglers working out at that new dude ranch. I wouldn't put nothing past 'em when they get a drink or two under their belts.''

Gabby stared at John from beneath his wiry brows. ''I told you I'd handle this. I only let you come along 'cuz Miss Lombardi was attacked on your land.''

''You didn't *let* me come along. I told you I was coming out here to talk to Matt and give him my two cents' worth. You just offered to let me ride with you.''

Tension simmered between the two men, creating a new series of doubts in Heather's mind. John obviously wasn't too confident of Gabby's ability to find the culprits. Should she distrust the sheriff, or was the running argument between the two men purely personal?

Matt stepped closer to John. ''What makes you think the men from the Galloping R might be involved in this?''

''I've seen 'em around town. They pamper the tourists during the day and then let off steam at night. Just last month Paul Ridgely like to have shot one of them for messing with his daughter.''

''Now, John,'' Gabby countered, ''you know Donna was as much at fault as the wrangler. That girl could get in trouble at a church social.''

Irritation rattled Heather's nerves. ''I don't think arguing about Donna Ridgely's morals is going to find the men who beat me up and planted a bomb in my car.''

"I agree," Gabby said. "Why don't you and I talk, Miss Lombardi, and John and Matt can do their conversing outside?"

Matt propped a booted foot on the hearth. "I don't think so. John and I can talk later. I want to be with Heather during *all* questioning."

Gabby raked weathered fingers through his thinning hair. "If that's the way you want it."

"That's the way it's going to be." Matt took Heather's arm and steered her toward the kitchen. "We'll sit at the table so we can take notes. John, I'll have to ask you to wait on the porch. Questioning of the victim is confidential at this point."

"Whatever you say, Matt. I'm just trying to help. But I sure wouldn't rule out those drugstore cowboys in their fancy shirts and tight jeans. Ben Wright's not one of us, and he don't do things the way they've always been done in Dry Creek."

"How's that?"

"He throws money around like it grew on trees, wearing them expensive Western suits, and he pays his wranglers extra to dance and flirt with the women who come to the dude ranch."

"None of which is against the law. But don't worry, we're not ruling out anybody." Matt threw John Billinger a look that made the man mutter and scowl as he stamped out the door. Then, kinking his foot around a kitchen chair, Matt dragged it closer to the table. He held it while Heather sat and then straddled one nearby. "I'd like to be asked in on this case, Gabby," he said, as the older man poured himself a cup of coffee.

"I kinda figured that." The sheriff pursed his lips disapprovingly.

"Is that a problem?"

"Not for me. It might be for you or your superiors. This isn't one of the high-profile murders they usually assign you to. And you said yourself, you're only here on vacation."

"I can extend my stay if I need to."

"I see." Gabby's brow knitted into a series of deep groves. "This thing might drag on for months, seeing as how we've got no clues."

"We have clues."

The same surprise Heather felt registered on Gabby's face. "That's news to me," he said, pulling his chair closer. "Fill me in."

Matt's voice was low and steady, as casual as if he were going over a grocery list. "Two men were involved. They were apparently taking orders from someone they simply referred to as 'the boss,' but one of them appeared to have an ax of his own to grind. My guess is he's come into town specifically to put a stop to Heather's nosing into the past of Kathy Warren. That means whatever happened twenty-five years ago stretches beyond Dry Creek. There could be more than one agenda in all of this, and Heather might not be the only one at risk."

Gabby shook his head. "Sounds good when you say it, but them's still slim pickings. You can't build a case on that kind of hogwash."

"I didn't say we had a case. I said we had clues. My suggestion is that we begin the search with ranchers who have at least two men who aren't family working for them. The ranch economy being what it is, that narrows the suspect field down considerably."

Confidence blossomed inside Heather. Evidently Matt did know what he was doing, and the endless questioning he'd put her through had accomplished something. For the first time since her abduction, she felt they were getting somewhere, that she might actually stop butting her head against the proverbial brick wall.

"I was out at the site of the attack at dawn this morning," Matt continued.

"Yeah." Gabby tapped his fingers on the edge of the table. "What did you expect to find that I didn't?"

"I was hoping for tire prints from the getaway vehicle."

"Not much chance of that. Worst drought we've had in ten years. The ground's hard as asphalt."

"You're right. I didn't find sufficient tire marks, but I did find something." Matt retrieved a plastic bag from the counter and laid it on the table. Peering through the plastic was a man's watch with a broken band. "I want it dusted for prints."

Gabby chuckled. "You do live up to your reputation, Matt McQuaid."

"I try. Now it's your turn, Gabby. I'm sure Miss Lombardi's anxious to get this morning's questioning behind her."

Gabby turned his gaze to Heather. "I reckon you're ready to do more than that. I'm sure you're itching to grab up your things and get out of this town. Can't say that I blame you, but I'm real sorry things turned out this way. We're usually a lot more hospitable around here."

"So I've heard. But I won't be leaving town."

His eyebrows drew together, and he leaned in closer. "You'll be making a mistake if you stay around here, especially until we get these men behind bars. The way it sits now, we don't even know what the hell we're dealing with." He looked to Matt for help.

Matt waved him off. "I told her that. She makes up her own mind. She's checking out of the motel though. She'll be staying at the ranch with me until we're sure she's out of danger.''

A frown cut deeper into Gabby's leathery face. ''Don't you Rangers have rules about getting involved with the victims of a case you're working on?''

''We're talking protection, not personal involvement.''

MATT WASN'T ANTAGONISTIC, but his tone left Heather in no doubt that this was just a job to him, and she was sure Gabby was convinced too. *She* was a job to him. The only reason she was at the ranch was that he believed her to be in imminent danger.

At the thought, fear knotted inside her. Last evening, fighting off two strange men, when the risk to her life had been palpable, terror and anger had surged inside her like suffocating clouds of poisonous gas. But now, in the bright light of day, the events of the attack seemed more like a bad dream that had been washed away by the dawn.

Only this wasn't an ordinary bright sunny morning. The pain that swam through her muscles and the ghoulish bruises that disfigured her face were proof of that. And these weren't just acquaintances she was chatting with. One was a Texas Ranger, the other a sheriff—undeniable evidence that her nightmare had substance.

''Miss Lombardi.''

The sound of her name jerked her to attention. ''I'm sorry, Sheriff. Were you saying something?''

''Just that I hate to put you through more questioning, especially when you seem a bit tired. It must have been tough sleeping after what you went through last night.''

''No, I'm fine. I was just lost in my own thoughts for a second. Fire away, and I'll answer as completely as I can.''

''Let's start with the note you received.''

Heather took a deep breath and plunged in, retelling the

story that repetition was burning into her mind. It was an hour before the two men across from her closed their notebooks and came up for air.

HEATHER BREATHED a sigh of relief as Gabby tipped his hat and headed for the door. Matt trailed him out, saying he needed to talk to John if they could find him.

Silence followed on their heels, but the solitude was welcome. Heather walked to the window and gazed out over land that seemed to stretch on forever.

Tufts of grass, tall and yellow-green, were splashed between clumps of scraggy mesquite trees. Yellow and red flowers danced in and between the spines of prickly pear cactus, and a hackberry at the corner of the house offered a few orange berries that a blue jay found to his liking.

Peaceful, but still, the land had a harshness about it, as though it issued the same challenge she'd heard voiced more than once over the last few days. Farming or ranching in south Texas was not for sissies.

Perhaps that was what had toughened the men who lived here, given them the rugged edge they wore with the same pride that Matt showed in his badge. Or maybe the land itself did the choosing, attracted the type of rugged, fierce men who had tamed the West originally and then stayed to see the challenge through.

The romance of the West. A charming idea, but the promise had turned sour for Heather. Every corner she turned slammed her against another barrier, each as barbed and impassable as the fences that crisscrossed the land that lay in front of her.

Matt swung through the back door, pulling her out of her reverie. "I need to make a couple of calls before we visit Cass Purdy. Do you want to come along?"

"Do I have a choice? I thought I was under house arrest."

"I wouldn't have put it quite that way, but you've got the concept. John offered one of his men for a few hours if I need a watchdog, though. He could come over and stay with you if you'd like to rest a while this morning."

"A watchdog. How flattering." She ran her hands down the front of her skirt in an unsuccessful attempt to remove the excess of wrinkles. "Actually, I'd like to go into town and get my things from the motel. This outfit is not the last word in fashion for ranch wear."

A smile touched the edges of Matt's lips and softened the lines around his eyes. "I don't think I've ever heard ranch wear and fashion used in the same sentence before, and definitely not when talking about my ranch." His gaze walked from her ankles to the above-knee skirt. "No one's complaining about your wardrobe, but I imagine you'd find jeans a lot more comfortable. Do you have any?"

"Of course I have jeans." Heather smoothed the wrinkles in her skirt with the palm of her hand. "I don't wear suits on weekends or when I'm not working."

"But you chose them for the wilds of Texas?"

"I thought I might get a little more respect and cooperation if I showed up in Dry Creek asking questions in a business suit rather than casual attire. Wrong again."

Matt propped his backside against the counter, his shadowed eyes belying the ease of his stance. "Your clothes have nothing to do with the reception party someone threw you last night."

"No, I'm sure they don't. Evidently the mention of Kathy Warren is enough to bring out killer instincts in some of the citizens of your fair town."

"Every town has a few buried secrets, most of them better off staying buried."

Heather walked over and stood in front of him, her back straight, her muscles suddenly tense. "I didn't come here to expose the town's dirty laundry. I'm only looking for the truth about one woman."

He waved her off. "Simmer down. I never said you were to blame for any of this. I just made an observation."

MATT WATCHED THE FIRE in Heather's eyes cool to a dusky shade of charcoal. She was quick to anger but just as quick to mellow. Either way, she was too damned attractive for her own good. Or his.

Not that it mattered. He had a crime to solve and then Miss Heather Lombardi could traipse back to Atlanta and the life she'd left behind. There were probably at least a half-dozen young men bemoaning her absence at this very minute. But how many of them had sat across from her at breakfast with her wearing nothing but their T-shirt?

An uneasy pang akin to indigestion settled in his stomach. He ignored it. "So, make up your mind," he said, tapping his fingers on the edge of the counter. "Do you want to tag along into town with me or not?"

"Of course I'm going. Who could refuse a charming invitation like that?"

"I'D LIKE TO STOP at the spot where we left my car last night."

Matt stared straight ahead, his eyes on the road in front of them. "I don't recommend it. There's nothing to see. Gabby took your car in as evidence."

"Still, I'd like to see the spot where the attack took place for myself."

"I don't see the sense of that."

"I don't see the sense of any of this. Whoever planted a bomb in my car intended to kill me. Yet last night one of the men who kidnapped me and beat me up insisted their orders were *not* to kill me.''

"It's a mystery, all right."

Heather sighed audibly. "Why do I always feel that having a conversation with you is like getting a confession of guilt from my six-year-old nephew? There isn't any limit on the number of words you can use in a lifetime, you know. You could just spout out a complete thought without waiting for me to coax every detail from you."

"The way you do."

"Damned straight. Now tell me your theory as to what's going on. No word limit."

Matt shook his head in mock disapproval, but laughter rolled inside him and escaped to split his lips in a grin. "Now that you've asked me so politely, I think there could be more than one person who wants you out of town. Someone may be more desperate than the other, or others."

"You didn't mention that to the sheriff. Why not?"

"Right now it's just theory."

"I still don't think you're telling me the whole truth."

"Really. What makes me think you're about to tell me what I left out?"

She twisted in her seat and faced in his direction. "You're curious as to why the sheriff didn't think about the same possibility you did. It's his job to notice things like that. He could be in on all of this. He might already know why people want me out of town, and he might be cooperating with them. He might even be masterminding this whole thing himself."

"Whoaaa. Old Gabby is not a suspect in this. He's just a good-ole-boy sheriff who's not used to dealing with much more than a family argument, a loud Saturday night drunk or a few schoolboys cutting fences. You've been reading too many detective novels."

"I don't read detective novels. I read news magazines. And romance novels. So if I came to the conclusion that this is not a one-man show, the idea should have occurred to Gabby as well."

"Point taken, but not necessarily valid." Matt slowed and pulled to the side of the road. "We'll have to climb between the barbed wire," he said, opening the door of his truck.

"Why? The man who was driving my car last night went through a gate."

"Yeah, that's John Billinger's gate. It's a few yards ahead, but Gabby had him lock it today. He doesn't want the crime scene tampered with until he's sure he's through with it. He's keeping out everything except cows and jack-rabbits."

"And us." Heather jumped to the ground and bounded around the car and toward the fence, a step behind the sure-footed Ranger. Matt put a foot on one wire and raised the top one with his hands, making a gap big enough for her to crawl through without serious risk to body parts.

Wary, but determined, she wiggled between the rows of wire. Her short skirt slithered up to her panty line. Planting both feet on the ground, she tugged it back into position.

"From now on, I wear jeans," she said, heat suffusing her cheeks.

"I'm not complaining." He took her arm and led her around a patch of cactus. "I'd recommend boots, though. Open-toed shoes in cow pastures can be dirty business." He pointed to a pile of cow chips to emphasize his point.

Heather stepped gingerly around it, and then Matt took her by the elbow and guided her past a thick clump of sage. For a second she was only aware of his hand on her arm, a gentle pressure that created a surge of unfamiliar feelings. Then she marched ahead of him into the open pasture.

There was no sign her car had been here last night, no sign that she'd been trapped in it with two men. Yet, standing here, in the exact spot... Goose bumps prickled her flesh. She shuddered and tilted her head upward.

Matt stared down at her, his eyes hot and liquid. Heather gazed back at him, an alarm sounding in her heart. Matt McQuaid wore the trappings of a cowboy and spoke the words of a lawman, but there was more to him than that. Close to him like this, their eyes locked, she felt it as strongly as she did her own heart beating inside her. Perhaps he had his own ghosts to deal with, just as she had hers.

"I know this is tough," he said. He slipped a reassuring arm around her shoulder, and for a second his fingers tangled in her hair. Unexpected warmth drove away the chill that had settled in her heart the minute she'd arrived on the scene. She was in over her head, but she wasn't alone.

Matt let his hand slide down her arm. "Heather." His voice was strained. "I don't know what's going on, but as long as you're with me, you'll be safe."

Impulsively, she rose to her tiptoes and planted a whisper of a kiss on the drawn lines of his mouth. "Thank you," she said. "I'll hold you to that promise."

She turned and walked back to the truck, head down, watching carefully where she planted her feet. And wondering what in the world had possessed her to make a move on the Ranger.

"WE'LL STOP at the motel first and pick up your things," Matt said, finally breaking the silence that had ridden between them ever since the impromptu kiss.

Heather continued to stare at the passing blur of fence posts. "While we're there, I'd like to change clothes."

"Fine. I'd like to talk to Rube a minute anyway. He's

been around town all his life, ran that motel for most of it, and he's usually up on the latest gossip. He's likely to know if there have been any strangers hanging around town.''

''I know you said you wanted to go see Cass Purdy. What other stops will we be making today?''

''The Galloping R.''

''The dude ranch John Billinger mentioned this morning?''

''That's it.''

''Do you think there's something to the accusations he made, that the wranglers who work at the ranch might be involved?''

''Could be.''

Her muscles tightened, tugging painfully at the swollen face. ''Okay, cowboy. Let's go for a sentence with more than two words this time. Who owns the Galloping R and what's the likelihood they'll be threatened by my asking questions about Kathy Warren?''

Matt shoved his hat back a little farther and gave a two-fingered wave to a passing motorist in a dark green pickup truck. ''Ben Wright owns the place,'' he said, rubbing the back of his neck with his right hand. ''It's only been operating as a dude ranch for a couple of years, but Ben's been in town for about ten. He retired from the rodeo circuit and bought up a stretch of land. Tried his hand at raising Brahmans for use in rodeos, but decided that was too much like work.''

''He's been here ten years? The way John Billinger talked, I thought he was a newcomer.''

''That's the way the long-timers see it around here. If you haven't been around a generation or two, you're a newcomer.''

''They seem to accept *you* as one of their own.''

''I was born in Dry Creek.''

"I didn't know that."

"Yeah. We lived here until I was almost eight. My dad had a small ranch on the outskirts of town. He raised a few head of cattle along with being the sheriff."

"Where are your parents now?"

"My dad's in Colorado."

"And your mom?" She was beginning to sound like Matt, speaking in fragments that left more unsaid than spoken.

Matt turned down the side street that led to the motel. "Rube will ask you a lot of questions when you check out. Don't volunteer any information about what happened last night."

"Why not? Is he a suspect?"

"I just don't believe in spreading the facts of a case around like fertilizer."

"Such picturesque speech." She settled into her own thoughts. Matt had avoided her question about his mother, either intentionally or because he'd grown tired of friendly conversation and wanted to get back to business. Either way, the message was clear. Their relationship was purely business, and his private life wasn't open for discussion.

Minutes later, he pulled into a parking space in front of the motel. He followed her up the walk and waited while she unlocked the door and pushed it open. The now-familiar musty odor greeted her—that, and a trail of mud.

"Looks like they forgot to vacuum," Matt said, scraping his own boots on the hewn-fiber mat.

"I don't know where they found mud," she said, eyeing the black gunk suspiciously.

"From in front of your window. Someone left the hose on that plant with the pink flowers."

Heather shook her head. She hadn't noticed. Grabbing a pair of jeans and a yellow cotton shirt from the hangers, she headed toward the bathroom. She'd change first and then pack. The whole process shouldn't take more than fifteen minutes.

Matt leaned on the door frame. "Anything I can do to help?"

She considered asking him to empty the contents of the dresser drawers into her bag but changed her mind. The thought of his rough hands on her intimate apparel, his fingers cradling her panties and bras, made her insides feel weak.

And weakness was not a good idea when dealing with the take-charge Ranger. She was in Dry Creek for only one reason, and it didn't include becoming romantically involved with Matt McQuaid. She needed to keep things strictly business, make sure he didn't read anything more than gratitude into her impulsive kiss this morning. "It'll only take me a minute to change," she said, "but you can ask Rube for a copy of my bill since you're going to see him anyway. That would speed things up a little."

He nodded in agreement and ducked out the door. Taking a second to check the progress of the bruising on her cheeks, she squinted into the mirror. Bad as she looked, it could have been worse. She could be dead.

She sighed and opened the door to the minuscule hole that masqueraded as a bathroom. The blood caught her eye first, a thick crimson stain splattered over the shower curtain and the wash basin.

Blood that soaked the tailored white blouse of the woman who lay at her feet and made sickening patterns on the blue linen suit. The dead woman's legs sprawled like those of a discarded mannequin, her eyes open and bulging.

Heather heard someone scream. Maybe herself. Shaking and weak, she stepped back and against the hard barrier of a man's body.

Chapter Five

"Rube? What are you doing here? What have you done?"
She tried to run, but he grabbed her arm.

"Are you all right?"

The answer stuck in Heather's throat. She pointed shakily
to the bathroom and the body.

Rube let out a string of curses that dissolved into a hoarse
cry. "Oh, no! It's Ariana!"

She watched as the man who owned the motel fell to his
knees beside the blood-soaked body of the young woman
on the floor. Hands shaking, he felt for a nonexistent pulse
and then closed the woman's bulging eyes with a stroke of
his fingers.

Heather backed away, grabbing the corner of the dresser
for support. Her limbs grew rubbery as the room spun dizzily about her, the walls getting closer and closer until she
thought they would swallow her up. Finally, a door
slammed behind her, and she forced her mind to function.

Matt crossed the floor in two strides. She longed to run
into his arms. Instead she forced her legs to hold her upright
and her voice to speak with a minimum of shaking.
"There's a body in my bathroom."

"What the…"

"It's Ariana," Rube said, backing from the bathroom to

join them. "The lady who helps out with the cleaning when my wife don't feel so good. Someone's shot her. She's dead." His words were uttered in a lifeless monotone, his mind obviously still tackling the reality of the scene.

Matt stuck his head in the bathroom and followed with his own string of curses. He stepped toward Heather and reached out a hand. She slid hers into his and trembled, her stomach still warring with her equilibrium.

"Are you all right?" he asked, his eyes dark and angry but coated in concern.

"No, but I'll survive," she said as reassuringly as she could.

"Then I need you to go into the main office and call the sheriff," he said.

She picked up the phone. "I can call him from right here."

"No." He took the phone from her hand, slamming it back into the cradle. Rube groaned, and Matt turned back to the bathroom where the man was leaning against the door, his face the color of putty. "Don't touch anything," Matt ordered. "I need a clean crime scene."

"Nothing clean about it," Rube muttered. "It'll take weeks to clean this place."

"That's not the kind of clean I mean. Just don't touch anything." He placed a hand in the small of Heather's back and guided her to the door. "Now go and call Gabby, Heather, and stay out of here until I send for you. This will be ugly."

"She's wearing my clothes."

The comment stopped Matt cold. "What are you talking about?"

"Ariana, the girl who was killed." Lips quivering, Heather continued. "She's wearing my clothes. The blouse, the suit, even the shoes. They're mine."

Matt said nothing but his big hands drew into tight, threatening fists.

"What do you think it means?" she whispered through a throat that was dry and clogged.

Matt gave no answer. Instead, he all but pushed her out the door. "Go into Rube's office and stay there," he ordered.

His strength was contagious. It stiffened Heather's spine as she raced toward the motel office. Punching in the sheriff's number, she was certain of only one thing. She couldn't be in better hands than those of Ranger Matt McQuaid.

MATT SOAPED HIS HANDS for the second time, in a fruitless effort to wash away the memories of the last two hours. No matter how many times he faced it or how many ways he replayed a murder scene, he could never fully wipe the sights and smells from his mind. And he wasn't through with this one. He'd have to go to the morgue later for the autopsy.

The other Rangers teased him about his meticulous approach, calling him a control freak. Maybe he was, but he liked to make sure nothing was overlooked in dealing with clues that might lead to an arrest and conviction.

The autopsy would have to wait until a fully qualified medical examiner arrived, and the nearest one was sixty miles away. Waiting for him would give Matt enough time for a needed break from crime-scene madness—and Gabby's endless chatter.

He needed to have a talk with Rube and his wife Edna, but first he wanted to check on Heather. She'd been through plenty in the last twenty-four hours, enough to send even a headstrong woman running in the opposite direction.

He almost hoped she was ready to run. She'd opened a

passel of trouble with her questions about Kathy Warren. Matt was sure there was more to come. In his experience, once a stampede started it didn't stop till *it* wanted to—unless it came to a cliff first. For her sake, Heather needed to get out of town, go back to Atlanta and leave the investigation to the authorities. For his sake…

The image of Heather across the breakfast table sidled through his mind, his T-shirt sliding to the edge of one shoulder, her hair loose and wild. His chest constricted. For his sake, he should be on his knees praying she left town today, before she took it into her head once again to scoot up so close to him that her lips brushed his. He was not the kind of man for long-term commitment.

But he was a *man*. He'd been achingly aware of that fact ever since Heather Lombardi had come into his life. In his house, in his bed, in his arms.

"Matt."

Heather's voice startled him. He turned to find her standing in the doorway, staring at him.

"I saw the others leaving. Are you finished in here?"

"For now."

"Is it okay if I get my things?"

"Sure, but try not to disturb anything else."

She walked to the closet and reached for the piece of luggage that rested on the top shelf.

He stepped behind her. "Let me help." Her back pressed against his chest, and he fought the ridiculous urge to forget the suitcase, to forget where they were and why and to take her in his arms and taste her lips. Not the tickling tease she'd offered this morning, but a kiss she'd remember all the way home.

As usual, his conservative side won out. This was the wrong place, the wrong time, and he was the wrong man. He tossed the case to the bed and opened it. "Tell me where to start, and I'll help you pack. The sooner you get out of this room the better.''

''I have some toiletries in the bathroom cabinet. If you could get those…'' She nodded her head toward the murder scene but averted her gaze. ''I know the body's been removed, but still…''

Her voice gave the only indication of dread, though Matt was certain her insides still quaked at what she'd witnessed earlier. He'd seen big burly lawmen in training faint or become violently ill when they made their first call to a homicide scene.

''I don't blame you a bit,'' he said. ''Fortunately there's no reason for you to go back in there. I moved all of your things from the bathroom into the bottom drawer of the dresser to keep them clean. Fingerprint dust was flying hot and heavy in there.''

''Thanks.'' Her voice dropped to a near whisper. ''For everything. I have a lot of questions, but they can wait.'' Her gaze traveled the room. ''I'd really just like to get out of here as soon as possible.''

''I'm sure.'' He took her hand and pulled her closer. ''The danger just doubled, Heather. Now I'm even more convinced you should go home and leave the investigation to us. No one would blame you, not even your mother if she were still here to talk sense into you.''

As he'd half expected, she lifted a bruised but determined chin. ''I can't go, Matt. Not now. I can't explain it, but I have to find out what happened to my birth mother. I owe her that.''

She shuddered, and Matt pulled her into the circle of his arms. Touch seemed to be the only comfort he could offer. All the words he could think of were too harsh, the hard truths he'd learned through years of living.

Giving birth did not make a woman a mother any more

than providing sperm made a man a father. Some women stayed even if the children they held in their arms and cooked and cared for were not their own. He knew one who had, even though the man who shared her bed denied her his name and treated her like a hired hand.

But other women ran out on their husbands and their children. That was life. He let go of Heather and walked over to stare out the dingy window. "Dry Creek is no place for you, Heather. Not now."

"I think it is."

The old floor creaked at her footsteps, and the flowery smell of her lightened the stale air of the room. Matt didn't turn away from the window, but he felt her presence behind him.

"I have my reasons for staying, Matt. They wouldn't make sense to you, but they're important to me."

He turned to face her. "The way I see it, your reasons are to dig up the past. You might be sorry. Unearthing old secrets sometimes has a way of burying pleasant memories."

"I'll take my chances."

"And risk your life doing it?"

"I'm not afraid of the truth, and I trust you to protect me from the evil. Matt McQuaid, Texas Ranger. If the name and title weren't impressive enough, I've seen you in action."

Apprehension swept through him. He gripped her shoulders. Holding her at arm's length, he locked his gaze with hers. "Don't cast me in your fantasy, Heather. I'm no hero from a Hollywood script. I'm just a Ranger. I do my job. You can count on me for that, but nothing more."

"Who said I expected—or wanted—anything more?" Eyes flashing, she broke from his grasp and dissolved the tension of the moment in a flurry of activity.

Heather yanked open a dresser drawer and grabbed a handful of lacy scraps of underwear and shoved them into the back right corner of the suitcase.

"I didn't mean to make you angry, Heather."

"No? What did you mean to do? You certainly weren't trying to reassure me that what I wanted and felt was important."

"I was trying to make life easier on you."

"That's not your job, Ranger."

"You're right. Call your own shots, if that makes you happy." He was never known for his patience, and Heather had a way of riling him almost as fast as she could arouse him. Dealing with her was the last thing he needed right now, but he might as well accept the fact that she was almost as hardheaded as he was.

"Just don't interfere with the investigation," he snapped.

She ignored him, folding a flimsy cotton nightshirt with a vengeance. She was too damn independent, a trait that could get her killed. He grabbed her hand and tugged her closer, tilting her head up with a thumb under her chin. "And don't even think about sneaking away from the ranch without me. If you're staying in Dry Creek, I plan to know where you are every second."

"Fine. Now if you'll pack the things you moved, I'll get the rest of my belongings and we'll be out of here," she said, tossing a couple of paperback books into the open suitcase. "I do want to stop in the manager's bathroom long enough to slip into jeans and a shirt of my own, though. That is if you'll let me out of your sight long enough to change."

"I'll consider it." Matt walked to the door and opened it, dragging in a deep breath. Getting into a fight with Heather wasn't going to keep her safe and it wasn't going to help him come up with answers as to who and what was behind the lunacy that had struck Dry Creek.

He packed the toiletries he'd stashed in the bottom drawer and then lifted the edge of the spread to peek beneath the bed. A white sandal with signs of excessive wear and tear rewarded his efforts. He picked it up and balanced it on his palm. Funny, Heather's feet looked much more petite than the empty shoe.

"Where did you get that?" Heather asked, walking over to examine the sandal.

"Under your bed, but I don't see the mate."

"It's not mine. Whoever stayed here before must have left it."

Matt lifted the shoe from his hand, holding the strap between two fingers. "Fresh mud, and the pattern on the sole matches the tracks we found on your floor."

"Then they must be Ariana's."

"Not likely. We found Ariana's shoes in a pile with her clothes. What size shoe do you wear?"

"A seven."

Matt held the shoe up and found the size inside. "This is a nine. And Ariana's feet were approximately the same size as yours. The pumps she'd taken from your closet fit her perfectly."

"But that would mean another woman was in here, that she walked in after the water was left running outside." Heather dropped to the edge of the bed, confusion knitting her brow above the blackened eye.

"It looks that way," Matt agreed.

"But why was she in here? Unless..." She flung up her hands in exasperation. "Do you think a woman might have killed Ariana?"

"Anything's possible." Matt went in search of the other white sandal. His quest was almost immediately rewarded.

The shoe was lying behind the pine desk, askew, as if someone had kicked it off or thrown it at somebody.

"Let's get out of here," he said, retrieving the sandal. "I need to talk to Rube and Edna and drop these shoes off for prints. After that we'll pay a visit to the Galloping R and see if any of John Billinger's theories are worth investigating."

While Heather changed, Matt called the sheriff with information about the latest find, then returned a call to his office in San Antonio. His assignment to the case wasn't official yet, but it would be any day. Homicides that didn't fit into the traditional household-passion variety were his specialty.

So were those that had gone unsolved for years, cases that had never been closed but had lost the sense of urgency over time. And if his suspicions were correct, this one had roots that went back two decades.

Matt mulled over what he knew. According to Heather, Kathy Warren had disappeared on an autumn night twenty-five years ago, the same year and season when another woman had been beaten and left for dead. Susan. His surrogate mother.

Kathy Warren and Susan Hathaway. Coincidence or connection? Was the tale of two women woven together by some intricate knotting of threads or were they merely isolated stories from the same time period?

His mind toyed and tangled with possibilities. A day ago he'd wanted only peace and quiet—now he yearned for answers with the same passion. He only hoped that finding them didn't destroy the faith Heather had in the mother she'd never met.

That responsibility lay heavy on his mind when Heather reappeared, clad in a pair of snug jeans, her hair pinned in a loose swirl atop her head. She smiled and his heart plunged to his stomach.

He'd have to watch his step every minute. The attraction between them grew with every touch and look, but he couldn't fool himself. No matter how attracted he was to her, when this was over, he'd walk away. It was his heritage.

The legacy of Jake McQuaid.

HEATHER TURNED from the truck window and the rush of unchanging scenery. "Tell me about the Galloping R."

"It's your typical dude ranch."

"That doesn't tell me anything. I've never been to a dude ranch before."

"Neither have I, at least not as a paying guest. The way I understand it, it's a bunch of tourists paying money to do what regular wranglers expect pay for. Except the truth is, there's not a lot of work available for regular wranglers anymore."

"Is that because of technical advances in ranching?"

"Partly. And partly because of a shortage of manpower. The idea of being a cowboy sounds romantic. The reality is different, so as wranglers became harder to find, ranchers turned to other methods, like dogs or helicopters to help in rounding up cattle. They use modern machines to do the work cowboys used to do."

A pickup truck passed them, heading in the opposite direction. Matt made eye contact with the driver and lifted his fingers, but not his hand, from the wheel. A typical cowboy greeting, friendly, but low-key and noncommittal. Heather was learning a lot about the ways of the modern West.

"Tell me about the reality of cowboy life," she said, not ready for Matt to return to his own thoughts and shut her out again. Besides, she liked the sound of his voice when he wasn't upset. It was low and slow, yet strong and rhythmic, like a western ballad that haunted the soul.

"A cowboy spends most of his time talking to cattle and eating dust. The pay's poor, the work's dirty, and the cattle don't even say thank-you."

"So why does anybody do it?"

"They can't help themselves. The life-style gets in some men's blood, like a drug. Wide-open spaces, the brightest stars in the universe, a mount who never lets you down, and dealing with men who stand by their word." A smile eased the taut lines in his face. "And then there's the quiet."

"Meaning I talk too much?"

"No, but more than I'm used to." His gaze left the road for the briefest of seconds and found and captured hers. "Under other circumstances, I'd enjoy having you around."

Heather's pulse quickened, and a titillating warmth rushed through her. It wasn't much of a compliment by normal standards, but coming from Matt McQuaid, the simple words were like a sonnet.

The puzzle was why what he said or felt mattered enough to make her blood heat and her cheeks flush. Danger, she decided. The imminent threat of danger always heightened the senses. Or maybe it was a natural reaction to a man who'd saved her from being seriously injured, or worse.

Whatever the reason, she couldn't deny the overpowering attraction she felt every time he was near. And, she decided suddenly, she wasn't going to shortchange herself. Every aspect of what was supposed to be a vacation/fact-finding mission had turned sour except for running into Matt McQuaid.

So if being near him aroused her sleeping sensuality, so be it. After all, if the killer who appeared to be stalking her had his way, it might be the last time her sensuality or anything else about her was aroused.

With that chilling thought, the warmth evaporated. They both sat quietly until Matt turned in at a metal sign that heralded the Galloping R, a picture of a bowlegged cowboy toting a pair of six-shooters.

''I'll get the gate,'' she offered. She pushed open the door and jumped to the ground as soon as the truck came to a full stop. As the gate swung open, an uneasiness swept through her. In minutes, she might be standing face to face with the men who'd attacked her last night, maybe even with the man who'd just put a bullet through the heart of a young woman named Ariana.

She climbed back into the truck and listened with unaccustomed meekness to Matt's instructions about leaving the talking to him as they drove the dusty road to the main building of the Galloping R.

BEN WRIGHT'S OFFICE resembled the set of a forties Western. The walls were rough pine planks, the floor Mexican tile, the ceilings beamed. Only the myriad of photographs hinted that this was a ranch devoted to pleasing tourists instead of raising cattle.

The Kodak moments that lined the wall were all framed glossies of paying guests participating in the Galloping R's offerings. Cookouts by a creek. Laughing children riding horses single file along a well-worn path. A half-dozen smiling wranglers line dancing with a group of gray-haired women in matching shirts.

Matt paced the floor. Heather squirmed in her chair. They had been left to wait while the young woman on duty went to find Ben Wright, and the jiffy she'd promised to be back in had already stretched to five minutes.

They both turned as the door opened.

"I'm sorry, Matt." The receptionist smiled and touched him on the shoulder as she passed.

Heather was sure she had never seen more obvious flirting. The woman's efforts were wasted. Ranger Matt plainly had nothing but business on his mind.

"Does that mean you didn't find Ben?" he asked, scooting to the front of his chair.

"I found him, but he wasn't in the tack room like I thought. I paged him and he called back from the cookout area on the Roy Rogers Trail." She wiggled onto the back edge of the desk and crossed her long legs, swinging them seductively beneath a short denim skirt.

Smiling, she turned briefly to Heather. "All our trails are named after famous cowboys. The Gene Autry Trail…"

"So how do we get to the cookout area?" Matt interrupted, clearly not willing to waste time on promotional small talk.

"It's difficult by car," she said, her winsome gaze returning to Matt, "but it's only a short ride by horse. Ben suggested you get a couple of mounts from the stable and ride up. He said he'd meet you here if you preferred, but he thought you'd enjoy seeing what he'd done to the area. Besides it's a lovely day for a ride."

Matt stood and motioned for Heather to do the same. "We'll ride up," he said, his boots clacking against the tile as he headed for the door.

Heather stopped cold. "I don't ride."

Both of them stared at her as if she'd just professed she didn't salute the American flag. "I live in the city. We drive our cars or take the rail system."

"Well, there are no train tracks on the Roy Rogers Trail." The receptionist laughed at her own joke and winked at Matt. "I could ride up with you, Matt, and

Heather could stay here and answer the phone. I'd love the chance to get out of the office for a while.''

Matt grabbed his hat from the chair by the door and slid it onto his head. ''This is as good a time as any for Heather to learn. I'll have them get her a gentle mount.''

Heather followed him out the door. She had misgivings about climbing atop a horse, but at least she, and not the flirty receptionist, would be the one riding off with Matt. After what Billinger said this morning and what she'd seen in the motel room, she had no desire to be left alone at the Galloping R.

A few minutes later, after a close-up look at the animal he'd chosen, she changed her mind. ''Can't you find me a smaller horse?''

''I could, but the wrangler on duty said Rosy's the most gentle mare in the stable. They save her for first-time riders and children. Talk to her softly as you approach her and don't be afraid. Horses always sense fear.''

''Then I doubt she'll be fooled by my talking softly.''

''There's nothing to be afraid of. These horses walk this trail every day, and they've never lost a rider yet. Well, hardly ever.'' Matt tightened the cinch on the saddle and placed his hand on the horse's head, whispering in the animal's ear that they were taking her for a ride. She neighed in appreciation.

Heather stepped closer. ''Rosy acts as if she understood what you said.''

''She understands the tone. I could have been quoting the day's cattle prices and she'd have reacted the same way as long as I'd kept my tone nice and easy.''

''Okay, Rosy. I'm not afraid.'' Heather ran her hand down the length of Rosy's long neck. ''That's not my heart you hear. It's friendly drums in the distance. You and I are going to follow the paths Trigger trod, and Trigger never threw Roy Rogers.''

''You'll be all right, Heather. We'll take it slow, walk until you're ready to go a little faster.''

Heather recognized Matt's tone. It was the same soothing one he'd used on Rosy, but it was working. She took a deep breath. After all she'd been through in the last two days, she'd surely survive a ride on a horse.

''I'll help you into the saddle and then show you how to use the reins. Controlling them will let you communicate with Rosy on the trail, let her know what you want her to do.''

Matt's mouth was at Heather's ear, his breath warm on her neck. Emotion rose inside her, unsettling, dancing along her nerve endings. ''I think we better get started,'' she managed, her voice weak and lacking conviction.

''Heather.''

Her name was a whisper, husky with tamped-down desire. She turned to face Matt, knowing what would follow.

Chapter Six

Matt's mouth claimed Heather's, and he reeled with the sensation. Even as the kiss deepened, he knew it was all wrong, yet he couldn't stop. Heather was in his arms, her breath mingling with his, challenging every aspect of his control.

Finally, it was Heather who pulled away. "I think we'd better go," she whispered, but the strain in her voice gave her away.

She'd been as consumed as he had by the kiss. The thought pleased him and then turned bitter. What the devil was he thinking of? Heather had been through enough the last two days without the lawman who was honor-bound to protect her taking advantage of her. A lawman who had nothing more to offer than a meaningless kiss and an investigation that might tear the heart right out of her.

"I'm sorry, Heather."

She looked him in the eye. "Sorry because you didn't like the kiss...or because you did?"

The challenge was plain. He let it ride. They both knew the answer. Bending down, he wove his hands together to form a step. "Put your right foot here," he instructed, eager to be moving.

He understood action, the same way he understood handling an investigation. Right now, he was itching to get back to both and to forget the desire that had rung his bells a few seconds ago.

Heather threw her arm around his shoulder and planted a foot into his hand. She swung her leg over the horse's flank and scooted into place on the saddle.

"Slip your feet into the stirrups. I may need to adjust the length."

"It's a long way to the ground," she said. Her voice fell in an uneven rhythm.

"You're doing fine. Just don't look down." He adjusted the stirrups and placed the reins in her hand. Their fingers brushed, and once again he knew he was in big trouble. He'd forget how to breathe before he forgot how it felt to kiss her, and long before he reached the stage where he didn't want to do it again.

Resolutely controlling his emotions, he demonstrated the use of the reins. In no time she had the simple skill down pat. He mounted the horse he'd picked out for himself and led the way out of the corral and down a winding path that led to Crockett Creek, which turned out to be a creek in name only. It was a trickle at best. He talked of the scenery, as they eased into Heather's first nervous moments of the ride.

The sun was at their back, the wind in their faces. It would have been Matt's idea of a perfect day if it weren't for the fact that a killer was on the loose, and the beautiful woman riding behind him had likely been the intended victim.

The woman who had been shot in her hotel room had been close to Heather's age, nearly the same size and dressed in her clothes. Was it a case of mistaken identity, or had the killer forced Ariana to parade around in Heather's clothes before he killed her?

The sickness of the image turned his stomach, but it was no sicker than he'd seen more than once in real life. And then there were the sandals. His mind swam in the stream of possibilities, but his eyes stayed on the trail, mindful of anything that might spook Heather's horse and cause her trouble. She was knee-deep in that already.

"I COULD GET used to this," Heather admitted before they'd covered the first mile, "especially with a horse like Rosy."

"Does that mean you're ready to take her to a canter?"

"I didn't say that."

Matt gave his horse a little more freedom, easing into a slightly faster pace that wouldn't frighten Heather. She and Rosy kept up easily, and the smile of satisfaction on Heather's face was proof enough she was handling the new speed with ease.

His mind drifted back to the motel and stayed locked in mire and details until they rounded a clump of sweet gum trees and were met by the sound of hammering—and loud male voices.

"Looks like you found the place," Ben boomed, as the sound of hooves alerted him to their presence. He left his spot in the shade and came lumbering toward them.

"We couldn't miss it," Matt said. "Once the horses set foot on the trail, they kept to it just the way you've trained them."

"It's a good thing. Some of those tourists get lost finding their mouths with a full fork."

Matt studied the group. The hammering was coming from a spot near a man-made pond where two wranglers were assembling a row of wooden picnic tables.

"You brought a guest." Ben smiled and walked over to offer Heather a hand in dismounting. "Nice of you to brighten our day with a beautiful woman.'' He flashed her a toothy smile. ''Miss Lombardi, isn't it?''

Matt climbed from his horse and tethered the animal while Ben tended Rosy. ''We've had some trouble, Ben. I guess you've probably heard about some of it by now.'' He didn't waste time on small talk. It wasn't his strong suit, as Heather had so bluntly pointed out to him on more than one occasion.

''If you're talking about what happened to Miss Lombardi, I heard about it,'' Ben said, hitching up his jeans. ''That kind of thing makes a man want to buckle on his .38 and go gunning for the skunks, the way we would have done in the old days.'' He took a long, hard look at Heather's face. ''Now that I see for myself what the bastards did, I'm even more inclined to go after them myself.''

''Forget the .38,'' Matt said. ''If you really want to help, give me some information.''

Ben's eyes narrowed into slits. ''Of course. What kind of information would that be, Matt?''

''Which of your wranglers were unaccounted for last night?''

''My help's all over twenty-one. I don't do bed checks.'' He shifted his weight from one foot to another and ground the toe of his boot into a tuft of grass. ''Have you got a reason to suspect someone from my ranch was involved in this?''

''You know me, Ben. I don't need reasons. I'm an equal-opportunity Ranger. I suspect everyone.''

''Then you better spread your suspicions around. It might not have even been local guys who did the dirty work. Somebody driving through town might be responsible.''

''Any reason for you to think that?''

''We haven't had trouble like this before. I don't see any reason why it would start now.''

"You're right." Matt said, his voice still friendly. "Still, I'd like the names of every wrangler who can't prove he was at the Galloping R between six and ten last night. I have to start somewhere."

"Does that mean you have nothing to go on?" Ben asked. He stepped closer, swatting at a gnat that was cruising the top of his earlobe.

"It means I don't have a suspect in custody."

"I'll be glad as the next fellow when you do. Tourists getting beat up doesn't help my business any. When do you want this list?"

"Yesterday."

Ben chuckled awkwardly. Matt waited a moment before he threw in the next bit of news. "The attack's not the only trouble. We had a young woman murdered this morning at the motel. You might have known her. Ariana Walker. She worked for Rube from time to time."

Heather watched and listened as Matt told of the horror of the last few hours in the same calm, steady voice he'd used to question Ben about his employees. His gaze never touched her, zeroing in on Ben. She recognized the tactic, but was amazed by his proficiency at it.

The talk circled around the murder and back to her attack. Heather stepped away, roaming down to the area where the wranglers were at work. For all she knew one of the men wielding a hammer could be responsible for her black eyes and bruises, but she was safe here, with Matt so close by. And if she was lucky, she might recognize a voice or notice one of her scratch marks on someone's face or arms.

"Howdy, ma'am." The wrangler closest to her laid down his hammer, tipping his cowboy hat as she approached.

"Howdy, yourself. You look like you know what you're

doing. You've put a table together in the short time I've been talking to your boss."

"I know what I'm doing, but I'm not doing what I like. I hired on to handle the horses, but I learned quick. When you work for Ben Wright, you do what needs to be done to keep the paying guests happy."

"And picnic tables will keep them happy?"

"Cookouts." He shook his head disdainfully. "Me, I'd take my grub inside in the air conditioning, but tourists thrive on heat and bugs."

"Have you worked at the Galloping R long?"

"Going on my second year. I'm saving money to buy a small spread of my own up in the hill country. At the rate I'm going, I won't get there until I'm too old to run cattle on it."

Heather looked up as another wrangler left his pile of lumber and ambled over to join them. She stepped backwards, her breath quick and shallow. The cowboy's hat was pulled low, but it didn't hide a cut over his right eye or the bruise that discolored his jaw.

She'd fought for her life last night, swinging her fists and clawing with her nails, but could she have delivered this kind of damage to one of her attackers?

Footsteps rustled the grass behind her, and she whirled around. Matt stepped behind her. "Looks like you fellows got a hot day for table building."

"It's not too bad." The guy with the bruise responded to Matt's statement, then turned to walk away.

Matt stepped in front of him. "Looks like you had a bad *night,* too. What does the other fellow look like?"

The wrangler snickered. "Right now, he looks fine, but his day is coming."

"Who'd you tie into it with?"

"This ain't a matter for the law." The cowboy cocked his head defiantly.

Matt stepped into the wrangler's space and flashed his badge. "Miss Lombardi here was attacked last night, and a woman was killed today in town. Right now *everything's* a matter for the law. If you don't like jail cells, I suggest you start talking."

"Tell him what happened, George," the other wrangler prodded. "The jerk that did that to you isn't worth going to jail for."

George used a finger to shove the brim of the hat off the cut. "Some guy got rowdy two nights ago out at the road-house, started harassing one of the waitresses. I told him to lay off, and when I went to get in my pickup truck, he jumped me. He came at me from behind, the coward's way."

"Do you know the coward's name?"

"Nope. Never laid eyes on him before the other night, but I'll know him when I see him again. Only this time I'll be ready for him."

"Describe him for me."

Heather sat on one of the picnic benches while Matt made notes in his ever-ready pocket notebook. She listened to the description, but nothing clicked. A scrawny fellow in jeans and a Western shirt, blond, middle-aged. Once again, the description fit a couple of dozen guys she'd seen in the last week. Even if it hadn't, she wouldn't have been able to match it to one of her attackers. Her assailants had worn masks.

Matt exchanged a few more comments with the wran-glers and then took Heather's arm and led her back to their horses. Once again, he helped her climb into the saddle, but this time the contact was cool and impersonal.

Ben walked over and stopped beside them. "Have you talked to Logan Trenton lately?"

"No, should I have?"

"He keeps his ear pretty close to the ground. He might know something. Besides, I'm not the only fellow around here who has help. You might want to question him about his hired hands, or is he too rich to get this kind of treatment?"

"I'm not going to waste my breath answering that question."

"I guess you'll be going to his big shindig Friday night though."

Matt was already turning his horse around. "It's hard to say where I might be on Friday. I guess it all depends on how long it takes me to find a murderer."

Heather waited until they were out of Ben's earshot before she began her questions. "Do you think Ben Wright could be the boss my attackers were talking about?"

"It's hard to say." He brought his horse alongside hers. "I'll find whoever's responsible, Heather. I just wish that was my biggest worry right now."

His answer surprised her. She studied his profile, straight in the saddle, his dark hair poking from beneath his hat. His skin was bronzed from the sun, his angles hard, his muscles taut.

He was a man of many facets. Last night when he'd tended her wounds, she'd glimpsed a hint of tenderness. Today, when they'd found Ariana's body, she'd felt his fury. And now she sensed something deep inside him that drove him, something that reached beyond his macho sense of duty to the badge he wore.

"What else are you worried about?" she asked.

He faced her, his gaze penetrating. "You," he said. "I'm worried about keeping you safe."

"I'm staying with you at your ranch. Surely I'll be safe there. Who in their right mind would touch a woman sleeping under the roof of a Texas Ranger?"

"That's the other thing I'm worried about."

"I don't understand."

"I'm worried how in the hell I'm going to stay in *my* right mind with you sleeping under my roof."

She didn't have time to answer before he broke into a faster speed and put a few yards between them.

HEATHER PACED THE FLOOR of Matt's ranch house, from the dining room to the kitchen and back to the bedroom. Matt had left her at the ranch while he drove to the autopsy site, and there was nothing she hated worse than being shut out of things.

He hadn't left her alone. She was a prisoner, well treated, but a prisoner all the same. Her assigned guard was Tommy Joe, one of Gabby's overzealous deputies who took his duties very seriously. For the first hour he'd dogged her every footstep, following her from one room to the next.

Finally she'd convinced him that in a house this small, he would hear her if she so much as whimpered, let alone called out. Now he was in the living room, reading an outdated copy of *Texas Monthly*.

She checked to make sure he hadn't shot himself with the gun he kept fingering and then went to the kitchen for a glass of the lemonade she'd made earlier. The sun was resting on the horizon, but the heat of the day lingered, defeating the efforts of Matt's window cooling unit.

Glass in hand, she shoved through the screen door, reassuring Tommy Joe that she would go no farther than the porch swing. It wasn't that she didn't appreciate Matt's concern about her safety. She did. She only wished she was doing more than waiting around while he did the leg work.

She'd had such high hopes for this vacation. She'd managed to save up so that she had three weeks off, but if something didn't break soon, she'd have to go back to work knowing no more than she had when she'd left Atlanta. As it was, the pile of work waiting for her return was probably already a small mountain. Still, she'd take every day she had coming to her. This was too important not to give it her best shot. After a lifetime of wondering, this was the first time she'd had both the time and the resources to actively search for her birth mother. She had so many questions. There were lots of valid reasons for a woman to give her baby away. And no matter what Kathy's reasons were, Heather didn't blame her.

It was just that she'd always wondered about her birth mother, wondered who she was, why she'd had to give up her baby. Heather couldn't explain it in any way that didn't sound hokey. She only knew that she felt a need to connect with the unknown part of her past, knew that she wouldn't be complete until she did.

Lost in thought, she didn't hear the truck approaching until the door slammed shut and Matt climbed out. Tommy Joe bounded out the front door and down the steps, probably eager to tell Matt what a lousy prisoner she'd been.

The two of them talked for a minute, but even straining, she couldn't make out the gist of the conversation. A few minutes later, the deputy waved to her and climbed into his own truck. He was probably as glad to be rid of her as she was him. He'd clearly wanted a clinging virgin to watch over.

She was neither.

The sun sank a little lower in the sky, painting streaks of orange across the paling blue as Matt stamped up the steps and onto the porch. Shadows fell across his face, but they didn't hide the worry that was etched into every line.

Still he managed a forced smile as he caught sight of her. "Got any more of that stuff?" he asked, eyeing her lemonade glass.

"Half a pitcher, unless my bodyguard finished it off." She jumped to her feet. "Would you like for me to get you some?"

"I'd love a glass, but only if you'll come back and sit beside me in the swing while I drink it."

"Don't worry. I'll be back. I want to hear everything you've learned since you deserted me here today."

"Be glad that I left you behind. An autopsy is not something you want to experience firsthand unless you have to. And the only other thing you missed was another talk with Rube. Gabby had him into his office for questioning."

"I thought this was going to be your case."

"It is. As of..." He pushed his shirtsleeve up and glanced at his watch. "As of forty-five minutes ago. But Gabby will still be involved. In most cases, we Rangers only assist the locals."

"Did you get anything new from Rube?"

"Only that he'd seen a strange car in town yesterday, a blue Camaro, late model, with some guy behind the wheel he hadn't seen around Dry Creek before. The car had New Mexico plates."

Matt dropped into the swing, hooking his hands behind his neck. A lump caught in Heather's throat. The seductive, tempting cowboy she'd met at the café last night had disappeared, replaced by a man who showed distinct signs of overwork and stress.

She left him there and went for the lemonade. When she returned, his eyes were closed and his head was slumped forward. She hesitated by the swing, hating to wake him. Finally, a horse neighed in the distance, and he opened his eyes.

Stopping the sway of the swing with his foot, he reached for her hand and pulled her down beside him. "Thanks," he said, taking the lemonade. His fingers lingered against hers a little longer than necessary.

The unexpected caress touched her, comforting but at the same time unsettling. She'd only known Matt twenty-four hours, and yet she was living in his house, bringing him lemonade at the close of a long and frustrating day, sitting beside him in a creaky porch swing.

The tug to her heart now was even more frightening than the attraction that smoldered between them, heating every look, every touch. It had to be the dramatic situation they'd been hurled into. If she read anything else into their relationship, she'd be fooling herself and making it more difficult for them to work together.

She waited until Matt had downed half the lemonade and the muscles in his arms and neck had started to relax before asking her first question. "Did the autopsy show anything unusual?"

He stared into the gathering dusk. "Nothing we didn't expect to find. Ariana was shot at close range, and it was definitely not suicide. The bullet was from a .44 Magnum. Rube says he doesn't own a gun like that. There were no contusions or scratches to the body except those from the bullet wound."

"So she didn't struggle with the killer."

"Exactly. Which means it could have been someone she knew or that she was taken by surprise. We're not even sure why she was in your room. She didn't have her cleaning supplies with her."

"Maybe she heard someone in the room and went to check it out."

"Possibly, but at some point and for some unknown reason, she decided to try on your clothes."

"Could it be that she just wanted to see how she'd look in a nice suit? Women frequently try on clothes for fun when they're shopping."

"Yeah," Matt stretched his long legs in front of him. "Or maybe someone else decided he'd like to see how she looked in your clothes."

Heather tried to imagine the scene. Ariana in the musty motel room with a man, a stranger or maybe a lover. Ariana slipping out of her own cotton skirt and faded work shirt and perusing the choices, choosing a silky cream blouse and a blue linen suit. The man waiting until she was fully dressed and probably preening before the mirror. Then he'd put a bullet into her heart and had stolen her life away.

Or maybe Ariana hadn't been preening at all. She could have been shivering with fear. The images clawed inside Heather. She took a deep breath and forced these thoughts away. She needed facts and reason.

"Was anyone close enough that they could have heard Ariana if she'd called for help?" Heather pulled a foot into the swing and tucked it under her leg.

"Rube said he was in the office most of the morning, plenty close enough to hear a scream. He didn't hear a thing."

"He sure got to me fast when *I* screamed."

"I asked about that. He said he'd seen you go in and was on his way over to see how you were doing. He'd already heard about your accident."

"New travels fast in Dry Creek. What about Rube's wife? Did she hear or see anything?"

Matt tapped his fingers against the glass. "She claims she'd taken medicine for a migraine and had fallen into a dead sleep."

"I detect a little doubt on your part."

Matt finished his lemonade and set the glass on the floor

under the swing. "She seemed a little nervous when I talked to her at the motel after the shooting. Shaky, but not out of it as she would have been if Rube had roused her from a drugged sleep."

"Couldn't the shock of hearing about Ariana have caused that reaction?"

Matt slipped an arm over the back of the swing and wound a finger in Heather's hair. "Are you looking for a job with the department?" The humor in his voice was strained. "I'm supposed to be the know-it-all Ranger, and you're supposed to stare at me with those big, gray eyes, admiring my brilliance."

"I would, but I can't see well enough to stare from under the swelling."

Matt traced the tender area around her eye and down her right cheek. "Does it still hurt?"

"Only when I laugh."

"Then I don't guess you'll be needing any painkillers tonight."

"Not likely." She felt Matt's hand come to rest on her shoulder. As always, his touch jolted her senses. No matter how grim the discussion, it never totally overshadowed the effect of his nearness. She'd have to work all the harder at staying focused.

"Do you think Ariana could have known something about Kathy Warren, that whoever was determined I not ask questions about her thought Ariana might talk?"

"I can't imagine what the connection would be. Ariana would have been five years old at the time your mother was said to be in Dry Creek."

Heather's mind flashed back to the body in the bloody bathroom. "So she was thirty. So young to die."

"Way too young." His mouth twisted into a frown. "Are you *sure* it would have been twenty-five years ago this fall that Kathy Warren was supposed to have been in Dry Creek?''

"That's what I was told. I'll be twenty-five the fifth of October, and I was only a few days old when she dropped me off.''

"A year of trouble in Dry Creek." His muscles tensed. "One woman beaten and left for dead, and another one who apparently left secrets that still haunt the town today."

"I'm not following you."

Matt leaned forward and propped his elbows on his knees. "I was just starting school that year, finally big enough to tag along with my half-brothers when they went hunting. It was about this time of the night, not quite dark but late enough—we were supposed to be home."

A coyote howled in the distance, and Heather shivered, but didn't interrupt. For once Matt was opening up, talking in more than clipped sentences that delivered cold facts.

"We heard a moan," he continued, staring into space. "I thought it was a wild animal and started to run, but my brothers went over to investigate. They found a woman, bloody and bruised. She was barely breathing, but she opened her eyes and looked at us. We went and got the pickup truck—my oldest brother was too young to have a license, but he knew how to drive. We put her in the back and took her home, never once realizing that we could have killed her in the process."

"Did she live?"

He nodded and leaned back in the swing. "She did. She always said our finding her was a miracle. My brothers and I agreed, but we thought the miracle was for us. She turned out to be the best cook in the county and the best nurse for stomach aches, poison ivy and bruised pride a boy ever had."

His eyes lit up, softening the rugged lines in his face and

easing the defiant jut of his jaw. "And the best all-around substitute mom in the state of Texas."

"The Susan who taught you to cook?"

"That was her. Susan Hathaway."

"You mean she stayed with you? What a wonderful story."

"She stuck with us like a poor uncle come dinnertime, as my grandfather liked to say."

"Did you find out why she'd been beaten?"

"No. She recovered slowly, but never remembered anything about the attack."

"Were the men who did it to her prosecuted?"

"They were never arrested. It was the one crime my dad never solved. Strange, don't you think, for a sheriff not to follow up on a crime that hit so close to home?"

"What does he say about it?"

"Jake McQuaid? He doesn't explain himself to anyone." The bitterness in Matt's tone left no doubt that he had *not* paid his father a compliment.

Heather scooted closer, envisioning Matt at seven, motherless, frightened at animal sounds. She stole her hand into his, reconciling the strength of him now with the boy of the past.

"So you have a long history of saving women who've been attacked," she said. "No wonder you're so good at it."

He turned to face her. She couldn't read the message in his eyes. They were dark as the night had become, piercing, but mysterious.

"I'm just thankful it wasn't your body I found today, Heather." His voice was low and husky.

Heather's insides quaked, emotion swelling inside her. How could a man she barely knew have such a devastating effect on her? "We should go in," she whispered.

"I know."

Their eyes met, kindling a crackling surge of desire that left her breathless. And then she was in his arms, his lips on hers. Lost in the kiss, she forgot everything except the passion soaring inside her.

She wasn't sure how many times the phone rang before they were aware of its jingling coming from inside. "I have to get that," Matt said, pulling away. "It could be about the case."

She nodded, and he headed across the porch and into the house. Wrapping her arms around her chest, she thought only of Matt, unwilling to lose the magic of the moment. But the magic died on her kiss-swollen lips the moment he reappeared.

"I'm afraid to ask," she said, "but what's happened now?"

"That was Rube. We don't have to wait for fingerprints. The white sandals belong to his wife."

Chapter Seven

"What does that mean?" Heather asked. "Why were her shoes in my room? Did Rube's wife see the killer? Is she involved in this?"

Matt shook his head. "Don't you have to come up for air?"

"Not when something like this hits. Why didn't she say those were her sandals while we were there this morning?"

"All I know is that Rube wants me to come over and see Edna. He said she's hysterical and won't tell him anything except that the white sandals are hers."

"I'm going with you."

"Right." He stepped to the edge of the swing and offered a hand. "You're going with me as far as John Billinger's house. You can stay with him and his family until I get back."

"No!" She jumped from the swing. "Look at me, Matt. I'm the one who got my face beat in. I'm the one who found Ariana's body. All of this started because I asked a few questions. You are *not* cutting me out of the good parts of this investigation. I've earned my right to be there."

"There are no 'good parts.'" He turned and headed down the front steps. "And you are not part of the investigating team."

She passed him at a near-run, opened the passenger door to the truck and climbed in. "I refuse to be left out of this. Don't even think of stopping at Billinger's place."

Staring straight ahead, she braced herself for an argument that didn't come. He simply revved the engine and backed out of the narrow drive and onto the dirt road without one look in her direction.

Matt's muscles tensed as silence smoldered between them. Things were galloping out of hand, and it was all his fault. His job was to protect innocent citizens and apprehend the guilty, not to seduce victims.

Yet twice now he'd given in to the overwhelming attraction he felt any time Heather was near, losing his control like some love-struck schoolboy. Nothing like this had ever happened to Matt McQuaid. Now the boundary lines between duty and personal feelings were jagged instead of clean and straight. Now every decision he made had dangerous repercussions.

"Why is it you feel the need to go back to the scene of the murder?" he asked, when his irritation with himself and Heather had cooled to just below the boiling point.

She crossed her arms, stuck her nose in the air and jutted her chin out like a strutting cock. "I didn't start any of this, but since I'm in the middle of it, I need to know what's going on and why. Ariana's dead. I could be next."

"You told me you trusted me to see that you aren't."

She twisted in her seat, finally turning to face him. "I don't want to argue, Matt. It won't get us anywhere. Besides, I'm not as good at these rapid mood changes as you are. One minute you can't keep your hands and lips off me. The next you're all but shoving me out of your way."

Seemingly of its own volition, Matt's mind swept back to the kiss. Losing control like that was unforgivable in this situation and as foreign to his life-style as champagne and caviar. ''I shouldn't have kissed you, Heather. It won't happen again.''

''Won't it?''

Matt's insides knotted. He knew what she was thinking, that his willpower hadn't been worth two cents so far. She was probably used to that reaction from men and expected more of the same. If he had anything to offer, she might get what she expected, but he was who he was, a man who'd never learned the art of making relationships work. Not even a woman like her could change that.

''I was out of order, Heather, a simple mistake. Don't go reading anything into it. I'm the kind of man you'd throw back if you caught me.''

''I don't have a line out, Matt.'' She undid her seat belt as they neared the gate.

He slowed to a stop. ''I didn't mean it that way. The kiss was my fault, not yours. But it will go better for both of us if we keep our relationship strictly business.''

She opened her door, but paused, capturing his gaze. ''All business? Fine with me. Only how are we going to ignore the fact that every time we get within touching distance or even are alone in the same room, the sizzle of hormones is louder than that bacon you fried up for breakfast?''

She was out of the truck before Matt could respond. He was fresh out of arguments anyway, especially when the hormones she talked about were raging inside him even now. But he was sure he could tamp down his feelings, tuck them away so deep inside him he almost forgot they existed. He'd done it all his life and for far less reason than he had now.

A coyote howled in the distance and an owl hooted overhead. Both creatures who knew how deceptive and dangerous nights in South Texas could be. There was a killer on the loose, with elusive ties to Heather. He'd have to work fast to untangle the knots and discover what was going on.

Her life depended on it.

IT DIDN'T TAKE a Texas Ranger to figure out that Rube's wife was lying. Heather knew it from the moment the woman opened her drawn mouth. But it wasn't the lies that made Heather's blood run cold. It was the fear that crouched in Edna's eyes and turned her warm-toned complexion to pasty Swiss cheese.

"What time were you in room 4, the room that was rented to Heather Lombardi?" Gabby repeated a question that had been asked before.

Edna recrossed her legs and wrung the tissue in her hands. "I don't know, sometime after breakfast. I went in to see if Ariana had cleaned. She hadn't. And she wasn't there either. I told you that already."

Matt eased between Gabby and Edna, his relaxed manner contrasting with Gabby's accusing one. "We're not blaming you for anything, Edna. We just need to know the truth so we can find the killer."

She nodded, but kept her gaze directed at the scarred wooden floor.

"How do you think your shoes got in Heather's room?" he asked.

"I don't know. All I know is I had on these old tennis shoes today." She stuck her feet in front of her as if that should settle the question. "The sandals might have been on the porch. I wear them outside when I'm working in the garden."

"That's quite a green thumb you have, Edna, to coax flowers out of this dry clay," Matt commented. "The flowers around the front of the building look great. You must water them all the time."

Edna's lips split into a smile. "Every day. We have a deep well, you know. Ariana always said I had the prettiest flowers in the whole town."

"You and Ariana must have gotten to be pretty good friends, what with her working here from time to time. Did you ever see her with anyone around the motel? A boyfriend, maybe?" Matt asked.

Edna's breasts heaved beneath the cotton shirt that hung outside a pair of denim shorts. "I don't know who Ariana sees. She's a grown woman."

"She *was*," Matt said. His tone was insistent. "Now we need to find out who killed her. Just try to remember. Have you seen any unfamiliar men around here on the days Ariana was working?"

"She's told you everything she knows," Rube complained, wrapping an arm around his wife's shoulders. "Can't you let it go at that? Both of you know she's not a killer."

"We didn't say she was, Rube." Matt kept his voice calm and friendly. "Answer the question, Edna. Have you seen anyone hanging around with Ariana?"

"No." She squirmed in her seat and scooted closer to Rube. "I didn't see anyone today either. I don't know anybody who would want to kill a sweet girl like that. I keep telling you that. Why don't you believe me?"

Heather breathed a sigh of relief as Matt said he'd hold off on further questioning. They had been at this over an hour, and Edna showed no signs of changing her story and blurting out the truth, whatever that might be.

Matt explained to Rube that neither he nor Edna should leave town and warned them not to talk to anybody but himself or Gabby about the crime. Rube agreed and led Edna away.

Gabby watched them go, hitching up his jeans so that

they could work their way back down and under his belly. "You can't count on nobody to cooperate with the law anymore," he muttered, stamping towards the door.

Matt took Heather's arm and they followed the sheriff outside. The night air had grown cooler, and she breathed in the tart freshness of it. They were almost to their vehicles before Gabby made his assessment.

"That got us exactly nowhere."

"I'd say a little further than that," Matt corrected. "We know Edna's awfully upset."

Gabby snorted. "As jumpy as spit on a hot skillet. She's scared, that's what she is, and upset about poor Ariana. They'd gotten to be friends."

Heather lifted her hair from her neck to let the breeze cool her skin. "I think she's lying."

Both men turned, eyebrows arched, as if they'd forgotten she was there. Matt leaned against the front fender of his truck. "You think she's lying about having had the shoes on?"

"I think she's lying about everything. She knows something, but she's afraid to open her mouth. Every time you asked her a question, she looked to her husband before she answered. Maybe she saw the man who killed Ariana, and he threatened to kill her too if she squealed on him."

"If that's the case, why would he threaten her?" Gabby asked. "Why didn't he just shoot Edna while he was at it?"

Heather didn't back down. "Maybe he didn't want to kill her. Maybe they're friends, or relatives."

Gabby shook his head. "This ain't the big city. We don't go around accusing our neighbors of murder around here, Miss Lombardi, unless we got strong evidence. Rube ain't got a mean bone in his body, and Edna's good as gold. She'd have no cause to lie to us."

Heather saved her breath and let Matt and Gabby make their parting comments. Now that the questioning was over, she wondered why she had insisted on coming. She was tired and hungry and more frustrated than ever.

Finally, Gabby crawled in his truck and backed out of the dirt drive. Matt stepped behind her. "Are you too tired for a walk?"

"So that you can tell me more about how I shouldn't think any citizen of Dry Creek could lie, much less commit a crime?"

"No." Matt kicked at the dirt with the toe of his boot. "I agree with you. Edna was lying, no doubt about it. But she was scared, too."

"So what are you going to do about it?"

"Give her a little time to stew. I had Gabby put a guard on this place tonight, though he argued there was no need for it. I want to know who comes around to talk to her after we've gone. And I want to make sure she's not the next target for shooting practice." Matt took Heather's arm and guided her away from the truck and down a dirt path that ran the edge of the highway.

"I don't get it," she said. "If you and I could both tell Edna was lying, why didn't Gabby see it? It's as if he chooses what he wants to believe and ignores the other evidence."

"That's a problem when you're policing people you've known all your life. Familiarity sometimes gets in between the investigator and the suspects and witnesses, and makes objectivity impossible."

They walked past the motel to the front of a restaurant that had closed for the night. The windows were dark, the wood of the building old and battered, the roof a slanting line of tin.

A shiver snaked down her spine. She could swear someone was watching them. The town did this to her, made her feel the presence of ghosts. Perhaps they were the remnants of her own life, the past she didn't know. "Does this walk have a purpose?" she asked, increasing her pace.

"This is the spot where Kathy Warren would have caught a bus if she actually did leave Dry Creek that October night."

Heather stopped and looked around. "This is a restaurant."

"It is now." Matt tugged her toward a creaking sign. "I asked a few questions today. Twenty-five years ago this building was a hotel that also served as a bus stop."

"It's not big enough."

"The back part burned in '79. The hotel had closed a couple of years before, and the bus stop had moved down by Grady's Mercantile."

Heather dropped to a bench that sat by the front door. "My mother might have waited in this very spot for a bus to take her away from me."

She trembled, and Matt dropped down beside her, taking her hands in his. She swayed closer, suddenly craving his warmth. "I wonder if it was dark and deserted like this. I wonder if she was afraid, if she felt all alone, if she thought about me."

Matt gathered Heather beneath the curve of his arm. He knew what she wanted to hear, but he couldn't say it. "There's no reason to think she was afraid. She was doing what she chose to do."

"But she was young, barely more than a teenager. Mrs. Purdy told me that. She didn't want to leave me. She made them promise over and over to take good care of her little Heather."

"Is she the one who named you?"

"Yes. My adoptive parents kept the name my birth

mother had given me. Mom said they wanted to do something for the woman who'd given me to them.''

The coils tightened in Matt's stomach as his own memories merged with Heather's. Only he had no illusions left.

''Your mother left, Heather. Either she couldn't deal with a baby or she was running away from something, or someone. We may find out which, but chances are you aren't going to like what we find.''

''So you've said before, but you can't know that.''

''You're right. All I know for sure is that she left you a hell of a legacy—people smashing in your face and planting bombs in your car. And there's a good chance that the bullet that killed Ariana today was meant for you. I shudder to think what waits around the next corner, all thanks to Kathy Warren.''

Heather pulled away from him. ''She gave me life, Matt. Part of her lives on inside me. And good or bad, I want to know the truth about her.''

''I hope so, Heather, because we've gone too far to back down now. The murder today made certain of that.'' Matt stood and extended a hand to Heather. She ignored it, standing on her own and stalking back towards the truck. He'd upset her again. No surprise.

As his Ranger captain had always said, he lacked the fine art of tact, always blurting out the truth when a white lie would be much more palatable. But what good did it do to coat a hard reality with sugar? It would still be bitter when the shell melted away.

Tomorrow they'd pay a visit to Mrs. Purdy and then he'd spend the afternoon digging up the past, his own as well as Heather's. And if it turned out the two were tied together in some bizarre web of murder, there might be all hell to pay—for him, too.

His father had been sheriff of Dry Creek twenty-five

years ago, and he had not found Susan's attackers. As Matt had told Heather, it was the only major crime in his district he'd let go unsolved...

Matt had his theories on the subject. He hoped this investigation proved him wrong. No matter what personal wounds festered between him and his father, he didn't want to be the man who tarnished the legend of Jake McQuaid.

"YOU MUST BE STARVING," Matt said, pushing through the back screen door of his ranch house and standing aside for Heather to pass. "It's nearly ten, and we haven't had dinner."

"I thought maybe starvation was part of the protection plan."

"No, but it's pretty standard procedure for a Ranger chasing after a murderer. Eat on the run, or do without."

Heather opened the refrigerator. "There's milk and bread." She pulled opened the crisper and peeked inside. "And makings for a salad. I'll throw one together."

"That'll do for starters."

"A salad's a meal."

"Sure, for a jackrabbit. I take mine as an appetizer before a steak, grade A beef, not long off the hoof."

"How carnivorous. I guess the steak you're salivating for used to wander about on your ranch."

"Of course. I raise beef cattle. Damn good ones. I'll fire up the grill."

He pulled a pair of fresh-thawed filets still wrapped in freezer white from the refrigerator, and she realized he'd planned ahead. Steaks for two, an intimate dinner. The prospect dissolved her fatigue. Only she wasn't really a guest. Her presence had been forced upon Matt, all in the line of duty.

"What's that you're using on the steaks?" she asked

when he came back in the kitchen after firing the grill and started brushing a dark liquid over the meat.

"The Hathaway special marinade."

"Not the McQuaid special? After listening to the locals talk, I'd expect the McQuaids to be best at everything."

"My dad was well-liked by his cronies."

"You're too modest." Heather poked the lettuce under the faucet and let the water splash over the crisp leaves. "Jake McQuaid is a regular folk hero around here. Rube and I had a long conversation this morning while you were with Gabby and the body. He told me how Jake McQuaid had cleaned up the town and put a stop to the fights and shooting that went on every weekend. He said there were men still behind bars that Jake McQuaid put there when no one else would take them on."

"That's the way I've always heard it." Matt poked in the refrigerator. "Would you like a beer?"

"Are you having one?"

"At least one. It's been a long day. I might even have a bottle of wine somewhere if you'd rather have that."

"No, a beer would be fine."

He opened the can and poured hers into a tall glass. He left his own in the can, taking a long drink before he took two plates from the shelf and set them on the table.

"You don't seem quite as impressed with your father's accomplishments as the men around town," she said, not willing to drop the subject.

"He's my father. Living with a legend's a little harder than just knowing one." Matt came up behind her, reaching around her to open the drawer that housed the eating utensils. He took out forks and knives and moved away.

A casual move in a cozy kitchen, but her heart raced erratically. Her breath came quick and shallow while she threw together the fresh greens and chopped a tomato. She mixed her own dressing, a light oil-and-vinegar, avoiding the rich bottled one she found in the refrigerator.

By the time Matt reappeared in the kitchen with the steaks, her pulse had almost returned to normal. He pulled out a chair for her, and she slid into it, suddenly ravenous and not feeling the least bit carnivorous.

"You make a great salad," he said, after he'd swallowed the first bite. "I could get spoiled having you around."

"But then you'd have to put up with conversation with your meal."

"On second thought, maybe I could just get your recipe," he teased.

She stuck her tongue out at him and then rewarded his devastating smile with a few minutes of silence. Besides, it wasn't polite to talk with your mouth full, and for once her hunger took precedence over her curiosity.

The steak was cooked to perfection, brown on the outside, a touch of pink in the middle, succulent juices escaping from every bite, and so tender it seemed to melt in her mouth. She moaned in appreciation.

"I take it the steak is to your liking."

"It's wonderful. I'll swap recipes with you. My salad dressing for your Hathaway marinade."

"It wouldn't be the same. You'll just have to show up at my door again when you want steaks this good."

"Only if you promise your neighbors won't throw another welcoming party."

"I'd never have taken you for a party pooper." He forked another bite of steak.

Heather chewed contentedly, and part of the weight seemed to lift from her shoulders. It must be the beer and the food taking effect. It certainly couldn't be the situation, although even Matt was making a stab at small talk.

"I have to admit it's kind of nice having a beautiful

woman across the table from me oohing and aahing over my steaks."

"So why haven't you married?" she asked, and then wondered where the question had come from. "You don't have to answer if that subject is too personal for the body-guard/protector relationship."

Matt looked up from his plate. "You're not thinking of proposing, are you?"

"So you *do* have a sense of humor."

"I try not to but it slips out every now and then." He wiped his mouth on the napkin. When he met her gaze, the teasing smile had vanished. "I've thought about marriage, even got engaged once."

"What happened?"

"The lady in question wised up in time to save both of us a lot of misery. She said I didn't need her enough, that I was married to my job and my cows."

"Didn't you fight for her, try to convince her she was wrong?"

Matt's gaze caught and held Heather's. "She wasn't wrong. And I had no argument for what she said."

"Where is she now?"

"Married to the guy who was supposed to be my best man. They have a baby, and they're very happy. Strangely enough, I'm happy for them. He's still my best friend."

"Maybe you two weren't right for each other, but that doesn't mean you wouldn't be perfect for someone else. Surely you wouldn't let one bad experience frighten you away from marriage and a family."

"I know my limitations, and I don't go looking for trouble." He finished his beer and went to the refrigerator for another, signaling the conversation about marriage had ended. "Want another?" he asked, holding up a can.

"I still have half of the last one."

"It's warm by now. I'll get you a cold one."

"Why not? A good meal and two beers, and I should sleep like a baby."

He returned with the beers and settled back into his steak. Heather pushed her plate aside. She'd had enough food, but not nearly enough answers. One woman had walked away from Matt, blaming his inability to meet her needs on his job and his cows.

Heather's guess was it was something more than the job and cattle that ruled Matt, something that made him afraid of intimacy and commitment, made him keep people a safe distance from his heart.

He'd said he wouldn't kiss her again. She wondered how he'd react if she got up from the table right now and walked over and kissed him full on the mouth. Her insides quivered as titillating images danced across her mind.

"You're awfully quiet," Matt said after he'd chewed and swallowed the last bite of his steak and finished off his beer. "You must be exhausted after the day you've had. Why don't you get ready for bed, and I'll clean up in here."

"I'm not that tired."

Matt started to the sink with their plates. Heather got up to help. Idle hands, paired with the thoughts she'd been entertaining, could definitely lead to trouble. And her cup of problems was already spilling over the top.

THE THREE MEN HUDDLED behind the barn, away from prying eyes and ears.

The short, stocky one glared at the man who'd called the meeting. "I told you I didn't want to be mixed up in murder. I told you that up front."

"You should have thought of that twenty-five years ago."

"I did. You promised then we weren't going to kill anyone. Just rough Billy Roy up and get his attention—that's what you told me and that's the only reason I went along with you."

The tall, lanky guy stepped between the other two. "Forget Billy Roy. Why'd you go and kill Ariana? She didn't know anything."

"I didn't kill Ariana. *You* shot her."

"No, I didn't—why would I?" He wiped his clammy hands on his jeans. "It's Heather Lombardi and Matt McQuaid who are causing all the trouble."

"If you didn't kill Ariana, who did?" The short man was sweating buckets in spite of the cool, dry night air.

"Probably someone who thought she needed killing, but it has nothing to do with us. It was just damn poor timing. Now Matt McQuaid's not about to let things alone down here." The man raked his fingers through his graying hair. He'd kept his two accomplices quiet for years, but they were getting awfully nervous now. He'd have to do something fast.

"Keep your cool, and keep your mouths shut for a little while longer. I promise you we are not going to jail for the murder of Billy Roy Lassiter or for anything else."

"How can you guarantee that?"

"The same way I take care of everything else. I'm not afraid to do what needs to be done."

HEATHER SAT bolt upright, startled awake from a dreamless sleep. She glanced at the clock by her bed—it was 2:30 a.m., but there was light shining beneath her door. Evidently Matt was up. Maybe the killer had struck again.

Slinging her legs over the side of the bed, she ran her toes around until they found her slippers. She didn't bother with a robe.

The noise stopped her before she reached the door. A

sharp, shattering crack, like a gunshot outside her window. Oh, no, not again!

"Matt! Matt!"

But only the echo of her own voice answered her call.

Chapter Eight

The back door stood open, and the wind shuffled the edges of the newspaper on the kitchen table. Heart pounding, Heather rushed to the door and stared into the night. Slowly her eyes adjusted to the darkness. The shadows and angles materialized into the swing, the porch railing, the pickup truck. But no Matt.

Something rustled the grass, and she zeroed in on the spot, focusing on one lone figure crouched beneath a tangle of brush. Moonlight glinted off something in his hand.

If the figure was Matt, why was he crouched in the bushes, and what had he shot? Not a person, she begged silently. *Please don't let it be a person.*

Heather's heart slammed against her chest, her dread so real it stole her breath away. She couldn't handle another senseless death, another body. She'd never bargained for any of this when she'd come to Dry Creek.

"Matt, is that you?"

He stood up and stepped into full view. "It's me, Heather. Go back inside."

But something was wrong. He was clutching his arm, and holding a gun. She rushed down the steps to meet him. "What's wrong with your arm?" Before he could answer, she saw the blood dripping down his sleeve. Her stomach rolled wildly. "You've been shot."

"No, it's just a scratch." He walked past her.

"How did it happen? What were you doing out here in the middle of the night?"

"The horses were acting up, neighing and kicking around in the corral. I figured it was a varmint spooking them, so I went out to check."

"Was someone there?"

"I didn't see anyone, but somebody had left my ax stuck between the shelf and the supports with the blade pointing out. My arm caught the edge of it." Matt tore the shirt from his body and held his arm over the sink. Adjusting the faucet, he maneuvered his arm under the spray.

"I'll call 911."

"Don't even think about it."

"You're hurt, Matt. You have to see a doctor."

"Not for this. The doctor would shoot me himself if I woke him up for something as minor as this. I'll stop by Dr. Cappey's office tomorrow and have him take a look at it. I need to talk to him anyway."

"Isn't Dr. Cappey the vet?"

"Yeah. If he's good enough for my critters, he's good enough for a scratch. Don't worry," he added, obviously reading the concern in her face. "My shots are all up to date."

"Here, let me help you." She took a towel from the freshly folded stack in the laundry room and wrapped one around his arm to catch the drips of water. The bleeding had all but stopped, but the wound was an angry red.

"I'll get the antiseptic and the dressing," she said, hurrying to the bathroom. Fortunately Matt had an adequate supply of first aid equipment. She'd seen it this morning while getting some more medicine for her own cut, which paled in comparison to Matt's.

She rummaged and found some peroxide and bandages and a disinfecting ointment. When she got back to the kitchen, Matt was at the table poring over a page of notes.

"You said someone left the ax blade sticking out. Who besides you would have been in your tack room?"

"Could have been any number of people. I have help out here checking on things when I'm tied up in San Antonio. The young guys get careless, but that's no excuse. I can't imagine why the ax would have been in the tack room to start with."

"Did you find out what was spooking the horses?"

"No, it doesn't have to be much to get them jumpy."

"But I heard a shot."

"Something slithered in the grass when I stepped on it. I wasn't in a snake-friendly state of mind."

A rattlesnake. Even the possibility sent new shivers flying up Heather's spine. If she had to choose, she'd take a killer with legs any day. She pulled her chair next to Matt's and unscrewed the top from the bottle of peroxide.

"This will only hurt a *little*," she said, mimicking Matt's tone and words from a night ago. Only one night ago…it seemed like weeks. So much had happened.

She'd been in Dry Creek for five days. The first four had been uneventful except for the note, but from the minute Matt McQuaid had walked into her life, the action had been nonstop, and none of it good.

Well, none of it except what passed between the two of them when they were alone. She propped his arm on the folded towel and poured a dash of peroxide over the wound. It bubbled like a witch's brew, but Matt didn't even wince.

"You treat this like nothing, which makes me think

you've seen far worse. Were you ever shot in the line of duty?''

''Depends on what you call duty. My brother Cameron shot me once, accidentally of course. I was six, and he was playing with a BB gun. It hit me in the backside.''

''A BB couldn't have hurt as bad as this cut.''

''Not far from it. The thing stung like crazy, and I howled like I was dying. It scared Cam so bad he didn't touch any kind of gun again for years. Now, he's probably the best shot in Colorado.''

''I meant, have you ever been shot with a real bullet?''

''I took one of those, too. I was shot in the chest about five years ago while making a routine traffic stop, back when I was with highway patrol. I learned real quick not to turn my back on anyone.''

Heather dabbed the wound with ointment and wrapped it in a clean bandage, taping the edges down. ''You were lucky,'' she said. ''You're around to tell about it.'' Her gaze ran to Matt's bare chest and the scar that tried to hide beneath the mass of dark, curly hairs.

Her fingers rolled across the scar, catching in the hairs. Every inch of him was male, strong, masculine, sinewy, yet everyone was vulnerable to something. If the bullet had been a few centimeters to the left, it could have wiped out his life in a split second, the same way Ariana's life had been stolen from her.

Matt's hand closed around hers. She looked up and met his gaze. The fire was there, hot and burning, feeding the desire that washed through her.

As if reading her mind, he lowered his mouth to hers. His lips devoured her, roughly, hungrily, as if he couldn't stop himself. She didn't even try to stop. She wanted to taste him, to swallow his desire, bathe in his need of her.

''I shouldn't...''

She ended his protest with her mouth. She had learned something in her baptism of fire in Dry Creek. *Shouldn'ts, wouldn'ts, couldn'ts* were for ordinary times. Not for nights when the preciousness of life stood in stark contrast to the reality of death.

Matt's hands splayed across her back, his fingers digging into her flesh while he pulled her closer. Finally, he pushed away. "If we don't stop now, I won't be able to."

"Would that be so terrible?"

"It could be. For you." He stood and walked away from her, his shoulders catching the glare from the overhead light. "I have nothing to offer you except protection and help in finding out how you're involved in the madness that's overtaken Dry Creek. If you start expecting more from me, you'll only be disappointed."

She longed to go to him, to wrap her arms around him and tell him she could handle the problems of tomorrow better if she found some fulfillment tonight. But making love to him would only make her want him more.

"Why don't you go back to bed and try to get some sleep?" he coaxed. "We'll need to get an early start to visit Cass Purdy in the morning."

"If you're sure you're all right."

"I'm not fine, but my arm is. I wish a scratch was my biggest problem."

She turned and walked to the door that led to the hall.

"Heather." She stopped.

"Thanks."

"For what?"

"For dressing the cut."

"That was the least I could do, especially since I've ruined your vacation."

"That's not your doing. Kathy Warren must have been some woman to cause this kind of trouble twenty-five years after her death. And who knows what tomorrow will bring?''

''Facts, I hope.''

''Yeah. Sleep well,'' he said, ''and, just for the record—''

''Yes?'' She turned and caught his gaze. His eyes burned with the intensity that underlay every thing he did.

''I'm not sorry I broke my promise not to kiss you again. I'd have hated to go through life knowing I missed a kiss like that.''

Warmth stirred inside her. Just when she thought she had him all figured out, the Ranger had thrown her a curve. ''You may go through life missing a lot more,'' she said. ''Let me know if you're ever brave enough to find out.''

With that, she padded down the hall and back to her bed. Danger all around them, as thick as Texas stew, and still her emotions rocked with the attraction she felt for Matt McQuaid. Go figure.

CASS PURDY WAS WAITING for them at the door when they arrived. Heather did the introductions, and Cass ushered them into a tiny living room that was stuffed with the keepsakes of seventy years of living.

Pictures of her family filled small tables and stood in zigzag fashion across the bookshelves that flanked the fireplace. A stack of magazines filled a basket at the edge of the sofa, and a vase of silk roses rested in the center of the round coffee table.

''You two look as though you've been in a cockfight,'' Cass said, eyeing their bruises and bandages.

''It was a…'' Matt and Heather both answered at once. Heather stopped and let him finish.

''Heather had an accident in her car. Nothing serious. Mine's just a scratch I picked up on the ranch.''

He lied with apparent ease, a fact that sat uneasily in Heather's mind.

"I thought you said you were a Texas Ranger," Cass said, eyeing him suspiciously.

"I am." Matt fished his badge out of his pocket and held it out for Cass to see. "But I also own a small ranch near Dry Creek. I don't get to stay on it much, but running my few head of cattle's a nice break from chasing the bad guys."

"I imagine it would be. It's awfully nice of you to help Heather find her birth mother's family." Cass pushed her wire-framed glasses back up her nose. "Her mother was a nice lady. I didn't get much of a chance to know her, but I'm a good judge of character."

"I'm sure you are," Matt agreed. "What kinds of things did Heather's mother do that convinced you she was nice?"

"Well, she sure was upset over having to leave her baby. If she hadn't gotten killed so soon after that, I expect she'd have changed her mind altogether and come back for Heather long before the Lombardis had a chance to adopt her."

"She must have been a very special lady for you to re-member her so well. Either that or something else about her must have stuck in your mind. Twenty-five years is a long time."

Cass chuckled. "Not so long when you're seventy. Be-sides I remember the old days just fine. It's what happened yesterday I have trouble with. I've already forgotten to offer you folks something to drink. How about some coffee?"

Heather shifted so as not to sink into the worn chair. "We wouldn't want you to go to any trouble."

"Land sakes, it's no trouble being hospitable no more often than I have callers. Besides, the coffee's already made."

''Then let me help you,'' Heather offered.

Matt waited while the women went into the kitchen. No matter how Cass dismissed it, he thought it was strange she'd remember one particular woman so well. She must have come in contact with hundreds of babies and their deserting mothers during that time. So how had one stuck in her mind?

The reliability of Cass Purdy as a informant was suspect, though Heather certainly didn't see it that way. Cass was feeding her exactly what she wanted to hear, that her mother had loved her and hadn't wanted to abandon her.

He couldn't blame Heather. He'd fed himself the same diet of lies and wishes for more years than he cared to think about. Only both their moms had walked away, ready to start a new life without them. Mother love. It wasn't for everyone.

Matt tapped his fingers on the arm of the sofa, waiting impatiently until Heather and Cass returned with steaming cups of coffee and a plate of tea cakes. ''Tell me everything you remember about the night Heather was dropped off at the orphanage,'' he said, after they'd settled back with their coffee.

Cass picked up her knitting and stabbed the needles through the yarn as she talked. ''Kathy showed up at the door looking like a scared rabbit. Most of the women did, but there was something different about her. Everyone noticed it.''

Matt leaned forward. ''How was she different?''

Cass squeezed her lips together and wrinkled her brow. ''The way she talked for one thing, kind of refined, and she didn't say 'y'all' or drawl her words. She was blond, petite, pretty, but too thin to have just delivered a baby. It made me think she didn't take care of herself during the pregnancy.''

"How old was Heather when she brought her to the orphanage?"

"I don't rightly recall, under two weeks, I expect. She was a tiny little thing."

"I was five days old," Heather said, breaking into the conversation. "That was what my adoptive parents told me when I was old enough to understand. They were always honest with me, in a very loving way."

Matt scribbled a few notes and turned back to Mrs. Purdy. "And you are sure that Kathy Warren was actually Heather's birth mother?"

"Oh, the baby was hers all right. She held on to Heather like it was tearing the heart out of her to let her go. I gave her a ride that night myself when she left. That's probably how I remember so many details. You learn a lot about a person in a slow ride down a lonesome highway."

"And that was the night you brought Kathy Warren to the bus stop in Dry Creek," Heather added. "You said she was going to catch a bus to New Orleans."

"New Orleans." Cass rubbed a spot over her right ear. "Yes, I do think it was New Orleans. I can't be sure about that, but I do remember she wanted me to drop her off at the bus station. She cried when she got out and made me promise to take care of her baby girl."

"And you're sure you let her out at the bus station in Dry Creek?"

"Oh, I'm positive of that. I was driving on into Del Rio to my daughter's house. My granddaughter was born that night. She's only a few days younger than Heather. Maybe that's why I bonded so well with little Heather."

"And Kathy Warren never returned?"

"She didn't get much of a chance to. A few months later, this nice young man came by. I think he said he was Kathy's brother." She took a sip of her coffee. "Or he might have said uncle. It's hard for me to remember that part exactly. I only heard about him.''

''So you didn't actually see the man who said Heather's mother had been killed?''

''No, but I heard all about his visit from the other employees at the orphanage. He made quite a hit with them.''

''How's that?''

''He was young, good-looking and very well-mannered. He said Heather's mother had been killed in a car wreck. It just broke my heart. That's how sad I was, knowing little Heather would never see her real mother again.''

Matt stole a glance at Heather. She was quiet and seemed pensive, but her eyes were dry. He doubted they'd been so the first time she'd heard this story. Cass Purdy had a way of squeezing every ounce of melodrama out of the account. He moved up to the front of his chair and looked her squarely in the eyes.

''I know it's been a long time, Mrs. Purdy, but it would really help us a lot if you could remember.'' Matt waited until he had Mrs. Purdy's full attention. ''Did Kathy say anything about why she wanted to catch the bus in Dry Creek instead of one of the other towns along the way?''

''No, she didn't plan to go to Dry Creek, not at first. She was going to ride all the way to Del Rio with me and catch a bus there.'' Mrs. Purdy screwed her face as if struggling to remember. ''We talked some. I asked a few questions about her life, but she didn't seem to want to talk about herself. All of a sudden she told me to let her out. She said Dry Creek would do as well as any place because every place we passed through looked the same.''

''So my mother just happened to pick Dry Creek at the spur of the moment. She couldn't have known a soul in town, much less been involved in any wrongdoing.'' Heather reached over and took Cass's hands in hers.

"Thank you, Mrs. Purdy. That's important for me to know."

"I told that to the friend of yours who was here the other day."

Matt jerked to attention, alarms blaring in his brain. "Which friend was that?"

"I don't remember… I think he said his name was Bob Smith, something like that. He came by here about three days ago asking questions about Kathy Warren's daughter. He'd gotten my name from Mrs. Hawkins, same as Heather did."

Heather's voice caught on a hurried breath. "You mean someone has been to see you this week? Exactly what did you tell him?"

"That you were in Dry Creek looking for some sign of your mom's family. He looked mighty pleased when he heard that. I figured he rushed right over and looked you up."

"No, but he could be part of my mother's family. They might be looking for me the same way I'm looking for them. I'll have to go back to the motel in Dry Creek and wait for him."

Matt swallowed a curse.

All he needed now was a description of the man, and then they would get out of here and back to Dry Creek fast. His guess was the man was no longer looking for Heather. He'd already found her. And though he had no idea why, there was a good chance it had been this stranger's calling card that had been left in shades of purple across Heather's face.

Now they needed to find the man.

"I'M REALLY EXCITED, Matt." Heather pulled down the mirror over the dashboard and applied a coat of pink lipstick. She smacked her lips together and smiled at her image. "If the man went to all the trouble to track down the daughter of Kathy Warren, he must be related to me in some way. It might be the uncle who told the orphanage my mother was dead. It might even be my real father."

"For your sake, I hope that's true, but I wouldn't count on too much if I were you."

"You're such a pessimist."

"I like to think of myself as a realist."

"Same thing. If this person who's looking for me is related to my mother or father, he might be able to answer all of our questions about what happened to her after she left Dry Creek. He might know the story behind why someone is so upset by my asking a few questions."

"The timing seems a little too coincidental for my liking. Some strange man turns up at Cass Purdy's looking for you a few days before two men attack you in your car."

"Mrs. Purdy said he was a nice man, and that he wasn't from around here. He tracked me through the former administrator of the orphanage, the same way I found Cass. He's obviously not connected with the trouble in Dry Creek."

"I'd never jump to that conclusion, and you can forget that ridiculous notion you threw out about going back to stay at the motel."

"I knew you'd say that." She touched the bruise around her eye, stretching to get a mirror view from all angles. "I look almost human again."

"Which is no reason to take chances."

"I know. After I thought about it, I realized that anyone in Dry Creek can probably tell the man where I'm staying."

"No doubt about it." Matt lowered his foot on the accelerator, inching his speed a few miles over the limit. "Tell me about your adopted family, Heather. Were you unhappy with them? Is that what drives you to search for a family that let you be given away?''

"Absolutely not. My adopted parents were wonderful. My mom was a secretary and very funny. She could make me laugh no matter how upset I thought I was. And my dad was super—a little strict, but very loving. They were honest with me from the time I was old enough to understand adoption. If they were still alive, they'd back my search one hundred percent. They'd know no one would ever take their places.''

"How long have they been dead?''

"My dad had a heart attack my senior year in high school. He died instantly. My mom had cancer. She fought it as long as she could. She passed away two years ago.''

"I'm sorry.''

"So am I. I'd like for them to have met you. Actually, they'd probably have flown down here the minute they heard about my attack. My mom would be telling you how to conduct this investigation. She was never at a loss for words.''

"Who'd ever have guessed?''

Heather hit him playfully on the shoulder and then nestled closer. A familiar ache settled in the area of his groin. The longer he was around her, the more she filled his mind and tore at his control.

If he gave her half a chance, she'd burrow into his heart so deeply he'd never be able to walk away when this was over. He'd start imagining they could have a life together, fool himself into believing he could make her happy over the long haul.

He'd be wrong. The spitting image of Jake McQuaid in every way. That's what everyone said about him, even Susan Hathaway, and she knew both of them better than anyone else did. She might be the only woman who could love either of them enough to put up with them.

She'd stayed with his dad through thick and thin, but Jake had never been the man she deserved. To this day he wasn't. He'd let her down, let Matt's mother down, too, but in a different way. The rest of the world might call him a legend.

Matt couldn't even call him a real man.

"Hey, this isn't the way to Dry Creek. You should have turned back there."

"I told you we're going to spend the rest of the afternoon looking up old records."

"I assumed you meant at the sheriff's office in town."

"No, we're going to my office in San Antonio. The local records have been transferred into a computer base. They'll be a lot easier to access in that form. Plus, I can check out everything where I have all the resources I need to cross-reference incidents and dates."

"You should have told me. I'd have worn something besides these jeans."

"You look all right."

"Thanks for that gushing compliment."

He snaked his arm over the back of the seat. Her hair brushed against his arm, and his heart plunged. "Actually, you look great," he added, "bruises and all."

She stared up at him, her eyebrows arched in surprise. "Why, Ranger McQuaid, I do believe that's the nicest thing you've said to me since we met."

"I told you, I'm not much at small talk."

"To a woman, a compliment is never small."

They rode in silence after that. It was one of the few conversations they'd had that hadn't ended in a confrontation or a kiss, and he was not up to either.

HEATHER RUBBED the small of her back with her right hand and stretched as far as she could manage in the high-backed swivel chair. They'd been going over records for hours. It seemed more like days, especially since they hadn't stopped for lunch. Matt apparently wasn't joking when he'd said starvation was part of the plan when he was on a case.

"There's no record of a Kathy Warren in Dry Creek or any other town in Texas in the months preceding her dropping you off at the orphanage."

"Meaning if she was around, she stayed out of trouble with the law?"

"Meaning I can't even find her listed as having applied for a driver's license or any kind of welfare or medical aid."

"Do you have access to all of those records in this one office?"

"No, I have other people running searches for me in various state databases. People are usually easy enough to find if you can pinpoint the area. Kathy Warren doesn't fit the mold. She either kept a very low profile or she gave birth to you somewhere else and then brought you to Texas."

"She might not have wanted her family to know she was having a baby."

"That's a real possibility."

"But someone in her family must have found out. That person came and told the people at the orphanage that Kathy had been killed in a car accident."

"Maybe she confessed on her deathbed. If she knew she wasn't going to make it, there would have been no point in keeping secrets." Matt stood and paced the room. "The only proof we have that Kathy Warren existed was that she dropped you off at the orphanage one night in October."

"Were there any crimes reported in Dry Creek that night?"

"Not in the records. In fact there are no records at all for October of that year."

"Isn't it strange for a town to have no records for an entire month?"

"Yeah, especially since I know of one crime that happened that month that was never solved."

"Susan Hathaway, the woman you and your brothers found. So where do we go from here?"

Matt shrugged. "Back to Dry Creek to talk to Logan Trenton. If anyone knows what happened to those records, it should be him. He was deputy under my dad and replaced him as sheriff when we moved to Colorado."

"Can we eat first? I'm starved."

Matt's beeper rang at his waist. He read the number from the display and grabbed the phone from the desk. "As soon as I return this call."

Heather drank a cup of water from the dispenser and willed her stomach to refrain from growling while Matt completed the call. "Good news, I take it," she said, noting his smile as he hung up the receiver."

"It could be. Rube just called Gabby. Edna's ready to talk."

"Did she say she saw the man who killed Ariana?"

"She hasn't said anything yet. Her talking has strings attached."

"What kind of strings?"

Matt grabbed his hat. "She'll only speak if you are present."

"Me? Did she say why?"

"Yeah. She says the man who killed Ariana is a friend of yours."

Chapter Nine

Matt had decided the interview would go better in his living room than in either Gabby's office or the motel. An unthreatening environment that was removed from the scene of the crime was what he wanted. He'd accomplished his goal, Heather decided.

So far the meeting had the ambience of an impromptu gathering of good friends. The men had chatted about the rising price of feed and the poor beef market before Rube and Gabby had walked out to the tack room to look at a saddle Matt was thinking about selling.

She wondered if Rube realized that every aspect of the session had been orchestrated by Matt and agreed on by Gabby before he and Edna had arrived.

It was the familiarity Matt had talked about, the problem with investigating and questioning people you had known all your life. And, of course, neither Edna nor Rube was an actual suspect in Ariana's death. Heather wondered how different the method of questioning would be if they had been. Somehow she couldn't see Matt engaged in the bad-cop intimidation routine so popular on TV and in the movies.

"Would you like some more coffee, Edna?"

"No, Matt. I'm ready to talk."

Heather sat up a little straighter in the rocker opposite the couch where Edna huddled against a plaid pillow.

"I should have told you everything yesterday," Edna continued, "but I was afraid. I still am." Her voice shook. "Somebody capable of killing Ariana in cold blood like that. I mean you don't know what they might do to you if you cause them trouble."

Matt patted her hand. "No one's going to hurt you, Edna."

She kept her head down but raised her eyes to meet Heather's. "I'm sorry, Heather, but your friend is a real mean man."

Heather wrapped her arms about her chest as a sudden chill settled over the room. "Why do you think the man is my friend?"

"He told me he was, but I'm not sure I believe him. But he knows who you are. You may not be safe as long as he's around."

Matt leaned in close to Edna. "The sooner we catch the guy, the safer everyone will be. Just tell us what you saw."

"I was outside watering the plant by the window."

"What time was that?" Matt asked.

"About nine. I had a headache and I'd asked Rube to call Ariana over to clean Heather's room and do the laundry. I just wanted to put the water hose to my bougainvillea before it got too hot."

"Then what happened?" Matt's voice was gentle, coaxing, the same tone he'd used to settle Heather's horse at the dude ranch.

"I heard noises coming from Miss Heather's room, but I didn't see her car anywhere. I didn't know then that the sheriff had it." She paused, her fingers clutched around the strap of her handbag. "I knocked on the door and called out, but no one answered."

"Were you alone at the time?"

"Yes. I hadn't seen Ariana, and Rube was in the office fiddling with that computer of his." She sucked in a deep breath. "I tried the knob, and the door was open, so I just walked in. I thought maybe one of the dogs had gotten in there and was tearing things up. That old cur of Rube's has been known to do that."

"But it wasn't a dog, was it?" This time Heather asked the question. Edna's hesitancy was driving her nuts. She wanted the facts spoken fast and laid out neatly.

"No. At first I didn't see anyone, but I noticed my shoes were getting mud on the carpet. I took them off and dropped them right inside the door. When I looked up the man was standing there watching me." Edna trembled and sank lower into the couch. "I've never seen such eyes, so cold, so evil."

"What did he do when he saw you?" Matt asked, keeping Edna on track.

"He asked me who I was. He talked rough-like, and he had a strange accent."

"Strange in what way? Did he seem like he was from another country?"

"No, but I don't think he's from around here."

Heather scooted to the edge of her seat. "Did he say he was looking for me?"

"Yes. He said he was looking for a woman named Heather Lombardi. He knew you didn't live in Dry Creek, but he said he'd heard you were visiting here."

"Did he say *why* he wanted to see me?"

"He said you were old friends, that he was here to reunite you with your past."

The fear pummeling Heather's insides mixed with hope. Edna could be wrong. The man might not have anything to do with the murder. He could be someone from her birth mother's family.

"Tell me about him," Heather begged. "What did he look like?"

"He was a thin man, rough looking as if he'd led a hard life. I'd say he was close to fifty, starting to lose his hair. What he had left was blond, but thin and set way back on his forehead. I don't remember much else, except that he was a mean-looking fellow. I thought so the minute I laid eyes on him."

Heather fought back a shudder. Edna's description was almost exactly the same as Cass Purdy's. Only Mrs. Purdy hadn't seen the man as evil. Worse, the wrangler who'd been at the dude ranch had described a middle-aged man with blond hair. Paranoia again. There was no way they could all be describing the same man.

Matt took over the questioning. "What else did the man say to you?"

"He wanted to know where he could find Miss Lombardi, only he called her Heather." Edna turned to face her. "He said not to tell you he was looking for you. He wanted it to be a surprise."

"Did he give his name?" Heather asked.

"No. He didn't really say anything else until I said I didn't know where you were. I told him he had to get out of your room. He told me he was leaving, but he'd be back."

"Did he leave then?"

"He was about to, but about that time a wasp came flying in and buzzed around his head. He swatted at it, hit it, too, but it didn't die. That's when he picked up my sandal and started beating it into the rug. He smashed that bug until it was nothing but mush. He tossed the other shoe aside and left."

"So you *were* wearing the sandals?"

"I'm sorry, Matt. I was just so afraid yesterday. I saw what he did to that wasp, and what he did to Ariana. I don't want him to come looking for me. And Rube…"

"What about Rube?"

"He doesn't want me mixed up in this. He's scared, too, Matt. He won't say it, of course, but I can tell. He's nervous, chewing his nails, jumping down my throat if I try to talk to him about anything. That's not like him. You know that."

"I know, Edna. We're doing all we can to find the killer, and Gabby's going to have one of his deputies stay at the motel for a few days."

"I appreciate that."

"You still need to be careful, but I don't think the man will be back. He's probably on the run."

"I hope so. I hated lying to you. Then after I did, I couldn't live with myself."

Heather only half listened to the rest of the questioning. It was a rehash of what she'd already heard, and her mind was spinning with possibilities. The truth was Edna hadn't seen this man with Ariana. It could have been anyone who killed the cleaning lady, a jealous boyfriend, an angry relative, a stranger passing through town. Edna honestly believed it was the man she saw in Heather's room, the one who had asked about her, but that didn't make it so. Killing a wasp—no matter how brutal the technique—didn't make a man a murderer.

There was no reason to believe a member of her birth family could be involved in Dry Creek's secrets when Kathy Warren had only been in this town by accident. Even Matt would have to see that.

Heather stayed lost in her own thoughts while the question-and-answer session droned on. Matt wrapped up the session about the time her right foot went to sleep in protest. A minute later, Rube and Gabby rejoined them. The men visited for a while at the kitchen table, sipping the lemonade Heather served them and munching on some store bought cookies.

Heather and Edna walked out to the porch and sat in the swing. Gabby's dog left his spot by his master's pickup truck and came over to sit at their feet, moving only when the need to scratch overcame his lethargy.

"I'm sorry things have been so hard on you, but I'm glad to know it's not one of Dry Creek's people that is responsible." Edna slipped her hand over Heather's. "You're a sweet lady, smart, too. You're real good for Matt. It's time that boy settled down with someone like you."

Heather jumped to attention. "Matt and I aren't living together. I mean we are, but we're not *together*. He had me move out here so that he could protect me."

"Maybe so, but I know what I see. Matt likes you a lot, and you could do a whole lot worse. He's a good boy, from good stock, at least on his dad's side. His mother wasn't much of a woman. She ran off and left her husband and her son. I've got no use for a woman like that."

"She may have had her reasons."

"What kind of reasons would make a woman leave her own child?"

"I don't know, but there are some. And for all we know, leaving might be a hundred times harder than staying."

"I never thought about it quite that way."

"I have. I've thought about it a lot."

"I guess you have," Edna said, "seeing as how you were left at that orphanage." She ran her hand behind her neck and gathered the wisps of hair that had escaped the knot at the back of her head. "I always wanted a daughter like you, but Rube and I just had boys. If I *were* your mom I'd tell you two things, Miss Lombardi.''

"Call me Heather. And go ahead and tell me. One can never have too many mothers."

Edna took Heather's hand and squeezed it. "I'd tell you to stay safe. There's evil out there, and it's looking for you."

"I'm trying hard to do that."

"And I'd tell you to get a hold of that man in there and don't let go. A good man like Matt McQuaid doesn't come along every day of the week. Look at my Rube. We've been married thirty years, and I'm just as in love with him as I was the day I met him. I may not get all gooey-eyed, but I love him all the same."

"Why, Edna, are you suggesting I seduce the Ranger who brought me out here to protect me?"

"I'm suggesting you do what you have to. If you don't, some other woman will, and she won't be half as good for him as you are. Don't ask me how I know that, I just do."

An easy sense of camaraderie had settled over them by the time the men came barreling out the screen door. For a second Heather almost forgot that somewhere in Dry Creek there was a killer walking the streets. Almost forgot that two nights ago she had been attacked by two strangers. Almost forgot someone had tried to blow her and her car into little pieces.

Almost, but not quite.

"ARE YOU GOING to go through those files all night?" Heather plopped down on one of the musty boxes Matt had crated over from the back room at Gabby's office.

"Probably, unless I find what I'm looking for first. Do you have a better idea?"

"I thought we might take a ride before dark. You have those beautiful horses just going to waste."

Matt peered over the file he'd been scrutinizing. "You must be bored if you're asking to ride a horse."

"When in Rome, or in this case, when in Texas. Besides, I kind of liked riding the other day after I got used to it. Of course, I'd want a gentle horse like the one I had at the dude ranch."

"Where's your spirit of adventure?"

"Worn out. Another victim of Dry Creek's warm hospitality."

"In that case, I have just the horse for you. Maverick. A pretty chestnut. He's big, but he's got more sense than most men I know. He won't fight you for control, unless you make him."

"How big?"

"Big enough you don't want to go flying over his head, but he won't let you. Why don't you go have a look at him while I finish this file? But do your looking from outside the corral. And don't wander off anywhere else. I don't want you out of yelling distance."

"Yes sir." Heather gave a mock salute and headed out the door. She still hadn't had a chance to shop for boots, but she had traded her sandals for her tennis shoes. When she shopped, she might even buy a hat. One like Matt's, except with a smaller brim.

Not that she'd ever wear the boots or hat again once she went home. Home to Atlanta. The thought seemed strange. As long as she'd stayed in the motel, Dry Creek had seemed like a foreign country. But she'd been at the Lone M five days now, and she was getting way too familiar with the ways of Ranger Matt McQuaid.

Sitting across the breakfast table from him. Seeing him fresh from the shower, his hair wet and dripping down his sun-bronzed face. Knowing he was a few steps away when she crawled into bed at night. And always dealing with the smoky desire his nearness kindled inside her.

She took a shaky breath and stepped onto the bottom rung of the corral. A chestnut came trotting over. So did a large horse that was more brown than red and a prancing horse with white legs that looked like he'd dressed in boots.

"Hello, baby," she said crooning to the booted horse who was nuzzling her hand. She scratched his face the way she'd seen Matt do the other day at the dude ranch. "Are you ready for a ride or do you just want a little attention?"

The wind picked up, waving the grass and whirling sand. Heather stepped back. She had the crazy feeling that she wasn't alone, that someone was nearby, watching her. Was it some sound she'd heard, or only groundless fear that twisted in her stomach?

Her first impulse was to run back to Matt, to fly into his arms and let him hold her until the shaking stopped. But what would she tell him—that she felt eyes that weren't there? She sucked a deep breath of air into her burning lungs. She'd almost convinced herself she was safe and alone when footsteps rustled the grass behind her.

She spun around. "Matt, it's you."

"I didn't mean to frighten you."

"I'm just jumpy these days."

"With plenty of reason. Our ride may help. There's a creek past the south pasture, fed by a spring. The water's cool and clear, and overhung with branches of the biggest oak tree in these parts."

"You do love this ranch, don't you?"

"Have you ever met a rancher who wasn't partial to his own spread?"

"Up until a week ago, I'd never met a rancher."

"And now that you have?" Matt swung open the gate

and Heather followed him inside, watching where she stepped.

"I'd say you're a fascinating breed. Other than that, the vote is still out."

"Good answer. You don't want to get too sassy with the wrangler who's saddling your ride."

"Is that from the cowboy book of lore?"

"No, it's from the gospel according to Matt McQuaid."

"Right after the chapter about why you don't need a woman."

"I never said I didn't *need* a woman." He pulled a saddle from the rack. "I *said* I'd make a lousy husband."

"And I think you're a coward, Matt McQuaid, afraid the woman you chose would run out on you and leave you here to explain your predicament to all of the McQuaid admirers."

"Oh, it's not the explaining I'd mind. But you're right about the fear. I'd be scared to death of letting a woman like you crawl into my bed, set me on fire and then go running back to the bright lights of the big city. I don't relish the idea of putting out that kind of flame with cold showers and lonesome nights."

He saddled two horses, then called her over to mount the chestnut. She stopped in front of Matt, and he wrapped his arms around her waist, pulling her close and nestling his mouth in her hair. "But even a coward gives in to temptation occasionally. So you better keep that bedroom door locked at night."

With that, he boosted her up and into the saddle. Her heart raced, but this time it wasn't the size of the horse but the mystique of the cowboy that had her gasping for breath. Edna's words echoed tauntingly in her mind. A good man like Matt McQuaid doesn't come along every day of the week.

It was time to act, to stop playing it safe. Tonight she'd make sure Matt knew the latch on the bedroom door was off.

Chapter Ten

Heather lay in her bed, staring at the shadowed ceiling. The afternoon ride had left her breathless, dizzy with excitement and hungry for more. This time, at Matt's coaxing, she'd grown comfortable in the saddle and taken Maverick through all the stages. A slow walk, a fast walk, a lope, and for a few glorious minutes, a full gallop.

She'd seen the land from the back of a magnificent animal, feeling as if she owned the world. No matter that her world was riddled with problems and spiked with danger. The romance of the West was creeping into her blood, invigorating her with its spirit.

But she knew part of the thrill this afternoon had been due to her riding companion. For once, Matt had shed the tough armor that usually kept her at arm's length. When they'd dismounted by the creek, he'd pointed out every plant, cut off a bite of pear from a cactus and given her a taste of it, even playfully splashed cold water on her when she'd teased him.

For a few glorious minutes, they'd behaved like new lovers, frolicking in the late-afternoon splendor of a perfect day. But all that had changed the minute they'd walked back into the house. Matt had dug into the stacks of files with a vengeance, as if he expected them to disintegrate in front of him if he didn't scrutinize every one before he moved from the spot.

She'd puttered in the kitchen and come up with pasta, flavored with ground beef, carrots, onions and sweet peas. But dinner had been quiet. Matt had avoided eye contact and answered her questions in his typical one-word style.

He'd given no reason for the abrupt change in their relationship, leaving Heather to conjure up her own theories. The man was either scared to death of involvement, or else there was someone else in his life back in San Antonio.

So now she was lying here wide-awake, the victim of her own poor judgment. She'd known it wasn't wise to get emotionally involved with Matt, but her heart had jumped ahead of her, seeing the side of him it wanted to see.

She wasn't sure if she was falling in love with him. All she knew was that she ached to crawl into his arms, that she longed to have him here beside her, sharing the rustic wooden bed. Knew that her insides trembled just remembering the taste of his lips on hers, the feel of his breath on the back of her neck, the sound of his voice, all husky with desire, when he'd whispered in her ear at the corral.

Heather kicked away the sheet that bound her legs. She refused to lie here like a virgin in heat. Matt wanted her every bit as much as she wanted him. No matter how he tried to deny the sizzle between them, it burned its way into every second of their time together.

If she was wrong about that, he could tell her so, get it all out in the open. She slung her feet to the floor and marched across the room, wrapping her fingers around the knob, only to have it turn in her hands without her moving it.

She stepped back as the door swung toward her. ''Matt.''

He didn't answer, but his hands were shaking as he locked them behind her and drew her close. Her surprise heightened to hunger as he claimed her lips, and Heather rose up on tiptoe, pushing her body against his.

"I was just coming out to talk to you," she murmured, when he pulled his lips away and leaned against the door.

"What about?"

"This." She caught his bottom lip with her teeth, nibbling and then sucking until she was lost in another kiss. She was clutching and grasping, digging her fingers into his flesh, her body so hot, she couldn't think. Weak with desire, she fell against his chest.

"What about this?" Matt asked, his hands kneading her shoulders, his thumbs riding her neck, to her earlobes and back down again in mesmerizing motions. "That you wanted it or that you didn't?"

"That I wanted you. That I had to know if you wanted me the same way."

His lips found hers again, kissing her until she gasped for breath. "Is this answer enough?"

"It's getting there."

He swept her into his arms and carried her to the bed, laying her atop the rumpled sheet. "I've wanted you since the night I found you in the brush, spunky as hell in spite of having just taken a beating."

"That's a rough way to catch a man."

"You could have saved yourself the trouble. One look at you across the breakfast table in that T-shirt of mine would have done the trick."

His lips found hers again, quick but thorough, and then left them to seek new places, each new touch driving her wild. Below her ear, down her neck, just above the ribbon that held her gown together. He caught the ends of the tie and tugged the front open.

"Without desperate measures," she reminded him, though her breath was so jagged she could barely whisper,

"I'd never have gotten to your breakfast table. You practically pushed me away in the restaurant where we met."

A moan swallowed the last of her words, as her body responded to Matt's mouth sliding down her stomach, his hands still cradling her breasts, kneading her nipples, coaxing them to attention.

"I knew you were trouble even then," he whispered, his breath hot on her flesh. "I just didn't know how much, or how sweet the danger." Words got lost in the passion, reason swallowed up in shivers of anticipation as his fingers dipped inside her.

Heather writhed under his touch. Her body ruled now, soaking up pleasure as if it might never come again, knowing it had never been like this before. Finally, she cried out in ecstasy, the passion so intense she could hold nothing back.

Seconds later, when the first glorious waves of climax had passed, she started her own exploration—kissing, stroking, reveling in Matt's maleness. "What about you?" she whispered, her voice rough with desire and her heart racing in the aftermath.

"I'm still here." He took her hand, guiding it to him. She wrapped her fingers around him, and he shuddered.

"Take me, Matt. I want to feel you inside me."

"I thought you'd never ask."

HE TOOK HER THEN, his own head swimming as his blood rushed and his body caught and matched the rhythm of Heather's movements. He'd never wanted a woman like this, never even suspected that he could. It seemed now as though every second of every day since he'd met her had been leading to this moment.

His willpower over the edge, he exploded inside her before he was ready, a shaking, overwhelming experience that left him weak and disoriented. But still he knew the moment had been all the sweeter because Heather had skyrocketed with him.

He rolled to his side and held her close and wished the world could always be this wonderful. But even now, doubts were edging out his contentment. He forced them aside as Heather snuggled against him.

Every man should have one night like this, and he wouldn't be robbed of his.

"HOW WOULD YOU LIKE to go to a party tomorrow night?"

Heather looked up from her nearly empty plate of pancakes. Matt had been up and on the phone by the time she opened her eyes this morning. Stomach growling, she'd hopped out of bed and scrounged in the kitchen for flour, milk, oil and eggs while he finished his conversation. She'd never known making love could make one so ravenous.

"What kind of party?"

"Logan Trenton doesn't need an excuse to throw a party, but his reason this time is that his stepdaughter just received her Ph.D. Word is this will be a shindig of magnificent proportions."

"Does that mean music and dancing?"

Matt grimaced. "There'll be some boot scooting. Unfortunately. But there will also be good food, and most important, the chance to talk to a lot of local people at once. This investigation is going dry faster than a watering hole in August, but someone in this town knows something. You can bet a prize steer on that."

Heather considered the prospect of attending a party with Matt. He'd be off talking cattle with every male in the place, of course, digging for clues in the process. Meanwhile, she'd be odd woman out in a group of people who had all known each other from birth.

She slid a bite of pancake through a river of cane syrup. "Why don't you go without me? I didn't bring clothes for a *shindig of magnificent proportions.*"

"You'd outshine everyone else even if you went in your jeans."

She beamed at his compliment. It was the first time this morning he'd given any sign that last night had happened, that he was actually aware of her as more than an inconvenient aspect of his job.

"Or…" He slid his chair back from the table. "We can stop at Ridgely's feed store this afternoon and you can do some shopping."

"A feed sack? No thanks."

"That wasn't exactly what I had in mind, but if the bag were skimpy enough, it might work." He smiled with his lips, though not his eyes. Heather recognized the signs now. Something worrisome was brewing behind his façade of pleasantries. He finished off his milk and took his empty dishes to the sink.

"Actually, Ridgely's wife has a clothing shop in the front of his feed store," he continued, as if there had been no pause in the conversation. "Lots of the ladies around here shop there. You could pick up some boots while we're at it."

"And a hat." The idea was growing on her. The party would provide another chance for her do what she'd come to Dry Creek for, to question people about Kathy Warren. That simple task was getting lost in the search for Ariana's killer, and so far they had no proof the two mysteries were even related.

"Will Rube and Edna be at the party?"

"Probably not. Now that Logan's playing with the financial big boys, he doesn't fraternize as much with his cronies from the old days."

"Do we know for certain now that it wasn't any of the guys from the dude ranch who kidnapped me the other night?"

"I'm not sure of anything, but they all had alibis, supported by their friends."

"Friends might lie."

"Exactly. That's why I had a check run on every last one of them." Matt picked up a fistful of faxes from the counter and dropped them to the table beside her. "Gabby brought these by this morning while you were still sleeping. They came in during the night from Ranger headquarters in San Antonio."

"What did you find?"

"Dan Granger, age twenty-one, was arrested in Dallas last year for passing a couple of bad checks. Merle Fitch, age thirty-five, has a battery charge against him. He got into a fight with a man in a bar outside of Carrizo Springs. Apparently, they both wanted to sleep with the same woman. In both cases, the charges were dropped."

"And there's nothing else?"

"Everyone else is squeaky clean, just wholesome young boys wanting to grow up to be cowboys."

"What about fingerprints?"

"We found a set in the motel and on the sandals that we couldn't identify. We're checking them out now. The watch had been out in the elements a while, so it was apparently not from the night of the attack. John says it looks like one he lost last summer. The car was clean, as we expected it to be."

Frustration dragged at Heather's spirits. "And I guess it's the same no-luck pattern with the files you've been scrutinizing."

Matt's face screwed into hard worry lines. "Not quite. I've found a pattern of missing files. Two weeks' worth of reports from right around the time your mother was reportedly in Dry Creek, and scattered missing files for months before and after that period.''

''You didn't mention that last night.''

''No, I wanted to wait until I'd gone through every box of files that Gabby had found in the attic. I finished that about daybreak and ran a computer analysis with the dates of the missing files. The pattern emerged. Before and after that year, there are no missing files.''

''And the missing files are from the period of time when your father was sheriff?'' The reason for his concern took shape in her mind.

''The inimitable Jake McQuaid. The man who never left a crime unsolved, at least never a record of one.'' He spit the last words out, as if he hated the taste of them in his mouth.

''But you don't *know* that there was a crime involving Kathy Warren.''

''No, but I know there was one involving Susan Hathaway. Somebody beat her to a bloody pulp and left her for dead on the side of the road. If my brothers and I hadn't shown up when we did, she wouldn't have lasted the night. That's a crime, no matter who's sheriff. And there's no mention of it in any record I could find.''

''Your dad *must* have tried to find out who did that to her.''

''I'm sure he did.'' He stuffed his hands into the back pockets of his jeans, his eyes dark and impenetrable. ''Unless he already knew. Unless there was some reason he decided to cover it up.''

Heather leaned against the counter, watching him in consternation. ''You shouldn't think like that about your father, Matt, not without good reason. It's not healthy.''

''A man can't help how he thinks.''

"That's not true." She moved toward Matt, but he turned away. She stepped behind him and put her hands on his shoulders, massaging the tight muscles. "Whatever's between you and your dad is eating you alive. You have to let it go before it destroys you."

"You know all of that in six days?" The sarcasm in his voice punctured her resolve.

"Maybe not. Maybe I don't know you at all, Matt McQuaid. I know the man standing in front of me right now is not the man I made love with last night."

He turned back to her, his eyes colder than she'd ever seen them, grim and brooding. The lines in his face were deep and drawn. "About last night…"

She put up her hands. "No, don't start that routine where you tell me you're sorry and it won't happen again. I don't buy it. Making love to me was right. It's this pretending you don't need anybody, not even your own family, that's wrong. So, your dad was human and not the perfect legend everyone thinks. Get over it. At least you *have* a dad."

She was shaking now, fighting back tears. She didn't care. With all she'd been through in the last few days, she didn't need this kind of garbage from the man who'd moved heaven and earth for her a few hours ago.

"I'm sorry, Heather. I didn't mean to drag you into this." He grabbed his hat from a hook by the door. "Be ready in thirty minutes. We're going into town."

The need to cry subsided as she washed the last of the dishes. She couldn't solve Matt's problems. He'd nurtured them too long, clung to them as a baby might a favorite blanket, taking a strange kind of comfort from his simmering resentment.

And he'd never even explained exactly why he resented his dad so much. But if Heather had to guess, she'd bet it had to do with Susan Hathaway.

Susan Hathaway and her mother, both with histories that touched Dry Creek at the same time, a period when criminal records had never existed or else had disappeared. There had to be a tie there somewhere, but what would they have to do to uncover it?

She headed to the bathroom for a quick shower, the gentle ache in her thighs the only reminder that last night had been the most wonderful of her life.

MATT MADE A LIST of necessary chores for his neighbor's son to take care of that day, things he'd originally planned to do himself while on vacation in Dry Creek. Instead he was spending his days working a puzzle where all the edges were jagged and nothing slid into place.

His nights... They were his biggest problem. Last night, to be specific. Heather saw this as a simple problem of a rift between father and son. Hell, if that was all it was, it wouldn't have been a big deal. He'd have gotten on with his life, forgetting he even had a father. Until Heather had fallen into his life, he practically had anyway.

The problem was not bad blood that stood between them but the blood that ran through their veins. He was like Jake McQuaid in too many ways, in all the ways that counted. His brothers Cy and Cameron were the lucky ones. They were different, always had been.

A human thread ran through them that had bypassed Jake and Matt. They had felt the same way he did about their father once, at least they'd claimed to, but they had never crawled inside themselves the way he and Jake did, didn't have trouble showing emotion, talking out their concerns.

Maybe that's because their mom had died. She hadn't chosen to leave them the way Matt's mom had, walking away from her son just so she didn't have to put up with the dark moods of Jake McQuaid or the sterile life he gave her.

Not that Matt remembered that. He'd figured it out from the little bit his dad and brothers had told him when they thought he was old enough to understand. The truth was he had no memory of his mom at all, and he blamed Jake McQuaid for that. Jake had robbed him of ever having known the woman who gave him birth.

Funny, how the old resentments had returned with such force now that Heather Lombardi had dropped into his life. Maybe it was the enthusiasm she felt for a past she didn't know that triggered his feelings of regret. But nothing changed the truth. He'd spent a lifetime as a loner, never able to connect completely with anyone, never able to take the risks true intimacy involved.

He couldn't give Heather what she needed emotionally any more than Jake McQuaid had been able to do that for the women in his life. The difference was that he was smart enough to know it. Heather thought she wanted him now, but that would change quick enough when the newness wore off, when she was faced with life day in and day out with a man who had nothing of himself to give.

He backed the truck from the carport, turning it around while he waited for Heather. Last night had given her the wrong impression of what he was about. He was nobody's hero. Nobody to fall in love with.

She pushed through the screen door, her curly hair pulled back into a ponytail and bouncing behind her. Her shirt was a soft yellow that draped over her perfect breasts. Her short denim skirt buttoned in the front and split open just enough to reveal a flash of thigh.

His heart plummeted to his stomach. Letting himself get mixed up with her was about as smart as squatting with your spurs on. Dumber actually. He'd feel the pain for a whole lot longer.

He reached over and opened her door and she climbed in.

"Where are we off to this time?" she asked.

"Logan Trenton's."

"I thought you'd already talked to him and he'd told you Gabby had all the records."

"I'd like to pick his brains before the party, see what he remembers from twenty-five years ago. As far as I'm concerned, the fact that the records from that time are missing is pretty convincing evidence that *something* was going on back then."

"I still don't see how a woman passing through town could have gotten mixed up in the trouble."

"She might have been in on it all along. We don't know where your mom was living before she dropped you off at the orphanage or what she did before that."

"If Logan Trenton knew anything, isn't it likely he was in on the cover-up? You said he was your father's deputy during that time."

"I've thought of that. My hope is either he was and he's ready to talk now or else he knows something he doesn't know he knows. Some bit of information that means nothing to him but will unlock a clue for me, if I get him to talk about it."

"Maybe he'd speak more freely if I wasn't around. Drop me off in town. I can visit with Edna or shop. You could pick me up when you finish."

"Sure, I'll drop you off at the motel, and, if it's convenient, the killer can drop by. After all, he was there a few days ago. He won't have any trouble finding the place."

"Then drop me off at the library. I can look through old newspaper files. Something may turn up there."

"Not in our library. We're too small. We have a few books and the capability of getting whatever you want from the state system if you have a few days to wait."

"Then drop me at Paul Ridgely's feed store. No killer is just going to march into a shop with a bunch of cowboys hanging around, all of them with a gun of some kind in their pickup truck."

Matt kept his gaze glued straight ahead. "Are you so eager to be away from me?"

"No, I'm just not cut out for the role of helpless female. I need to be doing something. At least at Ridgely's I might be able to ask a few questions myself, talk to some people I haven't met before."

"Okay. I'll drop you off at the feed store and ask Paul to keep an eye on you. He's as tough as anyone in town." He turned and captured Heather's gaze. "Ask all the questions you want, but don't leave the store."

"Yes sir, Ranger."

Matt slowed the truck. There was a blue Camaro pulled to the side of the road in front of them, the hood up. "Looks like someone's in trouble."

"A late-model blue Camaro with a New Mexico license plate. Matt, that's the same kind of car Rube said he saw driving around town the day before Ariana was killed."

Matt pulled off the road, coming to a stop behind the car. "You're getting good at this." He opened his door. "Wait here. I need to check this out."

"Be careful."

"Always." Matt touched his hand to the gun at his waist as he approached the car. There was no sign of movement. He circled the vehicle, peering through the windows. There were a couple of old blankets in the back seat and some dirty clothes on the floor, but not a sign of the driver.

Turning his eyes toward a nearby area where the brush

grew thick enough to hide a man, he touched his hand to the motor. Cool as a cucumber. He made a second trip around the car, examining the ground around the vehicle.

Pulling the driver's side door open, he reached inside the car and punched the trunk latch. As he did, he heard his truck door slamming behind him, and turned to find Heather striding toward him.

"I thought I told you to stay put."

"You did, but there's no one around here. I could see that."

She followed him to the back of the car and stood beside him while he yanked the trunk open. A string of curses escaped before he even thought about curtailing them.

Heather inched closer. "The man must have robbed a gun store."

"With the intent to equip a small army. There's enough assault rifles in here to conquer a Third-World country."

"What do you think it means?"

"That there's a dangerous lunatic on foot somewhere around Dry Creek." He went back to the truck and grabbed his cellular phone, punching in the number to get a license-plate check.

It took less than three minutes to determine that the car was a stolen one. Matt's next call was to Gabby.

"What's up, Matt? You just caught me. I was about to run out to Ben Wright's to check out a complaint on one of his wranglers who got a little rowdy at Cushman's Bar last night."

"This takes precedence. I just came upon a deserted vehicle on the side of the highway about a mile past the entrance to Billinger's place as you're coming into town. A blue Camaro, stolen, with a small arsenal in the trunk. We need it checked for prints, and we need the border guys out here with their dogs to do an intensive drug search."

"What kind of guns are we talking?"

"Five assault rifles and a sawed-off shotgun, nothing you'd need for hunting legitimate game."

"Which means the man probably has an automatic pistol or two in his pocket or strapped to his leg, possibly a *.44 Magnum.*"

"Don't go jumping to conclusions, Gabby."

"No, but I don't want to find any buzzards circling. I'll get a bulletin on the radio not to pick up any hitchhikers in this area."

"My guess is somebody already has."

"Okay, I'm on my way, Matt. I'll have the deputy here alert the state highway boys."

Matt broke the connection and turned to Heather. "I want you to stay in the truck with the doors locked until I get back. If you see anyone approach, lean on the horn and I'll tear back down here."

"Where are you going?"

"To check out the surrounding area, especially that cluster of thick brush to the left of the windmill."

Adrenaline shot through Heather, fed by a fear that was raging out of control. "You can't go out there alone."

"I'm a Ranger. This is what I get paid to do."

"Then wait for back-up."

"Haven't you ever heard the old quote, 'One riot, one Ranger'? Well, this is one criminal, one Ranger. The odds are all with me."

"You don't know there's only one."

"Yes, I do. From the appearance of the ground, only one person left the car, and that was from the driver's side."

"The ground may be too hard for prints on the passenger side."

"Footprints aren't the only sign a man's walked a path. There's bent and broken blades of grass, overturned stones, slight impressions in the dirt. I've tracked men along the border before with a lot less to go on than there is here."

"Do the tracks you see lead in that direction?" she asked, motioning toward the brush.

"No, I wish they did. They appear to lead from the car door to the front of the vehicle and then to the road, but I'd like to look around a little more anyway."

Heather's breath caught, burning dry in her lungs. She leaned against the back of the car to support legs that had suddenly grown wobbly beneath her. "If someone gave the man a ride, and he's the man who killed Ariana... Oh, Matt, we have to do something. Someone else could be in danger."

He nodded, his lips drawn, his eyes stormy. "So get in the truck and lock the door."

Heather did, all but holding her breath until she saw Matt heading safely back in her direction. The sigh of relief was short-lived, as terrible visions began to flash through her mind.

Was the man who'd deserted the Camaro the same man who had put a bullet through Ariana's chest? Was he the man who was looking for her? Were death and murderous strangers the legacy of Kathy Warren?

No. She couldn't think that way. There was no proof her birth mother was tied to this man *or* to Ariana. Still, she didn't put up an argument when Matt told her he wouldn't be dropping her off at Ridgely's store. She'd be going to Logan Trenton's ranch with him.

THE OVERALL-CLAD FARMER eyed the man he'd picked up on the side of road. "I don't know where you're going, unless it's to Trenton's country. His is the only place this far out of town."

"Yeah, Trenton, that's it. He's a friend of mine. He'll

give me a ride back into town and help me get the parts for my car.''

''Yep. I wouldn't leave my car on the road too long if I was you, though. Used to be a man didn't take nothing that wasn't rightfully his, but times have changed.''

''You're right. You never know what kind of man is on the road or what they're after.''

''Yep.'' The farmer fished a toothpick from his pocket and poked at his teeth. ''I don't ordinarily pick up hitch-hikers myself, but I hate to see a guy stranded with car trouble the way you were. I've been in that spot myself. In fact, one time I was—''

The man cut him off. ''You got a smoke?''

''No, I gave up cigarettes years ago. Where are you from, anyway? You aren't from around these parts.''

''Out west.''

The farmer slowed to a stop at the dirt road. ''It's a good ways from the gate to the house. I'd take you all the way myself, but I'm running way late for my doctor's appointment up in San Antonio.''

''Yeah, don't worry. I'll get where I'm going.'' He jumped from the truck without bothering with a thank-you for the ride.

Strange fellow, the farmer decided, as he watched him leave the road, crawl between the rows of barbed wire and trudge into the brush. Still, if he was a friend of Logan's, he was probably all right.

He revved his engine and pulled his truck back onto the road. He had a long, lonesome drive in front of him. He should have gotten his radio fixed. Then he could have at least had some music to keep him company.

Chapter Eleven

Logan Trenton swung open the door as soon as Matt and Heather knocked, and ushered them into a massive den, paneled in pine and studded with the heads of game he'd snared in remote parts of the globe. The room made a statement of masculinity and power. So did the man.

Heather studied him during the introductions. He was tall, his Western shirt and string tie impeccable, his white Stetson spotless, his voice commanding. Gray touched his hair at the temples, adding distinction to his sun- and wind-roughened face, and his smile was polished and quick, though it never quite spread to his eyes. He had more the air of a politician than a South Texas rancher. And Heather definitely couldn't see him as ever having been a small-town sheriff.

He took her hand, holding it firmly in his instead of shaking it, and she felt his eyes move over her body, sizing her up. "It's nice to finally meet you, Miss Lombardi. I've heard so much about you."

"Yes, I seem to be the talk of the town."

"Well, we're all very sorry about that. I hate to even think what kind of men would attack a defenseless lady. I've told Matt and Gabby that I'd be more than happy to share my resources, an extra man or two, my small plane, anything I have if it would help in finding and arresting the two men who were responsible.''

Matt fingered his hat. ''We appreciate that, Logan. Right now, all I need are some answers.''

''So you said.'' He offered a patronizing smile. ''I hope this doesn't take too long. I've got to be in Uvalde by noon on some business.''

''I suggest we get started then.''

Matt started across the polished wood floor of the gigantic den toward the couch. Logan and Heather were left to follow.

''Matt McQuaid.''

They all turned as a striking young woman in jeans and an embroidered western shirt popped into the room. She fell into Matt's arms, then pulled away to give him a once-over.

''I'd heard you were in town, but I didn't know you were coming out to the ranch today. You look great.'' Her voice was deep, her Texas drawl abbreviated, as if she'd been away for quite a while.

Matt gave her an approving smile. ''Not nearly as good as you. I'd say the last few years have agreed with you.'' Matt took Heather's hand and tugged her closer. ''Forgive my manners. Heather, this is Logan's stepdaughter, Sylvia.''

Heather extended her hand and finished the introductions herself. ''Heather Lombardi. And I hear congratulations are in order.''

''That's right. It took me long enough, but as of next week, I'll be *Dr.* Sylvia McCullough, child psychologist.''

''That sounds like an interesting career choice.''

''I'm a natural at it. I've analyzed myself for long enough. I tried it with Matt, as well, but he's resistant to exploring his feelings. Like most of the men around here, he pretends his skin is cowhide, too thick for anything to get through.''

''I've noticed.''

Matt grimaced.

Logan laid an arm around his stepdaughter's shoulders, and Heather couldn't help noticing how quickly she jerked away. But if her stepfather noticed the reaction, he didn't let on. ''We tough-skinned men need to talk business, Sylvia. I'm going to take Matt back to my office. Why don't you take Miss Lombardi out to the stables and show her your graduation present?''

''Please, call me Heather,'' she said.

Sylvia stepped away from Logan and nearer to Heather. ''Word is you're in Dry Creek to try and locate your birth mother.''

''Yes, so far without luck. Her name was Kathy Warren. I don't suppose *you've* ever heard of her?''

''Not offhand. You can tell me more about it on our way to the stables.''

Heather shot Matt a questioning look. He'd been specific that she was not to go off by herself.

He hesitated, his thumbs hooked in the front pockets of his jeans, his gaze somber. ''I don't suppose it could hurt to go to the stables with Sylvia. There'll be wranglers around,'' he said, though he didn't sound enthusiastic about it. He turned to Sylvia. ''But don't be long. I still have more stops to make today.''

''No, we won't be long.'' She tossed her head back and her long, straight black hair fell about her shoulders. She was a little older than Heather, closer to Matt's age. Heather couldn't help but wonder if there had been more than friendship between her and Matt in the past.

Who could blame either of them if there had been?

They said their goodbyes, and Sylvia led the way as they

left the men and went out through the back door, the same way Heather and Matt had come in. Even with a killer roaming the streets, Dry Creek was a back-door neighborly kind of town.

"We'll take my four-wheel-drive. That way we can take the short cut and not stick to the road," Sylvia announced, marching toward a red Jeep with the doors and windows removed.

"How far is it to the stables?"

"Not more than a mile the way we're going. It's a couple if you take the main ranch road."

"How big *is* this ranch?"

"The San Jose is 150,000 acres." She jerked the vehicle into gear. "When I hit thirty-five, half of it will belong to me."

"Sounds like a nice trust fund."

"It is. My grandfather saw to that before he died. It was a good thing, because Mom left her half to Logan and he's not a man given to sharing." Sylvia took her eyes from the bumpy dirt path and stared at Heather. "Looks like someone worked you over pretty good."

"Don't tell me you haven't heard the details. You'd be the only one in Dry Creek if you've missed out."

"I've heard a little. I quit asking questions about Dry Creek as soon as I turned eighteen and got the hell out of town. I've been back very seldom since." She slowed for a heifer that had wandered across their path. "If I'd known Logan was going to throw a prodigal-daughter graduation party, I would have stayed away a while longer."

"I imagine he's glad to have you home."

"No, it scares him to death to think I might want to come back and take control of my half of the McCullough estate."

"Do you?"

"No, not as long as I have to share the land with Logan. When he's dead, I may reconsider. Or maybe not. I've made a new life."

They rode in silence for a few minutes. In spite of all Heather had been through herself in the last few days, she felt sorry for the troubled woman who rode beside her. She had wealth, beauty and a new career ahead of her, but she obviously harbored a few family resentments. No wonder she and Matt were friends.

Heather ducked and leaned toward the center of the Jeep as they passed a little too close to the branches of a scrubby mesquite tree. "Were you and Matt childhood friends?"

"We were in the same grade. We became better friends when he came back to Texas to go to college." Sylvia swerved to avoid a rut in the worn path she was driving. "We were never anything more, though, in case you were wondering. Too much alike, I think, to be more than buddies."

"Then you went to the same college?"

"Yes, the University of Texas. Matt stayed and got his degree. I dropped out after my sophomore year and spent some time finding myself, so to speak, before I went back and picked up a few degrees."

"Sounds like you did a good job of finding yourself."

They made a sharp turn to the right along a fence line. Heather felt the first tinge of alarm as they approached a narrow bridge without any sign of side rails. One wrong move and they'd plunge into the water below. "Don't tell me we're going to drive across that thing," she protested.

"Relax, it's been here for as long as I can remember. The hands use it all the time to move equipment a lot heavier than my little Jeep." Sylvia barely slowed as they hit the bumpy wooden ties.

Heather held her breath, crossing her fingers for luck. She

wouldn't have trusted the structure to support a small dog, but somehow they made it to the other side and level ground.

Sylvia drove a few yards farther, swerved right and then stopped.

"This doesn't look like the stables."

"No, it's the family cemetery. I'd like to stop for a minute, if that's okay with you. Today would have been my mother's birthday."

"No problem. I'll wait in the car."

"Get out and look around. You might find some of the stones interesting, and I won't be long."

Heather followed Sylvia through the gate. Sylvia was right. The names and dates on the tombstones told their own stories, mostly of hard lives that took people before their time.

Carrie McCullough, born June 1, 1861, died August 8, 1862. *Our precious baby girl.*"

Jack McCullough, born April 14, 1898, died December 16, 1944.

Billy Roy Lassiter.

Heather studied the tombstone. Billy Roy Lassiter would have been about the same age as Kathy Warren and he'd died the same month of the same year. The day of the month was missing. Heather read and reread the strange inscription.

Killed at the hands of his fellow man.

"Did you find something interesting?" Sylvia asked, walking up behind her.

"As a matter of fact I did. Do you know anything about Billy Roy Lassiter's death?"

Sylvia ground a toe into the ground, staring at her boot as if it were worthy of deep study. "I know he was murdered." She raised her head, her gaze finally connecting with Heather's. ''And I know some folks think Jake McQuaid's responsible.''

A cottony lump caught in Heather's throat. Digging up buried truths. Matt had warned her about that. Maybe he had always been afraid the truths she uncovered would rock and sink his own world.

''That's a pretty serious accusation.''

''I'm not accusing, just stating a fact.'' Sylvia started walking again, and Heather followed her, feet dragging, her emotions churning.

''The crime was conveniently never solved.'' Sylvia bit at her lower lip. ''Did Matt tell you about the woman he and his brothers found beaten and left for dead?''

''Yes. Susan Hathaway.''

''Some folks think Jake McQuaid beat and killed Billy Roy in retaliation for what happened to Susan. My mother was one of those people.''

Heather's mind fought for reason. ''How would you know this? You were no more than a child at the time.''

Sadness drew the corners of Sylvia's eyes into deep grooves. ''I know because I heard my mother and Logan arguing the day after the man's body was found. They thought I was asleep, but my mother's screaming woke me. She accused Logan of helping Jake kill Billy Roy.''

''And then what happened?''

''Nothing. My mother died a few months later when her horse threw her. She was an excellent rider, but something spooked her mount, and he reared back, throwing her to the ground in front of him. His front feet caught her before she could roll away. At least that's the way it looked when one of the wranglers found her body.''

''I'm sorry.'' The words snagged painfully in Heather's throat, the hurt as much for herself as it was for Sylvia— and for Matt, and everyone else who'd ever lost a mother.

"It's okay. It happened a long time ago, and I've dealt with it and let it go. It's the good memories I try to hold on to now."

"Have you ever mentioned this to Matt?"

"No. I didn't want him to quit being my friend when we were youngsters. And, to tell you the truth, I hadn't thought of Billy Roy Lassiter for years, not until you called his name."

Heather started back to the car, and then jerked to a stop. Something had moved in the distance. She'd caught a glimpse of it in her peripheral vision. A quick darting. Perhaps a bird, a jackrabbit, a deer.

It was the events of the past few days that had her jumping out of her skin at every movement. That and the fact that she and Sylvia were in an isolated cemetery, so far away that no one would hear them if they cried for help.

She stared into a patch of thorny, head-high brush standing between them and a ragged persimmon tree. This time the darting movement was clear and unmistakable. Someone was out there, watching them, like a coyote waiting for his moment to spring on the helpless prey.

The hair on her neck stood on end. "Sylvia." Her voice was soft, meant not to carry beyond their immediate surroundings.

Sylvia eyed her suspiciously "What's wrong? You look as if you've seen a ghost. You're not going to faint on me, are you?"

"No, but I think there's someone in the bushes watching us."

"No one would be out here without a horse or a car. We're too far from the house."

The taste of fear settled like acid in Heather's stomach. She could feel a man's hands on her, feel a fist plowing into her face, almost as real as it had been the other night in her car. "Let's just get to the Jeep, fast."

The urgency in her voice must have gotten through to Sylvia. Both of them broke into a run, not slowing until they'd reached the Jeep. Sylvia's hand shook as she poked her key at the ignition, scraping metal before sliding into the hole. The engine sputtered and died, and Heather swallowed the curse that tore at her throat.

Sylvia didn't bother. "Damn! What a time for car trouble. Look again, Heather, see if you really see someone."

She didn't get the chance. This time the noise was from the west, and there was no mistaking the approaching horse and rider. Sylvia quit turning the key.

The cowboy tipped his hat. "You ladies lost?"

"No. I never get lost on my own land, but we could use your help. Heather thought she saw a man watching us from those bushes over there." She pointed.

The cowboy pulled on the reins, making a full circle with his horse, his gaze scanning the surrounding area before turning back to them. "More likely a momma cow making sure you're not out here to bother her calf, but I'll ride over and check out the scrub."

Sylvia turned the key, and this time the engine purred to life. "Are you ready to go to the stables, Heather?"

"I'd rather go back to the house. I promised Matt I wouldn't be too long."

"Then back to the house it is." She inched the jeep forward, then stalled as the cowboy rode back in their direction, smiling broadly.

"I scared up a bevy of quail. No sign of anything else." A broad grin cracked his lips.

"I guess I was mistaken," Heather said, sure she hadn't been, but afraid to push the issue with a man she knew nothing about. She was dwelling in a world of strangers where the unexpected was all she could count on. A world where secrets were deadly, and where the only man she trusted was a man she might be about to destroy.

The thought tore at her heart. Matt might bear grudges against his father, but that was a long way from believing he was a murderer. She could almost see the headlines now: Texas Ranger Arrests Own Father for Twenty-five-year-old Murder.

And all because a woman named Kathy Warren had passed through this town one dark night years ago.

And because Heather had fallen into Matt's life. A stroke of luck for her, but it might turn into a heartbreaking stroke of tragedy for him. And the last thing she wanted to do was bring pain to Matt McQuaid.

The Jeep bounced and rocked as Sylvia lowered her foot on the accelerator. "Will you tell Matt what we talked about today?"

"I don't have a choice, not since Ariana's been murdered. The killing has to stop somewhere."

"No, I guess you don't. I hope he understands why I had to tell you about his father." Sylvia hit the accelerator a little harder. "For what it's worth, I hope I'm wrong about Jake."

"So do I, Sylvia. So do I."

HEATHER WAITED until they were in the truck before mentioning her trip to the cemetery and sharing the information about Billy Roy Lassiter's grave. She avoided mentioning Sylvia's suspicions that Jake McQuaid might be involved in his death. Somehow the short ride to Ridgely's store didn't seem the opportune time to suggest Matt's father might be a murderer.

Just as well the topic hadn't been approached, Heather decided, sliding her right foot into the boot that Ridgely's wife had pulled from the shelf. Matt was already distracted and agitated after his talk with Logan, a talk he claimed had gotten him nowhere.

"Tug hard on those pull tabs to make sure your feet are all the way in," Matt instructed. "Then walk around in them. The leather should ride the top of your feet, but not cut into them."

She followed his instructions, pulling up on her jeans as she walked to get a better look at the plain black leather boots that Matt referred to as ropers. Her toes rocked against the new leather, and her heels settled against the solid backs.

"They're not as comfortable as my tennis shoes, but I think they fit."

"Hmmmpf." Paul's wife stuck her hands on her ample hips. "Boots aren't meant for walking or comfort. They're for riding horses. Or else they're for show." She lifted her ankle-length full skirt so that Matt and Heather could capture the full effect of the fancy boots she wore. "Aren't these a pair of doozies? I just got them in today."

"Very nice," Heather admitted, "but not quite what I need at the Lone M."

"No, these beauties are for prancing and dancing, and I plan to wear them half out at Logan Trenton's big blowout. Paul Ridgely hasn't taken me dancing in a month of Sundays. I'll be making him pay for that tomorrow night."

"What are you wearing besides the gorgeous boots?" Heather asked, drawn into Mrs. Ridgely's excitement in spite of herself.

"A full skirt, flowered, and an embroidered blouse. It makes me look even fatter than usual, but I don't care. I like a skirt twirling about my legs when I dance."

"You're far from fat."

"Not nearly as far as I was at your age. But it's fine with

me and fine with Paul, and we're the only ones who matter. He says he likes a woman he can hold on to.'' Her easy laughter rippled through the small shop.

Heather made another circle around the stool and then paused in front of a floor mirror. "This will be my first pair of Western boots."

"Then you better be careful, Matt." Mrs. Ridgely gave him a conspiratorial wink. "Nothing gets in a woman's blood faster than Western boots and Texas cowboys."

Heather turned to hide the blush that heated her cheeks.

"You know," Mrs. Ridgely said, walking over to stand in front of her. "I just got in an outfit that would look terrific on you, make you look like a real Texas gal. Come on over and take a look."

"Let me take these boots off first." Heather dropped back onto the low stool. She slid her hands under the tops and shoved.

"That's not exactly how you do that." Matt knelt in front of her. "Let me help."

One hand grasped the leather just below her ankle, one caught her leg above the boot line. The crazy sensation attacked her again, hot and sweet, rolling inside her and making her dizzy with unexpected desire. His gaze caught hers and held, invisible steam rising between them, stealing her breath away. The boot clunked to the floor beneath her foot. Matt backed away, flushed and fumbling. "You can get the other one," he said. "Now that you know how."

His voice was gravelly and unsteady. He shoved his hands into his pockets and stalked away, not stopping until he reached the far back corner of the store and a circle of men.

Mrs. Ridgely stared at Matt's back and then at Heather, no doubt noticing the flush in her cheeks. She smiled and nodded. "So, the rough, tough son of Jake McQuaid isn't a robot lawman without a heart after all. And you, Heather Lombardi, must be some woman to make him show it. Many a girl around here's tried without a smidgen of luck."

"I have no idea what you mean."

"You might be a nice lady, but you're lying through your teeth right now. Come on over here and try on that outfit I was telling you about. You might as well go all the way and brand him while he's weak and willing."

Heather followed Mrs. Ridgely across the shop, but she knew something the friendly woman didn't. There was nothing weak about Matt McQuaid.

THE SOFT SQUEAKING of the porch swing worked like a lullaby, and Heather's eyelids drooped until only a slit of afternoon sunlight filtered through. Matt had gotten back to the ranch about fifteen minutes ago, after being gone all afternoon. He'd left her guarded by the deputy while he went back into town.

But his beeper had been buzzing as he walked up the steps, and he'd been on the phone with Gabby ever since. She'd had no opportunity to speak of Sylvia's accusation against Jake McQuaid. And until she did, she couldn't get a minute's peace.

She looked up as the front door creaked open. "What was Gabby's problem?" she asked, moving over to make room for him on the swing beside her. Instead he settled on the top step and leaned against the porch column.

"He collected some prints from the car we found deserted on the highway, but he doesn't have a name as yet. They're running a fingerprint scan up at headquarters as we speak."

"Are there any leads in Ariana's death?"

"Nothing new. But at least we've had another crime-free day in Dry Creek. No bodies. No attacks. No threats." Matt set his hat on the porch beside him and stretched out, his long legs reaching all the way across the top step.

"And no clue as to what happened to the missing records?"

"Not unless you buy Logan's speculation that Gabby let rats get into them in that attic above his office and then threw the damaged files away."

"Evidently you don't believe that theory."

"Seems strange the rats would choose the exact records I'm looking for, especially if we're talking about four-legged rats."

Heather ran her fingers up and down the linked chain that held the swing. "Matt, I need to talk to you."

"I thought we *were* talking."

She swallowed past a lump in her throat. "Sylvia mentioned something today that I think you should know about."

The phone rang, and Matt started to get up from the step.

"I'll get it," Heather said, beating him to the draw. She couldn't sit on the porch and wait in silence now that she'd broached the subject with Matt. Better to be the one doing something.

She caught the phone on the third ring. "Hello."

"I need to talk to Matty. Is he there?"

Matty. The name was spoken like an endearment, but the female voice was shrouded in concern. Heather trembled, suddenly ill at ease and shaky. "Matt's here. I'll get him for you. Who shall I say is calling?"

"Susan Hathaway. I need to talk to him about his father." She hesitated. "But don't tell him that."

"No, I won't." Anxiety was playing havoc with Heather's nerves as she handed Matt the phone.

Chapter Twelve

Matt took the phone from Susan. "Matt McQuaid."

"Matty. It's Susan."

His fingers tightened around the receiver. "Is something wrong?"

"No, I wanted to hear your voice, to find out how you're doing. It's been so long since you've called."

"Yeah. I've been busy." The lie was bitter on his tongue. Not that he hadn't been busy, but it had little to do with the fact that he hadn't called. "How are you?"

"Older, slower. A few more wrinkles. Other than that I'm the same."

He tried to imagine Susan as old, but he could only ever picture her as the young woman he and his brothers had found in the ditch. The beautiful lady who'd moved into their lives like an angel dropped from the sky. He'd never see her any other way.

"Have you talked to Cy or Cameron lately?"

"They're both well, absorbed in their own families and careers, but they drop by when they can. They'd love to see you." Her voice shook slightly. "We *all* would."

All. She meant his father, of course, though they both knew that wasn't true. Matt had been a thorn in his father's side for as long as he could remember, a reminder of the wife Jake had needed, but never loved.

But Susan would always stand by and defend Jake McQuaid. She didn't need vows or legalities to be faithful and loyal. It was who she was.

"How is Jake?"

"Not as well as he should be. The doctor's warned him to take it easy, to watch his blood pressure. He doesn't listen to him or to me."

"That's Jake."

"That's your *father*. He'll turn sixty-five in two weeks."

"I'm sure you're planning a party. Wish him all the best for me."

"You need to do that yourself, Matt. I want you to come home for his birthday."

"I can't." He swallowed, his throat drier than south Texas earth. "I'm in the middle of a case."

Silence hung on the line, accusing, pleading. It was difficult to refuse Susan anything, but more difficult to return home and play the role of loving, respectful son, especially now.

"Think about it, Matty. If you won't do it for yourself or Jake, do it for me. I've caused a rift in this family long enough. I can't carry the pain of that to the grave."

"The problem is between Jake and me, Susan. It has nothing to do with you."

"It has everything to do with me. You think Jake robbed me of respectability. He didn't. Like you and your brothers, he paid the price for mistakes I made before I was old enough to know what life was about. You know the truth of that now and you have to accept it."

"I accept that you make it awfully convenient for Jake to do exactly as he pleases, to play life his way, by his own self-serving rules."

"He lives life the only way he knows how, the same as you do." Her voice fell to a pain-filled whisper. "Come home, Matty. A quick visit for your father's birthday. Is that so much to ask?"

Matt shifted the phone to the other ear. His gaze cut to the front door and the darkness that was settling like a veil over his world. "Don't count on me, Susan. Not this time."

Her sigh cut through the static that was forming on the line. "I am counting on you. I need you here and so does Jake. And *you* need to be here for yourself. You're a part of this family and always will be."

Left without an argument, Matt shifted the conversation to impersonal topics, the weather, the dry spell in South Texas that was threatening to turn serious. But the tension created by Susan's pleas continued to cloud the conversation, and by the time he hung up the phone, Matt was sweating.

He walked back to the porch, this time easing to the swing beside Heather. He rubbed his clammy hands together, then wiped them on the rough denim that covered his thighs. "I'm sorry for the interruption."

"You look upset. Is something wrong?"

"Jake McQuaid's sixty-fifth birthday is approaching. I was invited to the party."

"You'll go, of course."

"I have a murderer to catch. Speaking of which, where were we?"

Heather sensed more than saw the change in Matt, although the signs were not invisible. The cocky, self-assured Ranger had drawn inside himself, leaving his shoulders to sag and his eyes and chin to drop. She longed to question him further about Susan's call, but she knew it would be a waste of time. Matt talked only when he was ready.

"We were discussing the murder of Billy Roy Lassiter," she said, dreading more than ever what she had to say.

"Billy Roy." Matt drummed his fingers against the swing's wooden armrest. "The man whose grave you discovered in the McCullough family cemetery. I asked a few questions about him today in town."

"What did you find out?"

"That the mention of his name stops conversation cold." Matt tensed, his muscles drawn and pulling at the fabric of his shirt. His face twisted into hard, unforgiving lines. He turned to face her, his eyes a frigid shade of gray. "Tell me exactly what Sylvia told you."

Heather did, wincing inside as she uttered the words of accusation.

"So Sylvia thinks Jake killed Billy Roy Lassiter," he said when she'd finished the statement. "Evidently the rest of Dry Creek does, too. Why else would they clam up so tight at the sound of his name?"

Matt didn't protest the accusation. The only sign he gave that it affected him at all was the burst of energy that pulled him from the swing and had him pacing the porch.

"I didn't want to tell you what she said about your father, Matt, but in view of Ariana's murder, I felt I had to. But Sylvia's saying it doesn't make it so. And if everyone in town believed it, why didn't someone do something before now?" She stood and walked over to him.

"Why? Because it's Jake McQuaid."

"What will you do?"

"The only thing I can. If he's innocent, I'll prove it. If he's guilty, I'll prove that, too." He turned and faced Heather, his eyes dark pools of determination. "The only thing that doesn't add up is that the law was Jake's life, part of the code of justice that ruled him. It was more important to him than even his own children. It's hard accepting that he prostituted that the way he did his women.''

Heather slid into his arms. She needed his closeness, but even that didn't give her warmth tonight. "There are other Rangers who can take over this investigation. Give up the case, Matt. If you don't, it might destroy you.''

"I can't." He tilted her chin so that she had to look him in the eye. "I told you. My father's blood runs through me. I have to do what I have to do. That's why I'm no good for you, no good for any woman.''

"Or maybe you just never met a woman who could handle you until now, Matt McQuaid." His arms tightened around her, but she pulled herself from his grasp. She'd just thrown down a gauntlet, and she wasn't sure that she was ready to meet her own challenge. She didn't even know where the words had come from.

"I'll finish making dinner," she said, pulling the screen door open. She peeked her head back out, stopping the door just before it closed behind her. "You might want to clean up. We're dining by candlelight. Even on a ranch, a lady needs some social amenities.''

MATT SHUDDERED as Heather disappeared from sight. He felt as if he'd been turned inside out and back again in the last few minutes. The reminder that so many people apparently believed his father was a murderer had left a raw lining in his stomach—which could usually handle the hottest of chili peppers.

But he'd shower and play gentleman rancher for the lady of the Lone M if that's what she wanted. He'd play all her games, maybe even pretend for a few minutes that he was the man she thought he was. Hell, he'd ride a wild stallion for her if he thought it would make the next few days any easier.

Susan Hathaway, Kathy Warren, Billy Roy Lassiter and Jake McQuaid. Somehow, they were all tied together in a plot that someone would still kill to keep secret twenty-five years after the fact. He stuffed his hand into his pocket and ran his fingers along the jagged edge of the note that rested there. This time the warning had been delivered to Matt, stuck under the windshield wiper of his truck while it had been parked in town.

Ranger: Let the search for Kathy Warren end before the lives of good people are ruined over something that can't be changed. If you don't, you will live to regret it. You and your girlfriend.

But what were a few more regrets to a man like him?

It was Heather he was worried about now. He'd do whatever he had to in order to keep her safe, even if it meant defying the law he was sworn to protect. More of the legacy of Jake McQuaid.

As for Jake McQuaid, he prayed Sylvia was wrong, though he had suspected Jake might be involved from the first sign of missing records. If Jake were arrested on murder charges it would tear the heart out of Susan. She would never forgive Matt for digging up the past. Maybe he'd never forgive himself, though he had no choice now.

Every muscle in Matt's body ached as he headed for a hot shower. He felt like a grain of sand caught up in a dust storm, powerless to stop the events that whirled around him, powerless to dictate where it would all end.

HEATHER FISHED fresh green beans from the pot, spooning boiled potatoes around them in the serving bowl. She'd snapped the beans herself—a neighbor had brought over a gift of vegetables from her garden—and rummaged in Matt's poorly stocked pantry for seasonings.

His freezer, however, was another story. There were

packages of corn, squash, carrots and other summer vegetables, all zipped neatly away in freezer bags labeled with
dates and the names of one or another of his neighbors.

Evidently the women of Dry Creek took good care of
their resident Texas Ranger. And he had his own supply of
meat, every cut of beef imaginable. She'd made beef Stro-
ganoff, one of her specialties.

Standing back, she admired her handiwork. The plates
didn't match, but the colors of the food prettied up the table.
All in the presentation, that's what the few ladies' magazines she'd found time to read said. Hot pads in hand, she
added the finishing touch, a big bowl of sweet corn, still
on the cob.

Funny, cooking for just herself had always seemed a
chore. Scavenging around in Matt's much less modern and
meagerly stocked kitchen had actually been fun. Or had the
pleasure been in the anticipation of sitting across the table
from him, watching him eat, and listening to him talk?

He claimed to be all wrong for her, all wrong for any
woman, but every moment she spent with him convinced
her differently. Yet she couldn't help but wonder if the
attraction that pulled her to him would be this great if it
weren't for the danger that hung over her head like an anvil
about to drop.

She touched her fingers to her hair, pushing the loose
wisps back in place, and then went into the bedroom to
smudge a tint of color to her lips. Steam and the sound of
running water beating against the plastic shower curtain
seeped through the cracks around and under the door.

In her mind's eye she saw Matt, naked, streams of water
running down the angles and planes of his body, imagined
the hair on his chest, wet and curled in the running water.
The images churned inside her, and she leaned against the

door, weak with desire. How could she want a man she barely knew this badly?

The door squeaked open and she lost her balance, falling inside far enough to catch herself on the counter. Matt peeked around the edge of the curtain. "Are you all right?"

"Yes." Her voice came out too soft, shattered by the emotion reeling inside her.

"Come here, Heather." Matt pushed the curtain aside and reached out a hand.

"The floor is getting wet."

"Let it."

He grabbed her hand and pulled her closer. The heat from the shower mingled with the fire inside her. Breathless, she tried to pull away. "You're getting my clothes wet."

"We can take care of that." His wet hands slid beneath her shirt, his fingers hot and damp on her skin as he raised her shirt and pulled it over her head. She didn't move, barely daring to breathe as he wrapped his arms around her, loosened the clasp on her bra and let it drop to the floor.

Shaking, she stepped out of her shoes, and Matt tucked his hands under her arms and lifted her into the tub, jeans and all. Water splashed around and over her breasts and face, but all she felt were Matt's lips on hers.

When she came up for air, she was trembling, her hair straggling into her face, but she still felt more sexy and desirable than ever before in her life. "I usually shower alone," she whispered, "and with all my clothes off."

"What a waste of good water. This way you can do your laundry, make love and get clean all at the same time." He soaped his hands and rubbed them over her breasts until soft snowy peaks highlighted her nipples.

Heather returned the favor, soaping Matt's chest and then his buttocks between kisses. Laughing, he pulled on the waist of her jeans until the snap gave. Using his teeth, he unzipped her.

She nibbled his wet earlobe. "The hidden side of Matt McQuaid. Do the other Rangers know you have this knack for conserving water?"

"If they do, they know me better than I knew myself. I've never behaved like this before." He kissed her again, thoroughly, boggling her brain. "You bring out the worst in me," he whispered, peeling the wet denim from her body.

"If this is the worst, I don't know if I'm up for the best."

"We'll soon find out."

The next few minutes were a symphony of movements and feelings, of words and moans of pleasure. Heather drowned in pleasure time after time, only to come back to life with a new touch by Matt. By the time they climbed out of the shower, she was too weak to do more than wrap herself in a towel and collapse across the bed.

Matt, on the other hand, was obviously refreshed and raring to go. She heard him padding through the house, singing a country song and calling to her. "All that and you cook, too. But you better hurry. Our candles are burning out."

She struggled into a pair of dry jeans and a white shirt. "Don't tell me you have enough energy left to eat," she challenged as she fell into the chair opposite him.

"Are you kidding? I'm famished." He passed the bowl of beans to her. "Come to think of it, I don't remember stopping for lunch today."

He settled into eating, and within moments the quiet routine snatched away the few minutes of pleasure they'd stolen in the shower. Heather could almost see the worries of the day claiming him again, dragging his spirits down and changing his eyes from black gold to dusty coal.

But nothing could steal her happiness away. She wouldn't let it. She'd learned something about Matt in the last few days. The passion that drove him wasn't all for the law that ruled him. He could feel that same passion for a woman. She'd experienced that firsthand.

Maybe this was the gift Kathy Warren had left behind for the daughter she'd never known. A meeting with Matt McQuaid. Perhaps even now her birth mother was looking down from heaven and smiling on their union. If so, she still had her work cut out for her.

There was a murder to solve before either Heather or Matt could be free to go on with their lives. And she knew Matt still had to be convinced that he could handle a long-term relationship—that even though he was his father's son, he was still his own man.

Because Heather wouldn't settle for what Susan Hathaway had. When this was over, she'd only stay in Dry Creek as Matt's wife.

THE THREE MEN HUDDLED in the back of the barn. Outside, the sun flirted with the horizon, spreading rays of red and gold across the graying sky. Inside, darkness was winning, letting mere splotches of light sneak between the shadows.

"I never meant for things to go this far." The shorter man tugged at the neck of his shirt, pulling it away from his Adam's apple. A drop of sweat worked its way down his collar.

"What are you going to do now?" The tall, lanky man ran callused fingers through his graying hair. His question was directed to the man who always took control.

"We don't have a lot of choice, do we?"

"I don't like it," the short man complained again.

"Are you willing to go to jail for life, that is, if the jury's reasonably friendly? If they're not, you could be talking the death penalty.''

The tall man hooked his thumbs into the front pockets of his jeans. "I don't know. I just don't know."

"I do. I'll take care of everything tomorrow night at the party. My plan is foolproof."

"You're talking about killing innocent people." The stench of his words filled his lungs and the man moved toward the door for a breath of fresh air.

"It's no different than it was when we killed Billy Roy."

"It's a lot different. I was young, and drunk. And the victim then wasn't so innocent."

"Susan Hathaway was."

The old cowboy felt sick to his stomach. "She wasn't part of the original plan. I've always felt guilty for what we did to her. The both of you have, too. Don't tell me you haven't."

"Not a day goes by I don't regret what we done." The tall man leaned against a giant roll of feeder hay. "Maybe we should just hold off. No one's found us out for a quarter of a century. We could keep quiet and take our chances."

"And you think Matt McQuaid will pack up and go away? You know his reputation. He's tougher than nails and persistent as a hungry mosquito."

"He's Jake McQuaid's youngest son and the heart of Susan Hathaway." The shorter man backed away from the other two, suddenly loath to look at them. "I'll take no part in killing him or Heather Lombardi. It was bad enough when you hired those two ruffians that beat her up so bad. You'd promised they'd only frighten her into leaving town."

"Even the beating didn't frighten her enough to run her off. She's not reasonable, but you'd better be. We're all in this together, and we stick together or swing together. It's the only way." The man stepped closer to his reluctant friend.

"Then we swing together. We done the deed. We'll pay the price if it comes to that." The man who spoke thought of his wife and how she'd die of grief if she knew the truth about him. "I hope it don't," he said. "I sure hope it don't, but I'll take the risk."

The man in charge wrapped his hand around the knife in his pocket. He didn't like the spot he was in, but he'd do what had to be done. "You might be willing to take the risk, Paul, but I'm not."

HEATHER ROLLED THE PEN between her fingers. "Let's try another scenario, Matt. Suppose my mother had nothing at all to do with the death of Billy Roy Lassiter or Susan's beating. Suppose she just got out of Cass Purdy's car and caught a bus to New Orleans that night."

"That makes perfect sense except for the fact that as soon as you arrived in town asking about her, you fell into a heap of trouble." He wadded the sheet of paper in front of him and hurled it across the room.

"But that could be because I said she was here in mid-October, twenty-five years ago. If I'd killed Billy Roy, I wouldn't want anyone digging up the past, especially if the past correlated that closely with the time of the murder."

"I'd buy the possibility of that scenario if we only had the threatening note. I'd give it a scrap of consideration if we added some guys roughing you up. But throw in planting explosives in your car and killing Ariana, and it blows your theory out of the corral. A man doesn't kill to cover up a murder he's gotten away with for years unless he has damn good reason to believe his secrets are about to be uncovered."

"I just wish the man who'd gone to Cass Purdy's looking

for me, the one who showed up at my apartment the day Ariana was killed, would show up again. It's possible that he's a member of Kathy Warren's family, that he could unravel this mystery."

"You're clutching at a broken rein, Heather. I've told you before, the chances of that man being a member of your family are slim to none. He's more likely a paid killer whose job is to make sure you don't get the chance to find out too much."

She stretched her legs in front of her and crossed her arms over her chest, so tired of dead ends she could scream.

Matt leaned closer. "Are you cold?"

"A little. Inside."

"I'm afraid I can't do anything about that."

"But you do help, all the time. Just being with you helps."

He shook his head. "That's only because you see in me what you choose to."

"And you see in yourself what you choose to see. I like *my* vision better." She wouldn't give in to his demons tonight, not after he'd played and made love to her the way he had in the shower. He was flesh and blood, not some inhuman clone of his father, whether he cared to admit it or not.

"Tell me about Susan Hathaway, Matt."

"What about her?"

"You told me she didn't know a soul in Dry Creek, that she was only passing through town that night, when she was beaten and left for dead, but you've never really talked about her."

Matt put down the legal pad he'd been using to scribble possible matches between the skimpy evidence he'd collected so far and every man in town. "She was quiet, loving. She laughed a lot, but sometimes I'd come in and find her crying. I never understood that until recently, when we found out who she really was."

"What do you mean by that? Who was she?"

He walked over to the counter and poured himself a double shot of whiskey, drinking it down before turning back to Heather. "Susan kept her past a secret, not even letting my brothers know about it until just recently. I don't know how much she remembered or how much she wanted to remember before that, but I've honored her wishes to keep it her secret."

Matt returned to the couch. He took the end opposite Heather, working his feet from his boots. When the last one clattered to the floor, he propped his stockinged feet on the wooden coffee table. "In light of all that's happened to you, I don't think Susan would mind your knowing her story, but it's to go no further."

"Of course not."

His gaze met Heather's "Have you ever heard of Pamela Jessup?"

"Pamela Jessup? The name sounds familiar." Heather pulled her feet up under her. "Wait, isn't that the California heiress who ran away from home and joined up with some bank robber? I saw a TV show about her once."

"That's her."

"According to the show I saw, her family never heard from her again. Her body was found in some motel in Texas. So what does that have to do with Susan?"

"Pamela Jessup *is* Susan Hathaway."

Chapter Thirteen

Matt reached for the newspaper.

"Oh, no, you don't, Matt McQuaid." Heather snatched the paper from his hands and tossed it over the arm of the sofa and to the floor. "You don't nonchalantly announce you were raised by some infamous bank robber heiress and then turn away as if you'd given me a weather report."

Matt sighed and rubbed his forehead as if his head hurt, but he went on. "My brothers and I were raised by a homeless woman we found at the side of the road. Believe me, we never had a clue the woman who cooked our oatmeal and patched our jeans was a bank robber or an heiress. No one did."

"Can you imagine, a woman wanted for bank robbery found by the sheriff's sons. It was probably a good thing no one knew who she was." Heather tapped the end of her pen against her tablet. "But I thought Pamela Jessup's body was found in some motel in Texas."

"That was all a lie concocted to keep her family from looking for her. Apparently Philip Gould lost track of her about the time we found her. When her body didn't show up, he made up his own version of her disappearance. He admitted as much when he was finally arrested. He still claimed he wasn't the one who'd attacked her."

"It has to have been all one and the same, Matt. Your dad, Pamela Jessup, Billy Roy, my mother, all involved in something someone is determined to keep secret. You tried to tell me I might not like what I found out, but I couldn't have imagined that Kathy Warren might be involved with a bank robber."

"We don't have proof of anything."

"It still doesn't make sense. I can see how my mother could have been mixed up with Pamela Jessup. We know nothing about her, but Billy Roy was just a local wrangler."

"He could have just been in the wrong place at the wrong time. It happens, especially when there are two beautiful young women about."

Heather's insides churned. All she'd wanted was to find a connection with her past, learn something about her birth mother, but the old secrets she was discovering were actually hidden crimes. She turned around so that she could face Matt. "Tell me about Susan, or should I say Pamela?"

"She'll always be Miss Susan to me." Matt's tone softened. "She was different from the women around here. Her voice had a musical quality to it, and she had funny ways of doing and saying things. We laughed at her, but she was fast as the wind on the horse Dad bought her."

"It must have been difficult for her, going from a life of luxury to being the caretaker for a poorly paid sheriff and his three sons."

"I guess so, but we never noticed. We had no idea she'd ever been rich."

Matt shifted, and a smile touched his lips. Heather sensed he was lost in his own past, this time in the good parts of it.

"Susan and I bonded right from the first," he said, continuing the story. "I suspect I was a needy child, aching for a mother like all the other boys had. She gave me more than my fair share of love and attention. Not that she let me get away with anything. She was tough as nails.''

''According to the documentary that I saw, Pamela Jessup was a wild teenager who'd gotten involved in drugs and partying, a victim of too much money and loose morals.''

''There's two sides to everything.'' Matt reached in his back pocket and pulled out his wallet. He removed a small photograph, yellowed, the edges crinkled. ''This is the woman I knew. No drugs unless you count an occasional aspirin. And I don't remember a single wild party.''

He handed the photo to Heather, a smile curving his lips. ''But she could dance. She'd play the radio and boogie with the broom or the mop or one of us boys. That was the wildest I ever saw her. Unless you count the time my brothers and I let a snake loose in the house.''

Heather held the photo so that it caught the glow of the lamp. ''She was very pretty.''

''She still is.'' Matt fingered a loose string on the throw pillow that rested between them. ''You remind me of her.''

Heather studied the photo. There *was* a resemblance. Not the hair. Not the eyes or cheekbones, either. The mouth, maybe, or the shape of the face. A sinking feeling settled in her stomach. ''Is that why you took me in, Matt, because I reminded you of Susan?''

''I took you in because you were in danger.'' He stretched his arm across the back of the couch, catching a strand of her hair between his fingers, toying with it. ''I know what you're thinking, Heather. Forget it. The attraction between us is a hell of a lot more than my looking for a lost mother figure, and you know it.''

''You're reading my mind. I'm starting to get worried.''

''I'm worried myself, but not about my mind-reading abilities. More that I'm so comfortable having you around even after we make love." He pulled her to him, settling her in the crook of his arm. "That doesn't usually happen with me. Most of the time, I'm ready to clear out and be by myself."

"Have there been so many others?"

"Fewer than I like to admit."

The confession warmed her heart. She snuggled closer. "I'd still like to know about Susan. What made her so angry with her parents that she turned to a life of crime?"

"A lack of trust, I suspect." Matt paused, his fingers unconsciously rubbing Heather's arm. "She was raped by the son of a family friend, the same man who faked her death. Her parents refused to back her in pressing charges, saying that she would cause unnecessary embarrassment for herself and her sister, but she decided to press charges anyway."

"How sad, to have your own family turn against you after such a traumatic experience."

"It gets worse. After he raped her, Phillip Gould apparently paid one of his no-good friends to kill her. Instead, the guy kidnapped her and tried to collect a ransom."

"I remember that part from the TV show. David something or another. He was arrested later."

"David Eisman, a first-class louse. May he rot in the California jail where they stuck him."

"Wait a minute. Didn't she marry him while they were on the run?"

"Yeah. Apparently, he was a charming and very charismatic first-class louse. She was caught on the surveillance camera helping him rob a bank."

"But Pamela Jessup somehow wound up in Texas with Jake McQuaid and his three sons. This is a bizarre story." Heather slipped from the shelter of Matt's arms and picked up her pen and tablet again. The answer to the riddle of her own mother might lie somewhere in this muddle of facts. "So the notorious Pamela Jessup raised you and your brothers and none of you ever knew who she was until a few years ago."

"That's the size of it. We would probably never have known if my brothers hadn't discovered her identity while trying to solve another crime."

"Was she prosecuted then?"

"No. More than two decades after the fact, she was granted immunity and an annulment of her marriage to David Eisman. The best part was that she was able to keep her anonymity. It would have reopened the nightmare all over again if she'd been forced to become the focus of the media after all those years."

"Your father must have been thankful to have it all out in the open. Now, with her annulment and immunity from criminal prosecution, she was finally free to marry him. It's a beautiful story, Matt."

"It is the way you tell it." He rubbed the muscles behind his neck, the smile gone from his face, replaced by taut lines. "There's been no wedding."

"Maybe she doesn't need his name or a license. Maybe knowing he loves her is enough for her."

"Yeah, sure." Matt walked to the window and stared out into the murky darkness.

Heather moved over to stand behind him. She circled his waist with her arms, smoothing her hands over his chest. His muscles tightened, every nerve in his body urging him to move away, not to let her get too close, not to let her into his personal world.

"You should go back for your father's birthday. It would please Susan."

"Leave it alone, Heather. Family is a dead issue with me. I've made my life here in Texas."

"You've made an existence, not a life."

She buried her head between his shoulder blades. Part of him ached to turn and take her in his arms. Part of him longed to run like hell. He did neither.

"You told me when I first came here that I shouldn't dig up old secrets, Matt, that doing so might shatter the present."

"And I was right."

"Maybe, but it's no worse than what you're doing. You're letting the past eat away at the present, letting it make you just as afraid as your dad to show emotion."

"You've noticed. A chip off the old block, that's me. Being with you these last few days has convinced me of that more than ever. I should never have touched you in any intimate way while you were under my protective custody. Follow the rules when they suit me, ignore them when they don't. It's a family tradition."

Heather tugged him around to face her, rose up on tiptoe and met his gaze straight on. "Don't give your father blame or credit for what's happened between us these last few days. It was what we both wanted, and no matter what happens after this, I'll never be sorry we made love."

"Don't count on that."

Heather touched her lips to his, and seemingly unable to stop himself he wrapped his arms around her. The kiss this time was softer, sweeter than ever before. She shuddered, sensing instinctively that their relationship had moved beyond the savage sensual hunger that had driven them initially.

There was no denying the signs. She had fallen in love with Matt McQuaid, a man whose destiny remained chained to his past. A man who would never be able to love completely until he could learn to forgive his father and accept that he was his own man.

The phone rang then, and the next round of bad news hit home. Paul Ridgely's wife had come home and found him unconscious in the barn behind their house. He had been stabbed twice, once in the back, once in the chest. The good news was that even though he'd lost a lot of blood, he was still alive.

HEATHER STOOD in the waiting room of the small hospital. It was a good forty-five-minute drive from Dry Creek, but the room was filled with Paul Ridgely's friends and neighbors. John Billinger and his wife, Gabby, Rube and Edna, the pastor from his church, even Logan Trenton had shown up. There were others as well, some Heather had seen before, but she couldn't put names to the faces.

Most of the men were grumbling about the fact that a man wasn't safe on his own land anymore. Most of the women were consoling Mrs. Ridgely. She was dry-eyed now, but her red, swollen eyelids made it clear that she'd shed her share of tears.

"I hope Matt finds out who did this soon," Edna said, walking up behind Heather. "None us are safe with a murderer roaming the area."

"He's doing everything he can, Edna."

"I know. He's a good man, just like his dad was. Where is he now?"

"He's in the room with Paul."

"I hope Paul lives, I truly do." Edna shredded the tissue in her hands into tiny pieces. "But even if he doesn't, I pray he regains consciousness long enough to tell who did this to him. I haven't had a minute's peace since Ariana was killed. And Rube's as worried as I am. He's hardly eaten since he found Ariana's body, and I wake up in the night to find him walking the floor or staring out the window."

Heather turned as Matt stepped into the room. A group of men circled around him, all asking the same question. Did Paul give him a name?

Matt put his hand up to silence the anxious questions. "Paul is still unconscious. The doctor promised to call me when he's able to talk. In the meantime, we have a guard at his door to make sure the man who stabbed him doesn't come back to finish the job. Believe me, the problems in Dry Creek are top priority. Go home and get some sleep, but keep your doors locked."

"And your shotguns loaded," John Billinger muttered. There was a rumbling of agreement among the men.

"Just watch out who you shoot," Matt warned. "Nervous fingers on the trigger can get a man in a lot of trouble." He motioned for Heather to meet him at the door. She did, and he wasted no time in hustling her outside.

"Do you think Paul will live?" she asked, as they hurried down the corridor and to the car.

"He has a good chance."

"But he didn't tell you who stabbed him?"

"No, he was muttering, but not coherently. The only name I recognized was Billy Roy Lassiter."

Dread filled Heather, thick as smoke from a smoldering fire that refused to die. It burned her lungs and rolled in her stomach. The secrets that had lain hidden for a quarter of a century were ripping Dry Creek apart. She had been the catalyst for reawakening the terror.

And the end wasn't even in sight.

STANDING under a tree a few yards from the back door of Logan Trenton's sprawling house, Heather surveyed the scene, and marveled, "So this is how they throw a party in Texas!"

"It's how the wealthier ranchers do it." Matt grabbed a

couple of glasses of champagne from the tray of a passing waiter. He handed one of the crystal flutes to Heather.

"I propose a toast," she said.

Matt's eyebrows rose inquiringly. He lifted his glass and waited.

"To finding answers to all of our questions so that we can go on with our lives."

Matt clinked his glass with hers. "I'll drink to that," he announced, "and I propose another toast."

"What to this time?"

"To Lady Luck, for setting me up with the prettiest lady at the ball."

A blush heated Heather's cheeks. "I'm sure there are a lot of men here tonight who'd argue that with you."

"Let them. My eyes don't lie."

They clinked their glasses again, but when Heather looked into Matt's eyes, it was more than desire she read there. "Do you think there'll be trouble tonight?"

"Could be. I plan to keep my eyes and ears open. That's why we're here, to try to find a few more pieces to the puzzle."

Heather made a full turn, taking in the entire front lawn and the grassy area to the side of the house. Tables laden with food were sheltered from the late afternoon sun by huge white awnings. Brightly colored streamers and white lights hung from the branches of trees, and waiters in white shirts and black bow ties mingled with the festive crowd, passing out drinks and hors d'oeuvres.

"Even music," she said, as a trio of strolling mariachis stopped nearby to serenade a young couple.

"And more people than you can shake a stick at. Let me know if you see John Billinger. I'd like to catch him away from his wife and ask him a few questions."

"So, that's why everyone's avoiding you tonight. You've been harassing them with questions."

"I hope they keep on avoiding me. I can work better that way. Are you up for a little snooping?"

Heather's heart beat a little faster. "I'm up for anything that might produce results. What do you have in mind?"

"I don't see Logan, but I'm sure he's occupied now doing what he does best, schmoozing with people with money and power. It's a good time to take an exploratory look around his office."

"Without asking him?"

"That's the general idea. You can stand outside the door, let me know if he's coming."

"What do you expect to find?"

"I don't know. That's why it's exploratory."

Excitement battled with doubt. "Isn't breaking into someone's office illegal?"

"We're not breaking in. We're invited guests. If someone asks me what we're doing in that part of the house, I'll explain that we were looking for a little privacy." His eyes danced with devilment. "I'll tell them you couldn't keep your hands off me."

"You'll do no such thing."

"Why not? It's half true."

"It's you who can't keep your hands off me."

"That's the other half. Now take my arm and smile a lot. We'll go in the back door and take the hall off the den. Don't worry. Most of the people are outside where the food is."

Heather followed his instructions, the adrenaline rush making it easy to smile but hard to speak intelligently when Ben Wright stopped them to ask about Paul Ridgely and whether or not Matt was close to arresting a suspect in the stabbing incident.

Matt gave him a quick update on Paul's condition, but dodged the rest of the questions in his easy cowboy manner, short sentences that sounded friendly but said nothing. She followed him to the back of the house where a fiddler was tuning his instrument and a tall, skinny guitarist was adjusting a microphone.

"The dance band is warming up," Matt announced, pushing through the back door and into the cool interior of the house. "That should keep Logan busy. He loves to show off his fancy two-steppin'."

A couple of teenaged girls were giggling in the den. They didn't give Matt or Heather a second look. The hall was empty. Matt stopped at the door to the office and jiggled the knob. The door opened, and Matt stepped inside. His gaze traveled and settled on a window. He walked over and unlocked it, sliding it up a few inches and then shutting it again.

"An escape hatch in case I need it," Matt explained, walking back to the door. "Hang out in the hall. If you see Logan, call to him, loudly, so that I know he's around. Then keep him talking long enough for me to climb out the window."

"What if someone sees you?"

"I'll chance it, but it's not likely. The window's on the east side, and there aren't any tables of food set up there. Besides, we're not breaking and entering. We're invited guests. Now, are you clear on everything?"

"All clear." Heather swallowed a lump of fear. "This is my first lookout."

"Watch it. It gets in your blood. You might want to give up your job and become a Ranger."

"Not likely. *My* associates don't carry guns."

"You've got a point." Matt kissed her on the tip of her nose. "I'm counting on you, partner." He steered her away from the door with a hand on the back of her waist and then shut himself inside the office.

Apprehension balled inside Heather the first dozen or more times the back door opened. After that, she grew lax and weary of waiting. She tapped on the door. "Matt."

The door squeaked open. "What is it?"

"You've been in there so long I was starting to get worried."

"Look at this."

Heather scanned the file he stuck in front of her. "It's an insurance claim on Logan's wife."

"Right. The insurance company demanded an autopsy to prove the cause of death was accidental. Logan refused the autopsy, even though it meant losing two hundred thousand dollars."

"That seems strange."

"It got my attention. I need a few more minutes in here. If Logan shows up, stall him."

"How?"

"I don't know. Flirt. Ask questions. Do whatever you have to. Just buy me enough time to check the rest of these files."

Matt disappeared behind the closed door again. Heather paced nervously. It was clear she had the least exciting part of this mission. She had half a mind to forget Logan and go help Matt.

What would Logan do if he did find them inside? Shoot them? At the thought, images of Ariana's dead body filtered through her mind. *Someone* in this town would shoot to keep their secrets. But Logan? Not likely. He just seemed too much the gentleman.

She leaned against the wall, her toe tapping to the music that drifted in from the band stand. Suddenly, the back door swung open and Logan Trenton stepped inside. Unlike the others who'd come in, he noticed her immediately.

"Logan, I've been looking for you." She said his name extra loudly so that her voice would carry through the closed door. Her breath caught in her throat as he hurried toward her, the smile on his face not hiding his surprise at seeing her there.

"Well, you've found me, or I've found you. Now how can I be of service?"

"I wanted to tell you how much I'm enjoying the party. And—" she moved closer, the skirt she'd bought at Ridgely's store swishing about her legs "—I'd hoped to persuade you to dance with me. I heard you're terrific at the Texas two-step, and I've never danced it with a real cowboy."

He tipped his hat and smiled. "I'd like nothing better, but first I have to get something out of my office."

"Surely you wouldn't put me off to take care of business. Not at such a great party." Heather batted her eyes in what she hoped was a coquettish manner. Flagrant flirting wasn't part of her usual repertoire, but desperate times called for desperate measures.

"It flatters me to think you're that anxious. I'll take care of business quick." His stepped toward the door.

Faint, yell fire, throw myself into his arms. The options flashed through her brain. Instead she grabbed his arm. "Please, Logan, that's my favorite song. I'd hate to miss it."

He stared at her, his eyebrows at angles that indicated she was overplaying her role. "'Deep in the Heart of Texas' isn't much of a dance number. Besides, it's almost over. We'll request a much better tune when I'm finished." He pushed the door open and walked inside.

Heather took a deep breath and waited. A minute later,

Logan was back at her side, sliding a slender envelope into the inside pocket of his Western-cut jacket. She glimpsed the silver handle of a pistol peeking from a shoulder holster.

He took her arm. "Now, shall we dance?"

"Yes." It was all the answer she could manage, and it came out in a shaky whisper. Evidently Matt had made a quick, unnoticed escape through the window. Her relief was short-lived. Logan was leading her the wrong way, down the hall, away from the back door.

She stopped walking. "The band is outside."

He circled her waist with his arm. "Don't worry, the party will be going strong for hours. I have something I'd like to show you."

"No." She tried unsuccessfully to pull from his grasp.

"Logan, *there* you are."

He whirled around. Heather breathed a sigh of relief as she spied Sylvia rushing down the hallway.

"I've been looking all over for you."

"I'm a very popular man tonight."

"I wouldn't know about that." Anger burned in Sylvia's eyes, her muscles drawn tight in her face and neck. "I was at the cemetery a few minutes ago. Someone has dug up the area around my mother's grave. I'd like to know why."

"Probably just vandalism—but we'll talk later, Sylvia. This is a party, in your honor I might add. And right now Miss Lombardi has asked me to dance." He took Heather's arm again, practically dragging her down the hall, but at least this time they were going in the right direction.

The afternoon sun had vanished, leaving the yard in dusky shades of twilight. The air was still filled with laughter, music, tinkling glasses, and the odor of barbecue. Logan took her hand, leading her to the center of the sawdust-covered dance floor. She searched the crowd for Matt, but there was no sign of him.

The music started, and Logan fell into perfect step. He made her look good, leading her into twirls and guiding her around the floor with practiced steps. His boots seemed to only brush the ground, and he whispered in her ear that had he known she was such a wonderful partner, he wouldn't have even stopped at his office, much less considered wasting time showing her a painting he'd just purchased in Santa Fe.

He was charming, the perfect gentleman. Heather wondered how she could have imagined that he had been luring her to the back of the house for sinister purposes. Had the events of the last few days made her see danger in innocent events, made her think everyone she saw was a potential murderer?

For a brief second she wished she was back in Atlanta in her cool, gray office of glass and polished wood. Wished she'd never come to Dry Creek at all. Wished she'd never tried to find anyone from her distant past.

The next second, Matt was making his way through the field of dancers toward them. His light blue yoked shirt was open at the neck, his dark hair rumpled by the wind, his smile devastating. And all Heather's wishes to be back in Georgia evaporated the moment his gaze met hers.

He tapped Logan on the shoulder. "You can't hog *all* the beautiful women. You have to give us poor lawmen a chance."

Logan faked a grimace. "Don't you have crimes to solve?"

"Not when there's a party."

Heather slid into his arms. The tempo picked up, an upbeat country song. Matt took over where Logan left off, never missing a beat. If he had less expertise than her previous partner, he made up for it in charm. Every young woman they danced by turned positively green with envy.

"I thought you told me you didn't like 'boot scooting.'"

"I never said I couldn't do it. Miss Susan insisted all her boys learn to dance."

"I like Miss Susan better all the time. So, did you get what you needed from Logan's office before you made the fast getaway?"

Matt twirled her around and gathered her in his arms. "More than I expected. Are you ready to get out of here? I'll tell you all about it on the way to the cemetery."

Heather missed her step, scraping her foot against Matt's boot. She might have imagined Logan's motivation a few minutes ago, but the figure she'd glimpsed in the bushes behind the cemetery yesterday had been all too real.

To go back there now, on a dark, moonless night… Her stomach grew queasy, her pulse rapid. "What is it you expect to find in the cemetery? It's too dark to see anything."

"I have a flashlight. We'll see what I need to see."

"What's that?" She fought to keep the dread that churned inside her out of her voice.

"I just talked to Sylvia. I have a hunch that her mother's grave is either empty now or will be soon."

HEATHER PRESSED CLOSER to Matt as the truck skidded and bumped along the dirt trail. A shovel, borrowed from the back of a pickup truck belonging to one of Logan's unsuspecting guests, was bouncing around in the bed of the truck.

"You are surely *not* going to dig up the grave of Logan's late wife tonight."

"No, I'd just like to check the condition of the soil. According to Sylvia, it was rock-hard when the two of you were there yesterday. She said it's loose now, and that the spotty grass covering has been upturned."

"Why would someone dig up that grave?"

"For the same reason Logan refused to have an autopsy

done, to keep anyone from finding out the true cause of death.''

Heather looked up as they approached the narrow bridge that had sent her into spasms the day before. She shuddered and crossed her arms in front of her chest.

Matt circled an arm about her shoulders. ''What's the matter? You're not getting scared on me now, are you?''

''No, I've been scared ever since you saved me from the attackers last week.'' She took his hand and placed it back on the wheel. ''You need both hands to handle this bridge.''

''Nothing to it. I cross bridges like this all the time. This one will hold several tons more than my truck weighs.''

''So I've heard.'' She closed her eyes as they left the dirt for the rumbling wooden ties. She opened them as the truck came to a jolting stop. ''What happened?''

''A few boards must have worked loose. I didn't see that they were missing in time, and I think both front wheels are stuck in the hole.''

''I thought this bridge could hold tons.''

''Ordinarily it can. Open the door slowly and step out. But watch your step. There's quite a drop-off.''

''You want me to get out of the truck in the middle of this horrible bridge?''

''That's the idea.'' Matt opened his door and stepped out. Before Heather could follow, the crack of a bullet shattered the night air. Instinctively, she ducked. When she looked up, Matt was nowhere in sight.

Chapter Fourteen

Panic jangled Heather's thoughts. *Do something. Get out.* Her mind shouted orders, but her body refused to obey. Finally she slid over to the driver's side of the door and peered through the window.

Another shot came, this one crashing into the windshield, sending fragments of glass flying into her face and hair. She crouched, brushing away the glass, scrambling to the other side of the car. The passenger door eased open, and her heart jumped to her throat, then plunged in relief. It was Matt.

"Don't panic." His voice was surprisingly calm.

"I already have." Her voice was shaky and high. "What are we going to do?"

"Get out of the car." He tugged on her arm. "And stay down."

She managed to climb out the door without getting her head above the roof line and without drawing another shot. She stooped on the wooden bridge, and her gaze settled on the murky waters below. "Now what?"

"We jump."

"Oh, no. Not me. I'll just creep back across the bridge."

"The second you get out from behind this truck, you're a target for whoever ambushed us."

"Then let's stay here. You have a gun. Shoot them."

"When I count three, we jump." He took her hand.

"No, I don't swim."

"You won't have to. You can wade out. Heather, you've got to. It's jump or be shot."

"I don't like the choices."

"One, two, three."

Heather felt herself toppling over the edge, falling too fast to think. The next second she was gasping for breath, water in her face and mouth and nose. Pain shot through her right elbow, and when she tried to get up, she stepped on a sharp rock and slipped back into the creek.

Matt found her floundering in the water. "Are you hurt?"

"Yes, no, I don't know."

"You're not dead, so keep low, and keep moving. We have to get out of here fast."

He pulled her along, and she trudged to the shore, water filling her boots and soaking into her full skirt, weighing her down. Once her boot cleared the last gushing hold of the mud, she dropped to the bank.

Matt yanked her back to her feet. "We can't stay in the open. You'll have to make it to that cluster of mesquite."

She forced her legs to keep moving, but evidently not fast enough. A bullet whizzed by her head.

"Run," Matt yelled, "and don't look back."

Gunfire cracked through the air, and Heather's breath came in sputtering, burning gasps. Finally, she made it to the mesquite and dived under the branches. Matt wasn't behind her. He was still at the bank of the creek, half hidden behind one of the supporting beams, firing into the dark. He'd stayed behind intentionally, made a target of himself to save her.

The chorus of gunfire ceased for a few seconds, and Matt

was on the run, climbing the bank and heading toward her. She wrapped her arms around her own shaking body, fighting the urge to scream until he'd dived in beside her.

He cradled her in his arms, and she held on extra tight. "What do we do now?" she whispered.

"*You* stay out of sight. *I'm* going to try and work around, get behind the filthy cowards, see if I can identify anyone."

"You can't. That's too dangerous. "

"Heather, this is what I do. I fight the bad guys. It's my job."

"Not like this. I feel as if I'm trapped in a poor imitation of some spaghetti Western. Those men have guns."

He kissed her, more to stop her talking than anything else, she imagined. Then he left her there to wait for him to return. A few minutes later, crashing timbers startled her to attention. She looked up just in time to see Matt's truck plunge from the bridge into the water.

A second later he was by her side.

"Did you see anyone?"

"No, they drove away before I could get close enough. I saw the beam of their headlights on the dirt." Matt gathered her in his arms, and for a few minutes they sat in a silence broken only by the hooting of an owl and the sounds of Matt's truck sinking deeper into the mud beneath the shallow creek.

She leaned into him. "Tell me again how safe that bridge is."

"It wasn't the fault of the bridge. This was a planned ambush. Someone cut those ties loose."

"That couldn't have been planned for us. No one knew we were leaving the party and going to the cemetery."

"One person did."

"Who?"

"The good sheriff. Always helpful. Always insisting he

be included in every aspect of this investigation. If I find out that he's responsible..." Matt picked up a stick and broke it fiercely.

"Gabby couldn't have done it, Matt. Not by himself. Not in the dark. Not so fast. You only decided to come up here a few minutes ago."

"Actually, I didn't just decide to come out here. Gabby and I had already discussed my paying a visit to the cemetery tonight. I wanted to check out why someone was stalking you there yesterday."

"You told him about that? I haven't mentioned it to anyone but you, not after the wrangler practically convinced me it was my imagination."

"No, Gabby knew about it already. Apparently the man who checked out your story told Gabby about it. Gabby followed up on it and found a couple of Logan's hired hands digging up a grave. Logan showed up about then, and he wasn't pleased to find the sheriff observing the scene. He put a stop to everything, telling the guys doing the digging that there had been a mistake."

Heather wrapped her arms about her chest, suddenly chilled.

"I hate thinking Gabby could be responsible for all that's happened in the last few days, Matt."

"I don't think he is. But I have to consider that he might be in on it, either as an innocent pawn or a player. He's the only person I told we'd be on this road tonight."

"Pamela Jessup, Kathy Warren, Billy Roy Lassiter, Paul Ridgely and now Gabby." She pushed dripping strands of hair from her face. "Will it ever end?"

"Oh, yeah. It's going to end, and damn soon. And before this case is closed, more than one person is going to take up residence behind bars."

"We can't solve it out here." She shivered again as a

gust of wind whipped at her wet hair and clothes. "So, Ranger McQuaid, how do we get back to civilization?"

"My lines of communication all went down with the truck, and I don't think we could yell louder than the music from the party even if we weren't waterlogged." His arm circled about her shoulders. "That leaves only one option. We walk."

Her head flew up. "In wet boots? Through thick brush inhabited by rattlesnakes and coyotes? In my soaking skirt and ridiculously thin wet blouse?" She groaned.

"A piece of cake," he promised, standing and tugging her to her shaky legs.

"You saved me for *this*. And I actually thanked you!"

"You can always count on a Texas Ranger."

THE DAYBREAK PARTY at the collapsed bridge was anything but festive. A tow-truck team worked at hauling Matt's truck from the creek. Logan, Gabby, and Matt watched, circling each other like a pack of wild dogs.

Heather stood in the background, the memory of last night's dive into the creek and the game of dodge the bullets destroying any objectivity she might have otherwise mustered.

"You had no call to go snooping around my land, Matt McQuaid. You slink around like a skunk in the night and then have the nerve to accuse me of destroying my own damn bridge and having you ambushed." Logan stuck his nose in the sheriff's face, including him in his angry tirade. "You, too, Gabby. I know you started this, messing around where you have no business. I'll have you *both* investigated for improper procedures."

Matt stepped between Logan and Gabby. "You do what you like, Logan, but unless you come up with a fast explanation for why a section of this bridge was cut, and some ties removed, you'll be filing your complaints from a jail cell.''

"I told you, I had no idea the bridge had been vandalized." Logan waved his arms in frustration. "Hell, my own daughter travels this road sometimes. And I sure have no reason to hire gunmen."

"Your *step*daughter." Matt's eyes took on a frightening sheen, cold as death. "Someone around here attempted to murder Heather and me last night, and I know you well enough to know that nothing goes on around this ranch without you knowing about it."

Logan's hands knotted into fists, and his chin jutted defiantly. His accusing glare moved from Matt to Heather. "If you want to find the real roots of all the problems we've been having around here, Ranger, I suggest you let your brain—not some other part of your body—do your thinking.''

"Say what you mean, Logan. Forget the sarcasm. A man in the position you're in now shouldn't waste energy."

"I'm saying you need to look a little closer to home. We didn't have any problems in this town until Heather Lombardi showed up, prancing around in her short skirts, asking questions, pretending to be looking for her mother."

"I wasn't pretending, Logan. And I didn't ask for trouble. It came looking for me." Heather jumped into the fray.

"All I know is you drove into town, and trouble rode in right behind you. You made your moves on the Ranger, and he got sucked right in. You turned him against all of us.''

At that, Matt's face twisted into hard lines. "You've said enough, Logan."

"No, not nearly enough. If you weren't such a brown-nosing coward, Gabby, you'd tell Matt yourself."

"Tell me what?"

"That the whole town's talking about how you're just like your old man. The minute Susan Hathaway dropped into his life, he forgot the law he lived by, forgot his friends, forgot everything except protecting some skirt passing through town."

Gabby stepped backward. "You're about to say too much, Logan."

"No, just what needs to be said. Jake McQuaid took up with some tramp and forgot who put him where he was. He turned against the honest citizens of Dry Creek, the same way Matt is doing."

Tramp. The word stuck in Matt's gut, and every muscle in his body knotted. He lunged for Logan, pinning him against the trunk of the only tree in the area.

"You say what you want about me, Logan. You say what you want about my dad. We can take it, might even deserve it. But if I ever hear you say another word about Susan *or* Heather, your face will be mincemeat. Do you understand?"

"Yeah. I understand everything. I understand it all too well."

Logan met Matt's gaze, and Heather trembled at the rage that passed between them. She knew the fight was far from over. It would be continued some place, some time, and the results might be deadly.

Logan wiped sweaty hands on his jeans. "You better have a damn good case if you have me arrested, McQuaid. My lawyers will walk over you like..."

"Like your wife's horse walked over her."

"You sonofa—"

This time it was Logan who raised his fist. Gabby grabbed his arms. "That's enough, the both of you. This ain't how the law around here operates."

"What does any of this have to do with my mother?"

They all spun around at the sound of Sylvia's voice. She was mounted on a magnificent horse, the two of them rising like a centaur above a cluster of thorny cactus.

"What are you doing out here?" Logan demanded. "I told you to stay at the house."

"I'm not a little girl, Logan. You can't order me around any longer, especially not here. In three years, half the ranch will belong to me."

"Fine, then you stay out here with these sorry excuses for lawmen. I'm going back to work, and I'd suggest the sheriff and the Ranger do the same. One person has been killed in Dry Creek in the last week, and one stabbed nearly to death. Shots were fired again last night. And the best they can come up with is some damn fool notion that I'm involved in this."

Matt pulled his hat low. "Oh, it's more than a notion, Logan."

Logan headed toward his horse. "If you have evidence against me, spit it out now, Matt, like a man."

"I'll spit it out when the time comes. Like a *lawman*."

Logan climbed on his horse and turned it around, leaving at a fast gallop and not looking back.

"I'm sorry you had to hear any of this, Sylvia." Matt walked toward his friend.

She threw her head back, as a gust of wind caught her long black hair and flung it across her face. "What were you saying about my mother?"

Heather saw the defeated shrug of Matt's shoulders. He put a hand to Sylvia's horse, running his fingers through the flowing mane. "I have reason to suspect your mother's death may not have been an accident. I'm sorry. I know it's going to be hard on you, but I have to reopen the case."

"If you know something, Matt, tell me. I have a right to know."

"I can't say anything yet."

"Because you're a *lawman.*"

She spit the word at him, and Heather saw him wince. But he held his head high.

"Because I'm a lawman, and because I'm your friend."

"I can tell which carries the most weight." Sylvia turned her horse and galloped away, but not before Heather saw the glint of tears in her eyes.

The weight of the world appeared to settle on Matt's shoulders. He pulled his hat low over his forehead. "Let's get out of here. I've got work to do."

He yanked open the passenger-side door of the truck he'd borrowed from John Billinger. Heather touched her hand to his shoulder. "You did what you had to, Matt."

"Thanks. I'm glad somebody believes that."

"You wouldn't be a good Ranger if you didn't do what has to be done. You know that."

He took her hand and squeezed it. "Most of the time I know it, but it's a damn hard job when you have to hurt your friends."

"When it's all over, Sylvia will understand and be thankful to know the truth."

"Maybe, but what about the rest of the town? How will they react when I hang all their dirty laundry up for public inspection? And will my own family be thankful if I have to drag the name of Jake McQuaid through the dirt in order to find justice?"

"Let's hope that doesn't happen."

"Hope isn't in my job description." He jerked the truck into gear and revved the engine. In minutes they were heading back into town.

IT WAS LATE AFTERNOON before Matt finished up his business in town and he and Heather started back to the ranch.

Nothing was settled yet, but they were miles ahead of where they'd been yesterday. The paperwork was in process.

By tomorrow they'd have the insurance records on the death of Logan's wife, and legal permission to dig up her grave. If the body was there, an autopsy would be conducted to see if evidence indicated the death might not have been an accident. If the body was missing, that in itself still implicated Logan.

Not only that, but Paul Ridgely had regained consciousness for a few minutes and spoken for the first time since the stabbing. By tomorrow, the doctors had said he might be coherent enough for Matt to ask him a few questions.

Heather adjusted her visor, warding off the blinding glare of the sun. Watching her, Matt felt a crazy urge to stop the truck and take her in his arms, and realized how drastically the focus of his life had changed in the last few days.

He'd driven down this same road eight days ago, needing nothing but time alone at his ranch to satisfy his every need. It would never be that way again.

Now days at the ranch would be colored by the memory of Heather sitting at his breakfast table, her hair rumpled from sleep, her face bruised and battered and still so tempting. He'd see her in the swing, sipping lemonade, her lips wet and pink.

But the nights would be the worst. He'd be forever haunted by the moments they'd spent making love. He'd feel her beneath him, smell her fragrance, all flowery and intoxicating. He'd taste her lips and long to run his fingers across her velvety skin.

Damn. How had he let this happen? Even if she wanted to, he couldn't ask her to stay. His dad's blood ran too pure in his veins. The art of small talk, of cuddling, of making a woman feel loved and wanted, was as foreign to his makeup as branding cattle was to Heather's. He'd never be able to satisfy her, not over the long haul.

Or was he just unwilling to give it a try, because he was too afraid of failing?

Surprising himself, he made a sharp left turn, swerving onto a dirt road he hadn't been down in years. So much of the past had crashed down around him the last few days, a side trip to the scene of it couldn't make things any worse.

"Where are we going?"

He reached across the seat and took Heather's hand, tangling his fingers with hers. "To the old home place, the house where we lived before Jake pulled up stakes and moved us to Colorado."

"I'm glad. I'd like to see it."

"It's not much to look at—crumbling walls, broken windows, a leaky roof."

"Does the property still belong to your dad?"

"No, he sold it to Logan Trenton for less than it was worth, but I guess he was anxious to put Dry Creek behind him."

"I wouldn't put much stock in what Logan said about your father. Everything I've heard since I've been in this town indicates that the people thought your father was a saint."

"Yeah, most of them did."

"Give your dad a chance, Matt. He deserves that much from you." She slid closer as he pulled into an overgrown dirt drive and stopped in front of a dilapidated old house.

Matt opened the door and climbed out. She followed him, jumping from the truck to the hard ground. "Is this where you found Susan, out by this old drive?"

"No, it was down the fence line, close to that lean-to that's half gone." He pointed to what looked like a pile of boards a quarter of a mile down the road. "The grass was high then, the way it is now. She'd been thrown out of a car and somehow managed to roll under the fence and into that cluster of mesquite and hackberry, just west of the lean-to.''

''Why don't we walk down there before we go inside? I could use the exercise.''

''If you want. There's nothing there to see.''

They walked in companionable silence for a few minutes. Heather was mulling over the events of the last several days. ''I don't understand about Logan,'' she said at last, turning to Matt. ''If his wife owned such a big ranch, why was he a deputy under your father? Why did he want your dad's job of sheriff when Jake left for Colorado?''

''Talk is Logan's wife didn't give him much say in running the ranch while she was alive. He gave up the job of sheriff a few months after she died,'' Matt explained.

''But not so soon that he couldn't squelch an investigation into her death.''

''Exactly, and from the time the new sheriff took over, there are no missing records.''

Heather shivered. ''Death, murders, cover-ups. Even the possibility of Logan killing his own wife. I pray we find out that's not true.''

''Me too, for Sylvia's sake. But men have killed for far less than a ranch the size of Trenton's place, not to mention the enormous cash inheritance that provided the power he so enjoys.''

''Let's go back, Matt. I've seen enough out here, and I'd like to see the inside of the house before it's totally dark.''

Quietly, hand in hand, they retraced their steps. Heather had never felt closer to the rugged Ranger at her side. She wasn't sure why, except that he had once run this land as a boy, played chase with his brothers around this brush.

She could almost see him now, a smaller, less assured image of the man beside her.

He was opening up to her more and more. The trip here today was proof of that. For most men, taking a woman to see the home they grew up in might not mean so much. But Heather knew Matt well enough now to know that this was as intimate as making love, perhaps more so. He was tearing down another of his defensive walls and letting her peek inside. She knew this was a rare revelation.

"Go on inside," he said, when they'd reached the back steps. "I'll get a couple of soft drinks out of the cooler in the truck. I'm dryer than dust."

Heather started to wait, then changed her mind. Darkness was setting in fast now that a few clouds had blown in. If she wanted to get any kind of feel for the house Matt was born in, she'd better get moving.

She stepped inside. The door slammed behind her. And even before she felt the barrel of the gun boring into her back, she knew she was not alone.

Chapter Fifteen

"Logan!"

"Don't tell me you're surprised to see me."

Her mind struggled to accept the reality. Somehow she and Matt had stumbled into another trap. "Put the gun away. Matt's just outside."

"Put the gun away?" He poked the pistol harder into her flesh. "Why would I do a thing like that after I followed you all the way out here to kill you?" He grabbed her arm and twisted it painfully behind her back, shoving her against the rickety counter that housed the rusted kitchen sink.

"I didn't see your truck."

"You *do* take me for a moron, don't you? You and that damn fool boy of Jake McQuaid's. I knew where Matt was going the minute he turned off the main road. I came the back way, cut across my own land and left my truck parked out of sight. The better to surprise you."

Panic skittered along Heather's every nerve. She had to warn Matt. Her gaze roamed to the door. If she could see him coming, she could yell out to him.

Logan ran a finger across her cheek. "You're a pretty woman, Heather. I didn't want to hurt you. I sent you a note and warned you to get out of town, but you just wouldn't listen." He slid the gun from her back and nestled it against her right temple. "Now call your Ranger lover in here so I can get this over with."

She didn't have to. The footsteps on the back porch were heavy and quick. "Matt…"

Logan's hand slammed across her mouth, muffling her voice. She kicked at him and bit into his fingers, but his hold never loosened. Sick and shivering with fear, she watched Matt's face turn ashen as he walked through the back door and caught sight of the gun at her head.

"Hands out to the side, Matt. One rash move on your part and Heather Lombardi's brains will spray the room."

Matt did as Logan said, standing quietly while Logan reached over and yanked his gun from the holster, tossing it across the room. The sound of metal on wood echoed like thunder in Heather's brain, her senses soaking in each sound, each movement, as if it were her last.

Matt's eyes turned black as coal, his stance rock-steady. Only the perspiration dotting his brow hinted at the fear that had to be churning inside him.

"You won't get away with this, Logan."

"What makes you think that, Ranger?"

"Because too many people know what you've done. There's Paul, and Gabby."

"Paul hasn't told you anything."

"How do you know that?"

"I know Paul. And he knows what I'm capable of."

"We all know you're capable of murder."

Logan's grip on Heather's arm tightened. She fought the pain, determined not to give him the satisfaction of hearing her cry out. And she wouldn't keep quiet any longer. "You killed Billy Roy Lassiter, didn't you, Logan?"

"Smart little woman you have here, Matt. Too bad you won't get to enjoy her after tonight." He twisted the barrel of the pistol into her temple. "Billy Roy got what he deserved. He was messing around with my wife, no-good tramp that she was. She'd already had Sylvia out of wedlock, and still she had to have her men.''

Matt eased closer. "Is that why you killed her, too, Logan, because she wanted to dump you for another man?''

"She didn't want to dump me for another man. She was scared of me. That's why she wanted a divorce. But there was no way I was going to stand by while she cut me out of her will. She left me no choice but to kill her.''

Matt stepped closer. "But you made it look like an accident.''

"That part was easy. I delivered the killing blow to her head and then threw her under the feet of a horse that I drove to kick and buck.''

"And Jake protected you.''

"Jake McQuaid would have arrested his own mother for jaywalking. Only one person ever spit crosswise of the law and escaped his punishment.''

"Susan Hathaway." Heather didn't realize she'd spoken the name out loud until she heard her own voice.

"Yeah. Jake worshiped her, though she never told him the truth. If she had, it would have saved Heather a lot of trouble. She wouldn't have gone looking for a woman you and your brothers had already found.''

Heather swallowed past the lump in her throat. "What are you saying, Logan?''

"Do I have to spell it out for you?''

Matt eased closer. "Tell Heather all of it, Logan. Susan and Kathy Warren were the same woman. You stole Susan's ID after you and your buddies had beaten her and left her for dead.''

"Double jeopardy. I wonder how well you'd do in the lightning round. Too bad we don't have time to find out.'' He pulled back the hammer, cocking the pistol. "But you're right so far, on all counts. Kathy Warren—or should I say Susan—wandered from the bus stop crying. She stumbled behind the building and right into a little beating that turned real ugly.''

"And the good sheriff never bothered to find out that you were the one responsible?"

"Jake's priorities had changed by then. It wasn't me or Billy Roy or even my wife your dad was worried about.''

"Who was he worried about?"

"Susan Hathaway. He'd have killed to keep her safe, if it had come to that. Instead he took her and her secrets and left town. I don't think she remembered what she'd seen or even who she was at first. All Jake knew was that she was running away from something.''

"But why did you kill Ariana?" Matt asked, inching still closer. "You didn't mistake her for Heather.''

Logan sidestepped, moving so he could see out the window. Heather held her breath. The gun was cocked and ready to fire. One slip of his finger, and she'd be dead.

"Ariana's killing was none of my doing. She didn't know anything. No one does, except me and Rube and Paul. That's how you get people to keep secrets, Matt. You involve them in the crime.''

"Evidently Paul changed his mind about keeping quiet.''

"No more talking, Ranger. It's over. You first, then your pretty woman.''

Something rumbled above them and a rotten piece of lumber crashed through the ceiling and onto the floor. Heather ducked just as the pistol in Logan's hand fired, the bullet skimming the top of her head.

Matt lunged for Logan, grabbing his hand. Heather spun around, looking for something, anything, to slam into Logan's head. The gun. Matt's gun. Her gaze swept the room and then back to Matt and Logan.

One second they were scuffling. The next the gun had gone off. A horrible cracking noise thundered in her head as she stared at the dark crimson stain darkening Matt's shirt.

Heather swayed dizzily, her stomach churning wildly. She fell to the floor and placed her hand over the wound. "Matt, I'm here. Don't die on me. Please, don't die." Tears rolled down her cheek mingling with the blood as he stared at her through glazed eyes.

"No need to worry, Heather. You're going with him."

"No, Logan, please. Call an ambulance. You'll never get away with this, but if you get help for Matt…"

"No one will blame me for this tragedy. The stranger in town, the one whose car you found the other day, will make a perfect scapegoat. Folks around here will blame a stranger long before they'll blame me. I'm one of the good-ole-boys."

This time when the gun fired, Heather clung all the tighter to Matt's hand. At least they'd die together. She waited for the pain. It didn't come. She felt nothing but emptiness and the sting of the foul curses from Logan's mouth.

She turned and watched him sink to the floor beside her, his hands clutching his chest. And then she looked up and into the eyes of the man who'd just dropped from the attic and saved her life.

"So, we finally meet," he said, moving to stand beside her. "I'll say this for you. You're just as much trouble as your mother." The man kicked Logan's body, rolling it over.

Relief surged through her. "I don't know who you are, but I'm glad you're here. Get the cellular phone from the truck in front and call 911. And hurry. Please hurry." She bent back over Matt, feeling desperately for a pulse, whispering assurances in his ear.

"We'll call on the way out. I'd like to keep the Ranger alive myself. It would make life easier on me. Now get up. We're getting out of here."

"I can't leave Matt. He's been shot."

"You'll do as *I* say." He kicked her in the thigh to prove his point. "Get up and start walking." He yanked her to a standing position.

Confusion dulled her senses. She wiped away tears and stood, holding on to Matt's limp hand until the man forced her toward the door.

Middle-aged, thin blond hair. Edna's description of the man she'd seen in Heather's motel room rattled through her mind.

"Who are you?" The words stuck in her throat, scratchy and hoarse when they finally worked their way clear.

"David Eisman. Your dear mother's ex-husband. Now keep walking. I want you breathing, but I don't care what shape you're in, so make it easy or hard on yourself. It doesn't matter a bit to me."

"What do you want from me?"

"The ransom your grandparents should have paid years ago for your mother. But don't worry, I'll get the money this time. Pamela will see to that. She'll make the Jessups pay to keep her precious daughter alive. The baby she carried inside her bulging belly was the only thing I ever saw her care about."

Heather stumbled to the truck, David Eisman beside her, leaving a shot and bleeding Matt behind her. She'd finally come face to face with her past and discovered a horrifying nightmare. She no longer cared what happened to her, but, *please, God,* she begged silently, *don't let Matt die.*

GABBY STOOD OVER Matt's hospital bed. "Too bad we didn't ID the fingerprints on that deserted car a little sooner. Then we'd have known they matched the ones we found in Heather's motel room."

"Too bad we didn't know a little sooner that the ones in the motel room belonged to David Eisman." Matt's hands knotted into fists, his nerves ragged and raw. "David Eisman, out of prison early on good behavior. And now the filthy scum has Heather." Anger and frustration tore at his voice.

"I'm doing what I can to find her, Matt. Me and half the men in town have combed the area around your old home place looking for her, and the Rangers are sending help."

"All this and I'm lying up here useless. Did you find the truck I'd borrowed from Billinger?"

"No, I guess Eisman still has it. There's no telling where he's gone with Heather."

Matt wrung the sheet into a tight knot. "I just hope I get my hands on him. I'd like to tear him apart, limb by sorry limb."

"You better get a sight healthier than you are now before you tangle with anybody. You're lucky to be alive."

"I'm healthy enough. What I need's a vehicle. Get Heather's car for me."

"You're not going anywhere."

"I'll decide that. I want the car brought to the hospital. Do you understand?"

"You're not the only one who can find Eisman, Matt."

"No one else has done it yet. Just get me the car."

"I'll have it brought over first thing in the morning."

"I want it tonight. Now find my clothes. I'm tired of wearing this gown."

The sheriff backed toward the door. "The nurse said not to let you con me into anything."

"In that case, I'll get up and find them myself." Matt slid his legs over the side of the bed, and the room spun dizzily around him, round and round until the world went black.

Gabby lifted Matt's feet and laid them back across the bed. Then he pushed the emergency button and waited for the nurse.

HEATHER PICKED AT the sandwich of dry bread and smelly luncheon meat David Eisman had given her for lunch. For two days, they'd been holed up in a rattrap of a cabin. She had no idea where it was, except that they hadn't driven more than a few miles. At least Eisman had told her Matt was alive and recovering. To be stuck here without knowing whether he was dead or alive would have been unbearable.

She forced a bite of the sandwich down her parched throat. Eisman gave her little enough food or water, and she had to try to keep her strength up. Given half a chance, she'd run.

"Just a few more days, Heather," Eisman commented, sitting on a bale of hay and whittling on a stick of wood. "As soon as your Ranger friend gets out of the hospital, I have a message for him. He's the perfect emissary to deliver the ransom note. Matt McQuaid, the kid Pamela raised like her own son."

A low, sinister laugh rolled from Eisman's lips, and he dropped the piece of wood to the floor and walked over to stand in front of her. "The irony of all of this appeals to my twisted sense of justice."

"It would."

"You sound awful high-and-mighty. But you're nothing but the offspring of rich garbage. Your mom was no good, and your dad was worse."

"Who was my dad?"

His eyebrows shot up. "Don't you know?"

"I wouldn't have asked if I'd known. I only hope it's not *you*."

"You'd be a sight luckier if I was your father, but I'm not."

"I doubt you know who my father was."

"Oh, I know all right. Haven't you heard of the famous rape? No, I guess not. You wouldn't have been looking for your mom if you'd known how black your past really was."

His gaze walked across Heather and her skin crawled under his slimy assessment.

"Or maybe you would," he continued, picking strands of hair from her shoulder and releasing them to fall back about her face. "Maybe you're in it for the money, too."

Heather swallowed past a choking lump in her throat. Pamela Jessup and Phillip Gould. Her birth parents. No, Pamela Jessup no longer existed. Her mother was Susan Hathaway, the woman who'd loved and cared for Matt. A good woman, Matt had said so over and over. She wouldn't let herself think about Phillip Gould.

"Are you the one who went to the orphanage and told them Kathy Warren had died?"

"No, that was your loving father, protecting his own hide, as usual. Not that he didn't get it in the end. He's in jail now on other charges. Once rotten, always rotten."

Heather rubbed her hand along the cuts on her wrist. Her hands were free now, but they'd be in ropes again soon. Her legs as well. That was the way Eisman made sure she'd always be there when he got back. Wherever it was he went, he left her behind, with only the spiders and the wail of the coyotes for company. Still, they were better company than he'd ever be.

MATT WAITED UNTIL the nurse left the room and then spit the sleeping pill into a paper napkin. He raised himself to a sitting position, swallowing his moans and curses as pain shot through his body. He had to get out of this place, had to find Heather. He'd tried to leave yesterday when Gabby was here, but his body had refused to function.

Stretching, he grabbed his shirt from the hanger and shoved his arms through the sleeves. He didn't bother tucking it into his pants or buttoning it over the bandage that covered his chest. A second later he shuffled out the door and down the hall before anyone could notice and stop him.

MATT STUDIED the ransom note. It had been waiting for him when he'd gotten home from the hospital. Tucked under the front mat, one white edge stuck out so that he couldn't miss it.

I have Heather. I'll exchange her for a million dollars of Jessup money or I'll leave her dead. No tricks, Ranger McQuaid. I'm through playing games. Have the money ready before I call.

Eisman had to be the one who'd delivered the note. That meant he was somewhere in Dry Creek, waiting for the money. But where? Matt went to the sink and let the water trickle from the tap until it ran cool before filling a glass and drinking it down.

David Eisman had been in town for a while. Thinking back, Matt realized he'd probably been on the Lone M the night the horses acted up. He was probably the one who'd fooled with the ax. Perhaps it had been in his hand, a planned weapon for the middle of the night. The thought released a new surge of adrenaline, and Matt paced the floor of his small house.

Eisman had also been at the motel. And Matt and Heather had found his car deserted on the road between here and town. Matt scribbled a series of meaningless doodles on the pad at his fingertips, then began drawing a rough map. Here, the motel, the highway...

And Logan Trenton's ranch. Heather thought she had seen someone watching her when she visited Lassiter's grave the day before the party.

Matt's mind swung into overdrive. There was an old shack out there, between the cemetery and the stables. He and his brothers had played in it one time when they'd been out at the ranch with Jake. The shack, a former bunkhouse, hadn't been used in decades except by rats, snakes, and scorpions.

Matt grabbed a couple of guns and headed for his truck. He'd call Gabby on the way.

A COYOTE HOWLED outside the cabin, too close for comfort. Eisman pointed his shotgun in the direction. ''I don't know why anybody in their right mind would choose to live in this godforsaken dust pit,'' he muttered.

''Some people like it.''

''They can have it—soon. I'll give McQuaid twenty-four hours after he gets out of the hospital to get the money.''

''Does he know that?''

''Not yet. He'll find out when the time comes.''

''Will you be delivering the instructions for the exchange in person?''

''No. I'll call from a pay phone. He can meet me at the edge of town with a small plane and the money. Then he can come back here and find your body.''

Her body. She'd known all along he planned to kill her, but hearing it said gave it a finality that left her nauseous. ''Did you plant that bomb in my car, Eisman?''

''Yes, my only mistake, but it worked out in my favor. It was supposed to explode while you were in it.''

"You couldn't have gotten a ransom if you'd killed me then."

"I know. The ransom idea didn't hit me till later, but it was choice, don't you think? At first I only planned to kill you to get back at Pamela. The bitch walked away scot-free while I rotted in jail. A sorrier wife never lived, but I liked imagining her face when she opened a box with little pieces of her long-lost daughter inside."

The image turned Heather's blood icy cold. Still, she needed to keep Eisman talking, find out what she could, just in case she did get out of this alive. "You killed Ariana, didn't you? You just stood there and put a bullet through her chest at close range."

"The woman in your motel room? Yeah. I killed her. She was strutting around in your clothes. I guess the temptation of dressing up in nice things was too great for her to pass up. I came in and saw her preening in front of the mirror. I thought I was killing you. Imagine my disappointment when I realized my mistake."

"You poor guy."

"You're Pamela's daughter all right. Sassy like her. Pretty like her, too."

He ran his rough fingers down Heather's arm. She jerked away.

"You think you're too good for me, don't you?"

"I think *everyone's* too good for you."

He raised his hand and slapped her across the face. She reeled from the pain, but held her ground. If she was going to die anyway, she'd do it without his filthy hands on her body.

"I should have ruined you that night in your car, sliced you up so badly the Ranger would have gotten sick just looking at you."

"That was you!" She should have known. "But why, if you'd already planted a bomb in my car?"

"I ran into Logan Trenton at a bar outside of town right after the bomb didn't blow. My reputation was already spreading, thanks to the two-bit cowboy I'd roughed up the night before. Logan paid me and one of his cowardly hired hands to beat you up. Imagine getting paid for something that brought me so much pleasure."

He chuckled, and the sinister sound of it sent shivers up Heather's spine. "If Matt hadn't come along when he did, you would have killed me?"

"Lucky for me he did. Now I'll get my million and have my fun, too." Eisman jerked to face the door. "What was that?"

"A coyote. Why don't you go out and keep him company?"

"Not the coyote. The other noise."

"I didn't hear anything." She hadn't, but still, hope swelled in her chest. People would be looking for her by now. Matt would see to that. "Are you scared, Eisman?"

"Keep quiet."

"No, let's make noise." She grabbed a loose board and hurled it against the wall.

Eisman was on her in a second, wrestling her to the floor and pinning her under him while he tied her hands. "One more peep out of you and I'll feed you to the coyotes."

He pulled a pistol from his belt just as the door burst open and a bright light flooded the room. Heather squinted, barely making out Matt's form behind the light. She rolled away from Eisman as a shot rang out.

She closed her eyes. She couldn't bear to see Matt shot again, but this time it was Eisman's voice she heard yelping curses. When she looked up, he was on the floor, a few feet away from her, clutching a bloody wrist.

Heather jumped to her feet. Matt stood over Eisman, his gun pointed at the wounded man's head.

"You won't shoot me," Eisman taunted. "That badge you wear won't let you."

Matt kept the gun pointed. He could pull the trigger so easily. "Are you all right, Heather?"

"Yes, Matt. He didn't hurt me."

"I should have killed you. The tramp daughter of a slut."

Matt's hand tightened on the trigger. With one movement he could shut David Eisman up forever. His hand shook. Was this what it was like for Jake McQuaid? he wondered. Had he turned his back on the law for Susan the way Matt longed to do now?

Finally, he regained control. "You're right, Eisman. The badge won't let me kill you unless you make one foolish move. Just one, and I can pull this trigger with a clear conscience."

He reached for Heather, and she moved beneath the shelter of his outstretched arm, burying her head in his chest, holding on tight, breathing in the very essence of him. She fought a losing battle with the tears that stung the back of her eyelids.

Matt rocked her against him and then wiped her tears away with the tips of his fingers. "I thought I might never see you again."

"I wasn't worried for a minute," she lied. "I knew you'd come." She was still in his arms, his pistol still pointed at Eisman's head when Gabby led a team of Texas Rangers through the cabin door.

SUSAN HATHAWAY SCURRIED about the Colorado ranch house, feeling more lively than she had in months. Matty had called. He was coming home for his father's sixty-fifth birthday, and he was bringing a guest, a female guest.

Jake's middle son Cameron stamped into the room and reached past her to run his finger around the rim of the frosting bowl.

She tapped his fingers with her hand. "You'll spoil your dinner."

"It would take more than one bite of chocolate to spoil my appetite for your pot roast."

"Where's Cy? He and Amy should have been here by now."

"Relax. They're on the way. He'll be here before Matt and his new sweetie arrive." Cameron dragged a kitchen chair away from the table and dropped into it. "So what did you do to get Matt to show up for Dad's birthday?"

"I didn't do anything but invite him. He's part of this family. I don't know why you McQuaids are so suspicious."

"I'm not suspicious. I just know how you are about my kid brother. We all know he's your favorite."

Cameron was teasing, but Susan had to admit there was a bit of truth in what he said. She loved all three of Jake's boys as if they were her own, but Matt was different. He'd been so young when she'd come to live with them, so in need of the mothering he'd never known. She'd showered her love on him, praying that some woman somewhere was doing the same for her little Heather.

"I don't have favorites. I just want the day to be nice for Jake. But Matt did say he had a surprise for me. I think he's going to announce his engagement to the woman he's bringing home with him."

"More likely his surprise is a picture of a new horse he bought."

"We'll see. We'll just see. Is that a car I hear pulling up? Look out the door and see if it's Cy."

Cameron stopped at the screen. "No. It's Matt."

Susan fumbled with the ties on her apron, dropping it to the back of the kitchen chair and then smoothing her hair. Her pulse raced as she walked to the door. Matty was home at last.

Chapter Sixteen

Heather's heart pounded furiously as she climbed out of the car and got her first look at the woman who'd given birth to her. Susan was smaller than she'd looked in Matt's picture of her, delicate, but not frail. And even though she was smiling, Heather caught the gleam of moisture in her eyes as she hurried toward them.

Susan held Matt for a long time. When she finally let go, she turned to Heather and held out her hand. Heather took it, realizing that her own hands were shaking. She murmured a hello, her mouth so dry the greeting sounded strained and way too formal. Part of her longed to blurt out the truth, to hurl herself into her mother's arms, but another part shuddered in fear that Susan might not want her in her life.

The introductions went the way she'd asked Matt to handle them. For now she was just Matt's guest. When she told Susan who she really was, she wanted more privacy than the porch provided, more intimacy. It would be as much of a shock for Susan as it had been for her.

It would be different if Heather had been a love child, but she was the result of a traumatic rape, a tragedy that had changed Pamela Jessup's life forever, stolen her very identity.

Matt was joking with his brother Cameron, but he eased a reassuring arm around Heather's shoulders as they climbed the porch steps. His nearness helped steady her nerves, but now that she was here, she was anxious to finish what she'd come for, anxious to tell Susan Hathaway that she was the daughter she'd given up so many years ago.

But she would have to wait a while longer. Matt's brother Cy and his wife drove up, and a new round of hugs and greetings got under way.

THE BIRTHDAY PARTY was primarily a family affair—Matt's two brothers and their wives, Jake and Susan and a few close friends. Heather had barely tasted the food, managing to eat just enough not to call attention to herself while the men wolfed down more than one helping of pot roast, creamy potatoes, fresh butter beans, sliced tomatoes from Susan's garden and huge portions of chocolate birthday cake and hand-churned ice cream.

They had laughed and visited at the kitchen table, lingering over coffee, everybody talking at once. If anyone noticed Heather's nervousness, noticed that her breathing all but stopped when Susan's gaze focused on her, they'd been too polite to say so.

Finally, the guests and family members had said their goodbyes. Now it was only the four of them left in the den of the massive ranch house—Susan and Jake, Matt and Heather. Heather's pulse raced, her stomach a knot of nerves. She took a deep breath and signaled to Matt with an uneasy glance that she was ready.

Matt reached over and cradled Heather's clammy hands in his. "I told you I was bringing a surprise for you, Susan. Actually, it's Heather who has the surprise."

Susan leaned forward in the chair, her hands crossed in her lap. "I hope you didn't do anything special for me,

Heather. Just having you and Matt here is treat enough for us.''

"No, I didn't do anything.'' Her voice cracked, shattering into a whisper. "This is about something you did for me. Twenty-five years ago.''

The color drained from Susan's face. "What are you saying?''

Moisture burned at the corners of Heather's eyes. She bit back the tears, and plunged ahead, afraid to say more, but knowing she couldn't rest until she'd said the words that tore at her heart. "I'm your daughter.''

Silence filled the room, tension as thick as fog wrapping around them. Heather sat still, her insides trembling, but she met Susan's gaze head-on.

"No, this can't be happening.'' It was Susan who broke the deafening silence. Her voice faltered, and she wiped a tear from her cheek with the back of her hand. "All these years. All this time.''

"It's true,'' Heather whispered, her fingers digging into her sweaty palms. "I'm the child you gave up for adoption.''

Susan tried to stand, but her legs seemed to give way beneath her. Jake was at her side in a split second, his big work-scarred hand around her shoulder as she staggered across the floor and took her daughter in her arms.

"Heather. My own little Heather. Let me look at you.'' She cradled Heather's face in her trembling hands. "You can't know how many nights I lay awake thinking about you, wondering if you were happy, praying you were safe.''

Heather quit fighting the tears, quit fighting anything but the unfamiliar emotions churning inside her. "I was always safe, and usually happy. My adopted parents loved me very much, and I loved them.''

"You were so tiny when I was forced to leave you, so helpless."

Susan's breathing was ragged, her face pale. Heather held on to her as if she might dissolve in front of her, as if this might all be only a dream.

"You should have no regrets about leaving me at the orphanage. My new parents gave me everything I needed to grow into the woman I am today."

"The things that I could never give you, even though I loved you more than life itself."

Susan's eyes shone like diamonds in a mist, full of a love so strong Heather could feel it wrapping around her, warming her heart. If she lived to be a hundred, she'd never forget this night, this moment. It was as if Susan's spirit had bonded with hers, mother and daughter, joined for all time.

Finally, Susan pulled away, though she never let go of Heather's hands. Shoulders drooping, she dropped her head and stared at the rug beneath their feet. "I don't know how much you know about my life, Heather. I made so many mistakes."

"I know all I need to know about your past. It doesn't change the fact that you gave birth to me, that I'm part of you and always will be."

"Always." Susan's voice broke on the simple word. Tears spilled from her eyes again, this time running unchallenged down her sun-bronzed cheeks.

"Always, *Mother*. I've come home."

A knot the size of Texas welled in Matt's throat. He swallowed hard, emotion pummeling his gut, dissolving the tough shell he used as a shield. The two women he loved the most in the world were both crying and talking all at once, pouring out their hearts.

Jake touched his arm. "I think we may be in the way here, son."

Matt stared at his father in amazement. If he didn't know better he'd think that was the glint of a tear in Jake Mc-Quaid's eye.

MATT STEPPED into the kitchen and poured himself a cup of coffee. He and Heather had been in Colorado two days now, long enough for the events of the last few weeks to come out and be discussed in detail. And it was all the time either he or Heather could spare. She'd already extended her vacation long enough to see him through the touch-and-go days after Logan's bullet had torn through layers of flesh and muscle.

"You're up awfully early," Susan said, hurrying through the door. "Couldn't you sleep?"

"I slept fine, but my body's on Texas time now. Besides, I'm all grown up. I get up without being prodded, most of the time, anyway." He kissed her on the cheek. "Where's Jake?"

"Your *father* is in the shower. He'll be down soon. He doesn't move as fast as he used to."

"You're a saint, Susan, to live with that man all these years. You know my biggest fear in life is that I'm just like him, that I'll make some woman as miserable as he's made you."

"Miserable? Is that what you think, Matt, that I've been miserable living with Jake McQuaid?"

"Haven't you been? He grumbles and gives orders and does little else. If a compliment ever fell from his lips, we'd all expect the world to come to an end."

"Grumbling is not what this is about, Matt. Say it out loud. You're still angry with your dad because your mother left him."

"No, I was for a long time, but not anymore. Deserting me was her choice, and I can't blame him for that."

"You shouldn't blame her, either. You can't know a person's heart. You certainly don't know Jake's."

"You're right. How could I?"

Matt took his coffee to the table and sat down. Susan wiped her hands on her apron and dropped into the chair beside him. "Look at me, Matt, and listen to what I say. Jake never wanted things to be the way they were. He followed my wishes. I couldn't take his name legally, and I wouldn't take it any other way. If I was ever found out, I didn't want him dragged into it. He'd done enough already."

"It seems to me *you* did all the doing. You took care of us, cleaned the house, canned food from the garden. How is it you figure Jake had done enough?"

"Your father gave up his job as a lawman because he couldn't keep it and me, too, and that was practically the same as giving up his soul. He was too much a man to live a lie, to hide a woman wanted for bank robbery under his roof while he wore a badge. Besides, even before he knew about the bank robbery, he knew I needed protecting. He just didn't know who from."

Matt finished his coffee and pushed away from the table.

Susan grabbed his arm. "I'm not through, Matt. It's time you faced things the way they are. Your father bore the brunt of his sons' resentment for years, just so that he could protect my secrets and so that he wouldn't destroy the bond I shared with each of you. He all but gave up his life for me. So don't tell me he doesn't know how to love. And don't tell me you're worried about being too much like him. You are like him, and you should thank your lucky stars every day that you are."

"What's all the racket down here? You sound like a

bunch of clucking hens." Jake's boots clacked on the kitchen floor as he made his entrance.

"Just a friendly discussion," Matt answered, carrying his cup to the sink.

"Well, since you're talking anyway, you might as well fill me in on the rest of the details. What's the latest on Rube and Paul?"

"They're both out on bail. The district attorney has offered them a plea-bargaining agreement. I'm sure they'll take it. Just having people know what they did to Billy Roy and Susan has been tough punishment for them, and no judge in the country is going to think they're dangerous."

"What about Logan?"

"That's another story altogether. I talked to Sylvia yesterday. She said they're going for murder one for killing her mother. She wasn't as upset as I thought she'd be. I guess we've all grown up over the years. Now she just wants closure and to go on with her life."

"And that leaves David Eisman," Susan said. "It's hard to imagine I was ever married, even under duress, to a man as evil as he is. If he'd killed Heather or Matt..." Her voice trailed off into a sigh. "I can't even bear to think about it."

"Well, he won't be on the streets again for a long, long, time, if ever," Matt assured her. "Not only did he shoot me and kidnap Heather, but he killed Ariana Walker in cold blood and never showed a second's remorse."

Susan trembled. "I brought so much on all of you. I don't know how you keep on forgiving me."

Matt kissed her on the cheek. "Because we love you."

"Yeah, we do," Jake seconded. "But we can't spend all day standing around talking. I've got a corral that needs some repair work. You can help me with it, Matt, if you don't have anything better to do."

Matt stood and stared at Jake, really seeing him for the

first time since he and Heather had arrived in Colorado. The lines in his face were much deeper than Matt remembered them, his shoulders bent a little with age. "I think I could make time to help with the corral."

"Good." Jake poured himself a cup of coffee. "I'm glad you're home, son."

"Me, too, *Dad*. And no one is more surprised about that than I am."

MATT TOSSED in the twin-sized bed he'd slept in as a kid, a million thoughts galloping around in his mind. Things still weren't perfect between him and his father, but some of the resentment had eased. It was easy to see things in black and white, much more difficult to deal with shades of gray.

His father and Susan had dealt with the shades of gray and made a new life for themselves the best way they knew how. He understood that now. They'd found something in each other to hold on to, and years later, they were still together and happy. Who was he to argue with that? They were even talking about a wedding, a quarter of a century after the fact.

Matt had always loved Susan, just as much as if she had been his real mother. At some level he'd probably always loved Jake, too, but he was just now coming to terms with it. Hopefully, in time, the bond would strengthen between them, but it wouldn't happen in an instant, not the way it had with Susan and Heather. But then neither he nor his dad had ever been able to open up so freely.

Tomorrow he and Heather would leave Colorado. He'd go back to Texas, and Heather would go back to Atlanta. It would kill him to watch her walk away. She'd invaded every part of his life, every corner of his heart.

He knew she'd stay if he asked her, but how long would she be happy? He couldn't believe she wouldn't miss the city, expect him to be more romantic, to be someone he wasn't. He closed his eyes and tried counting cattle. He gave up as his bedroom door squeaked open.

"Are you awake, Matt?"

"Yeah. I can't sleep. I guess you're having the same problem."

Heather pushed his sheet aside and sat beside him. "I don't see it as a problem. My mind's just so full. I've never been so happy."

"I'm glad."

"My mother never wanted to give me away. It's nice to know that. She did what she had to do to keep me safe and to keep my life from being tainted with her past." She kicked off her slippers and pulled her feet onto the bed. "I think she needs me even more than I need her."

Matt tousled her hair. "You're easy to need."

"Do you need me, Matt?"

There was no missing the seriousness of her tone. He swallowed hard. "Not me. You're much too bossy for my style." He pulled her close, and his lips found hers, the need inside him eating away at his control. He struggled to keep the moment light. "Not to mention that you're a city girl and I'm a sh…a manure-kicking cowboy lawman."

"Since when did you launder your language so closely?"

"Since I stepped back inside Miss Susan's house. The taste of soap forever lingers on my tongue when she's around."

Heather ran her fingernails across his bare chest, and desire pitted inside him, hot and aching.

"You know, Matt, I may be a city girl, but I have boots now. A hat, too. It would be a shame to waste them."

"Whoa, hold on a minute." His insides tightened. "You're not getting caught up in the emotion of meeting your mom, and going off half-cocked, are you?"

"No, I know exactly what I'm doing." She dropped to the pillow and pulled him down beside her. "I want to sleep with you, Matt."

A strange mixture of relief and pain flashed through him. If that's all she wanted, he could definitely oblige. "Under your mother's roof? You are brazen." He started to kiss her again, but she rolled away from him.

"I want to sleep with you, but not just tonight. I want to do it forever. I want to sit across the breakfast table from you. I want to share your problems and tell you mine. I want to have your children."

"I doubt you know what you're asking for."

"I know. The question is do you want me, Matt? Do you love me?"

He buried his head in her breast. "You know how I feel about you. It's the *us* part that worries me. You'll stay a while, but what's to hold you forever? I'll get used to having you around, used to needing you, then you'll up and disappear."

"No one can promise forever, Matt, but I'm not your mother. I'm Heather, the same woman who has stood with you and by you. And I love you."

"What if I'm no good at being a husband?"

"You'll make a wonderful husband, maybe not for everyone, but for me."

Matt held her close. All his life, he'd been convinced he was too much like Jake McQuaid to ever make a woman happy. Susan had forced him to rethink that theory this week. Now Heather was in his arms, asking to be his wife. How could he say no to that? Why would he ever want to?

"You won't be getting much of a bargain. Just a cowboy lawman."

"I'll be getting the man I love."

Matt released his hold on her, his heart beating fast, as

if it were already reaching out for the happiness she was offering. "If this is going to be it, I guess I'd better do it right." He rolled from the bed and fell to his knees.

Heather sat on the edge of the bed, her nightshirt brushing her shoulders, her hair tumbling about her face. He studied the image, knowing the sight of her at this moment would live inside him forever. "Heather Lombardi Hathaway...Jessup...whoever you are, will you marry me?"

"Yes, I'll marry you, but you forgot the 'I love you' part."

He crawled into bed beside her. "I didn't forget anything. I'm a man of action, remember? And I'm about to show you exactly how I feel." He skimmed her body with his hands as his mouth claimed hers.

She moaned and squirmed beneath him. "Matt McQuaid, are you sure you want to do this in Miss Susan's house?"

He kissed her again, soundly, his body screaming its need for her.

"What Miss Susan doesn't know won't hurt her."

"I love you," she whispered.

"And I love you."

"You did say it."

"Of course. You can always count on a Texas Ranger."

Epilogue

Six months later

Matt walked Susan down the steps and then took his place with his brothers, all standing beside their dad. They'd waited for this wedding for twenty-five years. And they'd threatened to hogtie and drag Jake squealing to the altar if he backed out now.

Heather, his wife now, stood across from Matt, looking so pretty she took his breath away. His gaze fell to the swell of her stomach. He marveled every time he thought about his child growing inside her.

The service was short and to the point, tailored to Jake's specifications. Matt agreed with that philosophy. The sooner he got out of this stupid tie and ridiculous suit, the happier he'd be. A cowboy ought to get married in blue jeans and boots, the same way he lived. But neither Heather nor Susan had accepted that philosophy.

"Do you take this woman to be your lawful wedded wife, to have and to hold, to…"

Matt's mind wandered from the vows to events that had brought them to this point. All of a sudden he was aware of a crowd-numbing silence. The preacher was staring at Jake expectantly, waiting for a response.

"*Jake,* do you take this woman..."

Matt nudged his brothers. *"He does."* The answer was a chorus of McQuaid voices.

"I do," Jake agreed, snapping out of his temporary stage fright. "I wouldn't be standing here in this monkey suit in the middle of a work day if I didn't."

"Then I pronounce you man and wife." The preacher looked Jake square in the eye. "And you can kiss the bride, if she'll still have you."

"I'll have him," Susan whispered. She wrapped her arms around his neck and kissed him solidly on the mouth to the applause of everyone present.

"She kept me waiting twenty-five years," Jake announced in his booming voice. "But I can tell you one thing." He wrapped his arm about her shoulder and hugged her to him. "She's worth every second of the wait."

Cy, Cameron, and Matt McQuaid looked at each other and smiled their agreement. The secrets of the past had all been laid to rest. The McQuaid family was finally at peace, and life had never felt so good.

HOTSHOT P.I.
B.J. Daniels

Prologue

Clancy didn't know what had awakened her. She blinked, confused by the moonlight streaming across the third-story balcony, even more confused to find herself standing at the narrow log railing, staring down at Flathead Lake.

Waves lapped at the dock in the small bay below the island lodge. Clancy's heart rate accelerated along with her growing apprehension as she realized what was so terribly wrong.

The view. She shouldn't have been able to see the bay from this angle on her bedroom balcony. Behind her, the door to her family's lake lodge stood open. Past it, furniture huddled under sheets like ghosts. A corner of one sheet flapped softly in the night breeze. Clancy stared at the room, frantically trying to orient herself in a place haunted with childhood memories. The garret on the third floor—a room that hadn't been used in years for anything more than storage.

The early June breeze stirred the sheets and ran like a chill across her skin. She looked down, surprised to find she wore nothing but her nightgown. Her feet were bare—except for the sand. It was happening all over again! Fear raced ahead of her thoughts. Where had she been? What had she done *this* time? With growing panic, Clancy became aware of something heavy clutched in the fingers of her left hand.

A bronze sculpture of a cowboy, one of the first she'd ever made. It had been on the mantel downstairs. She shuddered as she realized how she and it must have gotten up here.

She hadn't sleepwalked in years. But the terror of waking up not knowing where she was or where she'd been wasn't something she'd forgotten from her childhood. She remembered with horror the last time she'd walked in her sleep. The night of the fire.

Clancy turned, wanting only to get back to her bedroom on the other side of the lodge, and realized she wasn't alone. Her heart slammed against her ribs. She fought back a scream as the moonlight spilled across the garret. Someone was on the couch. Sprawled, legs out at an odd angle. She stepped into the room, flipping the light switch. And stopped.

The bronze slipped from her fingers, hitting the hardwood floor with a thud, as she recognized the boots. Bright red cowboy boots. With wet sand on them. Just like her feet. Her heart thumped like a drum, filling the silence of the room.

Dex Westfall lay on the couch. His dark hair, normally coiffed to perfection, was now matted to the side of his head. Blood, once the color of his boots, stained the sheet covering the couch. His eyes stared, vacant, empty.

Clancy stumbled back, suddenly aware of the stickiness on her fingers. She stared at her left hand, her terror accelerating. How had she gotten blood on her? Her gaze leaped to the cowboy sculpture lying on the floor. Her heart rate rocketed, her pulse now a deafening roar in her ears. She didn't need anyone to tell her that the dark stain on the bronze was Dex's blood or that her former boyfriend was dead.

It was happening again. Only this time, her worst nightmare had come true. She'd killed someone in her sleep.

Chapter One

Ignoring the overdressed stranger on the dock, Jake Hawkins loaded the cooler full of groceries into his twenty-five-foot fishing boat, then reached for his tackle box and new rod and reel resting at the woman's high-heeled feet. He noted with no small amount of satisfaction that she'd finally gotten the message. Beneath the huge hat, she pursed her thin, lipstick-red lips and stripped off the large designer sunglasses to give him the full effect of her icy baby blues. The look she gave him shot off more sparks than all the diamonds weighing down her body.

He smiled to himself. From the moment he'd found her waiting for him on the dock beside his boat, there hadn't been anything about Mrs. Randolph L. Conners that he liked—from her wealthy smugness to her condescending certainty that he was about to go to work for her. And he especially didn't appreciate being bothered on his day off. It was Monday and he was going fishing for a few days. And nothing was going to keep that from happening.

"Like I said, I don't baby-sit heiresses," he repeated as he turned away from the Galveston skyline to take a whiff of the gulf breeze. "Especially heiresses who have just murdered their boyfriends." The gulf shimmered in the morning sun, beckoning him. He couldn't wait to hear his twin 150-horsepower engines rumbling as he crossed the water, the wind in his face.

"I don't think you understand, Mr. Hawkins," Mrs. Conners said, enunciating each word carefully. "I'm not hiring you to baby-sit. I'm hiring you to see that my niece is exonerated."

Jake pushed back his Houston Astros cap and laughed. She wasn't hiring him at all. He didn't have the time or the inclination. Not even the money could entice him right now. Not when he had a well-deserved fishing trip planned. "You need a good lawyer, not a private investigator. But I can give you a few names—"

"I already have the best lawyers money can buy," she said, sounding pained that she had to explain everything to him. "I need someone with your…talents."

He prided himself on what he called his hunches, and right now one was riding up his spine like a centipede wearing spiked heels. While his hunches were seldom wrong, he hoped this one was; he had a bad feeling that somehow he was going to end up working for this woman.

"My talents?" he repeated, also hoping he was wrong about where she was headed. He shook his head as if he didn't get it.

Exasperation gave her a pinched look that reminded him of one of those mean little hairless dogs. "I want you to prove my niece's innocence, Mr. Hawkins. Whatever you have to do. Whatever it costs. My niece will not be convicted of murder."

Jake jumped from the boat to the dock with a thud. "If you think you can hire me to tamper with evidence…" He found himself looming over her, his blood pressure up and running.

She tilted her head back ever so slightly until he could see her eyes shaded beneath the hat. If she felt even a little bit intimidated, it didn't show; her gaze glittered with brittle-hard certainty. "You misunderstood my intentions."

"Like hell I misunderstood," Jake said, locking his gaze on the woman. "If your niece is guilty, then she deserves to do time. And from what you've told me—"

"You are wrong, Mr. Hawkins," she said, her voice as hard and gritty as gravel. "My niece is a Talbott. A Talbott does not go to prison."

Talbott? He felt a jolt of recognition shoot through him. He squinted at her, telling himself Talbott was a fairly common name. Not that it mattered, he reminded himself; he wasn't going to take this case. But still he couldn't shake off the rotten feeling tap-dancing at the back of his head.

"Do you understand what I'm saying, Mr. Hawkins?"

He understood perfectly. The niece was an embarrassment and too good for prison. He couldn't believe the gall of this woman. And now she wanted someone to go in and clean up the mess. At any price. Well, she'd picked the wrong man. "Like I said, I can't help you. It's my day off and I'm going fishing."

Jake flung his duffel bag into the boat, hoping Mrs. Randolph L. Conners would take the hint. But he wasn't averse to throwing her into the gulf if he had to.

She squared her shoulders, straightening her expensive suit. "I'm sure after you've given it some thought you'll change your mind, Mr. Hawkins."

He pointed to the shore. "Don't count on it."

She smiled. "We'll see."

Fighting to control his temper, Jake watched her walk away. He hated having someone raise his blood pressure, especially this early in the morning and on his day off.

As he went to untie the boat, he noticed the envelope on the bow, underneath the cellular phone the woman had surreptitiously left to hold it down in the light sea breeze. The envelope was creamy white; the address engraved. He slipped it from under the phone, not surprised to find his name hand-printed on the clean white surface or the paper smelling of her expensive perfume.

He figured the envelope would be full of old family money, but it felt a little too light. Maybe she'd written him a check. Jake ripped open the envelope, planning to do the same with the check.

But it didn't contain a voucher of any kind. Nor were there any crisp large bills inside. Instead, there was a single sheet of paper, folded neatly. On the sheet were printed the words: Deer Lodge. September 30. 9:00 a.m.

At the bottom was her neatly signed signature: Kiki Talbott Conners.

Kiki Talbott. He should have known. With a curse, Jake crumpled the paper and threw it into the water, feeling his plans crumple with it. The phone began to ring. He looked out across the gulf, suddenly reminded of a photograph that used to sit on the mantel of his family's Flathead Lake lodge in Montana. Memories flooded him. Bittersweet memories that he'd spent ten years trying to forget. He picked up the phone.

"I've left you a ticket and triple your normal first week's salary at the airport," Kiki informed him in her no-nonsense tone. "Your flight leaves in less than two hours. You'll have to hurry."

"And where exactly is it you think I'm going?" Jake asked, anger making his words as hard as stones.

"Montana. You can buy anything you need when you get there," she continued. "Of course, I will reimburse you for all expenses."

"Montana?" Jake swore and pushed back his baseball cap, dread making his body ache as if he had a bad case of flu. "I think you'd better tell me just which niece of yours

we're talking about.'' He held his breath, waiting for the other shoe to drop.

Sea gulls squawked overhead; the gulf breeze tickled the sandy blond hair curling at his neck.

''Clancy Jones. Her mother was a Talbott. Her father was—''

Jake let out an oath. ''I know who her parents were, for hell's sake. And I know who *she* is! You don't seriously believe that I'm going to help *her?*''

Kiki's tone was coldly calm. ''Mr. Hawkins, you're very good at what you do. One of the best. That's why I've hired you. That's why you're going to do whatever you have to do to get my niece exonerated—in spite of your…former connections with her.''

Jake walked over to his duffel bag and, cradling the phone against his shoulder, dug through his clothing. ''Lady, the only reason you're *hiring* me is because you have something to hold over my head, and you damn well know it.''

Jake thought he heard a hint of emotion in her voice when she finally spoke. ''Please understand, I will do whatever I have to do to protect my niece. Including helping you on September 30. Or hurting you. And believe me, I'm in a very good position to do either.''

Jake carefully lifted the .38 nestled in its worn shoulder holster from the duffel bag. He wondered if Kiki had any idea what kind of man she'd just hired. Or how big a mistake she'd just made.

''How do I know you'll hold up your end of the bargain?'' he asked, glad she wasn't still on the dock, afraid of what he might have done.

She let out a long, impatient sigh. ''I'm a Talbott, Mr. Hawkins. Please don't confuse us with the Joneses. Our word is our bond.''

"Right."

"One more thing, Mr. Hawkins," she said, dropping her voice. "Because of your less-than-amiable association with my niece, I might offer you a tip as to how to best handle her—"

"Look, Kiki," Jake said as he snugged the .38 to his ribs. "I have a little tip for you. You can force me to take this job, although it's not the smartest thing you ever did. And you can force me to take your money and waste my time trying to find evidence that your niece isn't guilty of murder. But you can't tell me how to do my job."

"Now, Mr. Hawkins—"

"The truth is, Kiki, you can only buy so much with your kind of blackmail. And you've already bought more than you can handle."

Chapter Two

Awakened from a troubled sleep, Jake rolled over, forgetting where he was, and banged his head on the balcony railing. That rude awakening and the once-familiar view reminded him exactly where he was. As soon as he'd landed, he'd rented a boat to get to Hawk Island and his family's lodge. And he was there because of Clancy Jones.

Having no intentions of staying long, he'd just rolled his sleeping bag out on the balcony, wishing he was on the deck of his boat. The truth was he couldn't stand the thought of sleeping inside the lodge. It felt too musty and confining, brought back too many memories.

He'd gone to sleep cursing Clancy, while glaring through the railing at the only other dwelling on this side of the rugged island—an almost identical log lodge nestled in the pines across the small bay.

A single light had shone in one of the rooms on the second floor of Clancy's lodge until the wee hours. He'd seen an occasional shadow and wondered if she was alone. Angry that he couldn't sleep, either, he'd speculated on what she might be doing still up. Working in her studio? Or trying to sleep and not think, like him?

At one point, he'd considered going over to see her, getting it over with. But it was late, and he told himself waiting until morning was the best plan. He'd finally dozed off, only to be dragged from sleep by a loud noise, which did little to improve his disposition.

As he stared across the moonlit bay, trying to figure out what had awakened him, a movement jarred his attention into focus. Something was thrashing around in the water off the end of Clancy's dock. He saw what appeared to be a head surface, heard the choked cry before it disappeared again. Clancy?

Shedding his bedroll, Jake leaped from the end of the balcony, dropped onto the beach and took off at a run. He saw the head materialize again, dark against the silvery surface of the water, heard the cry for help and pushed his legs harder. All the time his mind raced ahead of him; the swimmer couldn't be Clancy. She swam like a trout and was much too smart to be swimming—drowning—at this hour of the night.

He sprinted down the weathered dock to the end as the person emerged once again—yards beyond his reach. Having no time to consider the consequences, he dove in. The sudden shock of the cold water brought him wide awake; he surfaced, gasping for breath. Just ahead of him he could see the swimmer start to disappear under the dark water again. He swam hard and reached out to grab the only thing he could. Hair. It was long enough he could bury his hand in it.

But to his surprise, the swimmer pulled him under with a force that almost made him lose his grip. Immediately he realized his mistake. The silly fool was struggling, fighting him, and he remembered why he'd never considered the lifeguarding profession. Too dangerous. At least in the private eye business you knew who you were dealing with: murderers, crooks, cheaters and liars. Not some novice in over her head in deep water, panicked to senseless desperation and determined to take you down with her.

Jake got a tighter hold on the hair and a grip on one flaying arm, and with all his strength kicked toward the moonlit surface. At first nothing happened, then they both rose in a rush, the swimmer choking and coughing as they surfaced. Jake used a no-nonsense half nelson to drag the person to the dock and, none too gently, hoisted the obviously feminine body onto the worn boards. He felt a moment of relief. This woman, whoever she was, wasn't Clancy. Not with *that* body. Her wet clothing molded to her curves—dangerously enticing, fully developed curves.

She leaned over the edge of the dock, fighting for breath, her dripping shoulder-length hair in her face. Slowly, she raised her gaze, sending a shock wave through him.

Clancy? Even under the wet mop of blond hair, even in the shimmering silver of the moonlight, there was no doubt about that face. Her hair was longer. Not quite as blond. But that face. That cute little nose. That slightly puckered, almost pouty mouth. That wide-eyed, curious deep brown gaze. If anything, she was more beautiful than he remembered. And certainly more…filled out. And in all the right places. That adorable seventeen-year-old tomboy he'd known was now one hell of a good-looking woman.

But he wasn't sure what shocked him the most. Seeing the change in her after all these years. Or realizing she was the swimmer he'd had to rescue. What had happened to the Clancy he used to know, the one who was much too smart to swim alone in the middle of the night?

"What the hell were you doing swimming at this hour?" he demanded, anger following his relief that Clancy was all right. He needed her alive, he told himself. His relief had nothing to do with any old feelings from their past, he assured himself, ignoring the flashes of memories of the two of them as kids. They'd been so close—best pals. More than that. Kindred spirits. The truth was, he'd thought he was in love with her.

"Swimming?" she said, choking. "You think I was swimming?" She coughed, then leaned back, her gaze settling on him with suspicion. "Someone tried to drown me."

"Wait a minute," he said, holding up his hands. "I was the one who fished you out of the drink." He felt something cold sprint up his spine as he looked into her eyes.

"Someone grabbed me and—" Clancy glanced around in obvious confusion, her eyes wild with fear. "You dragged me out?"

"Yeah." Jake studied her for a moment, wondering how long it would take her to acknowledge that she knew him. "About this *someone* who tried to drown you…you might notice there seems to be just the two of us on this whole side of the island." He glanced toward the still water, then at the empty shoreline, then at her again.

"Thank you for helping me," she whispered, still looking disoriented. And more than a little scared.

He'd known seeing her again was going to trigger a lot of old emotions, emotions he couldn't afford. He quickly reminded himself that Clancy hadn't only perjured herself on the witness stand and helped send his father to prison ten years ago, now she was facing a murder rap of her own. Forget that cute kid he used to build sand castles with on the beach and catch trout with off the end of this dock. Someone had bludgeoned Dex Westfall to death, and from what Kiki had told him, the police thought that someone was Dex's girlfriend, Clancy Jones.

"So what were you doing out here on the dock at this time of the night?" he asked, unable to keep the reproach out of his voice. He was wet and tired and didn't appreciate being awakened in the middle of the night. Especially by this woman.

"I heard someone…calling me." She sounded dubious.

Welcome to the club. "Someone calling you?" He glanced at the still water beyond the dock. The pines etched a dark, ragged line against the night sky. Then he looked over at her again. "Someone called you, so you walked down to see what they wanted in the middle of the night?" Perfectly logical.

He saw her look toward her lodge, her eyes widening. He followed her gaze, surprised to see that not a single lamp glowed in any of the windows. She hadn't turned on a light before coming down to the dock?

"I suppose you didn't recognize the voice calling you or see the person who pulled you into the water?" he asked, not even trying to hide his disbelief. He could read most people as easily as he could the cover of a tabloid from across the floor of a good-sized minimart. Clancy Jones was lying through her teeth, but for the life of him, he couldn't imagine why. He reminded himself that lying seemed to come easy for her.

"Whether you believe it or not, someone tried to drown me," she said, her voice breaking. She didn't sound any more convinced than he was, but she *was* scared. He could see it in her movements as she got to her feet, nervously tugging her wet clothing away from her body.

For the first time, he realized she wasn't dressed for a night swim. She wore a T-shirt and a pair of leggings. Both were wet and molded to her body. An amazing body, Jake grudgingly admitted. Her feet were bare, and she still wore her watch and a single gold bracelet. Both looked expensive. He ignored the voice of reason that questioned why she would have gone swimming wearing an expensive watch, why Jake had had to pull so hard to bring her to the surface. The questions wedged themselves in the back of his brain, a reluctant sliver of doubt.

"Right," Jake said. "And where is that someone now?"

When he raised his gaze to her face, he saw that she was staring at him again. Squinting, actually, as if the moonlight was too bright.

"Who are you, anyway, and what are you doing here?" she demanded.

He tried not to let it hurt his feelings. Why should she recognize him or even remember him? She'd only spent the first seventeen years of her life living right next door to him, spending most every waking moment with him from the time she could walk. And it wasn't as if he wanted to believe he'd made an impression on her just because she had on him. True, there'd been that kiss, the first for both of them, on this very dock, and she'd said she loved him, but hey—

"Jake Hawkins," he said, surprised at the hurt and anger he heard in his tone. And the bitterness. "Not that there's any reason you should remember *me*. But perhaps you haven't forgotten my father. Surely you recall that your testimony sent him to prison ten years ago."

"Jake." It came out a whisper. She seemed to wobble a little as she squinted harder at him. "It's been so long…you sound so different…and—"

He rolled his eyes. "Forget it." For a moment, he just glared at her, mad, irritable and just plain out of sorts. He shifted his gaze to the lake. Lights flickered on the mainland. The air smelled of fish and pines. He should have been at sea, drifting with the night clouds, catching stripers and sailfish. He should have been at peace, breathing salt air, not standing on a dock in the wee hours of the morning with a woman who'd forced him to remember things he'd only wanted to forget. A woman, who unlike him, seemed to have put at least some of that past behind her.

"Why now?" she asked quietly. "After all this time?"

Fueled on a mixture of hurt and anger, he answered, "Your Aunt Kiki sent me to save your butt."

"What?" The surprise on Clancy's face was worth the flight to Montana. It was almost worth missing his fishing trip. "You met my Aunt Kiki?"

"The Wicked Witch of the East herself." He'd never completely believed the stories Clancy had told after one of her required trips back East each spring to visit her rich aunt. He did now. "She's everything you said she was. And then some."

"I don't understand," Clancy said, frowning. "Why would Aunt Kiki send *you?*"

"Probably because I'm a private investigator and your aunt thinks her money and I can dig up evidence that will keep you out of prison." Even as he said it, he realized it didn't make that much sense to him, either. He had a hunch, one he was holding off like a bad cold. He told himself not to look a gift horse in the mouth. Kiki had provided him with the perfect opportunity. Why question it?

Clancy met his gaze; tears glistened in her eyes. "I see."

He realized she did see at least part of it: one of the only reasons he was here was because Aunt Kiki had procured his services. He thought it would give him more satisfaction than it did to hurt her. What had she expected? That he'd come back and forget what she'd done, forgive her? Not likely.

"It's unfortunate that you've wasted your time," she said, her words so faint, he almost missed them.

Wasted his time? What was she saying, that she killed Dex Westfall, that she was guilty?

She straightened, her glance shifting from her bare feet

o his face. "The last thing I need right now is...*you* helping me."

He stared at her. "It's not like you have a lot of choice n the matter. I doubt there's a line of private investigators knocking down your door to take *this* case."

She let out a small laugh; her hand fluttered for a moment n the air between them. "Jake, we both know you're not here to save me. Admit it, you'd love nothing better than to see me behind bars."

He started to admit it, but she didn't give him the chance.

"What was my aunt thinking?" With a dismissive shake of her head, she turned and headed down the dock toward shore. "Consider yourself fired."

"Wait a minute!" he called after her. "You can't get rid of me just like that."

She didn't even turn around.

Jake stood on the dock, shaking his head in disbelief as he watched her stride toward her lodge. Fired? He'd never been fired in his life. Especially by some woman who didn't have the good sense not to go swimming in the middle of the night. A woman who had the audacity to make up a story about an attacker calling her down to the dock to drown her— Jake glared at Clancy's ramrod back as she retreated up the beach. Once a liar, always a liar, he thought.

"Fine," he called after her. "Fire me. Say hello to my father when you get to prison."

Her lodge door slammed, leaving him standing alone in the moonlight. He cursed and started toward his own lodge. Matching her angry strides, he stomped down the beach but quickly slowed to a limp. The bottoms of his feet hurt like the devil from racing across sand, rocks and rough wood to save a woman who didn't even recognize him. He cursed himself for not only his unappreciated heroics, but also for that moment of weakness he'd had when he first saw Clancy again. For just that instant, he'd actually cared. How could he have forgotten, if for even a moment, the part she'd played in helping send his father to prison? He assured himself he wouldn't forget again.

CLANCY FELL BACK AGAINST the door she'd just slammed and tried to stop shaking. She'd promised herself she wasn't going to fall apart; she'd already cried too many tears and it had accomplished nothing. But just when she thought things couldn't get any worse—Jake appeared.

She hugged herself to hold down the shudders that welled up inside her. Confusion clouded her thoughts. Someone *had* called her down to the dock and tried to drown her. Or had they? She closed her eyes, searching through the darkness of her memory, fighting desperately to remember. Could it have been just a bad dream? But it had seemed so *real*. The hand coming out of the water, grabbing her ankle, pulling her into the water. Once she hit the water, she'd been wide awake. But had there really been someone else in the water trying to drag her under? Or had it been Jake fighting to bring her to the surface? It had happened so fast. And yet she remembered the voice. It had been familiar. Jake's voice?

Her eyes flew open at the thought. No, it hadn't been Jake's. His voice had a hint of a southern drawl.

Jake. A rush of emotions assailed her. Memories, as sweet as the warm scent of summer. Regrets that made her heart ache. She'd never expected to ever see him again. Never expected to have these old feelings come back with such force. Then to find him on her dock tonight. And now of all times.

She moved to the table to retrieve her glasses, anxious to be able to see clearly again, wishing she'd had them on earlier. Or at least had her contacts in. All she'd gotten was a blurred impression of Jake. Medium height and muscular. She smiled, remembering the boy she'd grown up with, the boy she'd fallen so desperately in love with.

She thought about the betrayed, angry look he'd given her that day at the courthouse ten years ago. Tonight, she'd heard that same anger and bitterness in his voice. He still blamed her for his father going to prison. And now he'd come to Montana to help her? She couldn't possibly let herself believe that.

But Jake had saved her life tonight, hadn't he? Clancy shivered, remembering the dark water and the hands pulling her under. Or had they been Jake's hands trying to pull her toward the surface? If there had been an attacker, where had he gone so quickly?

She shivered, hugging herself tighter. Right now she needed a hot bath and dry clothing. She didn't want to think about the fact that she'd walked in her sleep again; she particularly didn't want to think what could have happened if Jake hadn't been there.

She hurried upstairs, anxious to get out of her wet, cold clothing. But as she disrobed and stepped into the hot shower, exhaustion pulled at her, making her thoughts as clouded as the steam that rose around her.

She yearned to be warm and dry. To wrap herself in one of her mother's old quilts. To curl up in front of the fireplace. To forget everything. And sleep. She closed her eyes and leaned back against the shower wall.

JAKE QUICKLY SHOWERED and changed into warm, dry clothing, hoping it would soothe his anger and frustration. It had done neither by the time he dialed the private number Kiki had left for him at the Kalispell, Montana, airport along with another cellular phone. She'd evidently antici-

pated that he'd chuck the first one into the gulf, which he
had. It bothered him that Kiki thought she knew him so
well.

Kiki Talbott Conners answered on the fifth ring. With
more than a little satisfaction, he realized he'd awakened
her from a sound sleep.

"What time is it?" she groaned.

Way past *his* bedtime, he knew that. His eyes felt as if
they had sand in them. "A quarter after three."

"In the morning?"

"That could explain why it's still dark out." He could
just imagine her in a huge satin bed at the Bigfork condo
she'd rented, surrounded by plump pillows and pampered
poodles. "Your niece and I just got reacquainted."

"At *three* in the morning?" Kiki demanded, grogginess
turning quickly to surliness.

He walked to the window. "It's a long story." It looked
as though all the lights in Clancy's lodge were on. What
was she doing still up, he wondered. And why all the lights?
What was she afraid of? Surely she wasn't buying into her
own lies about a mysterious killer who came out of the
water like a shark from *Jaws*. "Let me cut to the chase.
Your niece doesn't want me on this case."

"That surprises you?" Kiki asked, adding an audible
"humph." "Perhaps she thinks you harbor a grudge against
her."

Kiki's words snapped his attention back like a short
rubber band. "Of course I have a grudge against her. And
for a damned good reason." He raked his fingers through
his hair, remembering what Clancy had said on the dock.
What could my aunt have been thinking? Exactly what Jake
wanted to know. "Which brings me to the reason I called.
Knowing that, why in the hell did you want me up here?"

A faint tinkling sound broke the silence. She was pouring

herself a drink. He felt as if he was going to need one, too. Kiki had enough money to buy the best private investigator in the galaxy. And if she wanted evidence tampered with, she could have bought that, too. For a price. But not from Jake Hawkins. So why hire a man who had every reason *not* to help her niece?

"The reason I hired you is the same reason you're not going to quit," she said simply.

He wanted to tell her just how wrong she was but that damned hunch of his was doing the lambada across the back of his neck to a little ditty called "Here Comes Heartache."

He heard her take a sip of her drink, taking her time. "Come on, Jake," she said impatiently. "You know the reason."

"Blackmail." He had a bad feeling that Kiki knew all the blackmail in the world couldn't make him do something he didn't want to do. He had his own personal reason for being here, and his hunch machine told him Kiki knew that, had known it all along. So what the hell had she hired him for?

Kiki sighed deeply. "Jake, we both know why you're in Montana, and it has nothing to do with blackmail."

He couldn't believe he was playing this game with her. "Why don't you spell it out for me, Kiki." He held his breath, afraid she was about to validate the strongest hunch he'd ever had.

"You're in Montana because you think Clancy's the key to proving your father's innocence."

Bingo. Jake squeezed the phone and closed his eyes. Clancy *was* the key. Had always been the key. She'd lied on the witness stand to protect her own father and let Jake's go to prison. And now Jake had Clancy where he wanted her. He'd taken this case for one reason only: to get the truth. And as certain as the coming sunrise, he'd do whatever he had to do to get it out of her.

He stared across the bay at Clancy's. "My motives for being here don't worry you?" he asked Kiki incredulously.

"No," she answered in that tone he'd come to despise. "I've seen how deep your loyalty runs. Unlike your mother. She could never forgive your father for disgracing her. She moved the two of you to Texas. She never visited him in prison. She forgot Warren Hawkins as if he'd never existed." Kiki sounded so damned sure of herself. "You, on the other hand, can't let go of the past. You believe in your father's innocence and would do *anything* to prove it. The same way you can't let Clancy go to prison for a murder she didn't commit."

"I wouldn't be so sure of that," he said, moving away from the window. Kiki thought he was a crusader for injustice? He wanted to laugh. Didn't she realize it was Clancy who'd done him the injustice? The woman was a liar; she'd proven that tonight. How could Kiki be so convinced Clancy hadn't killed this Dex Westfall guy? Blind loyalty? He'd once felt that for Clancy, and look what she'd done to him and his family. No, he suspected with Kiki it was simply a matter of saving the Talbott name.

"I'm quite sure of you," Kiki said, her tone downright haughty.

He wanted to tell her what a fool she was. After all these years, she'd just offered him the perfect opportunity to get what he wanted. The truth. And revenge at the same time. "What makes you think you know me so well?"

Kiki let out a long sigh. "I heard about how wonderful you were for years, Jake Hawkins. Did you forget that for a long time, my niece foolishly thought she was in love with you?"

Kiki hung up before he could respond. Not that he had a response for that one, anyway.

CLANCY'S EYES POPPED OPEN at the sound of the phone ringing and realized she'd dozed off standing in the shower! Panic came in hot pursuit of the realization. What if she'd fallen into one of her deep sleeps and sleepwalked again—this time totally naked?

Whatever it took, she had to stay awake. She cranked the shower handle and let out a shriek as the cold water made her skin ache. But just as she was being revived, the phone began to ring. She quickly turned off the water and reached for a towel.

Dripping, she hurried to the phone and picked up the receiver. "Hello." She could hear breathing at the other end of the line. "Hello?" There was no answer. Just what sounded like soft, labored breathing. "What do you want?" she demanded. No answer. Clancy slammed down the phone. A prank call. Someone who'd read about her in the paper. She'd get her number changed. Maybe even get an unlisted number.

She sat on the edge of the bed, suddenly too tired to move. The soft warmth beneath her beckoned her to crawl in, to cover her head and escape for a few hours in sleep. She stood and headed back to the shower, not about to make the same mistake she'd made earlier. After spending two nights in jail, she'd been running scared and not thinking clearly. She'd been so desperate she'd called her aunt Kiki who'd pulled strings and got her out right after the late afternoon bail hearing Monday. Clancy's plan had been to go to Bozeman and Dex's apartment as soon as she got out on bail. She'd come straight to the lodge to pick up a change of clothing. Unfortunately, after she'd hurriedly packed and started to leave, she'd spotted the flicker of a flashlight at the Hawkins' lodge and spotted the blue out-board tied at the dock. She'd assumed the county attorney had put a deputy on her.

She knew she was only out on bail because of Aunt Kiki and her money. She figured maybe the county attorney had gone along with the bail to please Kiki but had put a deputy on her to cover his political posterior.

So Clancy had foolishly sat by the window to wait him out—not knowing it was just Jake Hawkins, not some dep-uty, watching her. And she'd fallen asleep and sleepwalked.

She stepped back into the shower and let the icy cold water beat her body wide awake. She didn't dare let that happen again. Nor could she afford to wait until morning to leave. Although she didn't relish the idea of crossing the lake in the dead of night, Jake had left her no option. She'd wait until she could be relatively sure he was asleep, then she'd take her boat to the mainland marina where she kept her car. From there she'd drive to Bozeman, go to Dex's apartment and— She wasn't sure what she'd find there, but hopefully something that would prove she was innocent.

Sometimes she could almost forget about the upcoming trial. Almost pretend none of this was really happening. Then she'd get a flash of Dex Westfall sprawled on the couch in the garret. Murdered. And her standing over him with the murder weapon in her hand. One of her own sculp-tures.

Her heart told her she hadn't killed him. But reason ar-gued: how do you know you didn't? You were asleep. And look at all the evidence against you.

Exhaustion tugged at her, beckoning her to the one place where she didn't have to think. Sweet slumber. But with sweet slumber came somnambulism, and she feared her nocturnal wanderings. Look what had happened tonight.

What *had* happened tonight? She wasn't even sure. Her hands shook as she pulled on a pair of jeans and a T-shirt.

She clung to only one hope. That somehow she could prove her innocence. And the only place she knew to start was with Dex. She had to find out everything there was to know about him, including why he'd ended up dead in her garret.

She told herself going to Bozeman, to another county, wasn't really violating her bail. And anyway, she'd be back before anyone even knew she was missing. If she was lucky. But she'd take extra clothing, just in case. In case she found out something that would prove she had killed him and she decided to make a run for it?

Clancy was coming down the stairs, her hair wrapped in the towel turban-style, when she heard the pounding at her back door.

"Clancy, I know you're still up," Jake called. "You might as well open the door."

She pulled the towel off her head, shook out her hair and used the tip of the damp towel to clean her glasses. Maybe he was coming to tell her he was leaving, going back to wherever her aunt had found him. Hadn't she wished for the opportunity to really see him before he left?

If only her other wishes were granted that easily, she thought as she opened the door to find him standing on her step. He'd changed out of his wet jeans; he wore chinos and a white T-shirt that accented his broad shoulders and his tanned, muscular arms. A Houston Astros cap was snugged down on his sandy blond head; his hair curled at the nape of his neck still wet from a shower. His clean, spicy smell engulfed her.

"It's late," she said, but he didn't seem to be paying any attention. He was staring at her as if he'd never seen her before. The same way she was staring at him.

Her earlier impression of Jake hadn't done him justice. He'd been cute at nineteen; now he was strikingly good-looking. Strong features. A full, sensual mouth. Expressive gray eyes. A man with character. He had the kind of face she'd love to sculpt. A mixture of toughness and tenderness.

"You wear glasses," he said simply, sounding pleased.

She didn't tell him she'd worn glasses since she was fifteen—just not around him when she was a girl. "I can't see much without them."

He smiled then. "That's nice." He leaned one broad shoulder against the jamb.

She wasn't sure what she wanted him to say. Goodbye? Or maybe that he was sorry he'd hurt her. Or even that he understood she'd only done what she had to at the trial. "It's late," she repeated.

"Yeah," he said, the smile dissolving as if he'd suddenly remembered why he'd come over. "It's about your case."

She stared at him, telling herself she shouldn't be surprised. "I thought I fired you."

His frown deepened. "Your aunt hired me, and she's the only one who can fire me. And trust me, as much trouble as she's gone to to get me here, there isn't much chance of that happening."

Clancy could only assume her Aunt Kiki had lost her mind.

"So now that we have that settled…" He glanced past her into the lodge.

"Yes, I guess that settles everything." She yawned openly, not that the Jake Hawkins she used to know could take a hint.

"Except for one thing," Jake said, his voice deadly soft. "I had a fishing trip planned that your aunt interrupted to get me up here." He held up his hand to silence her before she could tell him what he could do with his fishing trip.

"Let me give it to you straight. I'm here for only one reason—to get the goods on you," he said, his gaze hard as his body looked.

She swallowed, the cold hatred in his voice making her heart ache, her eyes burn with tears. Only stubborn determination kept her from crying. She wasn't about to let him see how much he'd hurt her ten years ago, how much he could still hurt her.

"I'm going to find evidence I can use against you," he said. "And then you're going to tell me the truth about what you really saw the night of the resort fire, the night Lola Strickland was murdered."

Clancy started to tell him she *had* told the truth, but she knew it would be a waste of breath. He hadn't believed her at the trial, why would he believe her now?

She looked into his eyes, wondering what had happened to the boy she'd loved, the boy who had loved her. She saw nothing in all that gray but bitterness. But instead of hating him, her heart broke as she thought of all the years he'd suffered. Because of his father. Because of her. Jake should have trusted her. He should have known she wouldn't lie, she wouldn't hurt him or his father, and she wouldn't have thrown away their love without a fight, the way Jake had.

"In the meantime," Jake said, "you and I are going to be inseparable until you're acquitted—or sent to prison."

She bit back a curse. "You're making prison look better all the time."

His gaze met hers. "I think I know why you lied about my father, but no matter the reason, you're going to admit it to me. And very soon." He touched the brim of his baseball cap. "See you in the morning."

She slammed the door and dropped into a chair at the table, feeling incredibly tired and despondent. Aunt Kiki had brought Jake back knowing how he felt about Clancy, knowing how she'd once felt about him. That old familiar ache seized her heart in a death grip. How Clancy *still* felt about him.

Tears welled up in her eyes and spilled down over her cheeks, bitter on her tongue. She wiped at them. She still loved him. Through all the hurt, she'd never stopped loving him. Could never stop loving him. But like him, she felt betrayed. And angry with him for not trusting her. She knew she'd have to draw on that anger to keep Jake from knowing how she felt about him—and using it against her.

Emotional exhaustion and lack of solid sleep stole at her strength. She leaned her head on her arms and closed her eyes, telling herself she'd rest for a while, just until she could be sure Jake was asleep. Crossing the lake at night seemed less dangerous now. Much less dangerous than facing Jake Hawkins. If there was more incriminating evidence out there against her, Jake would find it.

She wished with all her heart that she could turn back the clock, back before the night of the fire and Lola's murder, back when Jake loved her. She closed her eyes. And saw Jake come sauntering up the sandy beach, sixteen and suntanned, that grin she loved on his handsome face. And she ran out to meet him, as carefree as the breeze that rippled the surface of the lake.

CLANCY OPENED HER EYES, shocked to find the sun streaming in through her bedroom window. Even more shocked to find herself curled in the middle of her bed, the quilt rough with sand from her bare feet. She lay perfectly still, her mind frantically trying to recall when she'd come to bed. No memory.

That's when she noticed her left hand clenched into a fist, as if she held something that might try to escape. With dread, she slowly uncurled her fingers. There in her palm lay a single tiny blue bead.

Her heart pounded. There was nothing unusual or unique about the bead. Except Clancy knew where it had come from. With a tremor of terror she remembered Friday night when Dex had called and demanded she meet him at the Hawk Island Café on the other side of the island.

He'd been holding a necklace of colored beads when she'd walked up to him. The outdoor café was empty that late at night and that early in the season. Dex sat at a table in a flickering pool of light from the Japanese lanterns strung overhead. She had looked at the necklace with growing dread, thinking it was another present, wishing she hadn't agreed to meet him.

He must have seen the expression on her face, because he gave a bitter laugh as she took a seat across from him.

"Don't worry, it's not for you," he'd said, holding up the string of beads for her to see. With a jolt she realized she'd seen it somewhere before. The tiny beads were pale blue. A handmade ceramic heart hung from the center of the necklace. It was painted navy with a smaller pink heart in the middle.

"Where did you get that?" Clancy asked, trying to remember where she'd seen it before.

"It's part of my mother's legacy," Dex said.

His mother? "What are you doing here?" Clancy demanded, wishing she'd never come, wondering how he'd even known where to find her. She'd never told him about the family's lake lodge. When she'd broken it off with him in Bozeman, she'd thought she'd never see him again. She felt a chill as she watched him hold the necklace up to the light and smile.

"What do you want, Dex?" Clancy asked with dread.

His eyes narrowed as he glared at her. "You're part of that legacy, Clancy."

She felt her fear level rise. How could she not have seen this side of him from the very start? "I thought we'd agreed not to see each other again."

"*We* agreed?" He reached across the table and grabbed her arm, squeezing it until she cried out in pain.

"Leave me alone, Dex. I'm warning you—"

He squeezed harder. "If you think you've seen the last of me you're—" He looked past her, seeing something that made his eyes widen. He released her arm almost involuntarily. She turned to look but saw nothing in the darkness beyond the café.

He lowered his voice. "I'm not leaving this island, Clancy. Not until I get what I deserve." He'd hurried off, leaving her sitting, head reeling, wondering what he'd seen in the darkness that seemed to frighten him. And what Dex thought he deserved.

Just hours later, he'd turned up dead in her garret.

Now she stared at the tiny bead in her palm, knowing this had to be one of the beads from the necklace. Apprehension rippled through her as she stared at her sandy feet. Something had triggered her night wanderings again. And she couldn't seem to stop them. Now she'd returned from sleepwalking with a single bead from a broken strand. When had it been broken? And where had she found this one blue bead? Even more frightening, how had she known where to look?

She slid her legs over the side of the bed and staggered into the bathroom. As she dropped the bead into the toilet and flushed, she watched it disappear with growing terror. She couldn't keep kidding herself. Like the broken string of tiny blue beads, her life was coming unraveled.

Chapter Three

Clancy glanced warily across the bay at Jake Hawkins's lodge. The shades were drawn; she could catch no sign of movement behind them. The blue outboard was still moored at his dock, a boat she assumed he'd rented to get to the island. She looked at her watch, surprised to find it was earlier than she'd thought. Then she turned her gaze again to Jake's lodge across the small bay. The coast looked clear. She picked up the overnight bag and her purse and opened the back door, expecting Jake to suddenly appear and block her escape.

As she stepped out onto the small back porch, she glanced apprehensively behind the lodge. While she found no one hiding in the lilac bushes that brushed the back side of the building, she did see something that stopped her cold. Slowly she put down her purse and overnight bag and moved toward the first lilac bush. Some of the branches along the lodge side of the bush had been broken. They hadn't been yesterday afternoon when she'd returned from jail. She was sure of it. She'd stopped on the porch to dig out her key and picked up the sweet scent of the lilacs, now in full bloom. And she wondered where she'd be this time next year when they bloomed. In prison?

Clancy brushed back the branches, not surprised to find

the grass beneath the kitchen window crushed where some-one had stood, looking in. Through the glass Clancy could see her coffee cup at the table, the chair pushed back from where she'd sat last night. Someone had stood on this very spot, watching her!

She crashed her way out of the lilacs as if the person was at her heels. Scooping up her purse and overnight bag, she rushed down the beach toward her dock. Who had been at the window? The same person who'd called her down to the dock and tried to drown her? It hadn't been a dream, her mind screamed. No more than the crushed grass beneath the window.

With relief she passed the old boathouse, and Jake didn't jump out of the shadows to stop her. All that stretched ahead now was the dock and her boat waiting beside it. The sun danced on the slick surface of the lake, golden. The tall pines shimmered, a silky green at the edge of the water. She took a calming breath. The air smelled of so many familiar, rich scents. Safe scents she'd grown up with. But she was no longer safe. From Jake. From the phantom in the lake. From the real live person who'd stood looking in her window. As long as she kept sleepwalking, she wasn't even safe from herself.

She reached the dock without incident and started down it, walking as quickly and quietly as possible. A sudden flash of memory tormented her. A hand coming out of the water. Grabbing her ankle. Pulling her. She walked faster, fear dogging her steps.

Just a few feet ahead she could see her boat, a yellow-and-white inboard-outboard; a coat of dew on the top and windshield glistened in the morning sunlight. Once she reached it and started the engine, Jake wouldn't be able to stop her. The thought buoyed her spirits.

She shot a parting glance toward his lodge. Jake must

still be asleep. He'd been so adamant about shadowing her every step last night, this seemed almost too easy. She smiled to herself, imagining his surprise when he woke and found her gone, as she untied the bow and started to swing her overnight bag into the hull.

"Good morning!"

Clancy jumped, nearly tumbling backward off the dock. She swallowed a startled cry, pretending she wasn't trying to get away and his catching her wasn't a problem. Jake grinned up at her from the bottom of her boat, where he lay sprawled on a sleeping bag, his arms behind his head.

"Going somewhere?" he asked, raising an eyebrow at the overnight bag still clutched in her hand.

She cursed under her breath.

"If you're set on a life of crime, Ms. Jones, you're going to have to be more devious," he said, getting to his feet. "And jumping bail." He wagged his head at her. "Bad idea."

Clancy groaned. This man was the most irritating— She took a breath, trying to still her anger as well as the silly sudden flutter of her heart as he vaulted effortlessly from the boat to join her on the dock.

"Level with me, Clancy," he said, his voice as soft and deep as his gray eyes.

The sound sent a tiny vibration through her, igniting memories of the chemistry between the two of them as teenagers. She wondered if it was still there and hastily brushed that errant thought away.

Having to deal with this man on top of everything else was too much, she told herself. She didn't have the time or energy for this. Nor did she need the constant reminder of what she'd lost ten years ago—or how much more she had to lose now.

"Where are you going so early in the morning?" he

asked as he stalked toward her, backing her against the edge of the dock, trapping her.

Clancy had to tilt her chin back to meet his gaze. He'd cornered her in more ways than one. And she acknowledged that it wasn't going to be easy to get rid of him. But getting rid of him was exactly what she had to do if she held any hope of clearing herself.

"If you must know," she said, coming up with the first plausible explanation that popped into her head, "I'm going to see my lawyer."

Jake pushed back his baseball cap. "Good, I need to see your lawyer, too."

She shot him a look. "You're going like *that?*"

He glanced down at his rumpled chinos and T-shirt, then looked up at her as he rubbed his blond, stubbled jaw. "It kind of makes me look dangerous, don't you think? Like a man who has nothing to lose?" He gave her a slow, almost calculated smile. "And anyway, what choice do I have? If I were to shower, I'd barely have the water turned on before you'd be hightailing it to wherever you're in such a hurry to get to."

That was exactly what she had in mind. She wished he didn't know her so well.

He stepped back to allow her room to get into the boat. "But I'm a reasonable man. I'll even let you drive your boat."

"You're so thoughtful," she said, but didn't move. Outwardly, she gritted her teeth and fumed. Inwardly, she plotted. She would dump Jake. And soon. She had to. She just didn't know how yet.

WHEN CLANCY DIDN'T make a move to get into the boat, Jake swung back in and offered her a hand. He'd hoped his disposition would improve with daylight. It hadn't. If anything, the late-night adventure, his phone conversation with Kiki and trying to sleep in the bottom of a cold boat with his clothes on had left him even more irascible. Add to that, the gall of Clancy thinking she could get away from him this morning.

He'd been on this case less than twenty-four hours, and he felt as if he'd been beaten up by somebody twice his size. He didn't like the feeling he was being manipulated by not one, but two females. Kiki had hired him for reasons he could no more fathom than he could walk on water. And Clancy. At one time he thought he'd known her better than he knew himself. But that was years ago and a lot of water under the bridge. For all he knew, she was a killer. Let her rot in prison for all he cared.

You've become a cold-hearted bastard, haven't you, Hawkins. Reluctantly, he admitted it was true. Something had died inside him that day at the trial. He'd lost Clancy, and he'd lost his father. Only, Clancy had voluntarily chosen to leave; his father hadn't.

He watched her flick a glance at his outstretched hand but make no move toward it or the boat. Instead, she brushed her hair back with her fingers and looked toward shore as if she were thinking of making a break for it. Silently, he dared her to try. So help him, he'd take her over his knee and—

"Clancy," Jake said softly. "There're a few things you should know. One, I hate being lied to. Two, these dirty little secrets of yours? I'm going to know them all before I catch a plane back to Texas, and you can bet the farm on that." He extended his hand again. "And three, if you try to run again, I'll track you down no matter where you go, and you won't like it when I find you."

He flashed her a smile. But to his surprise, she took his hand, stepped into the boat and came right up to him. If he'd thought he could intimidate her, he'd been wrong. Her gaze met his, challenging him, daring him to take her on.

"Jake, there're a few things *you* should know," she said as softly as he had. "One, I don't have the time or energy to lie to you. Two, I have no intention of helping you send me to prison. And three—" her smile deepened "—I'm going to ditch you just as soon as I possibly can." She moved past him to slide behind the wheel. An instant later she started the boat.

Jake smiled to himself as he took a seat next to her. He'd forgotten how much he'd liked Clancy Jones's spunk as a kid. He was glad to see it was one of the things that hadn't changed about her. Unfortunately, it didn't alter the fact that she'd lied about his father or that she was lying to him right now about not jumping bail. If she wanted to play hard ball, he'd play, too. But he doubted she was going to like his rules.

THEY PICKED UP the expensive bright red Mustang convertible he'd rented with Kiki's money at the mainland marina. The marina was one of several his father and Clancy's had owned as partners. Jake saw Clancy raise an eyebrow as she climbed into the car's leather seat and realized he'd dropped another notch or two in her estimation.

"Doesn't it bother you to take my aunt's money on the pretense of helping me?" Clancy asked.

"No," Jake replied, angry to discover that what she thought of him mattered.

"I thought you hate being lied to," she said. "Or do you overlook it when you're lying to yourself?"

He floored the gas pedal, sending gravel flying as he headed into town. Beside him, Clancy smiled. Jake cursed. What an impossible woman! He'd expected her to still be that cute little tomboy he'd grown up with, someone he thought he could handle—not some beautiful woman who knew how to push all his buttons. He swore to himself. What had made him think this job was going to be easy?

She smiled, seemingly amused. "You're certainly wide awake this morning. I don't remember you being such a morning person."

He didn't want to be reminded of their past or of the foolish, love-struck nineteen-year-old he'd been. Not that he was about to let that past distract or dissuade him from what he'd come to Montana to do. He'd come to settle an old score, and he had no intention of taking any trips down memory lane along the way.

"I'm *forced* to be wide awake at all hours around you," he said as he pulled out into the traffic and headed for the office complex. "Want to tell me why you were about to jump bail? Or do you want me to guess?"

"Guess," she said, looking out the side window.

"Look, why don't you just level with me. I'm going to find out, anyway."

She glanced over at him, and to his surprise, her eyes glistened with tears. "What if you're wrong, Hawkins? What if I didn't lie about your father?"

He felt a sharp stab at his heart, followed instantly by an unexpected desire to take her in his arms and comfort her. What was it about this woman that made him feel protective? Had always made him feel that way?

He shoved away the desire, the same way he'd shoved her away ten years ago. "You lied and we both know why."

She shook her head and looked away.

"You could tell me the truth now and save us both a lot of grief," he said, letting the old rancor replace any warmer feelings he might have had for her.

"And save you the satisfaction of blackmailing it out of

me?'' She shook her head. ''Not a chance, Hawkins. Let's find out just how good a private eye you really are.''

Jake drove toward Kalispell, furious that she could still get to him. He blamed it on that silly childhood crush he'd had on her. He'd opened up, letting her get closer than any other person in his life. Now he bitterly regretted having done that. It made him vulnerable. And it gave her the upper hand.

Okay, so she wasn't going to make it easy. She was going to make it pure hell. But what she didn't seem to realize was that he'd already been to hell and back because of her. And it was payback time.

CLANCY BREATHED A SIGH of relief when Jake finally pulled up in front of Lake Center, a large old hotel that had been made into an office complex. All she wanted to do was to get out of the close confines of the car and put some distance between the two of them. With a little luck, a lot of distance.

But as she started to open her door, he grabbed her arm. She pretended she didn't feel the jolt from his fingertips that seared her bare skin.

''I wish I didn't know you so well, Clancy,'' he said, sounding as though he meant it. ''Whatever's on that conniving mind of yours, forget it. We're going to see your lawyer and find out what evidence they have against you.''

She gave him what she hoped was one of her most innocent looks. ''All right. But I'm starved. Why don't I go get us some breakfast at that café up the block and bring it back. What can I get you?''

He laughed as he opened his door and got out. She stepped out of the convertible, only to find him waiting for her. She watched him lock the car, her overnight bag in the rear seat. Then he linked his arm with hers and steered her toward the building's front entrance.

She didn't resist the gentle strength of his persuasive hold on her. It wouldn't have done her any good if she had. But while she also wouldn't admit it under Sodium Pentothal, she liked the feel of his skin against hers; she liked his touch, as dangerous as it was to her future, to her heart. And she glimpsed something in his expression that made her wonder if he wasn't as immune to her touch as he wanted her to believe.

"Geez, Jones," he said as they headed for the elevator. "Breakfast? A bit too predictable and not very imaginative. But a nice try, nonetheless."

Too predictable, huh? Not imaginative enough for him? Well, she'd see what she could do about that.

JAKE STUDIED CLANCY as they stepped into the elevator and she pushed the third-floor button. She'd been like a kid in church, squirming in her seat on the way into town, glancing at her watch every few moments, tapping her toe to a nonexistent tune. She reminded him of a woman about to jump off a ledge. Actually, more like a woman about to jump bail, he corrected himself.

As the elevator climbed slowly to the third floor, Jake wondered what Clancy would have done this morning if he hadn't been there to stop her? With the depth of her bank account, she could probably disappear without too much trouble. At least for a while. But why run? Unless she was guilty of Westfall's murder and knew she was headed for prison.

But wouldn't a woman who planned to disappear forever take more than a small suitcase—or nothing at all—and buy what she needed when she got there?

The elevator doors thumped open, and it suddenly occurred to him that there might be a man—a man other than Westfall—in Clancy's life. That could explain the small suitcase. Jake realized he knew nothing about the nature of Clancy's relationship with the deceased. Kiki had said Clancy had dated Dex. But that didn't mean Dex was the only man, now, did it? Clancy could have dozens of men on the string.

"You don't mind if I step into the ladies' room a moment to freshen up, do you?" Clancy asked, breaking into his thoughts.

He grinned at her, hoping it hid his true feelings. "I'd hate to see you any fresher than you already are, but hey, it's all right with me since I'm coming along. Not that I don't trust you."

She scowled. "You can't seriously plan to spend every waking moment with me?"

"Every waking—and sleeping—moment." He took her elbow as they headed down the hall.

"That might be a bigger job than you think," she said cryptically. "And I suppose you want me to believe you're doing this for my own good, right?"

He held open the door to the ladies' room for her. "How can you doubt it?"

She shot him a drop-dead look.

"The truth, Jones, will set you free," he said, and smiled.

"Or send me to prison for life." She took only a quick glance into the rest room before she added, "I think you're right. I'm fresh enough."

As he let the door close, Clancy took his arm and smiled up at him as if he'd actually done something that pleased her. One side of her mouth crooked up a little, her brown eyes glinted with mischief, and just the hint of a dimple dented her left cheek at the corner of her lips. Jake had forgotten her smile could pack such a wallop. It hit him in the chest, taking away his breath and knocking him off guard.

He stumbled. Her smile deepened; humor glinted in her gaze. If he'd had any doubt before, he didn't now. She knew damned well the effect she was having on him, and she loved it. This was war. And for a moment, he wished there was another way, other than all-out war, to settle things between them.

He stared at her, wishing he could find the answers he needed in that face of hers. If only he could look into those brown eyes and know everything he wanted to about her. Like why she'd lied about his father. If she'd killed her boyfriend. Where she'd been going this morning in such a hurry. Why she'd betrayed him.

Instead, all he got were more questions from that adorable face of hers. And more suspicions.

She brushed against him as she stepped past, the silkiness of her skin sparking responses in him he didn't want to be feeling. Her scent filled him, branding his senses. He watched the provocative sway of her hips as she walked away from him. He assured himself he could handle this woman, that it would be a pleasure giving her some of her own medicine.

But that little voice of reason that kept him honest suggested the best thing he could do would be to get this case over with, pry the truth out of Clancy and head back to Texas lickety-split.

He swore softly to himself as he opened the door to the office with the sign that read Attorney Tadd Farnsworth, and watched Clancy waltz through, her bottom filling out her jeans in a way that should have been against the law. Clancy played him like a cheap guitar, but made him feel like he was a fine Gibson. Jake promised himself he'd have her dancing to his tune—and soon.

Chapter Four

"Jake? Jake Hawkins?" the handsome, prematurely gray-haired man said, coming around his large desk. "I didn't know you were back in town." Tadd Farnsworth's smile was as quick as his handshake and just as slick.

"I didn't know I had to check in at the border," Jake said, taking the attorney's outstretched hand.

"And Clancy," Tadd said.

Jake thought Tadd held her hand a little too long, his look a little too sympathetic and seductive.

Jake told himself he would have liked Tadd Farnsworth if the man hadn't been the prosecuting attorney who sent his father to prison. But he knew that wasn't true. At one time Tadd had been a regular at the island resort, always sporting a fast new boat, always a hit at the parties Jake's mother threw at the lake lodge. Jake remembered only too well how taken his mother had been with Tadd. That was plenty reason to make Jake dislike the man.

Seeing the way Clancy smiled at Tadd, Jake could see that even ten years older, Tadd still had a way with women. He decided he liked him even less.

"I was sorry about your mother, Jake" Tadd said as he returned to his chair behind his desk. "I heard she passed away a few months ago. My condolences."

"Oh, Jake," Clancy said. "I didn't know. I'm so sorry."

Jake nodded and took a chair beside Clancy. He didn't want to talk about his mother. Especially with Tadd. Nor did he want to talk about his father. He pulled his business card from his wallet and tossed it on the desk. "I'm here on the Dex Westfall case."

Tadd picked up the card. His eyes widened. "I'd heard Kiki had brought in some hotshot private eye." He laughed. "I'll be damned. So you're a P.I." He shook his head. "Interesting, her choice of investigators, wouldn't you say?"

No kidding. "I'd like to see what evidence you've got so far."

Tadd nodded. "Sure you wouldn't like some coffee? Or maybe a stiff drink?" His smile slipped a little as he looked from Jake to Clancy and back. "You're not going to like this case."

"There isn't much about it I've liked so far," Jake said. Clancy mumbled something under her breath and looked at her watch.

"Don't worry. This won't take long," Jake assured her.

"Do I look worried?" she asked with wide-eyed innocence.

The attorney excused himself and returned a few minutes later with a large manila envelope. He placed it on the desk in front of Jake and returned to his seat without saying a word.

Jake opened the flap, pulled out a stack of papers and flipped through them. He let out an oath without even realizing it.

"Told you you weren't going to like it," Tadd said.

The case against Clancy was overwhelming.

"I think I will take that coffee," Jake said to Tadd.

Jake sat stunned as Tadd buzzed his secretary. It had

been one thing telling himself the woman who betrayed him was a killer. It was quite another to realize it might actually be true.

"Why didn't the sheriff just hang her on the spot?" Jake asked Tadd after he took a sip of the coffee the attorney handed him, happily discovering it to be heavily laced with bourbon.

"Would have a hundred years ago. If she'd been a man." Tadd chuckled. "Instead, she's a woman. And a Talbott to boot." He shot Clancy a smile to say he was just kidding, but with one look from her, it died on his lips.

Jake wondered if she realized that she'd be cooling her heels in a cell right now if it wasn't for Aunt Kiki's money and the illustrious Talbott name. Not to mention what Kiki must be paying Tadd. Jake wouldn't be surprised if Kiki wasn't also making a large donation to the Tadd Farnsworth for County Attorney campaign for added incentive.

Jake thumbed through the rest of the evidence, including a list of Dex Westfall's belongings from the murder scene: a bloody western snap-front shirt, a pair of jeans and red cowboy boots. No socks. No underwear. Jake raised an eyebrow. Had Dex gotten dressed in a hurry for some reason? Or was that his usual attire? Jake made a mental note to ask Clancy.

There was also a list of items found at the cabin Dex had rented at the Hawk Island Resort, including Dex's wallet, watch, keys and some loose change.

"He didn't have his wallet or keys on him the night of his murder?" Jake asked Tadd, suspecting even more that for some reason Dex Westfall had dressed in a hurry.

"I guess he didn't need them," Tadd said. "No place to spend money and he sure couldn't drive anywhere. He probably took one of the island trails to Ms. Jones's."

''You don't know how he got there?'' Jake asked, surprised.

''Does it matter?'' Tadd said. ''He got there. We know that.''

Everything mattered, Jake thought. What Dex hadn't done was drive. There were no cars or roads on Hawk Island. That left two other options: he could go by boat around the island to Clancy's. Or he could take one of the many mountain trails. Because the sheriff hadn't found a boat at the scene didn't mean Dex hadn't had someone drop him off. And that meant maybe he'd planned to have that same someone pick him up again.

Dex was last seen with Clancy after the resort café closed on Friday night. That meant there wouldn't have been any place on the island for Dex to spend money. But Jake still thought it odd Dex hadn't taken his wallet. Most guys would grab their wallet, keys and watch out of habit. Some things you just felt naked without. Like underwear.

The wallet, according to the report, contained less than thirty dollars. He glanced through the photocopy of the items—a Montana driver's license, a few credit cards. Jake frowned. No photographs. Not even one of Clancy, the guy's girlfriend. No family photos. No receipts or junk like most people carried in their wallets. No mementos.

Dex Westfall's belongings reminded Jake of a new subdivision. No feeling of history. Everything of Dex's had been marked on the sheriff's list as in new condition. Jake found himself wondering just who the hell this guy was and what Clancy had seen in him as he glanced at Westfall's driver's license photo again. The guy was almost too good-looking. Jake had never figured Clancy for that type, but then, he reminded himself, he didn't know Clancy anymore. He looked over at her. For instance, what was she thinking about right now? He realized how little he knew about her. It worried him. A lot.

Taking out his notebook, Jake jotted down Dex's social security number and address from his driver's license, and took down the credit card numbers. He put everything back in the envelope and looked up at Tadd.

"What do you know about this guy?" Jake asked.

Tadd shrugged. "No more than what's here, and we won't know until his next of kin are notified." Jake noted Clancy's sudden rapt attention and wondered why this subject would interest her when nothing else about her case had.

"There's one other thing," Tadd said. Jake felt the bad news coming even before Tadd opened his mouth. "You should know the sheriff has two witnesses who overheard Westfall and Clancy arguing at the marina café the evening Dex Westfall was murdered. Both said they heard Clancy threaten Dex."

Jake groaned inwardly.

"One is a waitress at the marina café," Tadd continued. "The other is Frank Ames. You remember him?"

Yeah, Jake remembered the tall, pimply-faced kid six years his senior. Frank had always had a major chip on his shoulder, one that Jake had more than once wanted to knock off. Jake's father had given Frank a job at the resort, wanting to help him. But Frank's hostile unfriendliness had forced Warren Hawkins to let him go, making Frank Ames all the more bitter.

"Frank owns the resort now," Tadd said. "Maybe you'd heard."

"No, I hadn't." Jake hadn't heard anything about Hawk Island since the day he promised his mother he'd never say his father's name in her presence again. It had been the day they left Flathead Lake, right after Warren Hawkins had been convicted of embezzlement, arson and one count of deliberate homicide. They'd left town on the whipping tail of a scandal that had rocked the tiny community. Kiki had been right; his mother had insisted they leave without stopping at the Montana State prison in Deer Lodge to see his father even one last time.

Jake had kept his promise to her; he'd never mentioned his father's name. But several times a year he'd visited Warren Hawkins in prison. Jake had wanted to reopen his father's case and do some investigating on his own, but Warren had asked him not to. Jake had left it alone, not wanting to hurt his mother any more than she had been.

But now she was gone. And he was back in Montana thanks to Aunt Kiki. Back on Flathead Lake. And that hunch of his was knocking at the back of his brain, demanding to be let in. Demanding that he follow it, no matter where it might lead. Clancy was his ticket as surely as Tadd Farnsworth was a born politician. It was just going to be harder to get the truth out of Clancy than he'd first thought.

"Can I get a copy of this and the autopsy report?" Jake asked, tapping the envelope with his finger.

Tadd nodded.

"Give me call when it's ready." He gave Tadd the number from the cellular phone Kiki had given him.

"Here's my home number," Tadd said as he took out a business card and wrote on the back. He handed it to Jake. "In case you come up with something." He sounded more than a little doubtful that would happen.

Tadd pushed his intercom button and instructed his secretary to make Jake a copy of the Dex Westfall case, including the latest on Clancy's sleepwalking defense.

"What?" Jake snapped, telling himself he must have heard wrong. He glanced over at Clancy; she met his gaze for an instant, then looked away, her body suddenly tense.

Jake cursed under his breath. What else had Clancy and her aunt failed to tell him?

"I guess you didn't know," Tadd said, smiling sympathetically at Jake. "Clancy was sleepwalking the night Dex Westfall was killed. That's why she doesn't remember what happened."

Jake stumbled to his feet, feeling the weight of the world settle around his shoulders. He took Clancy's elbow and steered her out into the hall.

"Sleepwalking?" he demanded the moment the door closed behind them. He couldn't believe what a chump he was. Even when she'd lied on the stand, he'd figured she only did it to protect her own father. If Tadd was opting for a Twinkie defense like sleepwalking, it meant only one thing: Clancy'd killed Dex Westfall and she damn well knew it.

"Sleepwalking?" Jake demanded again, trying to keep his voice down.

"I guess I shouldn't expect you to believe me," Clancy said, jerking her elbow free of his grip. She started down the hall, but he grabbed her shoulder and whirled her around to face him.

He let his gaze rake roughly over her, telling himself not to be fooled by that face of hers with its cute little button of a nose or the crocodile tears in those big brown eyes. He pulled her into the first alcove and blocked her retreat with his body. "Another murder and you just happened to be sleepwalking *again?*"

Clancy found her gaze locked spellbound with his. There was something commanding about him. He demanded her attention, and ever since she was a girl, she'd been unable to deny him. She looked into his eyes; they darkened like thunderheads banked out over the lake. Everything about him, from his eyes to the hard line of his body, warned her of the storm he was about to bring into her life. Jake Hawkins was a dangerous man, one she'd be a fool to trifle with.

"I walk in my sleep. I have ever since I was a child."

He stared at her, suspicion deep in his expression. "Sure you have."

She wanted to slap his smug face. "I assume you've never walked in your sleep."

"No." He made that one word say it all.

She reminded herself that people who'd never sleepwalked didn't understand, couldn't understand. But she wanted Jake to, needed Jake to.

"It's frightening, because when you wake up you don't know how you got there. You don't recall getting up. Suddenly you are just somewhere else, and you don't remember anything. Not even where you've been." She met his gaze. "Or what you've done."

"How come I never heard about you sleepwalking when we were kids?"

She glanced away. "I was…ashamed. Wandering around at night in my pajamas, not knowing what I was doing. It was something I didn't want anyone to know about."

Jake nodded, eyeing her intently. "And you're trying to tell me that the night Dex Westfall was murdered you were walking around in your pj's, sound asleep, and you don't remember killing him? Not that you didn't kill him, but that you don't remember because you were sacked out?"

"I'm trying to tell you the truth," she said angrily, and wondered why she was even bothering. "Sleepwalking isn't something I have control over. It just…happens. Like last night."

"Last night?" He dragged his fingers through his hair. "You mean last night on the dock when you were sure

someone pulled you into the lake and tried to drown you?
Now you're telling me that you were asleep?''

She didn't like his tone. ''I was walking in my sleep.''
She took a breath and looked away. He'd never given her
the chance to explain ten years ago; he'd just assumed she'd
lied on the stand and he'd cut her off without a word. Without a goodbye. ''Just like I was the night of the fire.''

''How convenient that you were asleep at the murder you
committed,'' Jake said, bitterness oozing from his every
word. He slammed a palm to the wall on each side of her.
''And how inconvenient for my father that you just happened to wake up in time to see him kill Lola Strickland.''

''Yes.'' She ducked under his arm and ran down the hall,
blinded by tears and regrets. Behind her, she heard him.
The sound was a low, pained howl, the cry of a wounded
animal. It tore at her heart. She wanted to take him in her
arms, to comfort him. But nothing she could do or say
would do that. She'd told the jury the truth. She didn't
know what else had happened that night at Hawk Island
Resort because she'd been asleep—walking, but sound
asleep. Sleepwalking had always been her private shame.
A frightening weakness that was best kept a secret. Until
the night Lola Strickland was murdered. Now that horrible
memory had come back to haunt her—just the way her
sleepwalking had come back.

Jake slammed a fist into the wall, too stunned to chase
after her. Sleepwalking? She'd been sleepwalking the night
of Lola's murder *and* the night Dex Westfall was killed in
her garret? And last night on the dock? His brain tried to
assimilate this information but couldn't.

That's why her story had sounded like a lie. Could she
really not remember anything? Was that why there'd been
so many holes in her story? Because she'd been asleep? His

mind refused to accept it. Just as it had ten years ago. She was lying. Again. Sleepwalking! Again.

He charged after her, only to run headlong into a group of students on some kind of career day. The teacher tried to gather her flock, but they scattered like errant chicks. Jake forced his way through to reach the elevator door just as it closed. He watched the numbers overhead to make sure Clancy was headed down before he took off at a run for the stairs. She didn't really think she could get away from him, did she?

He burst out of the stairwell and into the main lobby as the elevator doors were closing again. He raced over to them, slapping the doors open and startling the only occupants, an elderly couple.

"Sorry," he said. "I was looking for a blond woman. About five six. Cute." Incredibly sexy. And innocent-looking. He started to make a curvaceous outline with his hands, but stopped himself. "Nice figure. Wearing a navy shirt, jeans and sandals?"

They both gave him a knowing smile. The elderly woman pointed across the hall to a door marked Women. "She seemed a little upset," the woman said, clearly blaming him.

"Thanks." As the elevator doors closed again, Jake made a beeline for the bathroom, cursing himself for letting Clancy out of his sight for even an instant.

He stormed through the doorway, propelled by a flammable fuel of high-grade anger. "If you think I'm going to believe this latest story of yours—" he said, taking up the conversation right where they'd left off.

His voice echoed off the tiled walls. A half-dozen women looked up, startled. Clancy wasn't at either of the two sinks powdering her nose. That left only the row of four stalls.

"Sir, you're in the wrong rest room," one woman politely informed him as if he didn't know.

He politely informed her that he didn't care, then he leaned down to look for Clancy's sandaled feet in the occupied stalls. No Clancy. The last stall appeared empty; someone had put a handmade Out of Order sign on it.

Most of the women had the good sense to flee from the room, though they did it in high indignation, telling him in no uncertain terms what they thought of his behavior.

You want to see bad behavior, he thought to himself, *wait until I get my hands on Clancy.* A couple of women stayed to give him grief. He ignored them, waiting for the stalls to empty out. As he glanced around the room, he assessed the situation. There was only one door. Clancy hadn't had time to come back out.

Jake waited for the last woman to exit. As she stomped past, he noticed that the summer breeze coming through the open window at the end of the room smelled sweet with the scent of freshly mown grass. Jake could hear the sound of a lawnmower buzzing just outside at ground level. In front of the window, someone had upended a trash can.

Jake cursed himself and his stupidity as he pushed open each stall door on his way to the window. All the stalls were now empty, just as he knew they would be. And on the corner of the metal window frame was a small scrap of navy blue material that perfectly matched the shirt Clancy had been wearing.

Damn her hide, she'd given him the slip.

Chapter Five

Clancy caught the first flight out of Kalispell. She thought she'd feel safe once the plane was in the air. Instead, she couldn't shake the feeling that someone was after her. And not just Jake Hawkins.

She glanced around at the other passengers but saw no one she knew. No one even appeared remotely interested in her. As the plane banked to the east, she looked out the window and told herself she had to calm down and think clearly. Her life depended on it. And yet she'd never felt more afraid, more alone.

Except for one other time in her life. The night of the resort fire. The night Lola Strickland was murdered. Clancy closed her eyes and tried to fight back the painful memories. But the memories came, edged with one penetrating truth: she'd walked in her sleep that night, just as she had the night Dex Westfall died.

It had been late that night ten years ago when she'd come down the stairs, awakened by the sound of her parents arguing. Her parents never argued. Until that moment, she'd led an idyllic life on the island. The only dark spot in her whole childhood had been her required yearly visits back East to see Aunt Kiki and get a little culture so she didn't grow up a wild heathen. Clancy had hated the visits, the stiff, prissy dresses, the long, boring lessons in social graces, her aunt's endless lectures on the value of money and the Talbott name.

But it was her aunt's low opinion of Clancy's father that made her call Kiki the Wicked Witch of the East. Kiki had always thought her sister had married beneath the family name when she'd married Clarence Jones. Clancy idolized her father.

Clancy had stopped on the stairs when she heard her father's voice saying that he couldn't go to the police, wouldn't go to the police. Warren was his best friend.

But her mother had argued that Warren was stealing from the businesses and had been for some time. Clancy felt a sick, sinking feeling, knowing that their lives had suddenly changed and would never be the same again.

When her father left by boat to meet Warren at the resort, Clancy followed by land, afraid for her father for reasons she couldn't explain then or now.

But when she reached the resort office, she could hear her father and Warren inside and decided to wait in one of the boats tied at the dock. She'd fallen asleep.

Later, she'd woken only to find that she'd walked in her sleep. To this day, she had no idea where she'd been or what she might have seen. All she remembered was waking to find herself standing outside the office.

Her father's boat was gone. Inside the office she could hear voices raised in anger. From the shadows, she watched in horror as Warren Hawkins struggled with Lola Strickland. Lola stumbled backward into an adjoining room. Both figures disappeared for a few moments, then Warren emerged at a run. Behind him the office burst into flame, and within seconds the fire consumed the building.

Just thinking about that night brought back the incredible regret. Lola's death and Warren Hawkins's arrest ended the life she and Jake had known on Hawk Island. Jake and his mother left Flathead; Jake left hating Clancy. Clancy's parents had moved to Alaska to start over. They'd lost everything. Kiki purchased the lodge at Clancy's pleading. Clancy had foolishly hoped her family would some day be reunited there. Two years later her parents were killed in a small plane crash outside of Fairbanks.

Clancy didn't come back to the boarded-up lodge for years and then only occasionally. At first the bad memories were just too painful. Then the good memories started to surface again.

She opened her eyes and looked out the plane window. She'd had such hopes when she'd returned. Had she made a mistake coming back? Was there a curse on the island and her? Some debt not yet paid?

She felt a chill as she thought of Jake. He'd believed his father's version of what happened that night. Warren Hawkins testified during the trial that he knew nothing about the missing money. After Clarence Jones left, he'd gotten out the books to go over them. Warren was in charge of that part of the businesses in the partnership with Clarence, but he'd turned a lot of the responsibility over to Lola, he'd said.

Warren said he'd heard someone in the adjoining office. When he'd gone to check, he saw two suitcases outside the door and found Lola cleaning out the safe.

He'd tried to stop her. Lola had poured gasoline around the office, obviously planning to cover her tracks. In their struggle, she must have lit the gas. The room burst into flames. That's when Warren swears he saw someone move in the shadows; someone else was in the office by the back door. When he ran out, Lola was still alive. He thought she was right behind him.

Warren said the other person in the office that night must

have taken the money from the safe, because it wasn't found in the debris from the fire and Lola certainly didn't get away with it. That person must have also murdered Lola. In the autopsy it was found that Lola had died from a head wound—not from the fire. That made Warren look all the more guilty.

In the end, the jury didn't believe there was another person in the office that night. Nor did they believe Lola set the fire. It looked too much like Warren had embezzled money from the businesses and tried to cover his misdeeds with the fire. Lola, who was leaving the island, just happened along at the wrong time. All of the joint businesses' books were destroyed in the fire. Warren couldn't prove his innocence. Nor could the police prove his guilt.

Clancy's testimony had clinched it. Warren was convicted of embezzlement, arson and deliberate homicide. He got sixty years at the state prison at Deer Lodge.

And because of Clancy's testimony, Jake had walked out of her life without a word. The hurt from that still made her heart ache. And now— Now he'd come back. For revenge.

Just what she needed, Clancy thought as the plane descended into Gallatin Field outside of Bozeman. An old boyfriend with a grudge on top of all her other troubles.

At the airport, Clancy rented a car and drove the eight miles into Bozeman to Dex's condo. She felt as if time were running out. Jake wouldn't be far behind her, she knew that. And he'd be furious. Boy, was that putting it mildly.

But she hoped that by the time he tracked her to the airport, discovered she'd flown to Bozeman and rented a car, it would be too late for him to stop her. By then she'd have searched Dex's place and hopefully found something that would help her case. Though she couldn't imagine what.

There was also the possibility that Jake would go straight to the county attorney. By the time she reached Bozeman, the police could be looking for her, as well.

Either way, she needed to get this over with as quickly as possible.

Dex owned a condo on the southside of town, set back against a hill overlooking Sourdough Creek. Clancy parked and sat in the car for a moment, watching the quiet street. No other vehicles cruised by. She told herself she was just being paranoid. No one was after her. Except Jake. And maybe the entire Bozeman police. And possibly the person who'd tried to drown her last night.

She picked up her purse from the seat and got out, closing the car door behind her. As she walked toward the front door of the condo, she searched the street. A florist's van passed by; the driver never even looked her way. She could only hope the spare key was where it had been the last time Dex locked himself out. Carefully, she slid the large flowerpot slightly to one side. Nothing but dust. She pushed it a little farther and was relieved to see the key.

Quickly she scooped it up, slipped it into the lock and turned. The door swung open.

Clancy stepped into the high-dollar condo, wondering whether the police had already been here, whether they'd already searched the place and found something that would further incriminate her. The cluttered condo didn't surprise her as much as the man who came out of the kitchen.

"Excuse me," he said, sounding annoyed and a little frightened by her intrusion. He was short, with rumpled dark hair and sunless pale skin, and he was wearing nothing but shorts. "How did you get in here?"

Her first thought was that the condo had been sold. Her second was that Dex had a roommate she hadn't known about. A roommate who was looking more than a little anxious.

"I'm a friend of Dex Westfall's," she said quickly, not sure that was exactly accurate, but it beat the alternative. That she was the woman the police had arrested for Dex's murder.

"Dex Westfall," the man said, shaking his head. Had he heard Dex was dead? She felt her heart rate accelerate. Worse yet, had he heard about her arrest? "I suppose he gave you a key."

She shook her head, wondering how she was going to explain what she was doing here. "I used the one under the flowerpot."

He swatted the air with the pancake turner in his hand. "Did Dex tell everyone where to find the key to my condo?"

"*Your* condo?" Clancy thought she must have heard him wrong.

"Dex Westfall was only house-sitting for me for a few months," he said, his tone increasing in both volume and irritation. "I come home to find he's run up my phone bill and failed to pay the utility bills, and now the police want to talk to me about God knows wh—" Behind the man, smoke curled out of the kitchen. He spun around and charged out of the room.

Pans clanged into the sink. A kitchen fan came on. A few moments later, he stalked back into the living room.

"Look," he said, his face flushed. "The guy's a deadbeat. Just give me the key and tell Dex I don't want to see him or any more of his girlfriends around here, all right?"

He didn't know Dex was dead. "The police called you?"

"I got a message on my machine," the man said. "I haven't had time to call them back." He seemed to resent her questions, but also seemed resigned to answer them. No doubt he felt sorry for a woman stupid enough to fall for Dex Westfall. "I just got back yesterday from Australia. I haven't even had time to unpack yet." He held out his hand for the key.

Clancy noticed the stack of newspapers by the door. Magazines and junk mail were piled high on a telephone table by the door. "Did Dex leave any personal items here?" she asked as she handed over the key. "He has something that belongs to me."

The man rolled his eyes. "Dex isn't completely stupid. He packed up and got out just before I returned home. Did you check his apartment?"

She stared at him. "His apartment?"

"You don't get it, do you," he said, his face growing redder. "Dex Westfall is a lying sleazeball. You aren't the first woman to show up looking for him. Or the last, I'm sure."

No, she *hadn't* got it. She realized how little she knew about the man she'd dated. The man she was now accused of murdering. "Where is his apartment?" Her voice came out a trembly whisper.

He reached over to snatch a scrap of paper and a pen from the phone table and scribbled something on it. "If you loaned him money, forget it. I'm sure it's long gone. Just like I would imagine he is. This is the address he gave me."

Clancy took the piece of paper. It had a northside apartment address on it.

"If you should catch up to him, tell Dex— Never mind, it wouldn't do any good," the man said disgustedly.

She figured he'd find out just how right he was as soon as he returned his calls.

He moved past her to open the front door. "Good luck," he said as she stepped outside, then he closed and locked the door behind her.

Clancy stumbled to the rental car and sat for a moment, too shaken to drive. She remembered the first time Dex had brought her to see his new condo. *His* new condo. He'd told her what a great deal he got on it. He'd insinuated that he'd purchased it with their future in mind and even talked about how easy it would be to build on a studio for her.

He'd been lying through his teeth. To impress her? Or con her? But out of what?

She started the car, anxious to get to Dex's apartment. Maybe the police didn't know about it yet. Maybe he'd left something that would help her.

Dex Westfall's apartment turned out to be a basement rental in an old run-down part of town. Clancy circled the block and, not taking any chances, parked behind the house. A short, worn path led from the alley to the basement entrance. Clancy stepped down the crumbling steps and peered through a dirty window into what looked like the furnace room.

"Can I help you?" The voice was elderly and shrill, with an irritated edge to it.

Clancy spun around to find a wrinkled woman; her pink curlers clung haphazardly to her washed-out gray hair. Her eyes were narrowed and mean.

"I'm looking for Dex," Clancy said, adding what she hoped was a friendly smile.

"Humph! Isn't everybody." The woman jammed her small fists down on her hips and glared at Clancy. "And just what do you want with him?"

"I'm his…sister," she said quickly. "I'm worried about him."

"His sister?" The woman eyed her. "Not much resemblance that I can see."

"Different fathers," Clancy said, caught up in her whopper.

The woman puckered her lipstick-cracked lips. "He owes me rent."

Clancy opened her purse. "How much?"

It took all of Clancy's charm, most of her cash and more flagrant falsehoods to get into the apartment. To her surprised delight, it didn't sound as though the police had been there yet. But then, they had their killer; they weren't looking for clues in Bozeman. Or maybe they'd only gotten as far as the condo, because that was the only address they had for Dex.

"Last thing he said to me was that he'd be back with enough money to buy this house and me with it," the woman said with a huff. "I've seen his kind before. Fancy dresser. Full of himself. Full of bull, that's what he was." She looked up at Clancy as she unlocked the apartment door. "Too bad you can't pick your relatives, huh? Don't take anything." With that, she left, her worn slippers shuffling up the cracked concrete steps.

Clancy closed the door and turned to look at Dex Westfall's apartment. Under the golden glare of a single bulb overhead, the cramped studio apartment looked seedy at best. An old couch hunkered against a dark paneled wall next to an overstuffed worn chair and a small kitchen table and two metal folding chairs. A blanket was neatly folded at one end of the couch. Dex's bed?

An old, hump-shouldered refrigerator kicked on in the kitchen area of the room, clanging a little before it settled into a tired, noisy thrum. Clancy reminded herself that she didn't have much time. Jake would be after her. And by now the man at the condo could have called the police back.

But still she didn't move. She stared at the apartment, trying to connect it with the man she'd known. Or thought she'd known.

On the makeshift counter next to the fridge was a sink

and a hot plate. Not far from it stood a tall, homemade pine closet, a bent wire hanger caught in its door. Past it, through a narrow doorway, she could make out a toilet, shower stall and a bathroom window, trash and dead weeds blown in on the outside.

This was the kind of cheap apartment college kids rented while they attended Montana State University. They hung posters on the paneled walls, had loud parties and spent most of their time playing hackysack over at the park or studying at the library. There was no way that Dex Westfall had ever lived here. There had to be a mistake. Even if Dex was short of money—

She reached to free the coat hanger from the closet door. The last thing she expected to find was any of Dex's clothing inside— She'd been right. All of his clothes were gone. But what she saw sent a shock of horror through her.

The wall at the back of the empty closet was covered with papers and pictures, all thumbtacked to the wood. One photograph in particular caught her attention. She shoved back the half-dozen bent metal hangers dangling from the galvanized pipe rod. It was a photo of a young woman.

Clancy moved closer, panic making her movements stiff, unsure. The photograph was of her. Next to it was a ten-year-old newspaper article about Lola Strickland's murder and Warren Hawkins's trial. Clancy's testimony had been highlighted.

Her heart slammed against her ribs as she saw that the entire back of the closet was covered with articles about the trial and that summer. She felt her legs quake beneath her and all her blood seemed to rush to her head. She reeled and caught herself, grabbing the closet for support. A photograph fluttered to the floor. Mechanically, she reached to pick it up.

It was a shot of her in a dark green suit coming out of

the gallery where she used to work in downtown Bozeman. She stared at the photo. It was a candid shot, taken from the other side of Main Street. She squinted as something in the picture caught her eye. A silver spot on the jacket's lapel. The pin her Grandmother Jones had left her when she died. Clancy drew the snapshot closer. She remembered that day! It was the last time she'd worn the pin. She'd gone to lunch and when she returned to work, the pin was gone. Lost. She'd run an ad in the paper, but the pin never turned up.

Her heart began to pound harder. It was the same day she'd met Dex. After lunch that afternoon. She'd been so upset about losing her Grandmother Jones's pin. And this man had walked into the gallery, looking for a sculpture. He didn't know the artist's name, just the artist's work. And he had to have the sculpture.

Clancy had been startled by Dex's good looks, his charm, his passion for an artwork he'd only glimpsed in a gallery window. And even more startled and pleased when the artist's work he was dying to purchase turned out to be her own.

Clancy gripped the photograph tighter. Dex had purchased one of her most unusual—and most expensive—sculptures. Then he'd asked her out for dinner that night, telling her he wanted to know more about the artist who did such magnificent work. And unlike her usual cautious self, she'd accepted.

Tears rushed to her eyes, fed by fear rather than regret. Fear and a fresh sense of panic. Dex had taken this picture of her *before* he'd come into the gallery, *before* he'd pretended he hadn't known the name of the artist he was searching for, *before* he'd ever met her.

Her pulse thundered, drowning out the thrum of the refrigerator, drowning out everything but one single thought:

Dex Westfall had known her! From that very first day. He'd known who she was. From the newspaper articles about the trial. He'd known. And he'd come after her.

Clancy clung to the edge of the closet. Why her? She let the photograph drop. It drifted to the bottom of the closet, where it lay staring up at her. A play program lay beside it. A play Clancy had attended. Just days before Lola's death.

A thud overhead pulled Clancy back. Pretty soon the landlady would be down here, wondering what was keeping Clancy so long. But Clancy continued to stare at the pictures and newspaper articles, shocked by Dex's deception.

Carefully she moved away from the makeshift closet. The hangers rattled softly behind her. She glanced toward the small, dusty ground-level window over the sink, that feeling that she was being watched even stronger than at the airport. She shivered, urging herself to finish her search and get out of there.

The rusted bathroom cabinet was empty. So was the chest of drawers she found tucked back in the corner. It seemed obvious that when Dex had left, he'd had no intention of coming back. He'd pretty much taken everything. Except for his wall of mementos. A shudder of apprehension rocked her as she stood before the closet again. Why had he thought he wouldn't need them anymore?

That's when she spotted the letter. The letter she'd written him, warning him not to contact her again. He'd tacked it on the closet wall, still in its envelope. She reached for it at the same time she heard the creak of the door opening behind her. Clancy grabbed the envelope, folding it in her hand as she turned, and smiled to greet the nosy landlady.

But the dark silhouette that filled the doorway was much larger than the landlady and much more threatening.

"Jumping bail *and* destroying evidence?" Jake asked,

that touch of a southern drawl doing little to take the edge off the anger in his voice. He stepped to her side in two effortless strides and, grasping her wrist, plucked the letter from her hand. ''You're just damned and determined to go to prison, aren't you, Clancy Jones?''

Chapter Six

Jake hadn't thought past finding Clancy. Hadn't thought of anything but catching her. And now that he had, he stood scowling at her, uncertain as to what to do with her. Several thoughts crossed his mind, surprising him in both content and fervor. "I ought to—"

Clancy stepped back as he advanced on her, stumbling against the open door of what looked like a homemade closet.

Jake stopped dead when he saw the bulletin board Dex had constructed on the back wall and recognized the subject. "What the—?" He swore under his breath, that hunch of his doing the Charleston in a bright red sequined outfit.

He shot a questioning look at Clancy and noticed how pale she'd turned and realized it wasn't even his doing. "Would you like to tell me what's going on?"

She didn't get a chance to answer. Car doors slammed out front. A moment later, someone pounded on the front door of the house overhead. The screen door creaked open and a woman's high-pitched, irritated voice demanded, "Don't tell me Westfall is in trouble with the law, too."

"Cops." Jake swore and glanced around for a way out. He grabbed Clancy's arm and shoved her toward the bathroom. "I know how fond you are of climbing out windows.'' He popped open the bathroom window, pushing aside the garbage and weeds, and hoisted Clancy up and out. A few moments later, he was through the window himself and leading Clancy down the path behind the house.

''Is that your car?'' Jake asked, hardly waiting for her affirmative response before he asked for the keys, opened the passenger door and shoved her inside. He climbed into the driver's seat, quickly started the car and pulled away.

''Where's your—''

''Parked up the block,'' he said. ''Don't worry, I'll call the rental agency to pick it up.'' His second rental car on this case was the least of his worries.

A few safe blocks later, he threw on the brakes, startling her, startling himself, at the depth of his anger with her.

''Do you realize the position you've just put me in?'' he demanded, unable to keep from yelling. ''It's not bad enough that you jump bail and I cover for you. Now I'm withholding evidence from the police on top of it.''

''I didn't ask you to cover for me,'' she said. ''You might recall, I fired you.''

He narrowed his gaze at her. ''Thank you for reminding me of that. I'd almost forgotten.'' The fact that she hadn't asked him to protect her, that he'd done it all on his own, only made it worse. Far worse. And to add insult to injury, she didn't even appreciate his heroic gesture. He reminded himself she hadn't appreciated it last night, either. One of them was a damned slow learner.

''I just compromised myself and my career, put my P.I. license on the line for you,'' Jake told her, laying it on a little strong.

She didn't look impressed. ''Let's not forget why you're really here.'' She glared at him. ''To get the goods on me, isn't that what you said?''

''I don't remember you being like this,'' he snapped,

forgetting he didn't want to be reminded of their past. He didn't want anything to weaken his resolve, and thinking about the two of them back then definitely made him weak sometimes. "You've grown into an amazingly irritating woman."

"Thank you," Clancy shot back.

Irritating. Conniving. Underhanded. Devious. Sneaky. All traits of a criminal mind, he noted. A murderer's mind. Why else had she jumped bail to get this damned letter? Wasn't that what really had him upset? That the reason for that mountain of evidence against Clancy was because she'd killed Dex Westfall.

He jerked the letter from his pocket where he'd shoved it before the impromptu climb out the window. "Is this what you didn't want the police to find?"

She started to say something, but he cut her off with a slash of his hand through the air between them. He pulled the letter from the envelope and quickly read it. There was no doubt it would be damaging in court. Clancy had dumped Dex in the letter, warning him not to contact her, to leave her alone. It sounded angry. And Jake couldn't help but wonder what the guy had done to prompt this letter. Was Dex the reason she'd quit her job at the gallery and moved back to Hawk Island? Jake suspected he was.

But the letter wasn't damaging enough to jump bail, to chance getting caught by the police, to climb out two windows in one day and race halfway across the state with the cops—and him—close at her heels.

No, Jake thought, glancing over at Clancy, nor did she look much like a criminal. She looked ashen. Shaken. Scared. He remembered the collection on Dex's back closet wall. "I take it you didn't know he had all that stuff on you?"

She bit her lip and shook her head.

Jake considered how he would have reacted to finding a closet wall covered with his life, complete with candid photographs. He thought about the guy tacking all that stuff up; Dex Westfall had to have been one weird bastard.

"He was obviously obsessed with you." Jake could understand that. "What is it you think he wanted?"

She shook her head. "He planned our first meeting." Her voice broke. "From the very beginning, he planned it all. But why?" She started trembling as if the summer day had suddenly turned ice cold. He felt a chill himself. But fear was a much safer emotion than what he felt as he watched Clancy try desperately not to cry.

That was the thing about the Clancy he'd loved, he recalled. All tomboy tough on the outside but tender and soft on the inside. Before he could consider how stupid it was, he pulled her into his arms. She resisted at first, her body stiff, almost brittle. He pulled her to him, gently rubbing his hand up and down her back. Slowly he felt her soften in his embrace, felt her let the tears out, her face buried in his shoulder. Her back warmed under his hand. He could feel her heart pounding next to his. He concentrated on the rhythmic rubbing of her back, forcing his thoughts to focus on Dex Westfall, a man he was beginning to hate, instead of the soft, wonderfully feminine feel of the woman in his arms.

The crying stopped; so did the trembling. She pulled away. He sat for a moment, less surprised by the sharp jab of desire he felt after having her in his arms than his longing to kiss away her tears, to protect and shelter her.

He growled at himself in disgust. Lust he understood. Clancy was one hot-looking woman. But anything beyond that would mess up his head—and his whole reason for being here. Just as she'd pointed out. He wasn't going to let anything change that.

He started the car, wondering about Dex's relationship with Clancy. In his business, he'd heard a lot of hard-luck stories from women who'd been screwed over by men. This was one story he wasn't anxious to hear. He had a feeling he was going to want to have killed the guy himself. "Let's get some coffee."

"HOW DID YOU FIND ME?" Clancy asked, cradling the coffee mug in her hands. He'd picked a truck stop just outside of Bozeman. Clancy looked small and vulnerable in the pea green upholstered booth, but some of her color had come back and she seemed a little less shaky.

"I added up a few things," he said, eyeing her over his coffee. At first, he'd been too furious to figure out anything. The fact that she'd run made her look guilty as hell. Not that everything else hadn't already made her look that way. The fact that she'd outsmarted him didn't help matters in the least.

But then he'd calmed down enough to replay it all in his head. From when he'd first seen her, hurrying toward the boat, anxious to get somewhere. The small amount of clothing she'd packed. He'd gone through the suitcase she'd left in the back of his rental car, hoping to find an address or phone number inside. No such luck. Instead, there was only what looked like enough clothes for an overnight stay. She hadn't planned to go far or for very long. An extra pair of jeans, a sweatshirt, one change of underwear, and a toothbrush and toothpaste.

Nor had she planned to go anywhere fancy. He happily threw out the boyfriend theory. No sexy nightgown. He added the fact that she'd seemed terribly anxious all morning, worried. She'd needed to get somewhere and in a hurry.

In the end, he'd felt a little better. Because unless he missed his guess, he knew where'd he'd find her.

"I placed a couple of calls, found out you'd taken a plane to Bozeman," Jake said simply. "It was just a matter of getting Dex's home address."

She looked up, surprised. "How did you—"

He smiled. "You'd be surprised what a motivated P.I. can find out. And I was *very* motivated after your devious departure."

"So, was it imaginative enough for you?"

He saw the beginning of a smile on her lovely face. "You want me to admit that you outsmarted me, don't you." He wagged his head at her. "All right, Jones, you got me. You happy now?"

Clancy smiled, her face transformed, sunshine after a storm. "You *are* good at your job, Jake."

He returned her smile, recognizing a reluctant compliment when he heard one. "It's what I get paid for." He hadn't meant to say that.

Her smiled faded. "Yes, I haven't forgotten that," she said, looking into her cup. "Or what really motivates you."

They finished their coffee, then he drove them to the airport where the small plane he'd chartered was waiting. He stopped for a moment to speak to the pilot, then ushered Clancy onto the plane. "I couldn't help but overhear. I didn't know you had your pilot's license," Clancy said as they boarded the plane.

"There are a lot of things you don't know about me, Clancy."

She was starting to realize just how true that was, she thought, hugging herself as if the afternoon had gone cold. Jake's arms around her had left an imprint, one she didn't want to forget. How could he have such compassion for her when at the same time he held such hatred for her? He'd just possibly postponed her going back to jail, and at the same time, risked his license and a brush with the law. She wondered if he even understood himself.

Still, she had been glad to see him when he showed up at Dex's. She'd needed someone desperately, and there was Jake. Just like old times. She'd almost run into his arms. Almost forgotten the bad blood between them.

"Thank you for helping me," she said, meaning it. "Again."

He mumbled something under his breath, then motioned to the empty plane. "Sit anywhere you like."

She headed for a window seat near the wing. Jake disappeared into the cockpit to speak to the pilot. A few moments later the plane began to taxi out to the runway. She was fumbling with the seat belt when Jake took a seat beside her. "I guess all of this sleuthing has made me a little nervous," she said, all thumbs. He took the seat belt strap from her and with practiced smoothness locked it into place.

"Try not to worry," he said, buckling up his own.

She clenched her hands together, her nerves a steady vibration running through her body like the whine of the plane engine as it readied for takeoff. The engine revved and the plane roared down the runway.

She looked out the window at the endless blue sky instead of at Jake's bottomless gray eyes. Only a few clouds huddled over the Tobacco Root Mountains. The rich green valley floor raced to the foothills and the pines. Below her, rivers ran to meet at Three Forks, the Jefferson, Gallatin and Madison converging to form the Missouri.

"Tell me about Dex Westfall."

She snapped back around in surprise, having momentarily forgotten the trouble she was in, both with the law and Jake Hawkins. "To help you put me in prison?"

Through the window across the aisle, the sun glistened,

blinding white off the plane's wing as the pilot banked toward Flathead Lake and home.

"Come on, Clancy, you know I don't want to see you go to prison." He almost sounded like he meant it.

"Right. You'd much rather see me hang."

Jake pulled off his cap and raked his fingers through his hair. "Look, I'm still going to get the truth out of you, but in order to do that, I need to find something that proves your innocence. I don't see any way I can do that without your help." He slapped the cap back on his sandy blond head. "The way I see it, that puts us on the same team."

"Not hardly." She locked her gaze with his, wishing for the look she'd seen earlier, wishing for the old Jake, the one she'd once trusted with her life, the one who'd trusted her. "I'm fighting for my life, Jake. You're fighting for redemption. You want me to tell you that you were right, that I'm a liar, and that I betrayed you and your father." His jaw tensed, his gray eyes darkened. "You want me to tell you that you didn't make a mistake ten years ago. Well, I'm sorry, Jake. You're wasting your time if that's all you came to Montana for. I didn't lie. And you'll have to judge just how large a mistake you made."

Jake stared at her for a long moment, then, unsnapping his seat belt, he stalked off to the front of the plane without a word.

Clancy sat stunned, surprised by what she'd said to him, surprised even more by her raw anger. She felt the same way she had the last day of the trial when Jake had pushed himself to his feet, his gaze finding hers just before he walked out of the courtroom—and her life.

That day she'd expected him to come back. She'd been wrong. Today, she told herself she was smarter: she didn't expect him to come back for the rest of the flight. He'd said he wanted the truth, but look how he reacted to it. She

cursed him for the coward he was and had worked herself
up into a pretty good mad by the time he returned. She
probably would have shared a few more choice words with
him, but those words died on her lips when she saw what
he'd brought her.

"I had the pilot pick us up a little something," he said,
handing her a soda, a bologna sandwich and barbecue po-
tato chips. Her childhood favorites; he'd remembered. "I
figured you haven't had any more to eat today than I have."

All she could think to say was "Thanks." She hadn't
realized just how hungry she was until that moment. She
took a bite, aware of his gaze on her as he sat down with
an identical lunch, just as they had a zillion times as kids.

They ate in silence, Clancy intent on her sandwich right
down to the last bite. "I feel like a prisoner on death row
eating my last meal."

"Clancy."

The way Jake said her name made her catch her breath.
That single, simple word broke down the barriers she'd
built around her heart. She could forget the past. She could
forgive. If only he loved her again.

"Yes, Jake?" she asked softly, wiping the last of the
bread crumbs from her lips. When he didn't answer, she
glanced over at him, half hoping, half afraid.

She found his gaze soft, his eyes a rich light silver. She
wasn't sure, but his expression seemed as hopeful as she
knew hers must be. Did he want to believe in her? Was
there a chance he could forget vengeance and remember
what they'd shared before the trial and really help her?

In the length of a heartbeat, whatever she'd witnessed in
his expression died. It blew out like a fledgling fire in a
strong wind. "Jake." It came out a plea.

He shook his head, the moment lost, then looked past

her to the plane window. "I forgot how incredible the sunsets can be in this part of the country."

Clancy turned to the scene outside, disappointed that he'd decided not to say whatever had been on his mind just then. The sunset was indeed spectacular. She couldn't remember the last time she'd seen anything so beautiful. Slivers of sunlight pierced the clouds like daggers of gold. The growing darkness dipped the peaks in deep purple while the dying sun painted the sky with a pallet of pinks.

The sight stirred something in her, giving her a feeling of strength and renewed hope. The sandwich helped, too. So did the truce, however uneasy, between them.

"I don't know what I can tell you about Dex Westfall," Clancy said after a moment. She didn't kid herself that Jake was on her side. But she needed his help. It was that simple.

"Dex planned our first meeting," she said, feeling a shudder at the memory of the bulletin board on the back of the closet. She told Jake about the day in late February when Dex came into the gallery pretending to look for the artist of a sculpture in the window.

Jake raised a brow when she told him she'd accepted a dinner date that very evening with a man who was a total stranger. She couldn't tell Jake that she'd been starved for a man in her life after Jake left her, but had never found one who even made her heart pitter, let alone patter.

"Dex was charming. He said and did all the right things." He'd swept her off her feet. At first.

But he never made her ache inside for him. Never made her deliriously happy at just the sight of him. Never made her want more. Like Jake had. Nor had his kisses ever made her feel the way nineteen-year-old Jake Hawkins's had. Nor had the kisses of any other man she'd dated.

"We dated for a few months," she said. "I never knew that much about him. He didn't like to talk about his past.

All he told me was that he was raised in eastern Montana, on a farm. His parents were very poor, and once he got away from there, he'd never gone back.''

"Why do you think he wanted to meet you?"

Dex had led her to believe he was as lonesome as she was. "He said he'd been looking for me all his life. At least that part was true." She grimaced at how gullible she'd been. "He told me he loved me."

"No kiddin'?"

She narrowed her gaze at Jake. "That surprises you?"

"On the contrary, in case you haven't looked in a mirror lately, you're not a bad-looking woman."

His compliment, although not eloquent by any means, warmed her nonetheless.

"What about you? Were you in love with him?" He balled up his sandwich wrapper and didn't look at her.

Did it bother Jake that she might have loved another man? Well, he needn't worry; there'd only been one love in her life, was still only one.

"I was flattered by the attention," she admitted honestly. "At first." At what point had the attention become too much?

"What made you finally write him off?" Jake asked.

She bit her lip. She'd literally written him off, and Jake had the incriminating letter in his pocket to prove it, not that the sheriff needed more evidence to convict her. "I just didn't want to see him anymore."

"So you were running from Dex when you went back to the island to live?" Jake asked.

She knew it had been more than that. Dex had frightened her in a way she couldn't even explain. But she'd also wanted to go home. She'd wanted to go back to a time when she'd felt safe. And loved. And that time had been on Hawk Island. "It felt like it was time to go home," she said.

Jake said nothing.

She'd had an uneasy feeling about Dex that she hadn't been able to throw. Now she realized she'd been right not to trust him. She felt almost a sense of relief to have her misgivings about Dex confirmed. Unfortunately, all that insight came too late. Dex was dead. And she'd be going to trial soon for his murder.

"Do you think he thought you had money?" Jake asked.

She'd considered that. "What money? I'm a struggling artist."

"Hardly," Jake said. "I've seen your work in galleries in Texas."

"I do all right, but not well enough for a man to want me for my money. And my parents lost everything after…what happened."

Jake winced. "And they blamed my father, I'm sure."

"No," she said with conviction. "They were horribly saddened by what happened to Warren." She looked over at him. "You lost your father to prison, but you can still see him. I lost both of my parents."

Jake looked away.

"The only thing I own is the lodge at the lake, thanks to Aunt Kiki," she said, then had a thought. "Unless he figured he could get his hands on Aunt Kiki's money."

Jake shook his head, seemingly happier that the conversation had returned to the case. "Kiki would have been a long shot. You're not her only heir."

She nodded, biting at her lip. "I still don't know what he wanted or why he came to Hawk Island." She looked out the window. The dying sun rimmed the mountains with gold. A deep purple filled the valleys and spilled over into the foothills. "That's why I went to Bozeman, to try and find out. Not to get that letter."

"Tell me about the night Dex showed up at the island."

She hugged herself against the memories of that night and related to Jake how Dex had called, insistent that he had to see her. She'd agreed to meet him at the café just to get it over with. Jake frowned when she told him how strangely Dex had been acting, talking about his mother, playing with that string of beads. Her legacy. "He said I was part of that legacy."

Jake's frown deepened.

She brushed her hair back from her face and took a calming breath. "I thought maybe he'd been drinking. He wasn't making any sense. Then he glanced past me into the darkness and saw something that…scared him."

"Something or *someone?*" Jake asked.

"I don't know, I turned, but whatever it was—if there was anything at all—was gone. Suddenly he became very agitated and said he had to go. He wasn't leaving the island until he got what he deserved."

"And maybe he got it," Jake said, his gaze intent on her face.

"I didn't kill him." She glanced away. At least she didn't believe in her heart that she'd killed him. "Why would I kill him in my sleep? What possible reason could I have had?"

Jake could think of a half-dozen reasons a woman might kill a man. And he figured a woman could think of at least six more without even being asleep. A woman who thought she could get away with murder because of her sleepwalking history could have any reason she wanted for killing Dex Westfall.

Well, Clancy might be able to dupe Tadd Farnsworth, who couldn't see beyond her shapely body and her aunt's money. But Jake Hawkins wasn't that easily fooled. He'd known Clancy. Maybe not as well as Dex had— Not wanting to continue with that line of thinking, he pulled a magazine out of the back of the seat in front of him and pretended interest in it he didn't feel.

After a few moments he looked over and realized the futility of his charade. Clancy was sound asleep. He stared at her beautiful face, peaceful in sleep, and wondered. Did she really sleepwalk? Did she kill Dex? Was it in her sleep?

He reached across the aisle for the manila envelope he'd tossed there earlier. He'd placed a call to the librarian while he was waiting to charter a plane. The envelope had arrived by courier shortly before his takeoff from the Kalispell airport. It contained photocopies of stories about sleepwalker murder cases. He'd been shocked by what he read on his plane ride to Bozeman.

Jake read case after case of what was known as homicidal somnambulism. One story, from medieval times, was about a woodcutter who thought he saw an intruder at the foot of his bed and, picking up an ax, killed his wife, who was asleep beside him.

The whole concept was too alien for Jake. Sleep-related violence. Out of the millions of Americans who had sleep disorders, only a small percentage became violent, picking up axes, guns or sculptures to kill while sound asleep.

He glanced over at Clancy, who was still sleeping peacefully, and tried to picture her. Her eyes would be open, her face bland. She'd be unresponsive to everything and everyone around her. In a hypnotic trance, functionally blind, the articles had said. She would pick up the sculpture, go up the stairs to the garret. Dex Westfall would be waiting for her up there. Who knew what for. And she would bludgeon him to death.

Her brain would be awake enough to allow her to do all

of this while the rest of her mind would remain unconscious to everything that was happening. She would wake to find herself standing over Dex's body and be horrified at what she'd done.

Jake shook his head. How could Clancy have stayed asleep through such a violent act and then have total amnesia from the time of falling asleep until waking? It was much easier to imagine her killing her boyfriend in cold blood.

They were approaching the Kalispell airport when Clancy stirred and looked up at him wide-eyed. "I fell asleep?" She sounded horrified by the idea. "I didn't—"

"Sleepwalk?" he asked, tucking the manila envelope away. She really didn't think he bought this, did she? "No, you didn't leave your seat."

He had his own theory on Dex Westfall's murder. One he didn't like to admit, even to himself. "Dex was seeing other women, wasn't he?"

She seemed startled, and he told himself he should have felt like a louse, catching her off guard, half asleep. He didn't.

"Yes," she said quietly.

"A jury might read that as possible motive. The woman scorned. You know?"

Clancy shook her head. "It wasn't like that."

Right. "When did you find out about the other women?" he asked, already knowing the answer and realizing how damaging it was going to be in court.

"Right before I left Bozeman, I found a note from some woman. I don't doubt there were others. The man he house-sat for mentioned Dex's other girlfriends. But I just used that as an excuse to break off the relationship. I'd been trying to break up with him for several weeks."

Jake scoured a hand over his face. He needed a long, hot

shower, a shave and a few hours of uninterrupted sleep in a real bed. "A note?"

"It was from some woman Dex had met in a bar."

"Some woman he'd—" He didn't have to finish; she anticipated this one.

"Some woman he'd been…intimate with," she admitted.

Jake groaned to himself. "Where is the note now?"

She shook her head.

The note would turn up, providing the prosecution with possible motive. Couple that with the letter in his pocket. "You wrote him a letter and broke it off right after that," Jake said, not even needing confirmation.

"Yes. Dex just wouldn't take no for an answer, so I thought if I wrote it down— Now I know he was after something else."

"Tell me about Friday night, the night you found Dex in the garret."

She shifted in her seat and looked out the window again. "I left him at the café and went home a little after ten," she said mechanically. Obviously she'd already recounted this story numerous times to the cops.

"Did you go by boat?" he asked.

"Yes." She seemed to be waiting for another question, but when none came, she continued. "I couldn't sleep. I went to my studio and worked for a while."

"Were you more angry or afraid?" Jake asked.

"What?" She sounded surprised by his question and not the least happy that he'd interrupted her again. She obviously wanted this over with as quickly as possible. "Why would you ask that?"

"I remember the year you started sculpting," he said, wishing he couldn't remember. "You used to work when you were upset."

"Both angry and afraid. I remember locking the doors. I never lock the doors at the lake."

"Then, you thought he might come over?"

"I guess I was worried that he might," she admitted.

"How do you think he got in? Did he have a key?" He felt her gaze burn his skin. "Did he come by boat or walk?"

"I didn't give him a key, if that's what you're asking." Her voice broke. "I don't know how he got there, what he was doing there, or how he got in. I don't know anything. I went to bed around midnight, exhausted. The next thing I remember is waking up to find Dex dead." She shuddered and hugged herself against the memory.

Classic homicidal somnambulism. No memory. Confusion. Horror at having done it. Right. "The murder weapon was in your hand. How do you think it got there?"

She didn't answer. Jake glanced over at her. He knew that look. He remembered it only too well as a kid. He'd stepped over the line.

"You don't believe me," she said. "You don't believe anything I tell you."

He could hear the anger in her voice. And the hurt. He just didn't expect the hurt to affect him the way it did. Damn her. He couldn't afford these feelings.

"You think I killed him?" Her face was flushed, but he had no idea whether it was from anger or something else. Like guilt.

"*You* aren't even sure you didn't kill him," he pointed out carefully. Then he went a step further, telling himself he had no choice. "It could have been a crime of passion."

"Passion?" she cried.

Jake wanted to back off. But he had to get to Clancy somehow, he had to get at the truth. "Don't tell me it didn't hurt you. The guy screwed around on you. You thought he was the man of your dreams. You were in love with him. He turned out to be a jerk. A jerk who wouldn't leave you alone.''

Her eyes flashed. ''You're wrong.'' She glanced away. ''I wasn't in love with him. I just wanted him to leave me alone.'' She raised her gaze to Jake's. He could feel the heat of it. ''How can you possibly hope to find something that proves my innocence when you believe I'm a murderer?''

Good question. And one Jake had worried about himself. He studied her for a moment. ''I don't know what to believe,'' he said honestly. ''All I know for sure is that Dex Westfall is dead and the cops think—maybe with good reason—that you did it.'' He flicked the torn sleeve of her navy blouse. ''And all you've done is dupe me. For all I know I'll turn my back again and you'll be gone, maybe for good this time.''

''You're wrong, Hawkins. And I'm going to prove it, with or without your help.''

Jake looked over at her, admiring her determination if nothing else. He didn't even want to think about what Clancy had told him. Or the things she'd told him that she hadn't meant to. Dex Westfall had hurt her. He'd had other women. He'd played her for a fool from day one. And he wouldn't leave her alone. He'd even followed her to the island. And what had Clancy done about it?

Did he really believe she could kill someone? Not the girl he'd known. But what did he know about this woman? Nothing, he told himself. And he'd been in the P.I. business long enough to know that anyone could kill—given the right circumstances. And the fact that he knew Clancy had already lied at least once, didn't help her defense.

As the plane made its descent into Kalispell, Jake placed his hand over Clancy's. He came up with several good reasons for doing it. None of them had anything to do with any feelings he might have once had for her.

The night air smelled of Montana summer. It was warm with a gentle breeze that stirred Clancy's blond hair as they walked to the Mustang.

"Tell me something, Hawkins," Clancy said as he opened the passenger-side door for her. "Has there ever been a case you couldn't solve?"

"No. And this one won't be my first."

He watched her climb into the car and started to close the door, but stopped as something caught his eye. "What did you do to your ankle?"

Chapter Seven

Clancy stared down at the scrape on her right ankle. Fear shot through her. "I don't know."

Jake touched his fingers to the discolored skin, tenderly, caressingly. She flinched.

"Does it hurt?" he asked, jerking back his fingers, obviously surprised by her response.

She shook her head, unable to speak. Hurt had nothing to do with her reaction to his touch. The pain of his fingers on her skin was a dull ache—far from her ankle.

"How did you get that?" he asked, frowning as he inspected the injury.

She flinched again, this time from a flash of memory. A hand coming out of the water. Grabbing her ankle. Pulling her—

"Last night," she whispered, staring out into the darkness. "On the dock when I was walking in my sleep—" She closed her eyes, trying to remember the moment when she'd awakened. It always felt like coming out of a fog with nothing ever very clear. Silver. A flicker of something silver coming out of the water. Then the hand and a sharp pain as the fingers reached out of the water and clamped around her ankle. Her eyes flew open. "He was wearing something silver on his wrist. It must have been a watch and it scraped my ankle.''

Jake stared at her. ''*Who* was wearing a watch?''

''The man who tried to drown me last night,'' she said, relieved she wasn't losing her mind. ''When he grabbed my leg and pulled me into the water, his watchband must have skinned my ankle.'' She shivered, her relief short-lived. If it hadn't been a dream, if she wasn't crazy, then the scrape and the memory added up to something far worse. ''Oh, Jake, I was right. Someone really *did* try to kill me.''

Jake stared at Clancy, unsure how to respond. He realized she believed what she was saying, but the evidence was against it. If there had been someone else there last night, where had he gone? Wasn't it more likely that she'd scraped her ankle when she fell from the dock into the water? And the memory of the hand and the watch? Part of a dream. She'd said she was walking in her sleep. If a person could believe that. Jake operated on solid evidence, not even putting much stock in his hunches, no matter how right they ended up being, until he had tangible proof to go with them.

''You think I'm making this all up?'' Clancy snapped. ''Then, how do you explain the scrape?''

He knew sharing his explanation with her right now would do him more harm than good. ''I can't.'' He barely got out of the way before she slammed him with the car door. He walked around to the driver's side and climbed in, wishing he could think of something to say that would cool her ire. Instead, he feared that anything he said right now would be wrong. So he kept silent, a male trait that he knew often only made her madder. But he'd risk it, he decided. It seemed the safest thing to do.

They drove with the windows down out past the lights

of the city, past Christmas tree farms and tiny resorts until they were running along the shoreline of Flathead Lake.

Through the pines, Jake caught glimpses of the lake. It never failed to move him. The largest natural freshwater lake west of the Mississippi. The most beautiful. Incredibly clear by day. But by night, there was something haunting about it. Especially when the lights of the tiny communities nestled around it shimmered at its shoreline as they did now.

Jake felt a dangerous pull deep within him. A pull for this place. And the people in it. One in particular.

Out of the corner of his eye, he could see that Clancy still had a good mad going. She wouldn't even look in his direction. That was probably just as well, he thought, dragging himself back from places he couldn't afford to go.

The moment he pulled into the marina parking lot, Clancy had her door open and was halfway out of the car. "You wouldn't believe me even if you caught someone with a knife to my throat," she said, slamming the door behind her.

She was gone before he could get in a word. "Women." Jake grabbed her overnight bag out of the back and followed her down to the docks where they'd tied her boat that morning. It seemed like days ago now.

Music and the smell of fried foods filled the night air. A band at Charley's Saloon a few doors down cranked out country, while french fries sizzled in hot grease at the Burger Boat across the street. It was June, and the small resort community bustled with tourists and locals. Kids cruised the drag, honking, squealing tires, revving engines, yelling at friends. Summer on the lake. Jake felt a stab of envy, remembering when he and Clancy were kids.

Clancy was already in the boat, behind the wheel, waiting. Waiting, he realized, because he'd taken the key that morning. He grimaced. If he didn't have the key in his pocket, she'd have left him in a heartbeat.

He stopped on the dock for a moment, trying to figure out what he was going to say to her. In the distance he could make out the lights at Hawk Island Resort. They flickered on the water, beckoning him, drawing him back to the island just as Clancy had. He untied the boat and hopped in.

"It isn't that I think you're making anything up," he said, sliding into the seat next to hers. Voices carried across the water, followed by laughter. "I believe you *believe* that's what happened."

"So you think I'm...what? Crazy?" She reached impatiently for the key, obviously annoyed that he'd taken it to begin with.

"I've never walked in my sleep, but I've had some doozy dreams where I couldn't tell reality from dreamland," he said, dropping the boat key into her hand. "They scared the hell out of me, they were so real."

Her fingers closed around the key. "But this *is* real, Jake. Someone is...after me." Her gaze shifted to the darkness beyond the shoreline. "This morning I found a place in the lilac bushes next to my kitchen window where someone had stood looking in. Someone's stalking me, just like Dex was. And I have no idea why." She flicked a look back at him. "You *do* think I'm crazy."

"No." That was the last thing he thought. "I think you're scared. And for a good reason." Someone *was* after her. Jake Hawkins. But he'd check under the lilacs. He was sure it had just been some kind of animal. "You're facing a murder rap. Anyone in your situation would be running a little scared."

Tears of frustration stung her eyes as she glared over at him, the skepticism in his tone still ringing in her ears.

"You think that's all this is? I'm just running a little scared? There's a mountain of evidence that says I killed Dex Westfall. I can't sleep at night because my dreams force me to wander to places I don't want to go. Now someone is trying to kill me." She fumbled the key into the boat's ignition, her fingers trembling with anger, frustration, fear. "And you say you can understand why I'm running a *little* scared? Great, Jake. At least on top of all that you're not here to help send me to prison."

She turned the key, the motor rumbled to life, and she gave the boat full throttle, roaring out of the marina, ignoring the no-wake buoys.

They raced across the smooth, dark surface of the lake. The night air felt cool and sweet, the speed of the boat pleasurable. Jake sat silent, his face dark with a scowl that she knew meant she'd hit a nerve. It gave her some satisfaction. But she knew she'd be a fool to rely on Jake Hawkins for anything but more heartache.

She felt her anger slipping away as the early-summer night soothed her senses, the lake calming her as it always had. But nothing could chase away the fear at the edge of the darkness. Someone out there wanted her dead.

Clancy pointed the boat toward Hawk Island. The wind from the speed whipped her hair. She let it blow away her thoughts, let the steady throb of the motor lull her, promising her she had nothing to fear on such a beautiful summer night, on an island that was her home.

But as they rounded the end of the island, Clancy saw a light flickering in her lodge and knew differently. "Look!" she cried.

"What?" Jake asked, suddenly alert.

"A light in the garret. Didn't you see it?"

It was obvious he hadn't, but still, as she pulled back on the throttle, he reached over and shut off the running lights.

"Are you sure it wasn't just a reflection?" he asked.

She ground her teeth together. "It was a flashlight. Someone's in the garret."

"Don't go to the dock," Jake said. "Pull into the beach."

She did as he said, silenced by fear as she steered the boat to the nearest stretch of shoreline and cut the motor. She had seen a light. She wasn't starting to imagine things as Jake kept insinuating.

As they reached land, Jake jumped out and pulled the boat up on shore. Clouds hid the moon, pitching the narrow stretch of beach into darkness. Jake tied the boat to one of the pines that grew almost to the water's edge.

"I'm not leaving you here alone," Jake whispered as he gave her a hand out of the boat. "Stay behind me, and if anything happens, get to cover."

Clancy followed Jake along the beach, hugging the rocky cliffs and the pines, her anger at him dissipating quickly. What would she have done if she'd come home alone? She'd sworn she wasn't going to rely on Jake, but right now she'd make an exception.

Water lapped at the shore as they crossed behind Jake's lodge. The light in the garret room had flickered like a firefly caught in a jar. What was someone doing in that room, the room where Dex had died? She felt a chill, although the summer night was exceptionally warm.

They were almost to her lodge when an owl let out a hoot. Clancy jumped, grabbing Jake's arm. He patiently unhooked her clawlike grip and motioned for her to stay low behind him.

They crept the last few yards in silence. Darkness draped the back of the lodge. Clancy held her breath as they climbed the steps and crossed the old wooden porch. The boards groaned under their weight.

"Is that your bike?" Jake whispered, motioning to the black mountain bike by the back door.

She nodded.

Jake tried the door. Locked. Clancy shook her head; she hadn't locked it. She could remember locking it only once in her life. And that night it hadn't kept Dex out, had it?

As she stood on tiptoe to reach above the door for the key, Jake groaned next to her. "Great place for a key. No one would ever look *there*."

Feeling Jake's reproachful gaze on her, she quietly slipped it into his waiting fingers and pressed against his back as he inserted the key in the lock. If he thought for a moment she was going to let him out of her sight, he was sadly mistaken. As she clung to him, she felt something hard. A gun.

The door creaked open. Jake drew the gun. Her heart dropped to her knees as she realized the danger she was putting him in.

"No," she whispered. He stopped and she collided with his back.

"What?"

"I don't want you getting killed because of me."

"How thoughtful of you. Now, shut up."

He turned and started across the kitchen floor, with her right behind him. Something thudded, and Clancy let out a squeal before she realized the sound had just been Jake crashing into her microwave cart.

"Quiet!"

"Jake," she pleaded, suddenly more afraid for him than herself.

"Stay right behind me," he commanded as he headed up the stairs. "And be quiet."

Clancy held her breath, afraid to breathe, as they started up the stairs. She followed, her heart in her throat, her hand gripping a handful of Jake's shirt. They were almost to the top when she looked back. She let go of Jake. The front door stood partway open. Starlight slipped through the crack and splattered onto the living-room floor. Clancy reached for Jake but he was several steps ahead of her. A shadow moved into the light.

"Jake." It came out little more than a whisper.

The shadow turned into a dark figure in a hooded sweatshirt. It looked up at her. A startled, pained cry escaped her lips. She caught only a glimpse of the face beneath the hood. But it was enough. Clancy screamed.

The figure disappeared out the open door and into the darkness as quickly as it had appeared.

Clancy dropped to the stair, her gaze locked on the wedge of light still spilling in from the night.

"Clancy!" Jake cried, charging down the stairs to her. "What is it?"

She heard him groping for the light switch but couldn't answer him. Instead, she stared after the intruder, too stunned to speak.

The living room was suddenly flooded with light.

"Are you all right?" Jake demanded, pulling her to her feet on the stairs. She fell into his arms. He held her tightly. "What happened?"

She stared over Jake's shoulder, her gaze fixed on the open doorway and the darkness beyond it. "I saw him."

"Who, Clancy?" Jake asked, pulling back to search her face.

She looked up. "Didn't you see him?" she asked, knowing he couldn't have. Pleading with him to say he had.

"Who did you see, Clancy?"

Her mouth opened but no words came out. She closed her eyes, willing away the image of the man in the dark hooded sweatshirt. "It was Dex Westfall. He's alive!"

Chapter Eight

Jake grabbed Clancy's shoulders and pulled her around to face him. "You saw Dex Westfall?" he demanded. He watched doubt flicker across her face. Worry settled in his stomach like a chunk of granite.

She tried to avoid his gaze. "I only got a glimpse so I can't be completely sure—"

"Clancy?" Jake asked, pleading.

She swallowed. Tears brimmed in her eyes. "It was Dex. I swear. It was Dex."

His grip tightened. "The *late* Dex Westfall?" He felt her flinch and let go of her, realizing he was hurting her. He led her down the stairs. The front door stood open.

"I know it sounds…crazy." She seemed to hesitate. "How could I have seen him when he's dead? I didn't get a really good look at him. He was wearing a dark gray hood that hid part of his face, but—" Her gaze flipped up to his, her eyes full of pleading. "It was him, Jake."

That rock of worry in his belly turned into a fifty-pound boulder. He went out on the deck and looked down the beach. Empty. He came back in and had barely closed the door when the breeze blew it open again, making them both jump. This time Jake closed the door and locked it.

"I know what you're thinking," she said, her voice barely a whisper.

Jake doubted she had any idea what he was thinking. He wasn't even sure himself.

"But I know what I saw," she said, the look in her eyes scaring the devil out of him. "It was Dex Westfall."

The cynical private eye side of him argued that Dex Westfall was dead; Clancy couldn't have seen him. She'd probably imagined it, or dreamed it, or she'd gone off the deep end.

But the man who'd fallen for her years ago made a good case that Clancy Jones had been one of the most rational, sensible and credible people he'd ever known. She might be a murderer, but he had his doubts that she was crazy.

"I'm telling you, Dex is alive," she cried. "Don't you see what this means? I didn't kill him."

Jake didn't want to burst her bubble, but it was time for a reality check. "If Dex isn't dead, then whose body did the sheriff find upstairs?"

Clancy blinked. Her face fell. She turned away from him to stare out the window. "I don't know. And no matter whose body it is, the sheriff thinks I killed him, right?"

That about sized it up. Jake knew how desperately Clancy wanted to believe she hadn't killed anyone. But the bottom line was someone had died in the garret upstairs and Clancy had had the murder weapon in her hand.

"If Dex is dead…" Her eyes turned dark with pain, her features drawn with fatigue. "Then his ghost has come back from the grave for me."

Jake glanced toward the darkness outside, his mind flashing on an image that freeze-dried his blood. The face of the woman his father had gone to prison for murdering. What if Lola Strickland's pretty face suddenly appeared outside his window one night? He shuddered at the thought. And reminded himself that no one came back from the grave. Not Lola. Not Dex.

He turned to lean with his back against the window, the last of the adrenaline ebbing. His body felt tired, his mind exhausted, as he settled his gaze on Clancy. Had someone been in the lodge tonight or had Clancy just imagined it? Like the person who'd tried to drown her last night?

"You first saw the light in the garret?" Jake asked after a moment. All he wanted to do was sit down, close his eyes, catch a few winks. He was too tired to think, too tired to try to figure out anything tonight. With effort, however, he pushed himself off the wall. "I'm going upstairs to take a look around. Why don't you—"

"I'm coming with you."

He looked at her, surprised she would willingly go back to the scene of the crime. "Look, I'm not wild about going up there. If I were in your shoes—"

"I'm coming with you," she repeated.

He nodded, recognizing that old familiar glint of persistence shining like a searchlight in her eyes and the stubborn way she stood when she wasn't about to budge an inch.

"There's nothing up there but old furniture," Clancy said as he led the way up the stairs to the third floor.

Old furniture. And bad memories.

The tiny room was indeed filled with furniture, Jake saw as he turned on the light and stepped through the open doorway. The single overhead light did little to illuminate the room. Shadows pooled everywhere. With the furniture covered in white sheets, the room had a ghostlike quality. Or maybe it was just the fact that Clancy believed Dex Westfall had come back from the dead that made it seem that way. It was enough to spook even nonbelievers, Jake thought.

The only bare piece of furniture was a couch in the corner

under the eaves. The sheriff's department had obviously stripped it, taking the blood-stained sheet and cushion as evidence, but left behind the couch.

"I'm not sure this is a good idea," Jake said, turning to shield Clancy from the view.

"I have to do this," she said, her tone brooking no argument. "Besides, I'm the only one who knows if something is out of place up here."

He nodded and stepped out of her way. As he watched her walk into the room he thought to himself: here is a woman to be reckoned with.

With all the courage she had, Clancy looked toward the couch where she'd found the body. Her fingers flew to her lips to stifle the cry that rose from deep within her. Memories of that night flashed before her, flickering images of horror. She staggered. Jake reached for her.

She motioned him away. "I'm fine," she said, knowing that if he touched her now it would be her undoing. She hugged herself to still the trembling, her gaze scanning the room, trying to remember every detail.

Before the night of the murder, she couldn't remember the last time she was in this room. How could she know if something was missing? On top of that, Kiki had hired a cleaning crew after the sheriff's department finished taking prints and collecting evidence.

Clancy stared at the garret. Bits and pieces of memory floated back from Friday night.

Dex— Her gaze leaped back to the couch. It had been Dex, hadn't it? Something had made her think it was, but what? The bright red cowboy boots. The moment she saw them she'd known it was Dex because of those stupid boots he loved. But had she really looked that closely at his face? All that blood— She shook her head, frustrated at her inability to remember any more.

As she walked around the room, she quickly realized it was impossible to tell if an intruder had been here. But how desperately she would have liked to prove he had.

She pushed open the balcony doors and stepped out, immediately assaulted by a memory. She gripped the railing. "Oh."

"What?" Jake asked, joining her.

She shuddered as she stared out at the lake. "Friday night," she said as it came back to her. "I remember waking up on this balcony." She glanced down; her head spun just looking at the dizzying drop to the rocky beach below her. "What was I doing out here?"

Jake followed her gaze from the rocky beach below to the lake, sprawled to the horizon, a dark, silent pool, its slick, silken surface a reflection of the star-splattered sky overhead. He had no idea what Clancy had been doing out here. No idea what she had been doing in the tiny room beyond them just moments before Dex Westfall died. God, how he wished he did.

"I remember standing here not knowing where I was at first," she said. "The view was all wrong."

"What do you mean 'all wrong'?"

"I thought I was on my bedroom balcony." But it was next to her studio and at the east end of the lodge. She couldn't see this bay from it.

Turning slowly, she moved back through the open doorway as if she were still sleepwalking. "At first all I saw was the furniture. The white sheets were blowing in the breeze from the open doors and I realized I was in the garret."

Jake followed her, watching her face as she relived the night of the murder. She stopped, her gaze going to the couch. "Then I saw him in the corner." She looked down at her left hand. "I guess that's when I realized I had the sculpture in my hand. I dropped it on the floor. My feet—"

"What was wrong with your feet?" Jake asked.

"I must have been to the beach, because the tops of my bare feet still had sand on them." All of the shore around Flathead Lake consisted of small flat rocks—no sand. But Hawk Island had sandy beaches.

"What the hell were you doing on the beach at two-thirty in the morning?" he demanded, then shook his head. "I forgot. Sleepwalking."

If she heard the doubt in his tone, she didn't respond to it. "Dex's boots had sand on them, too."

"Maybe he followed you up here." An unpleasant thought skittered past. "Or maybe you'd been on the beach together."

She stared at the stained arm of the couch as if there were things there she could see that he couldn't. From the horrified expression on her face, he was damned glad he couldn't see them.

"Where had I been that night?" Clancy asked, shifting her gaze to Jake. "I hadn't sleepwalked in years."

Not since the night of the resort fire, Jake thought bitterly. The night Clancy saw his father kill Lola Strickland. Or at least that's what Clancy would have him believe.

"Why would I suddenly start sleepwalking again after so many years?"

Jake wished he knew. He wished he could believe she sleepwalked at all. "What's the last thing you remember before you fell asleep?"

"I had been working late in my studio. I have, or I guess, that's *had* now, a show planned in August at a gallery in Bigfork. I was finishing up one of the pieces for the exhibit. As I headed up to bed, I couldn't help thinking about Dex, worrying about why he'd shown up here." She let out a long sigh. "That's the last I remember."

"Did Dex wear underwear?" Jake asked.

"What?"

"He wasn't wearing underwear the night he was murdered. Is that usual?"

"I would have no idea," Clancy said, turning away. "I didn't— I'm sure he wore underwear, but the subject never came up."

Jake smiled to himself, more pleased to hear that she had no idea than he should have been. "Unless I miss my guess, someone interrupted Dex that night, either from his beauty sleep or some other unclothed activity. He pulled on his jeans in a hurry and headed for your place."

"Who? Why?" Clancy asked.

"That's what we have to find out."

Framed in the balcony doorway, her hair shone golden, her face a pale porcelain. It surprised him just how beautiful she looked standing there. How small and fragile. And so terribly defenseless. Protecting her seemed as natural as breathing and had ever since they were kids. He felt a pull so strong, the force threatened to draw him to her against his will.

"I think we'd better get some rest," Jake said, stepping past her to close the balcony doors. He could smell her scent as he passed. It made him weak. He took a deep breath of the night air and closed the doors. When he turned, he found Clancy standing at the top of the landing, staring down the stairs.

"I'll stay here in the lodge with you tonight," he said, surprising himself even more than her. "If that's all right with you," he added. "I need a good night's sleep, and that boat of yours isn't all that comfortable."

"You think I'm going to run off, Hawkins?" she asked,

too tired to let his lack of trust do more than give her heart a twinge. The memory of Jake lying in the bottom of her boat, however, did offset the twinge some.

"I thought you could use some company," he said softly.

She studied his handsome features, trying to read motive in those bottomless gray eyes. The thought of staying alone tonight frightened her more than she wanted to admit. But was he suggesting staying here to watch over her? Or to keep her from jumping bail again? Did it even matter?

"I thought you didn't believe in ghosts," she said, reading nothing but concern in his eyes.

"I don't," he said. "Nor do I believe in taking chances until we know just what we're up against."

We're up against? Just hours ago, she'd warned herself not to rely on Jake Hawkins. But right now his words sounded better than a hot shower. After everything they'd been through today, couldn't she let herself rely on him for just one night? This whole day had made her realize what an incredibly strong, caring man Jake Hawkins was, just like the boy he'd been that she'd always loved so much. Only, she wasn't a girl anymore and he wasn't a boy. "You can take the spare bedroom. The sheets are in the hall closet. You know where that is."

He nodded. "Same place as my lodge."

He followed her down the stairs to the kitchen and, opening the refrigerator, pulled out two cold beers. He twisted the cap off one and handed it to her.

She took a sip, surprised at how good it tasted. "You don't believe Dex is alive and that he might be the one trying to kill me?"

His gaze, as warm and gentle as the summer night outside, brushed over her face. The kindness in his eyes made her want to cry. Slowly he twisted off the cap on his own beer. "The cops would know if it wasn't Dex's body," he said reasonably.

"Yeah, I guess so." She took a long draw on the beer. It tasted good. She leaned against the wall and closed her eyes. The beer made her drowsy.

"Why don't you go take a long, hot shower," Jake suggested. "I'll make sure everything's locked up for the night. Leave your door open."

"Thanks." She opened her eyes. His unruly sandy blond hair hung down on his forehead; the blond stubble at his jaw gave him a rugged, almost dangerous look that she found disarming. And appealing. Suddenly there seemed a million things she wanted to say to him, but she couldn't seem to sort them out. Nor did she trust her emotions. Not tonight. Maybe she'd tell him how much she appreciated him being here. Tomorrow. When she wasn't feeling so vulnerable. Or so tired. "Good night." She set her bottle on the table and turned to head for the stairs.

As she passed the telephone she noticed that the message light on the answering machine was flashing.

Clancy stepped over to it, hit rewind, then play. "Clancy?" Tadd Farnsworth's voice filled the room. "I didn't want to leave this on your machine, but I haven't been able to reach you and I wanted to be the one to tell you. The sheriff's having trouble getting a positive ID on the body you found in your garret. All he knows for sure is that the guy's name wasn't Dex Westfall. Dex Westfall never existed. At least not until five months ago."

Chapter Nine

The color drained from Clancy's face. Jake watched her strength and sanity empty with it. He knew only too well what it was like having his world crumble under him, no longer sure what to believe, who to believe. Wasn't this what he'd wanted for Clancy? In that dark, malevolent part of his heart, hadn't he longed for her to suffer the way he had? And now she knew what it was like to have her life destroyed overnight. So why did he feel like dirt?

He watched Clancy try to dial Tadd's number. On her second attempt, Jake took the phone from her trembling hand and hung it up.

"I don't understand," she said, her voice breaking.

Jake understood. It was just as he'd suspected. The brand new clothes. The leased car. The new-subdivision feel. No roots. No Dex Westfall.

He also knew that if the sheriff didn't get a positive ID in the first twenty-four hours, it could take a while to put a name to their John Doe—if they ever did. Clancy might never know who died in her garret. Nor why the man had stalked her.

"I have to call Tadd," she said.

Jake shook his head. "You have to take a hot shower. I'll call Tadd. I'll come up when I'm through."

Clancy nodded, looking shell-shocked and terribly vulnerable. She stumbled toward him.

He felt a rush of tenderness for her. He pulled her into his arms, aware of her soft fullness, her wonderful warmth, her need so like his own. She raised her gaze to his, her eyes as dark as her lashes. The look in those eyes—

Without thinking, he dropped his mouth to hers, hungry to taste her, hungry to feel her body molded to his. He knew her kiss would taste of sunshine and summer. Her arms would offer comfort and sanctuary. That's what he needed tonight. That's all he needed.

But when his lips met hers, there was nothing safe or comforting about it. The kiss fired his blood, sending desire streaking through his veins at the speed of a grass fire. He became a part of the blaze, losing himself in the heat and the hurry. Losing himself in her. The realization burned to the bottom of his black heart.

With a silent curse, he pushed her away. "Go take your shower. I'll be up in a moment, to tell you what Tadd says."

She stood just looking at him. He felt like the bastard he was. But he'd better get used to it. He would see a lot more hurt in those brown eyes before he was through with her. When she turned and ran up the stairs, he had to kick down the urge to go after her. He slammed his fist against the wall and cursed Clancy for the love he'd seen in her eyes. It changed nothing between them.

He waited until he heard the water running upstairs before he dialed Tadd's home number. It was answered on the second ring.

"Where's Clancy?" Tadd demanded.

"Here, at her lodge," Jake said. "What's this about Westfall?"

"Fake ID, nothing matches up, not his name, social security number or prints," Tadd said.

No prints on file? Then he'd never been in the armed services or in trouble with the law, Jake figured.

"The sheriff's sent out flyers to all law enforcement agencies across Montana and the Northwest. Maybe someone will recognize him."

"Clancy told me he grew up in eastern Montana, poor farming family. There might be some truth to it," Jake said. He'd found that people who lied often mixed in a little truth with their lies, just enough to hang themselves. He wondered if that was the case with Clancy. Would her lie about his father get her hung?

"I'll see that fliers get sent to the smaller towns back there," Tadd said.

"Anything new?" Jake needed to find out if Tadd had heard about Clancy's little trip to Bozeman.

"It looks like we might be dealing with some kind of nutcase." Tadd let out a long sigh. "The police in Bozeman found a closet wall full of background material on Clancy, including all that old stuff about your father's trial and Lola Strickland's murder. The landlady said Dex's sister had been there, paid his rent. Funny, but the sister's description sounded almost familiar." Bingo. "I thought Kiki hired you to keep Clancy in line."

"No," Jake said, his jaw tightening. "Kiki hired me to try to prove that Clancy didn't kill Dex Westfall—or whoever the hell he was."

Tadd didn't say anything for a moment. "How's Clancy holding up?"

"How do you think?" Jake snapped miserably. He hesitated, some old loyalty making him want to protect her. "Clancy thought someone was in the garret tonight."

"Someone broke into the lodge?" Tadd asked.

"Not exactly." Did he really believe there'd been anyone there earlier, especially someone who looked like Dex? "No sign of a break-in." In fact, the lodge had been locked, something Clancy said she hadn't done. Jake figured she'd just forgotten she'd locked it. Except for the front door, which had probably blown open.

"Was anything taken?" Tadd asked, sounding confused.

"We haven't searched the whole house, but it doesn't look like he was your run-of-the-mill burglar. There're valuables sitting all over and they weren't touched." Jake assured himself he owed Clancy nothing but grief for what she'd done to him. Clancy's lawyer needed to know about everything, even if Jake didn't like the guy. "She swears the man she saw in the house was Dex Westfall."

"Right," Tadd said. He laughed, then must have realized Jake wasn't joking. "You aren't serious?"

"Dead serious."

"Come on, we might not know who he is, but we do know he's not up and walking around."

"At least some guy isn't up and walking around." Jake pulled off his baseball cap and raked a hand through his hair. He felt one of his bad feelings doing a little polka at the back of his neck. "Could you send me copies of that stuff tacked up on the guy's closet wall and one of those fliers?"

Obviously following Jake's line of thinking, Tadd let out an oath. "The guy she knew as Dex Westfall is dead. Clancy IDed him the night of the murder. He was her damned boyfriend. Don't try to tell me that maybe her boyfriend's alive and we have someone else on the slab in the morgue."

"Then it can't hurt for her to take another look."

Tadd groaned. "I'll get you a flier," he said, not sounding the least bit pleased. ''Just try to keep her in the county in the meantime.'' He hung up.

Jake stood at the living-room window, staring out at the lake. He liked the quiet and the darkness. And the lake had always given him a sense of peace. Tonight it made him restless. Was the guy Clancy had known as Dex Westfall still out there? Or was it just Clancy's guilt making her see him everywhere she turned?

Long after he heard the shower stop running, Jake couldn't bring himself to go upstairs. His body felt leaden with fatigue. But the truth was, he didn't trust himself around Clancy tonight. It would be too easy to take her in his arms. Too easy to let her get to him. He felt a need for warmth tonight, and he'd seen the same need in Clancy's eyes. Along with love. It was the love that kept him from going upstairs.

He sat, put his head on the kitchen table and shut his mind to that kind of thinking. He thought of the past, letting the bitterness swell inside him.

THE HOT SHOWER did little to soothe Clancy. Her body ached with a need like none she'd ever known. She'd seen that same need in Jake's eyes. So why had he pushed her away? Because he wasn't about to make love to a woman he thought a liar? And a murderer?

And yet she came out of the bathroom half expecting to find Jake sitting on the edge of her bed, waiting for her. Half hoping. She reminded herself how much it had hurt when he'd walked away from her all those years ago. When would she ever learn?

She went to her dresser and, slipping off the silk robe, drew a long cotton nightgown over her head.

She couldn't trust her heart to Jake Hawkins ever again.

but nor could she seem to stop it or her body from aching for him.

She lay on the bed, staring up at the ceiling, wishing there was some way she could prove to him she wasn't the woman he believed her to be. If only there were some way to show him that she would never have betrayed their love. Never.

She closed her eyes, too exhausted to worry about the goblins that waited for her on the edge of sleep.

JAKE JERKED AROUND at the sound of soft footfalls behind him. For a heart-stopping instant, all he saw was a ghost—a figure shrouded in white coming from the kitchen. "Clancy?" He hadn't heard her come downstairs, hadn't heard her come into the kitchen, and he realized he'd fallen asleep at the table.

She looked up but didn't seem surprised to find him sitting alone in the dark. As she stepped into the shaft of light that spilled down the stairs, he caught his breath. She looked so beautiful, her face shiny and squeaky clean from her shower, her blond hair still damp and dark, lying in tendrils against her cheek. The long white nightgown cupped her full breasts and floated around her slim ankles. His gaze fell on her inviting curves for a moment, then flicked down to her feet and the floor behind her. She was leaving sandy tracks on the hardwood floor.

"What were you doing outside?" Jake asked, his pulse suddenly thundering in his ears.

Her gaze shifted to him and he looked into her eyes. An icy wind wrapped around his neck like the hands of an assassin. "Clancy?" She didn't answer. She stared past him, through him. Then slowly she turned and headed up the stairs.

He hadn't believed her story about walking in her sleep.

He still wasn't sure he did. He hurried after her, not knowing what he planned to do.

He found Clancy curled in the middle of her bed, her eyes closed, her breathing soft and rhythmic. As he stepped closer, he could see the sand still on her bare feet. She'd been outside on the beach. Doing what? He cursed himself. He'd have to keep a closer eye on her.

As he started to pull one corner of the comforter over her, he noticed her right hand balled tightly into a fist. It was the sand between her fingers that drew his attention.

Carefully, he touched her hand, expecting her to wake. She moaned softly in her sleep and her fingers opened like a flower to the sun. In her palm lay a single blue bead.

THE SUN CAME UP, filling the room with golden sunshine and warmth. Jake woke, sprawled in a chair at the foot of Clancy's bed. He sat up slowly, his body stiff and sore. What he wouldn't give for a good night's sleep in a real bed. He'd opted for the chair, pulling it over in front of the doorway, because he didn't want to leave her alone again, even for a moment. He'd hoped the morning light would bring him some peace. Instead, he woke with the same haunting questions he'd gone to sleep with.

He studied Clancy's face. She looked so tranquil, he envied her restful sleep. His dreams had been filled with dark shadows lurking at the edge of his subconscious. He'd awakened at the slightest sound, a creak of a floorboard, the cry of an owl outside the window.

He couldn't shake the memory of Clancy sleepwalking. He'd never seen anyone do that before. It was weird. And spooky. He could understand why it frightened her so. He couldn't imagine waking up and finding sand on his feet and realizing he'd been somewhere and had no memory of leaving his bed. And yet a part of him was still skeptical, even though he'd seen it with his own eyes. Hadn't he?

He tiptoed out of the room and down the hall, anxious to get a hot shower, a shave and a change of clothes before Clancy woke.

He was dressed in jeans, toweling his hair dry, when she stuck her head into his bedroom doorway.

"Good morning," she said, and smiled tentatively. She wore jeans and a blue shirt the color of a summer sky. Her hair was pulled back with a ribbon, and there was a freshness about her, as if the sunshine coming through her window had renewed her spirit.

"How did you sleep?" he asked, tossing aside the towel to pull on a fresh shirt.

"Great. For a change." Her smile faltered. "Did you call Tadd? The last thing I remember, you were going to come up and tell me what he had to say. I must have fallen asleep."

"You were sacked out by the time I came up," he said truthfully. "I didn't have the heart to wake you."

He ran a hand through his hair, studying her. She didn't seem to remember her little jaunt on the beach last night. Or maybe she was waiting for him to say something. Not a chance.

Last night he'd pocketed the bead, brushed the sand from her bed and covered her with the comforter. At the time, he'd wanted to protect her. But this morning, his suspicious mind wasn't ready to accept her sleepwalking. Not yet. If she'd staged it for his benefit, she'd made a fatal error. He suspected she no more sleepwalked than he did. And if he could prove it, he'd have her right where he wanted her. That kind of thinking made him feel more in control than remembering the way her lips had felt on his.

"Why don't I fill you in over breakfast." He smiled at

her, noticing with regret that she'd resurrected the wall be-tween them, her defenses safely back in place.

He told himself he should have taken advantage of the situation last night. What had made him think he might be vulnerable to her, a woman who'd betrayed him and still refused to admit that she'd perjured herself? He could have made love to her last night and maybe gotten to her and the truth. He promised himself he wouldn't pass up the opportunity if it presented itself again. *When* it presented itself again.

"What exactly did you say you were making us for breakfast?" he asked as he followed her down the stairs. He told himself sleeping with her would be a means to an end. Nothing more. And that the only reason he found him-self looking forward to it, was because it would mean get-ting this case over with and returning to Texas.

CLANCY BUSIED HERSELF in the kitchen while Jake made a small fire in the woodstove to take the chill off the room. The sun hadn't reached that side of the lodge yet, and even though it was summer, it was still cool in the morning. As she listened to him whistling to himself as he stacked kin-dling in the stove, her heart cried out for the old Jake. Was there any of him left in this hard-nosed cynical private in-vestigator?

"Buttermilk pancakes, my favorite," Jake said, taking a sniff over her shoulder. "Not with huckleberry syrup?"

She smiled at the pleading in his voice. "Of course."

He rolled his eyes toward heaven. "I may never leave here."

Clancy knew that wasn't true. She'd felt an urgency in him to get what he wanted from her and get out quickly. She wondered what would happen when he didn't succeed?

They ate in silence, Clancy watching in amusement as

Jake scraped up the last of the syrup and pancake from his plate before pushing it away with a satisfied sigh. He'd always loved her pancakes.

"Fantastic," he said, giving her a smile that warmed her more than the sun now beginning to shine in through the kitchen window. The smile faded as his gaze met hers.

She knew what was coming. "Can I get you more pancakes?" she asked as she stood. She didn't want to think about Dex Westfall or the upcoming trial or who she thought she'd seen on the deck last night. In the light of day, she wanted to believe she'd been mistaken about the face looking anything like the man she'd known. She feared she was losing her mind; she didn't want Jake to tell her those fears were well founded. "It won't take but a moment to fry up a couple more."

"Clancy." He took her hand and pulled her back to the table. "We have to talk about it."

Resigned, she sat.

He filled her in quickly about the phony name and social security number. "Whoever he was, he was carrying a fake ID that said he was Dex Westfall."

"But no Dex Westfall ever existed." She wasn't surprised after finding out that he'd lied about the condo, lied about everything as far as she knew. "Then, who was the man—"

"The sheriff should know in a few days, and maybe then we'll know what he wanted with you. I asked Tadd to send us the flier they're distributing. That way—"

"I'll know if the dead man is at least who I thought was Dex Westfall," she finished for him.

"Exactly. Meanwhile, we have work to do."

Work sounded good. She needed to do something. And the thought of doing it with Jake definitely had appeal. Especially since, as he'd said, she was running a little scared.

"I need to interview the two witnesses who overheard your conversation with Dex that night at the café," Jake said. "I was hoping you could tell me what you remember."

She leaned over her coffee cup and stared down into the black liquid.

"Tell me everything, no matter how trivial it seems," Jake instructed.

She nodded, remembering the summer night air, still remembering the sickening fried smells coming from the café. "Someone had been in the café working, cleaning the grill, I think. The air smelled of old grease. But the café was closed. There weren't any customers around. Dex was sitting at one of the tables on the deck. It was fairly dark."

"You're doing great," Jake encouraged her.

She drew a breath, letting it all come back. She told Jake again about the necklace, the legacy from Dex's mother, and how he had said Clancy was part of that legacy.

"What kind of necklace was this?" Jake asked.

Clancy looked up to find him watching her closely. "It was a string of beads like the hippies used to make and wear." She blinked. "Jake, how could there have been two witnesses who overheard the conversation? There wasn't anyone around."

"What about the person cleaning the grill?"

"Whoever was in the café couldn't have overheard us. We were sitting too far away."

"Did Dex give you any indication as to why he wanted to meet you?" Jake asked.

"No. I got the impression he had something he wanted to talk about, but whatever he'd seen in the darkness changed his mind." Clancy took a sip of the now-cool coffee. It tasted as bitter as the memory of Dex.

"What color was this string of beads?" Jake asked.

She looked up, surprised by his question. "Pale blue, with a tiny dark blue ceramic heart hanging from the center. Why?"

He shrugged. "Just wondering." He got up to take the dishes to the sink.

"The strange thing about the necklace was that I thought I'd seen it before," Clancy said, joining him. She shrugged and looked over to see Jake watching her. "I'm sure it doesn't matter. I just remembered something else. The clasp was broken."

"You think the beads are important in some way?" he asked.

"Maybe. The other night—" she picked up the dishrag, avoiding Jake's gaze "—I walked in my sleep again. When I woke up, I had one of the beads in my hand. I don't know where I found it. I just have a feeling that finding the rest of the beads might be a clue as to where Dex went that night."

Jake took the dishrag from her. He still didn't believe she walked in her sleep, she realized. She felt a hefty jolt of irritation. Why had she bothered to tell him?

"I'd like you to come with me to the resort," Jake said after a moment. "You'll have to wait in the boat while I talk to the witnesses."

Clancy told herself she shouldn't be hurt and angry at his lack of trust in her. "Let me see if I understand this: you'd like me to tag along so you can keep an eye on me, but stay out of the way so I don't hurt my case," she said, summing it up quite nicely, if she said so herself.

"I just don't want you staying alone. Or I could call your aunt Kiki to come over from her condo in Bigfork—"

"Don't even joke, Hawkins," she said. "Of course I want to tag along with you."

She didn't tell him that she had no intention of sitting by

casually while he did all the investigating. Her life was at stake, and she had a couple of things she wanted to check out on her own.

He shoved back his Astros cap and grinned, probably thinking he'd won. That it was his favorite hat was no secret to her. It looked as if it was the first thing he put on in the morning and the last to be discarded at night, and had been for years. The bill was stained and faded from the elements. The once-white *H* had bled into the once-bright red star. Even the cloth-covered button on top was missing.

When she came back from brushing her teeth, she found him outside by the lilac bushes, hunkered down at the edge of the window. "Did you find anything?" she asked.

He shook his head as he straightened. She tried to hide her disappointment as she turned and headed toward the dock.

"How did you get into the private investigating business?" Clancy asked when they reached the boat.

"You want to drive?" Jake asked, holding up the key.

She gritted her teeth, reminded that every time they stopped anywhere he'd taken the key for safekeeping. "Why don't you drive," she said as sweetly as she could muster. "*You* have the key."

He either ignored her sarcasm or missed it. But something told her he hadn't missed it.

"When I first moved to Galveston I met this old private eye who fished off the same pier I did," Jake said as he pulled the boat away from the dock. "We became good friends. He taught me everything he knew about people and secrets." Jake pointed the boat out of the bay. "'Everyone has a secret,'" he used to say. 'All that separates murderers from ordinary people is that they have secrets they'd kill to keep.'" They rounded the end of the island, the sky as clear blue as the water was green. "He used to say I was a natural private eye. Cynical and determined. If someone has a secret, I'll find out what it is. Or die trying."

She felt his gaze on her and wished she hadn't asked.

Chapter Ten

To Jake's surprise, Hawk Island Resort looked much as it had when he and Clancy were kids. The store and café had been rebuilt on the same spot overlooking the marina. A row of six original cabins that hadn't burned still stood in the pines off to the right. Jake felt a rush of nostalgia, followed by nausea. There were too many memories here. Just as at his family's lodge.

Although it was early in the season, a few boats had already been moored in the bay when Jake eased into a slip at the docks. The air smelled of motor oil, gas and fish. "You want to wait here or at the café?" Jake asked.

"I'll stay here and catch some rays."

Clancy leaned back into the seat and closed her eyes. He studied her for a moment, wondering if it was safe to leave her alone. "I want to be able to see you at all times, Clancy. So I know you're all right." Then, feeling like the louse he was, he pulled and pocketed the boat key. Her eyes flickered open; he didn't like the look she gave him.

"I won't be long," he said, unable to think of anything to say in his defense. She mumbled something he figured he didn't want to hear, anyway, and headed up the pier.

At the outdoor sinks, a man cleaned fish from the full

stringer of lake trout he'd caught. Jake was surprised when he saw who it was.

"Nice catch," Jake said, extending his hand to the man. "How have you been, Johnny?"

Johnny Branson looked up from his work. A smile crinkled his leathery face as he wiped his hand on his pants and took Jake's hand in his. "Jake Hawkins. I'd heard you were back."

Johnny was a large man with a full head of graying hair. He'd always reminded Jake of a Newfoundland puppy. Friendly. Loyal. And a little gangly. The former sheriff looked as though he'd lost some weight since Jake had last seen him. Johnny had been best friends with Jake's and Clancy's fathers since grade school. It had been Johnny who'd had to make the arrest and take Warren to jail. The strain of the trial had shown on Johnny, but the years since hadn't seemed to have been kind to him, either.

"I heard you retired right after the trial," Jake said.

Johnny nodded as he went back to cleaning his fish. "I'm a fishing guide now," he said, holding up a twenty-pound trout. "It suits me."

"Looks like business must be good," Jake said, not sure how to broach the subject on his mind. "I was hoping to talk to you while I'm back on the island. About my father's case."

Johnny didn't look up. "After ten years, can't be that much to say anymore, can there?"

He figured Johnny didn't want to drag up any of that old misery any more than he did. Johnny had taken his friend's conviction particularly hard.

"I was hoping you might be able to answer some questions I still have."

"That what brings you back?" Johnny asked, squinting past Jake to where Clancy waited in the boat. Idly, he rubbed the blade of his fish-gutting knife across one thumb pad.

"That and this mess with Clancy," Jake answered honestly. "I need to know if you thought my father was guilty."

"The jury thought Warren was, that's what mattered," Johnny said, cutting a clean slit up the fish's belly.

"I need to know what you thought. What you still think," Jake said. "Was justice served?"

"Life dispenses its own form of justice," he said as he ripped the guts from the large lake trout.

Jake shook his head. "I became a private investigator to ensure that justice gets done once in a while on earth. I'm too impatient to wait and let God set the record straight at the pearly gates." He met the man's gaze. "Just tell me if you think my father was an embezzler, murderer and arsonist."

Johnny chewed at his cheek for a moment as he looked out at the lake. "Sometimes people do things out of desperation, out of a feeling of helplessness and unhappiness."

He wanted to shake the big man and demand he answer his question, not dance around it. "Are you saying that's what happened to my father?" Jake asked, shocked by what sounded like an indictment against his father.

Johnny tossed the cleaned fish into the pile with the others. "I'm saying, leave it alone, son. No good comes from digging up the past."

The same thing Warren Hawkins had said to him. Jake walked away, heartsick and shaken. Not by Johnny's words as much as by the bitterness he'd heard in the man's voice. Was he really ready to find out the truth about his father? About Clancy? No matter how it came down?

As he walked up the steps to the resort store, he glanced

to the right, to the west end of the island. The Branson home sat at the edge of the cliffs. A wide deck ran across the front with an elevator platform next to a long flight of wooden stairs that dropped to a dock at the water. Jake could make out a figure sitting near the edge of the deck. Johnny's wife Helen, her wheelchair glistening in the morning sunlight.

CLANCY WAITED UNTIL JAKE was out of sight before she made her move. She headed for the row of cabins against the hillside, having spotted a cleaning cart parked in front of number three.

Johnny Branson waved to her as he left in his boat. She was shocked by the change in him. He looked so much older and slighter than he'd been. She wondered if Warren Hawkins's trial hadn't made him age more rapidly. She was thinking about the trial and the effect it had had on them all as she took the trail to cabin three.

"Hello?" Clancy called, sticking her head into the cabin's open doorway. Like the other five cabins, number three was small, with twin beds against the knotty-pine wall and a marred night table and lamp between them. A girl of about fifteen looked up from her bed-making, the tail of a sheet in her hand.

"This cabin isn't ready yet," she said quickly. "Check-in isn't until noon."

Clancy smiled and stepped inside. "I don't need a cabin. Actually, I need to find out if one of your guests left anything behind."

The girl let go of the sheet and straightened, but she didn't look all that happy for the interruption. "If they did, it would be in lost'n found. I can show you."

"It would have been cabin six," Clancy said. "On Friday."

The girl stopped in her tracks and looked up, her eyes narrowing. "That was the guy who got murdered."

"So what was he like?" Clancy asked casually.

The girl rolled her eyes. "A major hunk. But kind of a real pain."

"Yeah?"

"He was always bossing me around, asking me to run here and there for him."

It was obvious she hadn't really minded. "What did he want you to do?"

"Get him things and take messages— Why are you asking about him, anyway?"

"It isn't every day there's a murder on the island."

"He didn't die here, you know," she said.

"That's what I heard. But he stayed here a day and a night, right?"

"Two nights," the girl said.

Two nights? Dex hadn't called her until the second day? "So he had you running errands for him," she said, knowing she had to tread softly. "I hope he tipped you well."

The girl shook her head. "That part stunk, too."

"Really? If he had you taking messages to people…"

The girl looked wary. "You with one of those weird newspapers?"

This time it was Clancy's turn to shake her head. "No, the truth is, I dated the guy for a while," she said truthfully.

"No kidding?" The girl looked at her with misguided respect.

"That's why I wondered if he left anything behind, a message or letter, maybe…for me."

The girl gave her a sympathetic look. "Sorry, when the police finally let me clean the cabin, I didn't find anything." She went back to her bed-making.

"What about the messages he had you take for him?" Clancy asked.

"It was just one. I took it to the marina and left it under a bait can beside the repair shop."

Interesting place to leave a message. "What night was this?"

"The first night. Thursday."

"Didn't you wonder who it was for?"

"It didn't have any writing on the envelope."

Clancy took a long shot. "Was the envelope sealed?"

The girl looked up and grinned. "Yeah. I couldn't make out anything, even holding it up to a light. I didn't dare open it."

Clancy laughed. "Thanks for your help." She had more questions, but the girl was heading for her cart and another cabin and Clancy didn't want to press her luck. "Do you mind if I take a look around cabin six, just in case?"

JAKE FOUND FRANK AMES in the pumphouse behind the café, bent over, banging on a pipe, swearing.

"Frank?" Jake called over the racket.

He looked up, the wrench in his hand falling silent. Not much had changed about the tall, pimply-faced kid Jake had known. He was still thin, his narrow face pockmarked, his expression one of open hostility. "What do you want?"

"Just to ask you a few questions." He held out his business card. When Frank didn't bother to reach for it, Jake stuffed the card into Frank's shirt pocket.

Frank glared at him from dark, deep-set eyes that were just a little too close together. "Do I look like I have time to answer questions?" he demanded.

Jake had always wanted to knock that chip off Frank's shoulder. Only now, Jake's father wasn't here to keep him from doing it.

Frank must have realized that. "Hell," he said, pushing himself to his feet. "Make it snappy."

"You told the sheriff you overheard Clancy Jones talking to a man in the café Friday night," Jake said, disappointed Frank had given in so easily. He really wanted to thump that mean, nasty look off Frank's face.

"You know that or you wouldn't be here."

Jake smiled. He might get the opportunity to thump Frank yet. "What did you hear?"

"I already told the sheriff—"

"Tell me, Frank," Jake said between gritted teeth.

Frank slowly wiped the grease from his hands onto his worn jeans. "They were arguing about something."

"What?"

Frank shot him a contemptuous look. "How should I know?"

"You were listening to their conversation."

"I just happened to overhear Clancy threaten him, that's all."

"What exactly did she say?"

"I don't *exactly* remember." He shook his head at Jake's stupidity. "I got better things to do than memorize my customers' conversations."

Jake took a step toward Frank. "Try to remember."

"She said it was over between them. He said it was over when he said it was over. She said he was hurting her and he'd better leave her alone or else."

"Not bad for a conversation you can't remember," Jake said. "Where exactly were you when you overheard this conversation? I thought the café was closed."

He gave him a nasty sneer. "I was walking by."

Jake nodded. "This waitress who overheard this same conversation—"

"Liz Knowles. She's up at the café."

"Was she walking with you?"

"I think it's time for you to leave, Hawkins." Frank turned to go back to his plumbing problems.

"One more question. How was it you were able to buy this resort?"

Frank picked up a pipe wrench from behind the pump and hefted it into both hands. "I'm through answering questions. You don't own this place anymore. Your old man's behind bars, your girlfriend's a murderer, and you're nothing but some punk P.I. who doesn't know squat. So don't you come around here hassling me no more—or you'll regret it."

Jake smiled and pushed back his baseball cap. "One of these days I'm going to kick your ass, Frank. And that's a promise."

CLANCY KNEW THERE probably wasn't anything to find in cabin six, but she still had to look, and she hoped the cabin girl's curiosity would get the best of her.

Just as the girl had said, the cabin wasn't locked. Nor did it look much different from number three. Except the beds were made. Clancy glanced around in all the corners, under the beds and behind the door. Nothing, just as she'd thought. Then she took a closer look, inspecting the cracks between the worn pine plank floor and the crevices between the floor and baseboard. No tiny blue beads.

Disappointed, she stood for a moment in the middle of the room, thinking about Dex. Where were the rest of the beads from the necklace? It was obvious the necklace hadn't been broken here. Some of the tiny beads would have gotten caught between the floorboards. Common sense told her she'd find the beads closer to home. They were near enough to the lodge that she'd walked to them in her sleep. But where? And what did the broken beads signify?

Probably nothing. Her sleepwalking was often illogical, she reminded herself.

It made as little sense as Dex coming to Hawk Island. If it was to see her, then why hadn't he called her the first day? Why had he waited? And whom had he left a message for on the dock? As far as Clancy knew, Dex didn't know anyone up here but her.

"Find anything?" the girl asked from the doorway.

Clancy smiled to herself, glad she hadn't been wrong about the girl's curiosity. "Is it possible the message he wrote was for some woman he'd met here?" she asked, knowing that was more than a possibility.

The girl looked away.

Clancy knew she'd hit paydirt. "Dex always had a way with women."

The girl looked up, a smirk on her young face. "There was this one waitress."

Of course there was. "Which waitress?"

"Liz. Liz Knowles."

What a sleaze Dex had been! All the time he'd been dating her he'd been seeing other women. Then he'd come to Hawk Island supposedly to get her back and he was making time with one of the waitresses at the resort. Maybe she *had* killed him. "So the message from Dex was probably for her?"

The girl shook her head. "I passed Liz on my way down to the docks. She was already headed for his cabin."

"Maybe Liz just missed the message or picked it up later."

The girl brushed a speck of lint from her sweatshirt and, looking at the ground, shook her head. "Later I went to check. The message was gone. Liz hadn't left his cabin."

"Do you know if anyone else came to Dex's cabin that night?" Clancy asked on impulse.

"No." The girl looked disgusted, and Clancy realized her impulse had been right. The poor thing had hung around outside the cabin waiting for Liz to leave. All Clancy could think was how lucky the girl had been that Dex hadn't taken advantage of her schoolgirl crush.

But if the message hadn't been meant for Liz Knowles, then whom? Clancy felt a sudden chill as she remembered that night at the café when Dex had looked past her into the darkness and seen someone. Or something that had frightened him. She wondered what Dex had had to fear. And from whom. The person who killed him? "What about the night he was killed?"

"I had to work at the café. But I know Liz planned to go to his cabin that night."

Clancy remembered what Jake had said about Dex not having any underwear on when he was found dead. Liz Knowles might be the explanation for that. But if Jake's theory was right, who had interrupted the two?

"The only time he left the island was that first afternoon Thursday," the girl was saying.

Clancy's head snapped up. "He left the island?"

She nodded, looking unhappy. "He was all dressed up."

The girl obviously figured he'd had a date. She was probably right. "Do you know where he went?"

She shook her head.

Clancy had a thought. "He came back and *then* wrote the message you took to the dock that first night?"

She nodded, looking miserable. "He was in a really good mood."

THE FIRST THING JAKE noticed when he left the pumphouse and Frank was that Clancy was no longer in the boat. In fact, she was nowhere to be seen. He swore under his breath. This should not have come as a surprise. No, this was absolutely predictable. Anyone who knew Clancy would know better than to think she'd just sit idly by in the boat as he'd asked her. She'd never done anything he ever told her. Needless to say, that part of her hadn't changed a bit.

He spotted her finally by the cabins, talking to a cabin girl. Questioning a cabin girl, he corrected himself. Damn her hide. Well, at least he could see her, and she was all right. For the moment. He'd take this up with her when he finished interviewing Elizabeth Knowles.

The Hawk Island Resort café was actually little more than a grill that served burgers, hot dogs, fries and soft drinks. All the seating was outdoors at wooden tables under a canopy of pines and Japanese lanterns. Cheap plastic checked tablecloths flapped in the summer breeze. A woman in her early twenties in shorts and a tank top was busy putting out condiments.

"Lunch isn't served for another half hour," she said when she saw Jake. She had the harried, tight expression of a young woman who was already tired of her summer job and it was only early June.

"I'm looking for a waitress named Knowles."

She looked up.

He saw fear flicker in her eyes.

"I'm Elizabeth Knowles."

He asked her the same questions he had asked Frank. But got different answers.

"What makes you think they were arguing about money?" he asked, his interest piqued not only by the difference in how she and Frank related the conversation, but by this woman's obvious sympathy toward Dex.

Elizabeth shrugged. "He said she owed him money. But it sounded like she'd dumped him, too, and he was upset about that."

Funny, but money had never come up in the conversation, according to Clancy. And Frank. Jake glanced around the café. "Where were they sitting?"

She pointed to a far table at the back edge of the deck flanked by two large pines.

"And where were you when you heard this conversation?"

Her gaze flickered away. "I was working. I had to close the café that night."

She must have been the waitress Clancy saw cleaning the grill.

"You couldn't have heard their conversation from inside the café," Jake said quietly.

She flushed to the dark roots of her blond head. "I wasn't. I was...in the trees. I had to run an errand."

Right beside the deck. "Did you see anyone else while you were there?"

She shook her head. "I was only there a few minutes."

"Just long enough to overhear their entire conversation," Jake said.

"I gotta get back to work," she said, turning to walk away.

"What was so interesting about that conversation that you hid in the pines to listen?"

Her steps faltered, but she didn't stop or turn around. Nor did she deny it. "I was just curious," she said flatly. "There's no law against that."

No, if there was a law against curiosity, Jake would be doing time right now, he thought as he watched Clancy hurry down the dock to her boat. What had she learned from the cabin girl that had put a spring into her step? More important, how could he convince Clancy she wasn't going to be doing any more investigating on her own?

CLANCY STRETCHED OUT in the back of the boat, pretending to be asleep. It was hard to do since she couldn't help but steal a peek at Jake from under her large straw fishing hat. Jake strode down the dock, his cap pulled low over his eyes, his jaw set in concrete. She didn't have to see his eyes to know he was furious. Or to know who he was furious with. Obviously he knew that she'd left the boat.

"I thought you agreed to stay here where I could see you," he said the moment he reached her.

She leisurely pushed back her hat and looked up at him. "I *did* stay in the boat. For a while." She grinned, too pleased at what she'd discovered to hold it in any longer. "Don't you want to know what I found out?"

"Dammit, Clancy, I won't have you messing up my investigation with your amateur sleuthing." He glowered at her.

"I found out some pretty good stuff," she said. "For an amateur, of course. Dex was romantically involved with one of the waitresses."

"Liz Knowles."

She stared at him. "How did you know that?"

"She's one of the witnesses who overheard your conversation with Dex."

Clancy sat up. "Really?" How interesting. "Wait a minute, why didn't I see her that night?"

"She was hiding in the pines right beside the deck."

Excitement coursed through her. "Then, she wasn't the person Dex saw in the darkness. It *was* someone else, just as I suspected." She hurriedly told Jake about the note the cabin girl had left under a bait can and how Dex had been on the island an extra day and night before he contacted her. Also how he'd left the island Thursday to meet someone, maybe a date, and returned in a good mood. "That's when he left the note."

She waited for Jake's reaction, expecting him to be as excited about this as she was. He bent to untie the boat, and, if anything, he seemed more angry.

"Don't you realize what this means?" she demanded. "Dex knew someone else on the island, someone he left a note for. He also left the island to meet someone. It's a lead."

Jake looked up, leveling his gray-eyed gaze at her. "Clancy, I realize telling you what to do is a waste of my breath," he said. "But it would help if you'd let me do the job I've been hired to do. And if you'd just stay put like you're told. This is my case, and whether you believe it or not, I know what I'm doing."

"No wonder I keep firing you," she said in exasperation. "This may be your case, Jake, but it's my life. Even if I trusted you to do the job my aunt hired you to do, which you have already admitted isn't why you're here, I couldn't stay put. Someone tried to kill me. The sheriff isn't even looking into other leads because he believes he already has his killer, and you don't believe I'm innocent any more than he does. If I stay put, I might end up dead. At the very least, in prison for life."

Jake jerked off his cap and raked his fingers through his hair. "Dammit, Clancy, sometimes I'd like to—" He slapped his cap back on his head and leveled his gaze at her. "You were always like this. Too independent, stubborn and fearless for your own good. Remember that time you went swimming off Angel Point in the storm?"

She'd almost drowned. Probably would have if it hadn't been for Jake. She'd only done it because he'd told her not to. What he was saying was true. Often in the past, she'd let her stubborn pride get her into trouble. "You're wrong, Jake. I'm not fearless. I'm scared to death."

In one swift motion, he pushed off the boat and stepped

in. "You should be scared. There's already been one murder. If you didn't kill Dex, or whoever he was, then the killer is still out there. It's too dangerous for a—"

"Woman?" She raised a brow at him.

"Amateur," he said with that soft southern drawl.

She pushed back her sunglasses to glare up at him.

"We'll discuss this back at the lodge." He tossed her the boat key. "You can drive."

She caught the key easily enough but bristled at his tone. It sounded as if he thought he was going to have the last word on this. He was even going to let her drive her own boat. And then take the key again when they got to the lodge. She tossed the key back to him. "Some things aren't debatable," she said, pulling down her sunglasses as she stretched out on the seat in the sun again.

She heard him mumbling as he started the boat and pulled away from the resort. She had the feeling that Jake Hawkins was used to women he could mold like soft clay. Well, not this woman. And he had a fight on his hands if he thought he could.

It was more than her stubborn pride, Clancy told herself. She was tired of feeling like a criminal. And while she appreciated Jake's help, she had no intention of letting him investigate her case alone. She had to prove her innocence. And she couldn't depend on anyone to do it for her. Not even Jake Hawkins. Especially not Jake Hawkins.

Jake slowed as they rounded the island. Clancy pretended to sleep until she felt the boat bump the dock. She sat up, studying Jake out of the corner of her eye to see if his mood had changed.

He still looked irritated with her, but as he passed on his way to tie up the boat, he handed her the boat key. That simple sign of trust touched her more deeply than she wanted to admit.

''Jake?'' She started to tell him that she was glad he was here. That she liked being around him, even when he was ill-tempered. That his being here made her feel like she had a chance to prove her innocence. He gave her strength. And hope. Even if he was here for all the wrong reasons—
''Thanks.''

He grunted in response and offered her a hand out of the boat. ''I still don't want you interfering in my investigation.''

She smiled. ''But you're smart enough to know that I will whether you like it or not.''

''You are the most disagreeable woman I've ever—'' Before she knew what was happening, he grabbed her and hauled her out of the boat—and into his arms, into his kiss. It was a kiss that brooked no arguments. He took her lips, the same way he took her body to his. Her lips responded to his demands, parting of their own volition to allow him access to her. Against her counsel, her body answered his, molding its softness to his hardness.

''Excuse me?''

Clancy's eyes popped open as she recognized the voice and realized it was directly behind her. Abruptly Jake broke off the kiss and swung Clancy around, shielding her before he realized just who had joined them in the small bay.

''Sorry to interrupt,'' her attorney said from his boat, which now bumped the edge of the dock. Funny, but Tadd didn't sound sorry. Nor could Clancy remember hearing his motor when he pulled into the bay. She had a feeling he'd cut his engine and drifted in when he'd seen the two of them kissing.

But then she'd heard nothing but the throb of her heart against Jake's chest, felt nothing but his lips on hers. Now she felt her face flush, wondering how long Tadd had been watching them.

"I'd ask you how the investigation was going but I can pretty well see the course it's taking," Tadd commented.

Jake swore and released Clancy. She stumbled and fought to regain her composure.

"Did you bring the flier?" Jake said a little hoarsely.

Clancy tried to still her pounding heart, not even kidding herself that it was Tadd's sudden appearance that had caused it to pound, not Jake's unexpected kiss.

"Why don't we go up to the lodge," Tadd said, his look growing serious. "I've got some news you might want to sit down for."

Chapter Eleven

Clancy led them into the living room. Tadd took a seat on the western-style couch her family had bought when she was a child. It had horses embossed in the thick leather and wide wooden arms. She stood, too nervous to sit, remembering the night of the resort fire when she'd come down the stairs to find her parents sitting on that same couch, arguing about Warren Hawkins and the missing money.

Clancy had that same sick feeling now as she looked at Tadd. He sat on the edge of the couch, at odds with the warm, inviting character of the room with its large rock fireplace that Jake now leaned against, the rich golden pine floors, the bright-colored rugs.

Tadd pulled a sheet of paper from his shirt pocket. "The sheriff needs to know if this is the man you knew as Dex Westfall," Tadd said, unfolding the flier.

Clancy found herself unable to move. Instead, Jake crossed the room, took the paper from Tadd's hand and brought it over to her.

She could feel his gaze on her as well as Tadd's. She took the flier in her hands, a zillion thoughts whipping through her mind. The last thing she wanted to do was look at the photograph she knew she'd find reprinted on the sheet of paper. What if it wasn't the man she'd dated? What if it was?

She braced herself, her gaze flicking to Jake, his look sympathetic, supportive. She looked at the face in the photo. Her heart leaped into her throat.

"Is that the man you knew as Dex Westfall?" Tadd asked again.

She nodded, looking away from the dead man's face to stare into the darkness of the empty firebox.

Jake took the flier from her. "Are you all right?"

She nodded, avoiding his gaze. She wasn't all right and wondered if she'd ever be all right again. The man she'd known as Dex Westfall was dead. So who had been snooping around her lodge last night? Who had she seen who looked like Dex? Who'd run out of the lodge? Who had pulled her into the lake and tried to drown her?

"Have you got an ID on the body yet?" Jake asked Tadd as he handed back the flier.

Out of the corner of her eye, Clancy watched Tadd carefully fold the sheet of paper and put it into his shirt pocket. He's stalling, she thought, and faced him, realizing he'd brought news. Bad news.

"The sheriff got a positive ID from the family this morning," Tadd said. "What Dex told you, Clancy, about being raised in eastern Montana on a farm turned out to be true."

The air in the living room crackled. "Who was he?" she asked, her voice no more than a whisper.

Tadd's gaze shifted to Jake. "His real name was Dexter Strickland."

"Strickland?" Jake asked.

"Strickland?" Clancy repeated, the name not registering.

It was Tadd who answered. "Dex Strickland was Lola's son."

Lola. A chill stole across her skin. "Lola Strickland, the

resort secretary?'' The woman Jake's father had gone to prison for murdering.

Clancy looked over at Jake. He stood, his muscles tensed, all his attention on Tadd.

"Dex was her son?" Jake asked, sounding not all that surprised.

"I never knew she had a son." Was Clancy the only one shocked here? "I didn't even know she'd ever been married."

"No one did," Tadd said. "Dex lived with his father on a farm near Richey. The father had custody. I guess Lola just up and disappeared one day, leaving her husband to raise his infant son alone. Allan Strickland never heard from her again."

"What about during the trial?" Clancy asked. "It was in all the papers. Surely he would have heard about his wife's death."

"From what I can gather, Allan Strickland's farm is pretty isolated," Tadd said. "But you're right. He knew about her death. He says he was trying to shield his son."

Clancy's legs wobbled beneath her. "If Dex was Lola's son…"

"The murders have to be connected," Jake said.

"We don't know that," Tadd said. "But it could explain why Dex had the newspaper clippings of the trial in his closet and why he might have wanted to meet Clancy."

"Why Clancy?" Jake asked.

Clancy saw the pain etched in his face and wished with all her heart that she wasn't responsible for him being here, for him having to relive all this. They were talking about the woman his father had been convicted of murdering.

Clancy wanted to reach out to Jake but knew she was the last person he'd take sympathy from. Especially right now.

"Why wouldn't Dex come after *me?*" Jake demanded. "If he wanted retribution, it was my father who…he believed killed his mother."

"Who knows what Dex had in mind?" Tadd said. "Maybe he was just looking for some connection to his mother."

"Or to his mother's murder," Jake interjected.

That seemed more a possibility now that Clancy thought about it. "He did say something that night about his mother's legacy and how it linked the two of us."

"But what was that legacy?" Jake asked.

"Well, it seems to be death," Tadd said quietly, making the hair stiffen on Clancy's neck.

Dex had stalked her. With a shudder, she realized Dex was still stalking her. "Did Dex have any brothers?"

Jake's gaze swung around to meet hers.

"I already thought of that," Tadd said. "I asked Allan Strickland if there were any more like Dex at home."

"And?" Jake asked impatiently.

"Dex didn't have any siblings."

Clancy felt the air rush out of her. The floor wavered and threatened to come up to meet her.

"You should sit down," Jake said, suddenly appearing at her side.

She gave him the best smile she could manage. "I'm okay. I'm more worried about you."

He seemed surprised that she would be worried about him right now. He returned her smile. "Thanks, but I'm tough."

She knew that. And tender. Her heart ached to take some of the pain from those gray eyes. She wished she *had* lied on the stand about his father. At least now she could rectify things. "I think I'll get a drink of water."

"I'll get it for you," Jake said, already heading for the kitchen.

She stopped him. "Please, I need a little fresh air. A few moments alone."

He studied her for a long moment, then nodded.

Was he worried about her? Or just worried she'd jump bail? She felt a stab of annoyance. Just when she let down her defenses, he'd remind her again exactly what his stake in her case was. Revenge. Nothing more. She was on her own, now more than ever.

She left the two of them in the living room and went straight to the porch, where she gulped the summer afternoon air and tried to quit shaking. Dex was Lola Strickland's son. She couldn't even comprehend all the ramifications of that. What had Tadd said? Maybe he was just looking for a connection to his mother. Or to his mother's murder, Jake had added. Is that why he went to so much trouble to get close to her?

A connection. Like the string of beads. Dex said the beads were a legacy from his mother. But Lola was dead, and all of her belongings had burned in the fire. So where had he gotten the necklace? From someone who was still on the island who'd known Lola? Or someone on the mainland?

That silly necklace, why was it so familiar? The memory came in a flash. The string of tiny blue beads. Light glinting off the small dark blue ceramic heart. Clancy knew she'd seen them before. Now she knew where.

The memory brought her little pleasure. She'd seen them the night Jake Hawkins had promised her *his* heart. That's why the tiny navy heart had stuck in her memory. She reminded herself that not only had Jake broken that promise—he was now on the island to, as he put it, get the goods on her.

Grabbing her mountain bike from where she'd left i
against the porch railing, Clancy took off up one of the
trails without thinking of anything but reaching her desti-
nation and getting back before Jake missed her. If she was
right, she might have some answers to keep her out o
prison when she returned.

THE LODGE SEEMED EMPTY after Clancy left. Almost eerie
Jake found himself pacing, too keyed up to sit.

"I'm worried about Clancy," Tadd said, leaning forward
as he watched Jake wear out the rug in front of him.

"You should be," Jake said, stopping his pacing for a
moment. He fought the urge to check on Clancy again. No
long after she'd gone outside, he'd looked out to find her
standing on the back porch. He wanted to give her the space
she'd asked for, but not too much. She couldn't get into too
much trouble for a few minutes on her own back porch in
broad daylight, right?

"She thinks someone is trying to kill her," Jake said
resuming his pacing. He told Tadd about the near drowning
incident and filled in more detail about last night's supposed
intruder. "She thinks someone who looks like Dex Westfal
is still stalking her."

Tadd gave him one of those calculated lawyer looks. "I
that what you think?"

Jake didn't know what to believe. "There's a scrape on
her ankle, and if you'd seen Clancy's face last night— She
saw something," Jake said in Clancy's defense. "Someone
Someone she thinks looks enough like Dex to make her
believe he's still alive."

"You don't believe Strickland's come back from the
dead?" Tadd inquired.

"Of course not." Jake pulled off his cap and rumpled
his hair with his hand.

"At some point, Clancy's going to have to see a sleep specialist and have some extensive tests run on her," Tadd said. "If we can prove she has a sleeping disorder. That Dex's death was the result of noninsane automatism, an act committed by a sane person but without—"

"Intent, awareness or malice," Jake interrupted. "I know, I've read about it." He shook his head at Tadd. "If Clancy killed Dex, it wasn't in her sleep. Dex Strickland stalked her, lied about who he was, cheated on her. All the more reason for Clancy to want him dead. Add to that the mountain of evidence against her—"

"I *have* to sell the jury on the sleepwalking defense or she's going to prison," Tadd interrupted.

Jake groaned, realizing how true that probably was. "Unless I can find some evidence that proves she didn't kill him." And if he couldn't? Then he'd have no bargaining chip. Funny how that didn't matter as much as it had just a few days ago. "She thinks Dex has come back from the grave for her."

"Ever read any Edgar Allan Poe?" Tadd asked.

"There's no heart thumping under the floorboards here. Unless it's Lola Strickland's."

Tadd gave him a long look. "You think Dex came back to either avenge his mother's death or solve her murder?"

"You have to admit, both are possibilities," Jake said. "But if he believed my father was guilty, why wouldn't he come after me instead of Clancy? Unless he believes Clancy's father, Clarence Jones, is somehow involved."

"That's what you think, isn't it?" Tadd said as he got to his feet. "Maybe you should solve one murder at a time, preferably the one you're being paid to solve."

"The murders are connected."

"Maybe. Maybe not. My only concern is for my client. What's yours?"

"Clancy," Jake said, realizing that was true. "But these murders are connected."

His entire theory rode on the premise that the two murders were connected, and Dex turning out to be Lola's son only supported that. The hunch discoing at the back of his brain was that whoever killed Dex had killed Dex's mother. Clarence Jones could have embezzled the money, either used Lola to do it or killed her because she found the discrepancy, and started the fire to cover his own misdeeds. Warren Hawkins had come along after the fact, just as he said, and tried to save Lola and the books to prove his innocence.

But Clarence and Lola were dead. And Warren was in prison. So where did that leave Jake? All the prime suspects were now out of the picture. Too many things were blowing holes in his hunch.

Not only that, ten years ago he had found it easier to believe that Clancy had perjured herself than he did now—perhaps being around her had altered his perspective.

"I don't see how the murders could be connected," Tadd said.

"Clancy's the connection," Jake insisted. "Maybe she saw something that night that someone doesn't want her to remember."

Tadd lifted a brow. "They waited ten years to shut her up?"

Jake admitted it didn't make a lot of sense. But what did about this case?

Tadd let out a long sigh. "I'm worried about Clancy's mental state. I'm concerned she might be on the verge of a major breakdown. The sooner we get to trial, the better."

"I beg your pardon?"

They both swung around at the sound of a sharp, female voice from the doorway.

"Kiki!" Jake said. Her name came out like an oath.

"I can assure you my niece is not on the verge of a major breakdown, as you so delicately put it," she said firmly. She stormed into the room, giving them both withering glares. "Nor is she a murderer."

Jake wondered how long she'd been standing in the doorway listening. He didn't have to wonder long.

"If my niece says someone is trying to kill her, I expect you to believe her," Kiki said, biting off each word.

Tadd was on his feet, trying to explain himself, but Kiki cut him off.

"How can you fools *not* believe her?" Kiki snapped, some of her highly bred composure slipping. "Clancy's no murderer. She didn't care enough about the man to kill him. Asleep. Or awake." She narrowed her eyes at Jake. "Why aren't you out looking for the real killer instead of sitting around speculating on Clancy's mental health?" She shook her head in disgust. "Where is my niece, anyway? I came by to see how she was doing."

Jake stared at Kiki. "Didn't you pass her on your way in? She was out on the porch just a—" He was already racing toward the back of the lodge. He pushed through the door and out onto the porch. "Clancy?" She was nowhere in sight. A breeze rippled the water. The tops of the tall pines swayed overhead. Her boat was still at the dock. The beach was empty. He glanced around, thinking she might have just gone for a walk.

Then he noticed her mountain bike was gone. He swore, knowing he'd never be able to catch her on foot. Nor did he have any idea which trail she might have taken. The island was a labyrinth of trails.

"It's a small island," he heard Tadd trying to reassure Kiki. "How could she get into trouble on such a small island in broad daylight?"

"Find her. Hurry." The emotion in Kiki's command clutched at Jake's heart. He felt the tentative strum of a hunch at the base of his spine. He knew the name of this tune. Trouble. And Clancy, as usual, was right at the center of it.

Chapter Twelve

Clancy rode up the narrow mountain trail through the cool pines. The sun sliced down, making patterns of gold on the dry pine needles covering the path. The trail climbed the steep terrain through a series of switchbacks to the top of the ridge. The exertion felt good; she pushed herself harder, stopping at the top to catch her breath.

The lake stretched for miles, a mosaic of blues and greens. The Mission Mountains rose up from the valley floor to the east. Pines, dense and dark as the ones around her, edged the other side of the lake as far as the eye could see. To the north, boats churned the water in a bay near the resort. Laughter and the roar of engines drifted up the mountainside, making Clancy ache for happier summer days.

She headed down the main trail that ran along the ridgeline. Occasionally she'd catch a view of the lake from the dense pines. The island was a web of narrow trails; most she'd ridden at one time or another during her childhood. Ridden with Jake, she thought. Back when their lives had held nothing but promise.

As she rode, she tried to understand everything she'd learned over the last few hours and where she fit into it. Some things started to make an odd kind of sense to her.

Why Dex had stalked her. Why he'd followed her to the island. This is where his mother had died, and Clancy Jones had been the only witness.

That is what tied her to Dex Strickland. The same thing that distanced her from Jake.

JAKE AND TADD SPLIT UP and, lacking a bicycle, Jake began his search for Clancy on foot. Tadd opted to go by boat. Her bike tires had left no tracks on the needle-covered path, so Jake had no way of knowing which way she'd gone or where she was headed. He took the trail directly behind the house.

He stormed up the trail, that hunch of his dancing to that same old little ditty. Clancy was the key. Had always been the key. Now that he knew Dex was Lola's son, there was no doubt in his mind that their deaths were connected. Nor did he have any choice but to dig into the old murder and his father's case.

What bothered him like a bad headache just getting started was his father. Why had Warren Hawkins asked him not to get involved? Well, Jake was involved now. And he was going to learn the truth. About his father. About Clancy.

But first he had to find her. She couldn't have gone far, he told himself. Jake couldn't believe she'd taken off again. He knew the shock had thrown her—just as it had him. But if she really believed someone was trying to kill her, how could she have taken such a chance?

Because she was too impetuous, independent and stubborn for her own good. But Jake knew he was partly to blame. He'd made it clear to her that she couldn't trust him. She was alone and scared. Now he had to find her before she got into more trouble.

CLANCY CRUISED DOWN the mountain on a narrow trail that came out directly behind Johnny and Helen Branson's place at the edge of the cliffs.

Helen spotted her as she came out of the pines and waved from the kitchen window for her to come on in.

Helen was petite with short blond hair that showed no gray, blue eyes and fair skin. Unlike Johnny, Helen didn't look as though she'd aged at all the last ten years. In fact, Clancy noticed with surprise, Helen looked as if she might be closer to thirty than she was fifty.

"I hope I didn't catch you right at dinner," Clancy apologized as she was met with the smell of pot roast.

"Don't be silly," Helen said from her wheelchair in front of the stove. Johnny had built the house to accommodate Helen's disability; everything was wheelchair level. "Stay for dinner. Johnny should be here any moment. We'd love to have you."

Clancy's stomach growled, and she remembered she hadn't eaten anything since breakfast, but she declined the offer. She had to get back before Jake called out the National Guard.

"Maybe some other time," she told Helen. "I just stopped by to ask you something."

"I heard about all that nasty business. I've been so concerned for you."

"That's why I wanted to talk to you. You remember Lola Strickland, the secretary at the resort?"

Helen frowned. "Why, yes."

"That man, the one who was killed upstairs at my lodge. His real name was Dex Strickland. He was Lola's son."

Helen's eyes widened. "My word. The woman had children?"

"One," Clancy said. "A son."

"But how can that be?" Helen asked. "I never saw her with a child, and she certainly never talked of children."

Clancy felt a surge of hope. "Then you did know her fairly well?"

Helen chuckled. "It's a small island, dear. Everyone knew her. But it sounds like you know more about Lola than I do. I didn't even know she had a son."

"Oh, I thought you might have befriended her," Clancy said.

"What would make you think that?" Helen asked as she turned to take a peek into the oven at her roast.

The smell was enough to make Clancy drool. "I remembered that you were both involved in the Flathead Community Theater Company in Bigfork that summer."

Helen laughed. "I just did some of the makeup and helped with costumes."

"Didn't Lola star in one of the plays right before her death?" Clancy asked.

Helen frowned as she reached into the refrigerator and pulled out a bowl of salad. "It's been so long, but now that you mention it, I think she did. Why do you ask?"

"I remember the play," Clancy said, suddenly hesitant. Earlier her theory had made sense. Right now it seemed silly. "I wondered if you knew what happened to the necklace she was wearing opening night?"

"A necklace?" Helen asked in surprise. She wheeled over to the dining-room table by the window with the salad. Clancy noticed the table settings for the first time. Fresh flowers, cloth napkins, candles and fancy china?

"Is it your anniversary?" Clancy asked, even more ashamed for interrupting Helen's cooking.

"Oh, dear, no." Helen smiled. "I just wanted to spoil my husband tonight. He's been a little under the weather lately."

Clancy felt tears pool in her eyes. They threatened to overflow and spill down her cheeks.

"I'm so fortunate to have a man like Johnny," Helen said, straightening the napkins she'd folded by each plate. "We've been married for almost thirty years. We were childhood sweethearts, you know." She turned and seemed surprised to find Clancy near tears. "Are you all right, dear?"

Clancy hadn't thought much about true love, marriage or love-ever-after. Not since Jake had left the island ten years ago. Dex certainly hadn't made her realize what she'd been missing. But standing here, smelling pot roast, seeing this romantic dinner scene, having earlier kissed her own childhood sweetheart—

"What's wrong?" Helen asked again.

Clancy made a swipe at her tears. She was exhausted. Overstressed. Overemotional. But then, why wouldn't she be? She was a suspected murderer who wasn't even sure she was innocent, and a dead man was after her. That would make anyone a little teary at unexpected moments. "I'm fine." She wondered how many more times she could say those two words before she started to scream.

"You're not fine," Helen said, taking her hand. "Tell me what's wrong."

Clancy found herself pouring out her heart. From Dex's death, to the hand coming out of the water and scraping her ankle with the silver watchband, to Jake.

Helen smiled kindly when she finished. "It sounds like Jake being back might be putting even more stress on you. You have feelings for him, haven't you?"

Clancy tried to deny it and couldn't. She brushed away her tears, feeling relieved to be able to talk to someone who believed her. "Thanks for listening to me."

"Anytime, dear. I'll always have a strong shoulder for you to cry on. Now, what can I do to help you?"

"Was there anyone else involved in the theater company that summer who might still be around?" Clancy asked.

Helen seemed to think for a moment. "Frank Ames. I believe he helped with some of the scenery." She straightened one of the place settings. "Why are you looking for a necklace of Lola's, dear?"

Clancy knew it sounded ridiculous. What could a string of tiny blue beads have to do with finding Dex's murderer? "I just thought she might have given it to a friend. Or left it with someone for safekeeping."

"You thought I was that friend." Helen smiled kindly. "I was probably as close as anyone to Lola, but I wouldn't say we became friends. I'm sorry, dear."

Johnny came in then. "Clancy, what a nice surprise. Something sure smells good. I hope you're staying for dinner."

"Pot roast," Helen said, sounding pleased. "Wash up. I tried to get Clancy to join us, but she can't. I want her and Jake to come to dinner soon."

"Real soon," Johnny called as he headed down the hall.

"What did this necklace look like?" Helen asked.

"Tiny blue beads. Like hippies used to wear. There was a small handmade dark blue ceramic heart at its center."

Helen seemed surprised. "I thought maybe it was diamonds. You made it sound so important."

Clancy knew she must seem irrational, worrying about a string of beads at a time like this. "Dex had it the day he was killed. I just wondered where he might have gotten it." And where it was now.

"I wish I could have helped," Helen said.

Clancy thanked her and made a hasty goodbye, promising she'd come back soon. Once on her bike, she headed for home.

The air felt cool against Clancy's flushed cheeks. It had been hot in the kitchen, she assured herself. She wasn't flushed and embarrassed about her silly behavior. Crying over nothing. As she rode through the shadowy trees, she made excuses for her tears back in Helen's kitchen. They had nothing to do with Jake Hawkins. Nothing at all, she told herself.

JAKE REACHED THE TOP of the ridge and stood for a moment, scanning what little of the island he could see through the dense pines, disappointed Clancy was nowhere to be seen. Down the mountain at the resort, an American flag snapped above the treetops in the wind; whitecaps dotted the water beyond the bay. Jake wondered if Clancy had gone back to the resort. Or if she was just out riding and thinking. Or maybe making a run for it?

He'd tried not to think on his hike up the mountain. It made his head hurt, trying to put together pieces of a puzzle he'd spent ten years trying to solve. Worse yet was worrying about Clancy. And that latest stupid kiss.

Not that he regretted either kiss. Unprofessional, yes. Totally out of line, unquestionably uncalled for. And yet he couldn't get either one out of his head, let alone out of his blood. He'd planned to do more than kiss her when the opportunity arose. But the kiss on the dock had been as unexpected for him as it was for her. The real problem, however, was the effect it had on him.

Now he was out wandering in the woods looking for the most frustrating woman in the world. Stubborn. Hell-bent determined. Too brave for her own good. Grudgingly, he admitted he admired her.

Under normal circumstances. But now he worried that

Clancy might not have just gone for a bike ride. He worried she might have taken off. Tricked him again.

There was one way to find out. If she'd run, she'd need a boat to get her off the island. As he hurried down the trail, he realized he'd spent most of his time on this case chasing that woman.

At the resort office, the clerk assured him that no one matching Clancy's description had rented a boat.

Jake used the phone to call the lodge, hoping Clancy had returned by now. He hadn't seen Tadd since they'd split up to search for her. Aunt Kiki quickly informed him that neither Clancy nor Tadd had returned.

He hung up, more worried. Unless he missed his guess, Clancy was still on the island. The question was where?

As he started to leave the phone booth, he remembered the Bransons and dialed their number.

"Clancy was here, Jake, but she left just a little while ago," Helen told him. He could hear the clatter of dishes in the background and apologized for interrupting her dinner. She assured him they were just finishing. "I invited Clancy to join us, but she said she had to get home."

He hung up, wondering why she'd gone to the Bransons', and started back up the trail. So she was headed home. That was a good sign. He told himself he'd known she hadn't taken off again, at least not far. But he still felt a sense of relief that lifted his spirits. All right, maybe he'd started to trust her a little and he was glad she hadn't broken that trust by skipping the island to parts unknown.

Come on, Hawkins. When are you going to be honest with yourself? You desperately want to believe in Clancy's innocence. You're such a chump, you even want to believe she didn't perjure herself at your father's trial, that maybe there's another explanation.

Jake cursed his own foolishness. As he topped the mountain and started down the other side, he spotted Liz Knowles. Two things struck him as odd. One was the way she was dressed. The other was her hurried pace. He went after her on the side trail she'd taken, wishing he had enough time to tail her secretly and find out where she was headed in such a hurry.

"Hello," Jake said, catching up to her.

She jumped, startled. Scared, too, he noticed. Like a turkey on Thanksgiving morning. He couldn't help but wonder if he was the cause of her fear. Or someone else. After all, if the cabin girl was right, Liz had spent some quality time with Dex right before his death.

"You haven't seen Clancy, have you?"

"Clancy?" She wore a freshly ironed shirt with matching shorts and sandals. Her hair was pulled up, her lips painted pink, her cheeks flushed with blusher, and she smelled of perfume. He figured she had a date and must be meeting him on the trail somewhere since there was nothing but rocks and trees the way she was headed. She seemed a little overdressed for a roll in the pine needles.

"Clancy Jones, the woman you said you overheard threaten Dex Westfall on the day he died," Jake said through gritted teeth.

"Why would you ask if I'd seen her?" The drone of a dirt bike broke the stillness. Liz glanced up the mountain, her look agitated. He was keeping her from something. "I don't even know the woman. Of course I haven't seen her." When she looked again at Jake, she seemed all the more anxious to be on her way.

He decided to let her go. She started down the trail, turned once to see if he was following her, then took a side trail that headed off to the west. He had a feeling that wasn't the way she'd intended to go, that she'd changed her plans because of him.

Jake headed down a trail that would eventually lead him back to Clancy's lodge. As he walked, Clancy crowded his thoughts. Flashes of her making pancakes. Lounging in the boat with that silly fishing hat hiding her eyes. Standing in his arms. Looking up at him, her eyes filled with— He stumbled and swore. Love.

CLANCY HEARD THE BUZZ of a dirt bike coming up the mountain. The engine whined, the bike bucking as it climbed the steep terrain. The sound grew louder. She felt a chill and realized how dark the sky had gotten. Shadows hunkered in the pines. A wind blew up from the lake, swaying the tops of the trees. She pedaled faster through the growing darkness of the approaching storm, anxious to get back to the lodge. And Jake. Her sense of security ebbed with the light.

She was almost at a trail that dropped down to her lodge when she heard the dirt bike behind her, saw its headlight flicker in the trees in front of her as the bike gained on her. The bike was coming up behind her fast. Too fast. Didn't he see her? She took a side trail, stopping partway down the narrow path, waiting for the motorbike to go by.

She didn't realize she'd been holding her breath until she heard the biker stop. Clancy looked up to see a figure wearing a shielded dark helmet standing astride an old motorbike. She couldn't see his face behind the helmet, but she could feel him staring at her. Her heart thundered at the thought of whose face was hidden behind the shield.

She jumped on her bike and took off down the tree-lined trail, wanting only to get home. Above her on the mountainside she heard the bike motor rev. In horror, she realized he was chasing her. Panic tore through her. She pedaled as if the devil himself were at her heels. But when she stole a glance back, the trail behind her was empty, and she could hear the whine of the dirt bike dying off into the distance.

Clancy's heart thumped wildly in her chest. Paranoia. Maybe Jake was right. She *was* imagining things. Her legs felt weak and shaky from her scare. What had made her think that biker was chasing her? Was it the same thing that had made her think someone had tried to drown her? The same thing that made her think she saw a light in the lodge last night? Made her think she saw Dex?

The sky darkened to charcoal overhead. In the distance, she heard the rumble of thunder. The wind picked up, whipping the tops of the pines. Ahead, the trail forked, the trees opened a little. The path to the left circled up the mountainside to the east end of the island, the one on the right dropped rapidly in a series of switchbacks to the beach and her lodge. Clancy relaxed. She'd be home soon. An image of a furious Jake filled her mind. Even he would be a welcome sight.

A bolt of lightning splintered the sky above the treetops, making her jump. Thunder boomed, drowning out the sound of the dirt bike.

The biker appeared in a flash of movement. Leaping from the pines. All she saw was a blur. All she felt was the bike hit hers. A scream caught in her throat. The ground came up to meet her. She hit it hard, knocking the air from her lungs. Then she fell, tumbling down the steep mountainside.

Chapter Thirteen

As Jake wound his way through the dense pines, he heard the unmistakable whine of the dirt bike again. It cut through the softer evening sounds, irritating his already fried nerves. He cursed himself with each step. He was handling things poorly. He should have stashed Clancy with her aunt Kiki. Or had her bail revoked. At least if she was in jail, he wouldn't have to worry about her. And right now, he was worried.

One of his faithful hunches pounded at the back of his brain to a little ditty that had started the moment Kiki Talbott Conners had set one high-heeled foot on the dock beside his boat in Galveston. It reverberated like the thunder overhead and promised a darkness far beyond the storm bearing down on the island.

THUNDER RUMBLED and the sky darkened like night. Clancy's skin was cut, scraped and gouged as she fell, plunging down through brush and branches, dirt and rocks. She fought to find purchase, grabbing at anything, everything, to keep from tumbling all the way down the steep mountain to the beach below. Finally, when she thought she'd never stop, she plunged over a large, old fallen log, decayed from the years, dropped into a hole rimmed by a thicket of fresh new pines and slammed to a halt.

That's when she felt the pain. It shot through her, making it hard to tell if she was seriously hurt or not. She tried to get to her feet, but her body screamed with pain for her to lie still a little longer.

Overhead, thunder clapped with a startling closeness. She glanced around to see that she'd fallen into a hole below the rotted log. Squirming away from the prickly pines, she leaned back against the warm earth, stared up at the blackened sky above her, and assessed her injuries. None fatal, few that required more than a bandage. She'd been very lucky. Again.

She replayed the accident over in her head. Then slowly she sat up, her heartbeat accelerating to breakneck speed. It had been no accident. The biker had waited in the pines and deliberately hit her. But why? And where was he now?

She glanced up the mountainside but couldn't see past the fallen log blocking her view. Suddenly the day seemed too quiet. In that deafening silence before the storm, she heard a sound above her that congealed her blood. The soft scuffle of footfalls, half stumbling, half sliding, coming down the mountain.

A flash of lightning electrified the sky and illuminated the darkness. The light died in an instant, leaving thunder to rattle across the treetops. Dirt showered down on her, cascading over the log, as someone drew closer. The biker. Her mouth went dry, her pulse pounded so loudly she feared he could hear it.

She didn't move, just waited, knowing that any moment he would peer over the log and see her lying there.

A voice in her mind, which sounded a lot like Jake's, yelled for her to move under the log. And yet she waited, with a sickening sureness that he'd find her before she could move. Then the lightning splintered the sky; thunder boomed. Clancy scrambled under the log, wedging herself into the small, narrow space between rotting log and earth. She held her breath and waited.

A boulder cartwheeled over the top of the rotted log with a resounding thump, then crashed through the new pines below her and on down the mountainside to the rocky beach below. It was followed by the thud of boots on top of the hollow-sounding log. She could almost feel him standing up there, looking down the mountainside, looking for her. To finish the job?

Rain splattered on the ground next to her, large, hard drops that pummeled the earth. Clancy closed her eyes, praying he wouldn't come any farther down the mountainside. If he did, he'd surely see her and— She squeezed her eyes tighter, concentrating on Jake's handsome face, the sound of that soft southern drawl, the feel of his arms wrapped around her. She prayed for Jake, clinging to the log and hope as she waited.

THE FIRST DROPS OF RAIN pelted down, angry and wet, as Jake would soon be. He told himself that when he found Clancy, he'd wring her neck. He'd bodily carry her to her aunt's for safekeeping. He'd take her over his knee and—

The dirt bike. It took Jake a moment to realize why the sound had pulled him from his frenzied thoughts. Its engine. Revved to the max. He looked up to see the headlight coming out of the blackness of the storm. The light flickered wildly as the bike roared down the pine-lined trail. Jake had only a moment to realize its rider didn't see him, couldn't see him in the rain and the darkness. He leaped from the path as the bike sped past.

Jake watched it go, not surprised to see Liz Knowles on the back of the bike, her russet hair blowing in the wind.

He cursed the biker and his close call. Then he turned and headed down the trail, following the path he knew would take him directly to Clancy's lodge. He hadn't gone far when something glinted in the trail ahead.

Dread clamped down on his heart as he thought he recognized the object at the edge of the trail. His breath caught as he drew closer. A bicycle, broken and twisted. His legs forced him forward, his mind arguing it wasn't Clancy's. Couldn't be hers. Clancy's ruined bike lay mangled at the edge of the steep drop-off in the rain.

"Clancy!" Jake screamed her name, a cry of fear and anguish, hope and despair. He stumbled past the bike to stare down the mountainside. The wind howled in the pines; rain bit into his skin, hard as stones. He bent down, saw the tracks where she'd slid down the mountainside and practically threw himself down the slope after her.

CLANCY THOUGHT SHE HEARD the high-pitched whine of the bike fade. But she stayed wedged beneath the log, afraid to move. Had he really left? How could she be sure?

In the end, it was thoughts of Jake that made her slowly edge out of her hiding place. The wind whipped the pines, making them groan. The rain splattered down, wet and cold, promising a torrent shortly. She looked up, half expecting to see the biker standing on the log above her, his body in silhouette, his face as black as the shield he'd hidden behind earlier.

But no one waited on the log.

Had he really gone? And more important, who was he? Why did he want to harm her?

Clancy pulled herself to her feet. Her body throbbed with so many pains she couldn't isolate one from another. Her right hip ached with a dull throb where she vaguely remembered hitting it on something as she tumbled down the

mountainside. The rain stung her skin, but she hardly no
ticed. She thought she heard her name on the wind. She
thought she heard Jake's voice because she'd wished it so

JAKE'S HEART THREATENED to burst from his chest as he
slipped and fell his way down the mountainside. He didn'
even realize he'd screamed her name until he heard her cal
out to him and look up. He saw her just below him.

Her face was covered with a mixture of dirt and blood
her clothes were torn and stained, her hair a nest of weed
and decomposed wood. He thought she'd never looked
more beautiful.

"Clancy?" His voice came out a whisper and wa
quickly carried away by the wind. "Clancy."

He stumbled down to her, grabbed her and pulled her
into his arms. "Oh, baby. Are you all right?"

He felt her nod against his chest as she tightened her
hold on him. Relief washed over him, making him weak
The rain began to fall in sheets, drenching him and every
thing it touched.

"He tried to kill me again," she said, her words muffled
against his chest. "The man on the dirt bike. This time you
believe me, don't you?"

He pulled back to look into her face. Words stuck in his
throat. "Yes," he whispered. "I believe you." He swept
her up into his arms and took her to the closest shelter—
his lodge.

CLANCY COULDN'T STOP shivering as Jake kicked open the
door and carried her up the stairs, straight to his room and
the shower. She leaned against him as he got the water
going, refusing to give up the warmth of his body or breach
the bond between them even for a moment.

He turned and, without breaking contact, pulled her int

the shower with him. The warm water felt wonderful, but not as wonderful as Jake as he drew her to him. He cupped her face in his hands. His mouth dropped to hers, taking her as his own, possessing her in that single kiss in the same way he'd possessed her heart for more than a decade.

His lips lingered on hers, savoring her, seducing her with his lips, his tongue, his breath. He drew back. She looked up at him, breathless from the kiss, from the look in his eyes. "Jake," she whispered, a plea.

Slowly, his gaze on hers, he unbuttoned her shirt, opening her bare skin to the warm water and the fire of his touch. She leaned into the spray and him, letting the water wash away the dirt and blood, letting Jake wash away the years of hurt.

He caught his breath as her shirt dropped from her shoulders to the shower floor. His gaze alone hardened her nipples, making them ache with longing. He reached to unhook her bra, freeing her breasts to his gaze, to his touch, to his mouth and the rough, wet feel of his tongue.

Warmth sprinted from her hardened nipple through her body, making her weak. She ached for the feel of his skin on hers as she hurriedly unbuttoned his shirt, pushing aside the wet cloth to brush her palms across the solid wet heat of his flesh.

With a groan, he stripped off her jeans and panties and dragged her to him. Her pulse matched the thunder outside as he backed her up against the shower wall, trapping her there, her body now at his mercy. She surrendered as he devoured her swollen breasts, sucking her nipples red and hard. Then his mouth trailed down her belly to her open thighs, where he consumed her with the same kind of desperate need. She buried her fingers in his hair, arching against his mouth, as a hot current raced through her. There was no need for words; for once, they completely understood each other. There were no walls. No fences. Nothing to keep their hearts from running free.

"Jake," she whispered as she unbuttoned his jeans. A plea. A promise.

Jake stepped out of his wet jeans and lifted her, hip to hip. He breathed her name, husky with desire. "Clancy." Not a question. An affirmation. He thrust her against the shower wall, his gaze locking with hers. She gasped as he filled her so completely, and with each drive, he took her spiraling up, the water pounding them as the rain beat down on the skylight overhead. As the thunder rumbled and lightning lit the sky, he took her higher and higher, further and further, until they both soared like hawks over the island.

Jake said nothing as he pulled her into his arms. She buried her face in his shoulder, hugging him tightly, grazing his skin with a kiss. He placed a hand on the back of her blond head and gazed down at her. So small. So strong. So beautiful. He should have been surprised by his feelings for her. But instead he was more surprised by her feelings for him. After everything he'd done to her, she still loved him.

She leaned back to look up into his eyes. Then she picked up the bar of soap and gently glided it over his skin, lathering his shoulders, his chest, his belly.

He watched her eyes, still dark with pleasure, and he knew he had to have her again. One time would never still the need inside him. He doubted a hundred thousand would.

He took the soap from her and slowly slid it over her, from the pounding pulse at the hollow of her neck, over her luscious, full, rounded breasts, down to the hollow of her stomach, to the silken V of her thighs.

She groaned softly, her eyes darkening as her hands trailed over his skin.

He pulled her to him, their bodies slick and slippery. He buried himself in her again, losing himself in her body, in her eyes, in her.

CLANCY CAME OUT of the bathroom, her wet hair curled at her neck, her skin pink and bare except for the towel wrapped around her. Jake tossed another log on the fire and closed the screen.

"Do you want to go home and get something on your scrapes and scratches?" he asked as he closed the distance between them. "You must hurt all over from your fall."

She shook her head. Thunder boomed overhead, rattling the windows. Rain streaked the glass and pounded the deck. "I've never felt this wonderful."

He laughed as he swept her up and carried her to his bed. Before he joined her, he picked up the cell phone and dialed Clancy's number. Kiki answered on the first ring.

"Clancy's fine," Jake said. "She'll be back in the morning. Go home." He hung up and pulled Clancy into his arms. They lay together watching the storm rage outside, the fire crackle and glow inside until they fell asleep, spooned together in the middle of the bed.

THE NEXT MORNING, Clancy woke to find Jake propped up on one elbow, looking down at her. He smiled as he brushed hair back from her forehead and planted a kiss between her eyes, then dropped to place one on her lips.

She lay on her back, watching his face. When she'd first opened her eyes she'd caught him frowning down at her. She'd gone to sleep happier than she could ever remember being. Now she felt as if an elephant had just sat on her chest. "What is it?"

He seemed surprised by her question, then his smile faded. "You really don't miss anything, do you?" He trailed a finger across her shoulder.

She could almost hear the wheels turning in his head as she sat up, pulling the sheet over her bare breasts and leaned against the headboard, bracing herself. Outside, the storm had let up. The lake lay slate gray and flat. Water dripped from the eaves. In the distance, Clancy could see a slit of blue sky on the horizon.

Jake pulled himself up and leaned back against the wall next to the bed so he could face her. "Clancy, I've never been closer to anyone than I am to you."

She feared what was coming. She promised herself she wouldn't cry. "Why don't you just say it. This was a mistake."

She started to get up but he grabbed her arm and kept her on the bed.

"No, dammit, I'm trying to tell you that making love to you has made me realize that now more than ever, I want— I *need* to know—"

She knew the words before he said them.

"The truth. I have to know, Clancy. For my sanity's sake. For…our sake."

She stared at him. For a few hours she'd forgotten why he'd come back to Montana. Didn't he say he'd get the truth out of her at any cost? "Is that why you made love to me?" she asked. She shoved him away and got out of bed, anger soothing the dagger of hurt that was stuck in her heart. "Is that what this was all about? You thought if you got me naked and in a weakened enamored state, maybe I'd break down and confess everything?" She remembered her clothes were still on the shower floor, soaking wet.

"No! Dammit. You're not listening to me."

"Oh, I hear you just fine, Jake." She jerked a pair of jeans from Jake's closet. From the few items of clothing he'd brought, he obviously hadn't planned to stay long. Just get the truth out of her—whatever it took, even seducing her. Then he'd be gone back to Galveston. Oh, what a fool she'd been. Did she really think making love meant anything to him? Just a means to an end.

The jeans were way too big, but that didn't stop her. She tugged them on, grimacing at her aches and pains. Just hours ago, she'd felt nothing but pleasure in Jake's arms. But this morning, her sore body reminded her painfully that some things hadn't changed. Making love with Jake had solved nothing.

"Dammit, you're wrong," Jake said, flying out of the bed to tower over her. "You think last night was just part of my plan?"

She looked up at him. "Don't tell me it didn't cross your mind."

His gaze slithered off. "I'll admit it did cross my mind but—"

"That's what I thought." She shoved her way past him to the closet and jerked one of his shirts from the hanger.

"Listen to me, woman. I used to imagine making love with you." He took her bare shoulders and drew her around to face him. "Nothing in my imagination would ever come close to actually being with you."

"Now, if I'd just quit lying to you, everything would be perfect, right?" She shucked his hands from her shoulders and tried to get the shirt on without him seeing how hard she was shaking. She didn't want him to see how much he'd hurt her. She didn't even want to admit it to herself.

"Where do you think you're going?" Jake demanded, stomping around to face her in all his nakedness.

She pushed past him. "Leave me alone, Hawkins."

"I can't stand this between us. Can't you understand that, Clancy?"

She angrily thrust one arm into a sleeve, then the other,

making him have to step back to keep from getting slugged. "Nothing I can say or do will ever convince you."

"You can't just stomp off. Not now." She stepped back when he reached for her. He raked a hand through his hair and let out a frustrated curse. "Are you forgetting that someone tried to kill you?"

She fumbled with the buttons, not caring which holes they went in. "No, Jake, something like that doesn't exactly slip your mind, especially when I'd been telling you someone was after me all along and you didn't believe me." She stuffed her feet into her wet sandals and headed for the door.

"Just a minute, you aren't leaving like this. Let me get dressed. You took off by yourself yesterday and look where it got you."

She turned to see him hopping on one foot as he tried to pull on a pair of jeans. He looked so flustered, so much like the boy she'd fallen in love with. She cursed the emotions that drew her to him, the heart that threatened to break at just the sight of him. "Damn you, Hawkins. There are worse things than having a crazed killer after you. Like having a crazed ex-boyfriend who pretends to want to help you. Especially one you've been in love with your entire life." She turned and left, slamming the door on the way out.

"WHERE HAVE YOU BEEN?" Aunt Kiki demanded the moment Clancy slammed into the lodge. "Are you all righ—" She glanced from Clancy's flushed, scraped and scratched face to Jake's shirt, improperly buttoned with one tail hanging lower than the other. Clancy had to hold up the much too-large jeans with one hand.

"I'm fine," Clancy snapped, sweeping past her, feeling like a teenager caught necking. "Someone on a dirt bike tried to kill me. Other than that—'' She turned and walked to her aunt, whose eyes widened in obvious disapproval at this inappropriate display of emotion. ''And *someone* brought Jake Hawkins back into my life. If the guy on the bike doesn't get me, Jake will convince the state to hang me instead of just send me to prison. Other than that, I'm just fine. Didn't Jake tell you to go home?''

Kiki looked highly offended, but then she often did. ''I don't take orders from Mr. Hawkins. And believe me, *this*—'' she waved a hand at Clancy's postcoital condition ''—isn't what I had in mind when I hired him.''

It gave Clancy some satisfaction to see how displeased her aunt was over Clancy's liaison with Jake Hawkins. ''Sometime you'll have to tell me just what it was you *did* have in mind when you hired him. In the meantime, I will just continue to assume that you've lost your mind.''

Clancy turned and, with all the dignity she could muster, limped toward the stairs, her body hurting with each step.

''By the way,'' Kiki said behind her, ''your lawyer called. It seems he fell while looking for you and broke his leg. He's at the hospital but said he plans to be home later. You might want to call him. That's if you are still interested in not going to prison.''

''Actually, prison is looking better all the time,'' Clancy said without turning around.

She heard her aunt sniff in disapproval, then leave quietly. Always the Talbott, she thought, thankful that she had enough Jones in her to rant and rave and show some good, honest emotion.

Clancy started up the stairs, changed her mind and went back to lock all the doors. The last person she wanted to see again was Jake Hawkins. She'd much prefer Dex Westfall's ghost.

As Clancy climbed the stairs, she concentrated on the

pain from her fall instead of the warmth inside her where
Jake had been. Her skin still simmered from where his skin
had touched hers. She used anger as a salve. What had she
thought? That once they made love, Jake would realize she
couldn't have possibly lied? That she was a woman who
would never betray her man? That he'd been wrong? Oh,
sure. A man as stubborn, intractable and incorrigible as Jake
Hawkins? Fat chance.

JAKE TOOK A FEW frustrating minutes to try to find a shirt,
then gave up and went after Clancy, realizing that all he'd
done in the three days since he'd hit Montana was chase
this woman and he was getting damned tired of it.

He threw open his front door to find Kiki poised under
the dripping eave ready to knock. It didn't take a genius to
see that she was madder than an old wet hen. She glanced
at his bare chest with distaste. She was lucky he hadn't
come to the door stark naked. He almost wished he had just
for the shock value, although he doubted much could shake
up Kiki.

"What?" he demanded. Before she could speak, he
added, "Whatever it is, I don't have time for it."

"Perhaps we misunderstood each other, Mr. Hawkins,"
she said, her look darker than the storm that had passed
through. "I hired you to help my niece, not seduce her."

He bit back a nasty retort and tried not to bite off her
head. "It's none of your business who Clancy…sleeps with
or doesn't." In his case, it would be "doesn't" in the future, he was sure, but he wasn't about to tell her that.

Kiki narrowed her gaze at him. "Please don't be offended, but you're not right for my niece. She deserves
better than some…private investigator. Her mother married
poorly. I won't let that happen to Clancy. I hope that's clear
enough for you."

"Marrying your niece isn't even an option," Jake snapped.

Kiki's look would have frozen boiling water. "How nice to hear. Do you know who killed Dex Westfall yet, Mr. Hawkins?"

"No, as a matter of fact, I don't. If I could keep your niece from disappearing every time I turn around, I might be able to find out."

"See if you can do that." With a haughty flip of her head, she turned and headed for her boat.

Furious, he slammed out of his lodge and stalked the distance to Clancy's. *Some private investigator.* The nerve of that woman. He'd marry anyone he damned well pleased. As he stormed up Clancy's steps, he wasn't sure who he was the most angry with. Kiki. Clancy. Or himself.

He'd blown it, plain and simple. The case. But mostly Clancy. And, he realized with a start, he didn't give a damn about anything else. But she was right; what the hell was he doing making love to her when he still thought she was a liar and possibly a murderer?

Because I'm in love with her! He felt like he'd been struck by lightning. *You're in love with a liar and a possible murderer?* He stood for a moment, trying to get his bearings. He'd prove she was neither, dammit. He'd prove it to himself and then... And then what would he do? Throw himself at her mercy? Good luck.

But first he had to get back into her good graces somehow. It wasn't going to be easy. But for once, he thought he knew what to do.

CLANCY WAS CURLED UP on the couch in her robe, a heating pad on her back, a bag of crushed ice on one ankle, her scrapes, scratches and cuts disinfected and bandaged, when Jake burst in.

''I thought I locked that door,'' she demanded.

''Like everyone else in the world, I know where you keep your key.''

She gave him a sour look. ''Did you come to make love to me again to see if I'd crack this time?''

He cocked a brow at her. ''I want to make love to you again, yes. But not for the reason you think.''

Her look, as she got up to escape to another room, said his chances of that weren't good.

''But I'm not going to make love to you,'' he said.

She stopped and raised a brow at him. ''No kidding.''

''You were right. There's enough going on in your life right now without me complicating things by making mad, passionate love to you. We have a killer to find.'' He moved toward her, wanting desperately to take her in his arms and do exactly what he was about to promise he wouldn't. ''We have to concentrate. For now. So, I promise I won't even kiss you.'' He reached out to run his thumb along her lips. ''Or make love to you. Not until you ask me to.''

''Well, there's no chance of that.'' Clancy took a ragged breath. Just when she thought things couldn't get any worse, he'd promised not to even kiss her until she asked him to. Right. How could she be around him and not beg him to kiss her, beg him to make love to her? Prison was starting to look like a picnic.

''So, we'd better get back to business. We have to go to the resort and talk to Liz,'' Jake said. ''She knows who was driving that bike.''

Clancy told herself at least now he believed someone really was trying to kill her. She supposed that was something. Although, she did wonder about this sudden turnaround of Jake's. What was he up to with this promise of his? Something.

Out of the corner of her eye, she looked into his wonderfully handsome face and felt her dark mood lighten like the blue sky through the window. Even as a kid she could never stay mad at him.

"All right," she said, hoisting herself up from the couch. The parts of her body that weren't bruised, scraped, scratched or gouged, ached. All of her still ached for one man. She gave Jake a resigned look. "Let me get some clothes on."

He gave her a wide berth as she passed. Fool that she was, she already missed his touch.

IT LOOKED LIKE OFF-SEASON at Hawk Island Resort. The storm that had hammered the island most of the night still had everyone curled up inside their cabins. Only a handful of hard-core fishermen bailed their boats at the docks for a morning fishing trip. Everything dripped, wet and cold. June in Montana.

"I'd tell you to stay here—" Jake started, then smiled "—but what would be the point? You might as well tag along. One look at that scraped-up face of yours and Liz is bound to talk."

"Thanks a lot," Clancy said, climbing out of the boat and sweeping past him.

But when they reached the café, the only person banging around at the back of the small kitchen was Frank Ames.

"What do you want?" Frank said, glancing up from the dirty grill.

"We're looking for Liz Knowles," Jake said.

Frank cursed and continued scraping the grill with a large metal spatula. "Isn't everybody."

"What does that mean?" Jake demanded, amazed at how quickly he could lose his patience with Frank.

Frank gave him a smirk. "She didn't show up for work this morning."

A bad feeling settled in the pit of Jake's stomach. "When was the last time anyone saw her?"

"I wouldn't know," Frank said, throwing down the spatula in disgust. "What's the big deal with you, anyway? I'm the one who has no waitress."

Jake leaned over the counter toward Frank, hoping he wouldn't have to cross it to get what he wanted out of him. "Did you check her cabin?"

Frank had the good sense to look a little nervous. "Of course. She hadn't slept in her bed. One of the cabin girls said she had plans last night with one of the dock boys. He says she never showed up for their date. She probably left the island with some guy she met. Happens every summer." He turned back to his dirty grill.

"Who has a dirt bike on the island?" Jake asked.

Frank stopped scraping and turned around slowly. "Why?"

Well, that answered that question. "Who besides you?"

Frank looked suspicious. And worried. He laid down the spatula again. At this rate, he'd never get that grill cleaned. "No one. Why?"

"Someone on a dirt bike tried to kill Clancy," Jake said.

"What?" His gaze shot to Clancy, surprise registering in his expression when he saw her injuries. "Just a damned minute here," he said to Jake. "You're not pinning me with that. I haven't ridden that bike since last summer."

"Where is your bike?" Jake asked. "I want to see it."

Frank ripped off his apron and threw it down on the counter. With a mean look, he led them to the back of his place and a dilapidated shed. Frank swung the door open and stood for a moment staring into the semidarkness inside.

Frank's shoulders sagged. He swore but didn't turn around.

Jake stepped past him to look inside the shed. Junk had been piled waist-deep in a U-shaped heap that left only a small, narrow space at the center. Just small and narrow enough for a dirt bike. But there was no bike.

"Someone stole my bike," Frank said. "Not that I'd expect you to believe me."

Jake didn't. "How could someone take it? Where was the key for it?"

Frank avoided his gaze. "I always left the key in it and the helmet on the seat."

"That's handy," Jake said.

"It was handy," Frank snapped.

Jake couldn't believe this. "And I suppose everyone knew the key was in it?"

Frank kicked at the shed door in answer. "No one's ever stolen it before, so why would they now?"

"Is there any reason anyone would want to incriminate you in a murder?" Clancy asked from behind him.

Frank's head flew up. "You mean someone took my bike to make it look like I tried to kill you?"

"Bingo." Jake watched Frank's eyes widen in surprise, then narrow in meanness.

"No. No one." The lie seemed to catch in Frank's throat. "That's the craziest thing I've ever heard."

"If Liz turns up, have her call me," Jake ordered.

Frank nodded distractedly.

Jake would have given a penny for his thoughts.

ON THE BOAT TRIP BACK to the lodge, the sun burst through the clouds, making the morning golden if not exactly warm. A few thin clouds scudded across the blue. A light breeze rippled the top of the water, bringing with it the smell of wet pines.

Jake's obvious disappointment in not finding Liz or the

bike hung like a dark cloud over him. Clancy knew he was
worried about Liz. Had Liz seen the biker run Clancy off
the trail? Is that why she'd disappeared? Then, what had
she been doing on the back of the bike just after that? She
must have known Clancy's assailant. Did that mean Liz was
part of whatever was going on? She *had* spent time with
Dex.

Clancy felt a shiver as she and Jake walked up the beach
toward the lodge. As hard as she tried not to, she kept
seeing Dex's face beneath that bike helmet.

As Clancy opened the door, she could hear the phone
ringing. She raced to it. "Hello?"

Silence.

Her heart began to pound. Another one of those crank
calls. She motioned for Jake to pick up the extension in the
living room. "Hello? Is anyone there?"

For a moment all she could hear was the labored
breathing. Then came the distinct sound of a match being
struck as the person on the other end of the line lit a cigarette and took a long drag. "Please say something,"
Clancy urged.

"Clancy Jones?" The hoarse voice was a woman's. At
least Clancy thought it was. "I need to talk to Clancy
Jones."

"This is Clancy."

"I need your help." The woman sounded scared. And
maybe a little drunk. Clancy wondered if that wasn't why
she'd finally decided to speak rather than hang up like she
had the other times.

"My help?" Clancy asked in surprise.

"My name is Glenda Grimes," the woman said. Clancy
could hear her tapping nervously on something as she
spoke. "You don't know me. I'm Lola Strickland's sister.
Half sister."

Clancy looked across the room at Jake. His eyes widened in surprise. He nodded for her to keep talking.

"What can I do for you?" Clancy asked.

"Could you come up to Somers? I've got to talk to you. It's about Dex. I know who killed him."

Chapter Fourteen

Jake turned off Highway 93 and drove the Mustang through downtown Somers, a community with little more than a bar, post office, café and hardware store. He drove up one of the dirt streets to the top of a rise and parked in front of a small dilapidated cottage overlooking the highway.

"Are you feeling all right?" Jake asked. "You've been awfully quiet."

"Just thinking." Clancy brushed her hair back from her face and gave him what she hoped was a reassuring smile. After what Jake had told her, she was worried about Liz Knowles. She agreed with Jake; there was a killer out there and she felt if they didn't stop him, he'd kill again. As she opened her car door, she hoped Glenda Grimes really did know something that could help them.

A woman in her sixties answered the door with a cigarette and a beer. She held little resemblance to her half sister, Lola. A bright-colored scarf tied around her head hid most of her frizzy dyed red hair; a faded chenille robe the color of dirt hid most of her body, except for a pair of bony bare feet poking out the bottom of the robe, the toenails painted bright red. The same color as the lipstick smear on her beer can.

"Yes?" the woman asked, suspicion as much a part of her face as the wrinkles.

"Glenda Grimes?" Jake asked.

Eyes narrowed, she looked from Clancy to Jake and back. Clancy could smell her perfume. A mixture of cigarette smoke, beer and perm solution. At one time, she might have been pretty, Clancy thought. But not as pretty as Lola.

"What do you want?" She had the voice of a woman who'd spent a good deal of her life on a bar stool. She took a drag off the cigarette and blew the smoke out the corner of her mouth as she eyed them.

"I'm Clancy Jones." It didn't seem to register at first, and Clancy felt her initial rush of hope dissolve. Either the woman was a crackpot or Glenda Grimes hadn't called her at all.

Glenda looked around warily before she settled her gaze on Jake. "Who's he?"

"He's a private investigator," Clancy said, then added, "and a good friend of mine."

Glenda studied Jake for a moment, then glanced past him as if she thought someone might be watching them. Hurriedly she pushed open the screen and ushered them inside, closing and locking the door.

And Clancy thought *she* was paranoid.

Clancy stepped into a small, cramped living room. The place was filled with...stuff. Every flat surface had something on it from chipped figurines and old perfume bottles to ashtrays with the names of Montana bars.

"All I have is beer," Glenda said, shuffling into the cluttered kitchen to swing open the door of an old fridge with so many magnets on it Clancy couldn't tell the color.

Both Clancy and Jake declined, and Glenda finished the beer in her hand and pulled out a fresh one. It was obvious she'd already had a few as she came into the living room.

"Sit down." She motioned to a broken-down couch in a dark corner and dropped into a faded chair across from them. Clancy watched her put her beer next to an overflowing ashtray beside her chair. Her fingers trembled.

"There's something I don't understand," Clancy said. "If you have information about Dex's murder, why did you call me instead of going to the police?"

The woman took a drag off her cigarette, then fumbled it back into the ashtray. She popped the top on the beer and took a long drink as if she thought it would steady her nerves. Clancy wondered what Glenda Grimes had to be nervous about.

"You're the one they arrested for Dex's murder, right?" Glenda asked.

Clancy nodded, wondering where this was going.

"I figured you'd care more than the police about who really killed Dex."

That made an odd kind of sense to Clancy. "On the phone you said you knew who killed him."

Glenda reached for another cigarette, fingers shaking violently. "I did."

"You?" Clancy asked incredulously.

"I wasn't the one who bashed his head in, mind you, but I killed him just as sure as you're sitting here." Glenda reached for her beer and a tissue.

Clancy shot a look at Jake. Glenda Grimes was a crackpot, just as they'd feared. A morose woman who cried in her beer and blamed herself for her nephew's death. Another dead end.

"Why should you feel responsible?" Jake asked.

"I was the one who got him all stirred up about the past." She started to cry. "Got him digging into things that should have been left buried."

"What kind of things?" Jake asked.

Glenda just shook her head and cried. "I've never been to Vegas. I'm an old woman. I want to go before I die. That isn't too much to ask, is it?"

What did that have to do with Dex's death?

"So you really don't know who killed your nephew," Jake said, getting to his feet. "Why did you call Clancy and waste her time?"

Glenda wiped her tears and narrowed her eyes at him. "I don't know who actually killed him. But I know why," she said, anger making her cheeks pink.

"Why?" Jake demanded. When she didn't answer, he swore softly under his breath. "Two people have already died. If you really do know something—"

"Somebody doesn't want all that old stuff about Lola coming out again. You've got to find the murderer before he finds me." Glenda finished her beer as if it were an antidote.

"Why would someone want to kill you?" Jake asked. "What is it you know?"

"It isn't what I know," she cried. "It's what he might think I know. Don't you see, I talked to Dex and he figured it out. If the killer finds out I talked to Dex, he might think I know more than I do and come after me."

"Wait a minute," Clancy interrupted. "How do you know Dex figured it out?"

Glenda studied the end of her cigarette. "He came by here the night before he died. He told me he knew who killed his mother."

Jake shot Clancy a look she recognized instantly. Total disbelief. "He didn't tell you who that person was?"

"He didn't want to get me involved," Glenda said. "Just believe me, Dex was positive he'd figured it out."

"Based on what?" Jake demanded.

Glenda shook her head. "He'd collected everything he could find on his mother's murder."

The newspaper clippings, Clancy thought.

"He'd even hatched some lamebrain scheme that involved getting to know Clancy, thinking, I guess, that she might know something. I told him the rest, about the trial, his mother..." Glenda said with a look of disgust.

Clancy thought of the beautiful, dark-haired woman who had worked at the resort office. "I don't remember very much about Lola. Can you tell us what you told Dex?"

Glenda let out a long sigh, making Clancy think it was going to be a long story. "Lola looked like her daddy. All that dark hair, those dark secretive eyes, a face that stopped traffic."

"You didn't have the same father?" Clancy asked.

"No, my daddy died when I was young. Mama remarried and had Lola." Glenda wagged her head. "Lola was spoiled, wild and foolhardy from the get-go. She ran off at sixteen and got herself into trouble. Then she goes and runs off again after Dex is born." Glenda leaned back, as if that pretty much covered Lola's entire life history.

"Did you see much of her when she lived on the island?" Jake asked.

"She'd stop by just to lord it over me. Tell me about the parties she'd been to, important people she'd met."

"Do you know where she was going the night of the fire?" Clancy asked.

Glenda raised a brow. "She *thought* she was taking off with her lover."

"Her lover?" Jake and Clancy asked in unison.

Glenda seemed surprised by their surprise. "Lola always had a lover, but this time she thought she'd met her Prince Charming." She rolled her eyes. "But he turned out to be just another loser."

"You knew who this man was?" Jake asked.

"Lola never told me, just that I'd find out soon enough and I should expect fireworks," Glenda said. "Lola loved drama in her life."

"You think he was married," Jake said.

Was Jake thinking of his father, Clancy wondered.

"Could be why Lola kept him a secret." Glenda made a production of lighting another cigarette. "Who knows? But I can tell you this, he was no Prince Charming."

"What makes you say that?" Clancy asked.

"Where were his suitcases if he planned to run off with her?" Glenda asked. "All her talk about how sweet he was, loving, caring, considerate. I knew he sounded too good to be true."

"You think he's the one who killed her?" Jake asked.

"He could have been," Glenda said as she got up and headed for the fridge. "Probably over the money."

Clancy and Jake exchanged a glance. "What money?" Clancy asked first.

"The money Lola stole." Glenda gave them a look as if to say they weren't as bright as she'd hoped.

"Are you talking about the money that was missing from Clancy's and my father's businesses?" Jake asked. The money Warren Hawkins had gone to prison for embezzling. "Lola stole it?"

"If there is one thing Lola loved even more than men, it was money." Glenda dug around in the fridge. "I wonder if she ever really planned to run off with this guy."

"What do you mean?" Clancy asked.

"She could have led the guy on, planning to double-cross him all along," she said as she slammed the fridge door and popped another top. "Maybe he found out and killed her."

"If you thought Lola embezzled the money, why didn't you come forward during the trial?" Jake demanded.

Clancy could have cut the tension in the room with a dull knife.

Glenda came back into the room, sat and dug another cigarette out of a half-empty pack. "Why? I don't know she did it. Why get involved in something I didn't know squat about?"

"You were her sister," Jake shot back.

"Half sister. Maybe I didn't want anyone knowing I was related to her. It wasn't like she told anyone about me. Anyway, she'd made someone mad enough to kill her. I didn't want to get involved."

"But you did get involved," Clancy pointed out. "When you told Dex. Why did you decide to tell what you knew now?"

Glenda looked toward the front door as if she expected someone to come bursting in at any moment. "I want to go to Vegas before I die."

It took Clancy a moment. "You told Dex because you thought he would uncover the missing money."

Jake swore.

Tears filled Glenda's eyes. "How did I know it was going to get Dex killed?" she demanded. "I just thought he might be able to solve the mystery of what happened to that money."

"What made you think the money was even still around?" Jake asked, sounding surprised. "It had been embezzled over a period of time. What makes you think the embezzler didn't spend it as fast as he stole it?"

She shrugged. "I figure if Lola stole the money, she would have been real careful. She'd know better than to spend it. So she'd hide it somewhere. She was probably going to pick it up that night but she got killed. Her lover might or might not have known where she'd hidden the money. Either way, he probably didn't have time to rehide it before he was arrested for her murder.''

That was quite the theory, Clancy thought. *If* Lola took the money.

"But now Warren Hawkins is coming up for parole," Jake said, an edge to his voice. "You wanted to get to the money before he could. Just in case he was that man."

Glenda took a swig of her beer.

"Wait a minute," Clancy said, frowning at the woman. "You're saying now that you don't believe it was Warren Hawkins?"

"Someone murdered Dex because he was getting too close to the truth," Glenda said with certainty.

Jake shook his head. "You had to have told Dex more than this for him to figure out who killed Lola."

"I told you everything I told him," Glenda said stubbornly. "When he came by, he wasn't here long. We talked, he looked through a box of junk Lola left here, but he didn't take anything except for some silly necklace, and he left."

Clancy's head jerked up. "Necklace?"

"What box of junk?" Jake demanded with a pained look.

"What did this necklace look like?" Clancy questioned.

"Just a string of beads," Glenda said.

Clancy felt her heart rate accelerate. "Pale blue with a navy ceramic heart in the center?"

Glenda nodded, eyeing her suspiciously. "How did you know that?"

"Dex showed me the necklace. He said his mother left it to him."

The woman snorted. "Lola didn't leave him nothing. She could have cared less about the boy. It was just some stuff she dumped here and a few personal things the police turned over to me after the fire."

So Glenda had come forward after the trial to collect her sister's valuables. Only they hadn't turned out to be valuable.

"You should have seen the way that boy rifled through that box," Glenda was saying. "Like he thought she'd left him buried treasure or something." Glenda wagged her head. "It was pathetic to see—"

"You still have the box?" Jake interrupted.

"It doesn't have a thing in it that's worth anything," she said. "That's probably why Lola left it with me."

"I'd like to see the box," Jake insisted.

With effort, Glenda pushed herself out of the chair and went into one of the rooms off the living room. She returned a few minutes later with a shoe box and handed it to Jake. He set it on the coffee table and carefully removed the contents. Clancy slid closer.

Glenda was right. It contained little of monetary value. Several pressed dried roses. Ticket stubs from the local theater. A faded fishing lure. A plastic bubble with fake snow falling over a fat, red-cheeked Santa. A cheap dime-store mood ring. A pair of tarnished silver half-moon earrings. An envelope of photographs from the resort, mostly scenic, Clancy noticed as she flipped through them. A stack of play programs, ones Lola had had roles in. A handful of greeting cards. It reminded Clancy of the kind of things a young girl keeps from her first love affair.

It seemed odd that Dex would take nothing but the bead necklace. Had he just taken it because it belonged to his mother? Then, why didn't he take some of the other things? "Was the necklace in the box when Lola gave it to you?"

Glenda shook her head. "She must have been wearing it. The cops gave it to me with that ring and those earrings." She pointed to the mood ring and the half-moon earrings Jake had pulled out of the box. "That's the lot of her belongings,'' Glenda said with disgust. ''And all that talk about her ritzy friends.''

Jake handed Clancy the photographs he'd found. She leafed through them, stopping in surprise at a photo of Lola with a man she recognized. The man stood next to Lola on the dock in front of the resort, his arm around her shoulders, a smile on his face as he looked down at her. There was what Clancy would describe as a longing in his eyes. The man was Tadd Farnsworth.

''Could this have been Lola's Prince Charming?'' Clancy asked.

Glenda squinted at the photograph, then shook her head. ''Why the fuss over keeping it a secret if she was going to pose right in front of the resort with him?''

Clancy had to agree. She suspected Lola's great love had been a forbidden one. She just wondered why.

Jake glanced through the greeting cards, then handed them to Clancy. They were all in the same hand, all the kind of cards a man in love might buy a woman, all with the same inscription: ''With love, your Teddy Bear.''

Glenda nodded with a smirk. ''Teddy Bear. Can you believe that?''

It didn't sound to Clancy like anything a grown man would call himself, but what did she know about men? She put the cards back into the box.

''Do you think Teddy Bear was this man she planned to run off with?'' Jake asked.

Glenda shrugged. ''If a guy who calls himself Teddy Bear doesn't have something to hide, who does?''

''This stuff meant something to her,'' Clancy said, glancing at the odd items from the box. ''That's why she brought it here.'' But why? Was she worried that something might happen to her? Was there a clue in this box as to who killed her and had Dex recognized it? Then, why had he taken only the necklace, which hadn't even been in the box?

Out of the corner of her eye, Clancy saw Jake slip one of the cards into his pocket when Glenda wasn't looking. Clancy hoped he hadn't taken it because he'd recognized the handwriting as his father's, and that Teddy Bear was Warren Hawkins. If Glenda's theory was right, Lola's lover was still on the loose—and a killer. And if that were true, then Warren Hawkins had gone to prison for a murder he hadn't committed.

"Do you mind if we take this photograph?" Jake asked, holding up the one of Lola and Tadd.

"Take the whole box," Glenda said. "I want it out of here."

Chapter Fifteen

Clancy was too quiet as they left Somers. Jake drove along the lakeshore, his own thoughts tangled. The storm had left the day cooler than usual, but Jake cracked his window, anyway, to let in some of the fresh air. He found himself going over what Glenda had told them, trying to fit the odd-shaped chunks of truths and lies together. It made his head ache.

"Glenda Grimes knows more that she's telling us," Jake said with a silent curse. He looked over at Clancy when she didn't respond. "Want to tell me what's bothering you?"

They'd gone a few miles along the Flathead Lake shoreline, everything lush and green after the storm. He suspected Clancy had seen him pocket the card. She didn't miss much. Or was he losing his touch?

"You've never believed your father was guilty," she said quietly. "So who did you think was?"

Jake knew this discussion had been coming for years. Actually, he was surprised they hadn't gotten into it sooner. He pulled the Mustang over at the first wide spot and turned off the engine. Sunlight flickered on the water. A canopy of clouds still hung over the mountains. It had seemed clear to him. "Your father," he answered.

"That's what I thought." She didn't sound angry, jus
sad.

"It was the only thing that made sense," Jake admitted
"I knew you wouldn't perjure yourself except to protec
your father."

"That's what you think I did, knowing what it would do
to you?" she asked. "Jake, I adored my father. But I didn'
love him as much as I loved you. I would never have liec
for him. He wouldn't have let me."

Jake felt a pain at heart level stronger than any he'd eve:
known. "At the time, all I saw was that either you'd liec
to save your father or that my father was not just a thief
but a murderer and an arsonist."

"And now?" Clancy asked.

He shook his head. "Now everything seems differem
than it did then." Because of the large amount of money
that was missing, it seemed that one of the two partners
Warren Hawkins or Clarence Jones, had to be guilty
"Maybe Lola did embezzle the money. All I know is tha
now I can see that there might be another explanation, ever
though Lola's dead and the money's never turned up."

"Maybe she spent it or gave it to someone. Maybe it'
still hidden somewhere like Glenda thinks it is."

He looked over at her. "You don't want my father to be
guilty any more than I do, do you."

She smiled. "I never did, Jake."

"The problem is, if Lola had been skimming that mucl
money from the businesses, my father would have caugh
it." Warren Hawkins had been in charge of the financia
end of the businesses.

"Your father may have been…distracted," Clancy said

He glanced over at her. Had everyone known about the
problems his parents had been having or just Clancy? He'
always believed his parents would have worked things ou

f his father hadn't gone to prison. Now he wasn't so sure of that. He knew they'd been having financial problems partly because of the way his mother had liked to live, throwing large, extravagant parties. She loved to entertain, and there was nothing wrong with that. They could afford it. Couldn't they?

"I thought we'd stop by Tadd's and ask him about that photograph," he said as he started the Mustang.

"You think he's Teddy Bear?" Her tone made it clear she didn't.

"His name is Theodore."

THEY FOUND TADD AT HOME, his leg up and a ballgame on the television.

"How's the leg?" Jake asked, taking the chair Tadd offered. He noticed Clancy didn't sit. She'd gone to the mantel, where she seemed to be inspecting a series of framed photographs.

"Hurts like hell," Tadd said, grimacing. "Doctor says I'm lucky I didn't break my neck." His gaze followed Clancy. "How are you, Clancy?"

She turned. "Sore, but otherwise just glad to be alive."

He nodded, and continued to watch her inspect the photos. "The sheriff called. They found the dirt bike."

"Where?" Clancy asked.

"Paradise Cove." Tadd seemed to hesitate. "They also found Liz Knowles's body."

"Oh, no," Clancy said, slumping down into a chair by the fireplace. "She wasn't…"

"She'd drowned," Tadd said. "She was wearing the bike helmet."

Jake slammed a fist down on the arm of the chair. "No way. Someone else was driving that bike when I saw her.

Whoever it was killed her as sure as I'm sitting here. Don'
tell me the sheriff thinks it was an accident?''

"He's waiting for the results of the autopsy," Tadd said
"But it looks like Liz might have ridden the bike off the
cliffs and drowned."

Jake swore. "What about the bike?"

"Belonged to Frank Ames, all right. He's sticking to hi
original story that someone stole it."

"With Liz gone, we don't know who was driving tha
bike and we can't prove Frank's lying," Jake said.

Tadd nodded. "I think Frank Ames is up to his neck i
this. I asked for a copy of the police report." He reached
beside his chair, picked up a manila envelope and handed
it to Jake. "These are the photocopies of the evidence yo
asked for along with Dex Westfall's autopsy report and cop
ies of the clippings from Dex's closet wall."

Jake took the envelope but he didn't open it. He studied
Tadd, a dozen suspicions buzzing around in his head like
angry wasps. "Where were you when Liz went off tha
cliff, Tadd?" Jake asked, trying to keep the accusation ou
of his tone.

Tadd's eyes widened. "What?"

Jake saw Clancy tense. "You used to own a dirt bike.
remember when you raced in local competitions. You wer
pretty good."

Tadd let out a laugh. "You can't be serious. I haven'
ridden in years. I'd kill myself."

"Or break your leg," Jake added.

"Wait a minute," Tadd said, holding up his hands
"Why would I want to kill Liz Knowles and my own cli
ent?"

"Because of Lola," Jake said quietly.

"Lola?" Tadd asked, looking uncomfortable.

"We had an interesting talk with Lola Strickland's sister this morning in Somers," Jake said.

Tadd looked surprised. "Lola had a sister?"

"Half sister. Glenda Grimes. She told us she thinks the person who killed Lola also killed Dex."

"You're not accusing me?" Tadd laughed. I told you what happened. I got out of the boat to look around and fell. Fortunately I wasn't far from the boat and could get to the hospital. I had the doctor call as soon as I could."

"Lola's sister told us something else interesting," Jake said. "The night Lola died she thought she was running off with some man she'd fallen in love with."

"No kidding," Tadd said.

"Were you that man?" Jake asked.

"You aren't serious. I was engaged to marry a senator's daughter. Why would I run off with Lola?"

"Because you were in love with her," Clancy said as she reached into her pocket and pulled out the photograph Glenda had given them. She handed it to Tadd.

He took it with obvious reluctance and stared down at it for a long moment. "Where did you get this?"

"From a box of special mementos that Lola left at Glenda Grimes's house. This was in the box along with numerous cards from her Teddy Bear."

He looked up and seemed surprised at their expressions. "You think I'm Teddy Bear?" Tadd asked, sounding amazed.

"Isn't your real name Theodore?" Jake asked.

Tadd groaned. "I've never been called Teddy in my life. I certainly wouldn't call myself Teddy Bear."

"We think the man who wrote the cards is the same one Lola planned to run off with," Clancy told him.

Tadd laughed. "You've got the wrong man."

"But you did have an affair with her," Jake said.

Tadd let out a groan. He met Jake's gaze. "Okay, I had
an affair with her. But it was just that, a brief affair. When
she threatened to go to my fiancée, I bailed out."

"But you never married the senator's daughter," Clancy
pointed out.

Tadd nodded. "When I broke it off with Lola, she went
to the senator. Not only did Suzanne drop me like a hot
rock, it set my political career back a good ten years."

"What did you do about it?" Jake asked.

Tadd laughed. "It was too late to do anything. I'd lost
Suzanne and the senator. By then, Lola had already moved
on to her next victim. Lola didn't go long without a man,"
he said bitterly. "I got over it." He looked up and must
have seen their skepticism. "Come on, you don't really
believe I was Teddy Bear. I'm a lawyer. I'd never put anything in writing."

Jake didn't want to, but he believed him. He'd also com-
pared the handwriting on the back of the business card Tadd
had given him with the note on the Teddy Bear card. The
handwriting wasn't even close.

"Any guesses who this Teddy Bear might have been?"
Jake asked.

Tadd shook his head. "I'll tell you who used to have it
bad for Lola. Frank Ames. He was always hanging around
her like a lost puppy." He turned his gaze on Clancy.
"Well, are you going to fire me?"

"You have more reason than any other attorney to keep
me out of prison. The upcoming election and Aunt Kiki's
money. That's good enough motivation for me."

"I've been doing some research on sleep disorders,"
Tadd said. "Did you know that severe stress or some type
of trauma often triggers sleepwalking?"

"You mean like being arrested for murder?" Clancy
asked sarcastically.

"I was thinking more like Dex Westfall showing up on the island," Tadd said.

"Or showing up at the lodge after he's dead?" Jake asked.

CLANCY WAITED UNTIL they reached the car and Jake started to pull away from the curb before she asked, "I've walked in my sleep again, haven't I?"

"Yes."

"Oh, my God." She buried her face in her hands for a moment. "What did I do? Where did I go?" When he didn't answer, she looked at him. "Why didn't you tell me?"

He shrugged.

"You thought I was faking it." She turned to look out the passenger-side window, a volatile mix of emotions making her want to strike out at him.

"I'm not sure where you went—somewhere on the beach," Jake said. "You had sand on your feet. And—"

She looked over at him, her pulse rate accelerating. "And what?"

"You had something in your fist. A tiny blue bead."

Clancy let out a groan. "You weren't going to tell me?"

"I haven't really had a chance."

"You could have said something when I told you about the necklace and my other sleepwalking episode when I came back with a bead."

Jake said nothing. But then, what could he have said in his defense?

"Don't you realize your lack of trust in me is hampering this investigation? Can't you, the professional P.I., see that?"

"I should have told you."

No kidding. "Just like you should have told me about the card you took from the box."

He reached into his pocket. "Here." He handed her the greeting card. "I was going to tell you."

"Sure you were." She opened the card, wondering if that were true. The card was like the others in Lola's junk box. Only this one had a sailboat on the cover with a man and a woman watching a sunset. They presumably were in love. Inside it read: Each day with you is a dream come true. It was signed: Your Teddy Bear. "Do you recognize the handwriting?" Clancy asked.

"It's not my father's, if that's what you're asking." His voice had an edge to it. He knew that was exactly what she was asking. "You want to talk about trust here?"

He was right. But it was that lack of trust between them that was breaking her heart.

Jake took the card from her and turned it over and returned it to her. Written on the back in an entirely different hand were the words: I have to talk to you. Meet me at the usual place. Frank.

Clancy looked up at Jake. "Frank and Lola?"

"Lola seems to have been a busy woman. Makes you wonder, doesn't it? I'd like to pay Frank a visit. What do you think?"

"Why not?"

CLANCY COULD FEEL the weight of the few days' events on her sore and aching body as they parked the car at the marina and went by boat to the island resort. She wanted this case over with as quickly as possible so Jake could go home to Texas. Being around him wore down her heart. She told herself it would be easier not to see him. Not to be near him. Not to hear his voice. Not to know he was just down the hall.

Frank wasn't in his cabin. He didn't come to the door when Jake knocked and the door was locked.

"He's not home" came a male voice from the darkness.

Clancy recognized the youth as the dock boy she'd seen working the day before. "Do you know where he is?" she asked.

The boy shrugged. "He left earlier by foot." He pointed to the mountain.

Frank didn't seem like the hiking kind.

"You didn't happen to be around the night Dex Westfall was murdered?" Jake asked.

The boy looked up, surprise in his expression.

"I was wondering if Dex might have taken a boat out that night."

He shook his head. "The only time Mr. Westfall left the island was that first day. He rented a boat."

Jake looked disappointed. He thanked the boy and they started back down the trail.

"Mr. Westfall did have a visitor who came by boat the night he died, though," the boy added from behind them. "A woman."

Clancy stopped and turned slowly. "Can you describe this woman?"

The boy smiled. "Oh, yes." He proceeded to describe her in detail.

Clancy shot a shocked look at Jake.

Jake swore. "Kiki." He turned to the boy. "About what time was this?"

He shook his head. "It was late, well after dark. She went up to Mr. Westfall's cabin. I didn't see her leave."

"Did you tell the sheriff this?" Clancy asked.

The boy shook his head. "No one ever asked me. I figured it wasn't important."

Jake thanked him again. They walked back to their boat.

"Kiki?" Jake exclaimed the moment they were out of earshot. "Had your aunt ever met Dex?"

"Not that I was aware of." She bit her lower lip, feeling sick. "You don't think she—"

"Is somehow involved in his death?" Jake asked. "No, but I've thought from the very beginning that Kiki knew a lot more about this than she told either of us."

JAKE DOCKED THE BOAT in front of Kiki's rented condo in Bigfork. The condo hung over the water, a huge monument to commercial development. Clancy didn't wait for him to tie up the boat. She jumped out, charged up to her aunt's door and pressed the doorbell.

Kiki opened the door in a caftan with a champagne-colored poodle under her arm and what smelled like a banana daiquiri in her hand. "What a nice surprise," she said.

"You might not feel that way when you find out why we're here," Clancy said.

Kiki raised a finely sculpted brow as Clancy stepped past her. "Can I offer you something to drink, dear?"

"I'd love something to drink," Jake said from behind her, although Clancy noted Kiki hadn't offered him one.

Jake closed the door, then he and Kiki followed Clancy into the living room.

Clancy spun around to face her aunt. "What were you doing on the island the night of Dex's murder?"

"I'll fix that drink myself," Jake said to Kiki, and headed for the wet bar.

Kiki set the poodle down. It was the only color in the room. Everything else was white. Even the marble fireplace was white.

"Visiting Dex Westfall," Kiki said, and took a sip of her drink.

"Where's the ice?" Jake called from the bar.

"In the bucket," Kiki called back, her voice sounding a little strained.

"I didn't even know you knew Dex!" Clancy cried.

"I made his acquaintance shortly after the two of you met," Kiki said, walking over to sit in one of the large white chairs in front of the fireplace. "I offered to pay him not to see you anymore. Are you sure you wouldn't like something to drink?"

Clancy gasped. "You tried to buy him off?" Her aunt had always interfered in her life, offering unwanted advice, but this was way beyond that.

"What was I to do?" Kiki asked, nonplussed. "He wasn't the right man for you."

"Did he take the money?" Jake asked from the bar.

"No," Kiki said in disgust. "He said he deserved much more and he intended to get it."

"Aunt Kiki, I can't believe you'd do such a thing," Clancy said. "What else did you do?"

"If you're asking if I killed him, of course not," Kiki said. "But I can't say I'm sorry he's dead. He was a deplorable man."

"If he refused your money the first time, why did you go to the island to see him?" Jake asked as he joined them. He handed Clancy a glass of brandy she hadn't asked for and went to sit across from Kiki.

"To offer him more money," Kiki stated flatly. "I knew he had a price, I just had to find it."

Clancy rolled her eyes. Life was so simple for her aunt as long as she could solve her problems with money. While she almost appreciated Kiki's efforts, she resented her aunt's continued attempts to control her life. Had always resented it.

"Dex didn't take it?" Clancy knew no large quantity of money had been found in Dex's cabin or on his body. Although, she was surprised that Dex hadn't taken her aunt up on the offer.

"The opportunity didn't present itself," Kiki said with a sigh. "I caught him with some woman and did the next best thing."

"Let me guess," Jake said. "Blackmail."

Clancy glanced over at him, keyed to the way he'd said "blackmail." Was that how Kiki had gotten Jake to Montana? She felt sick.

"While blackmail is always a possibility," Kiki said, smiling at him, "it really wasn't necessary. He was planning to leave the island that night, anyway."

"But he didn't," Jake pointed out.

Kiki shot him a dour look. "Something must have kept him from it. Someone. He told me his business on the island was finished. He seemed quite pleased about leaving."

"Who was the woman?" Jake asked.

Kiki shrugged. "I never saw her, but I smelled her perfume. It was expensive."

"Did he look like you'd interrupted something?" Jake asked.

"He was clothed, if that's what you're asking," Kiki replied primly. "But yes, now that I think about it, I did see him kick something under the bed. A pair of white Jockey shorts, I believe."

Kiki didn't miss a thing, Clancy thought, and took a sip of the brandy. It burned all the way down. She took another.

"I was astounded to hear the next morning that he'd been murdered," Kiki continued. "Even more appalled to learn the sheriff thought Clancy had killed him."

Clancy drained her glass and stared dumbfounded at her aunt. "What do you do when you can't buy what you want or blackmail someone to get your way?"

Kiki studied her niece for a moment. "The problem's

never come up." She glanced pointedly at Jake. "But I could see how it might."

He finished his drink and got up to take Clancy's empty glass from her fingers. "You ready to go?" he asked her.

"Yes." She marched to the door, opened it and stopped to look back at her aunt. "One of these days you're going to go too far. Maybe you already have."

Jake tipped his baseball cap at Kiki on the way out. He didn't say anything until he and Clancy reached the boat. "She's something, isn't she?" he said, and laughed.

"It's not funny, Jake."

"Oh, come on. It's her way of trying to protect you. As strange and twisted as it is. And you have to admit, her instincts about Dex were right."

Clancy spun on him. "How can you defend her?" She narrowed her gaze at him. "How did she get you up here, anyway? Money? Or blackmail?"

"Money?" He sounded insulted.

She studied him for a moment, remembering that she'd heard his father was coming up for parole soon. "If not money, then it had to be blackmail. Initially."

He tried to look insulted, but she knew her instincts had been right. "What makes you think I didn't come up here because I wanted to?" Jake demanded.

Clancy glared at him. "I remember how mad you were that first night when you had to save me from drowning. Then, when you realized you could get revenge—"

"Hey." He grabbed her and spun her into his chest. "You're wrong. Maybe at first. But surely you realize it isn't like that anymore."

"Isn't it?" she asked, looking into those gray eyes. The lights from the marina came on, making them gleam a slick silver. She felt the strength of his grip on her arm as he pulled her to him. For a moment, she thought he'd kiss her.

Hoped he would forget his promise. Hoped he'd take her in his arms and tell her he believed her.

With an oath, he let go of her and climbed into the boat without another word.

Clancy said little on the boat ride back to the island.

"I need to do some work," she said the moment they walked into the lodge. Jake watched her disappear up the stairs to her studio, kicking himself.

He couldn't stand the wall between them. But at the same time, he seemed incapable of tearing it down. He cursed himself and went to his room just down the hall from Clancy's studio. He dumped the envelope of evidence in the middle of his bed. He had to find out who killed Dex and keep Clancy from going to prison. Maybe, if he got lucky, he'd also find Lola's killer. For his father. For his own sanity. But he wondered if by then it would be too late for him and Clancy.

He picked up the cellular phone and called Tadd.

"I need to know if Frank Ames inherited a bunch of money. Or maybe won the lottery. I need to know how he bought Hawk Island Resort. Now."

"Tonight?" Tadd croaked.

"Tomorrow would be fine," Jake said.

"I'll put my secretary on it at daybreak."

After Jake hung up, he felt restless. The lodge seemed uncommonly quiet, the summer night almost too still. He didn't want Clancy to think he was checking up on her. But he couldn't help himself. He couldn't get her off his mind any more than he could forget the feel of her in his arms. Or her steadfast conviction that she hadn't perjured herself, hadn't lied about his father.

Quietly, he sneaked down the hall. Clancy's studio was a second-floor addition that overlooked the bay. It had been a surprise birthday present from her father for her fifteenth birthday. Johnny Branson, who'd been a carpenter back then, had built it. That was before he ran for sheriff.

Jake heard music filtering through the open doorway. He stopped. Classical? He and Clancy had grown up on country music. The long-haired stuff coming off her stereo only reminded him of how much had changed between them. He was wondering if she ever listened to country anymore when the song ended and another came on. A Don Williams tune. One he used to know all the words to. He smiled to himself. Maybe things hadn't changed that much.

The actual studio was a large room with a bank of windows on three sides to catch the light. As Jake peeked in, he remembered the times he'd come here, moving quietly, hoping not to disturb her. He remembered how seriously she'd taken her sculpture. That's one reason he'd loved to watch her work.

Now he stood at the edge of the doorway, just looking at her. Watching the way her fingers molded the mound of clay on the table in front of her. She pinched, prodded, slicked and smoothed. Her fingers strong, her movements precise. He studied her face, not surprised by the intensity of her expression. Clancy had been fourteen the summer she confessed to Jake she wanted to be an artist. She'd felt it was a frivolous desire. How many artists actually made a living with their work?

But Jake and her parents had encouraged her. And surprisingly, so had her aunt Kiki. Kiki saw to it that Clancy got her first sculpting lessons. Jake could still remember Clancy's first work. It was crude but showed potential, her art teachers had said. Hell, one of her first pieces was a part of the breakwater at his beach house in Galveston, he thought with a curse.

Clancy frowned now as she stepped back to inspect her latest creation. She wore her glasses instead of her contacts.

He liked them on her. They made her look even more sexy, if that was possible. The frown deepened as if she wasn't quite satisfied with it. That would be the perfectionist in her. She stepped forward again and began to reshape and resculpt, working quickly, meticulously, totally immersed in the clay and the vision inside her head, totally oblivious to everything else. Including him.

So intent on studying her, Jake hadn't even noticed the sculpture she'd been so engrossed in until she suddenly pushed it back to inspect it again. The back of it faced him. A bust of a man's head.

She gave the sculpture a turn. It slowly revolved around on the lazy susan. Jake caught his breath as he saw the face she'd molded into the clay. The likeness was so striking it shocked him.

It was *his* face in the clay. Younger. His nose straighter than he remembered it. His face far more handsome than he'd ever been. But he could see the resemblance to the boy who'd grown up on this lake with Clancy.

It unnerved him, reminding him too much of the past and the way things had been between them.

He stepped back into the hallway, pressing against the wall. Emotions surged through him, waves that threatened to wash away everything he'd believed, everything he'd held on to for ten years, everything he'd let go of ten years ago. What if he'd been wrong?

He thought about the sculpture, the man she'd somehow captured in the clay. He felt moved and, at the same time, torn.

He sneaked back to his room. Clancy's phone rang. He heard her pick it up. He listened to her tell Helen about Lola's half sister. From the conversation, it seemed Helen didn't know about Glenda Grimes, either.

He turned his attention back to the evidence on the Westfall case. The answer was here, somewhere, and damned if he wasn't going to find it.

JAKE SIFTED THROUGH the pile of papers again, his head aching from lack of sleep and the craziness of this case. At some point, he could always feel the pieces start to fall into place. There'd be that rush as he started to see glimpses of a pattern. But not in this one.

He pushed back the papers and stretched, surprised, when he glanced at his watch, at how much time had gone by. Surely by now Clancy had gone to bed. But he hadn't heard her.

He walked down the hallway. Her door stood open. He peeked in. The covers were thrown back on her bed. Her shoes were by it on the floor. But her room was empty.

This time, he made noise as he went down to her studio. But when he rounded the corner, she wasn't sitting at her worktable. The sculpture of him wasn't on the table anymore, but a large mound of battered-looking clay sat in its place. His face was long gone. And so was Clancy.

Panic rocketed through him. "Clancy?" He raced down the stairs, calling her name as he went. "Clancy?"

The kitchen door stood open. He charged outside, wondering how much of a head start she had on him.

That's when he saw her. She looked ghostlike walking down the beach, her long white nightgown billowing around her bare ankles. He went after her, telling himself she was fine. But he couldn't throw off the bad feeling.

He'd almost reached her when she suddenly stopped and, in slow motion, bent to pick up a small piece of driftwood in her path. An icy chill shot up his spine as she started walking again, the driftwood dangling from the fingers of her left hand, forgotten.

He felt a stab of shock as he caught up with her and looked into her blank face, the face of a sleepwalker.

"Clancy?" She moved along on some agenda, programmed like a robot. The only problem was that the program was often flawed, senseless. Or was it? Was Clancy headed somewhere she really wanted to go? But she was headed for the end of the island and the cliffs.

"It's time to go to bed." He touched her arm. Hadn't he read that you shouldn't wake a person who's walking in her sleep?

But she didn't wake. Nor did she fight him. He turned her toward the lodge, then trailed along beside her. Almost home, something must have clicked, some kind of wake-up call. She blinked. "Where—"

"I'm here," Jake said quickly.

She turned in surprise to see him there. Tears flooded her eyes. "I did it again," she whispered. "Where did I go?"

"Just down to the beach. I saw you and brought you back."

She looked down, startled to find the piece of driftwood in her hand, and dropped it quickly as if it were a poisonous snake. She began to shake.

Jake swept her into his arms and carried her inside the lodge and up to her bed. He sat beside her, holding her hand until she fell asleep again.

He took the chair, positioned it in front of the door, and made himself as comfortable as possible. It was going to be a long night.

Chapter Sixteen

Thursday morning, Jake woke to the ringing of a phone. He hurried down the hall to his room and picked up the cell phone. "Yeah?" He could hear a television in the background.

"No inheritance. No lottery," Tadd said, sounding as sleepy as Jake felt. "No bank loans. Frank Ames couldn't have bought a candy bar with his earning power before he purchased the resort."

"Then, how did he?" Jake asked, starting to wake up.

"Good question," Tadd said. "As long as he put the money down as income on his tax returns, he's legal and there's no way we can track it. Hold on." Jake heard Tadd turn up the volume on the TV. "Lola's sister lives in Somers right? Glenda Grimes?"

"Why?" Jake asked, afraid he wasn't going to like the answer.

"Her house is on fire and her neighbors think she's inside."

Jake hung up and raced down the stairs to turn on the television in the living room. Glenda Grimes's home was nothing but a ball of flames.

"What is it?" Clancy asked from the stairs. She still had

on her nightgown, her expression worried and afraid. Not as worried and afraid as Jake was for her at this moment.

"Glenda Grimes," Jake said, turning off the TV. "She didn't make it to Vegas."

CLANCY STOOD IN the hot shower, letting the water pound her skin. Desperately she tried not to think about Glenda. Had Jake been right? Had Glenda known more than she'd told them? Well, her secret had died with her.

Clancy shifted her thoughts to something more pleasant. Jake. Knowing he was just outside the door gave her a sense of security and well-being. She'd seen her own fears mirrored in his face. Was she next?

When she reached for the soap, Clancy had a quick flash of her shower with Jake. Her skin tingled, and that ache low in her belly almost brought her to her knees. Having him right outside the door made her more aware of her naked body. Having once had it, she now ached for Jake's touch. She remembered his fingertips on her skin. His mouth. His tongue. The weight of his body on hers. She groaned.

"Clancy?" Jake asked on the other side of the door, his voice full of concern. "Are you all right?"

"Fine!" she called back quickly, and turned up the cold water. Well, he wasn't going to make love to her until she asked, and she couldn't ask until he believed that she wasn't a liar and a murderer. The way things were going she would never know the feel of him again.

When she came out of the shower wrapped in her modest robe, she heard Jake on the phone. He hung up when he saw her. "What is it?" she asked.

"I just talked to the sheriff's department."

"Arson?"

Jake nodded. "And deliberate homicide. Glenda was inside. She'd been bludgeoned to death before the fire was started.''

Just like Lola. Clancy clutched the front of her robe, the look in Jake's eyes making her more afraid.

''We've got to find this guy, Clancy. And soon.''

Clancy couldn't agree more. ''How would you suggest we do that?''

He hesitated. ''Helen was close to Lola. Didn't you say they were involved in summer theater together?''

Clancy nodded. ''You think Lola might have confided in Helen about this mystery lover of hers?''

''Maybe.'' He rubbed a hand over his stubbled jaw. His hair hung over his forehead. He looked as though he hadn't gotten a lot of sleep last night.

Clancy felt a twinge of guilt for that, but had to admit Jake Hawkins had never looked more handsome to her.

''Even if Lola never told her, Helen still might recognize something in Lola's keepsakes that at least would give us a lead,'' he said, and stopped. ''What are you smiling about?''

Clancy quickly looked away. ''I was just thinking that I could make us some breakfast while you—''

''Do I look that bad?'' Jake asked.

She shook her head. ''You look—'' Sexy. Seductive. Wonderful. ''Fine.''

He grinned. ''I won't take but a minute. Promise me you'll be here when I get back.''

Clancy had to laugh. ''I promise.'' There was no place she wanted to be more than with Jake, she thought with a curse.

Jake was as good as his word. He was back by the time she had the eggs and toast ready. He'd showered, shaved and changed into a shirt and chinos. He looked good enough to eat.

"Not bad," she said, sliding a plate of food in front of him. As she sat across from him and picked up her fork, she realized her sudden hunger had nothing at all to do with food.

"WE'RE GOING ON the assumption that Teddy Bear killed Lola, right?" Clancy asked as they took her boat to the Bransons'. "And he's still killing to keep his secret?"

The lake's surface mirrored the clear, sunny sky overhead. The air smelled fresh and clean. In the distance, she could hear a boat's motor running.

"Because he's never come forward, I think that's a pretty good assumption," Jake said. "Or he knows who did. I'm not sure how Frank Ames fits into all of this. I talked to Tadd this morning. No one knows where Frank got the money to buy the resort."

"You think it's the missing money?" Clancy asked.

"Maybe," Jake said. "If it is, then Frank had to have someone on the inside embezzling it for him."

"Lola." Clancy looked up at the cliffs as they rounded the end of the island. The Bransons' place sat on the highest bluff, with the elevator Johnny had put in for Helen running from the dock up to the house. There were also wooden stairs that switchbacked up the face of the cliff.

"Clancy, could you see Frank Ames as Teddy Bear?" Jake asked.

Clancy laughed. "Not hardly. But maybe Lola did. Frank would have been a lot younger. From what Tadd said, Frank had a huge crush on her."

"Yeah, it sounds like she enjoyed attention," Jake agreed.

"Maybe she encouraged that attention," Clancy said.

"That's what I was thinking," Jake said as he pulled

alongside the Bransons' dock. "Especially if Frank could be useful to her."

"Like helping her hide the embezzled money?"

Jake looked over at Clancy. "Yeah. Then maybe he got greedy. More than likely he found out she was seeing other men. I mean, Frank's note to Lola is on the back of one of the cards. Frank could have decided to get rid of Lola and keep the money for himself."

Clancy tried to imagine Frank's face behind the motorbike helmet, in the water off the end of the dock as he dragged her under, beneath the sweatshirt hood as he ran out of her lodge. But all she could see was Dex Strickland's.

Jake closed the door on the cagelike elevator and pushed the button. It lurched with a noisy groan and began to climb. He'd been disappointed to note that Johnny's boat wasn't tied at the dock. Jake had hoped Johnny would be here.

The elevator grumbled to a jerky stop. Jake opened the door and Clancy stepped out.

"I've always wondered why Johnny would build up here, especially with Helen's handicap," Clancy said quietly.

"You have to admit, it's an amazing view," Jake said, joining her at the railing. "And it's isolated. I get the impression that since the accident they pretty much keep to themselves."

Jake stood on the top deck. He couldn't help but admire the Bransons' house. Johnny had always been a master carpenter, but he'd outdone himself on this place.

It was built on three levels, all connected by ramps in such a way that they didn't call attention to Helen's handicap. Along the side of the house were three decks set at the same levels as the house, also with ramps. It gave the place a spacious feel. Each deck had a view, but the top deck, where he and Clancy stood now, was the most panoramic.

They found Helen in the pool on the second deck, swimming laps.

"Sorry, I didn't hear you come up," she said from the side of the pool. "I force myself to get exercise every day, and today was so beautiful—"

"Don't let us keep you from it," Clancy said.

"No, actually, I was just finishing," she said, hoisting herself up onto a step.

"Here, let me help you," Clancy said.

"No." Helen smiled to soften her words. "I have to do it myself. I refuse to be an invalid."

"You look great," Clancy said as Helen lifted herself into the wheelchair, making it look effortless.

"So what are you up to this morning?" Helen asked, pulling a white robe around her shoulders.

"We brought something we'd like you to look at," Jake said, indicating the small shoe box under his arm.

"Come on in," Helen said. "I think Johnny put some coffee on before he left."

They followed her into the living room, which opened up into the kitchen to the left and what looked like bedrooms off to the right. It had that same open, airy feeling inside as it had out. A two-way radio near a large window squawked as they went past.

"Where's Johnny?" Jake asked. "Fishing?"

"No, he had a doctor's appointment," Helen said on her way to the kitchen. "He hasn't been feeling well lately."

Jake saw that Clancy had stopped in front of a glass cabinet filled with trophies. He joined her, noticing a photograph of a smiling Helen beside a balance beam.

"Gymnastics. It was my first love," Helen said from the

kitchen. "Then I got into theater and met Johnny and found my true love."

Clancy followed Helen into the kitchen. "You and Johnny both were actors?"

Helen laughed and shook her head. "Johnny on stage? No, he built sets. That's how we met. I'd seen him around at school, but he was so shy. So I joined the drama club, hoping he might notice me. I liked acting, but found helping with the costumes and makeup put me closer to Johnny. The rest is history, as they say."

Helen poured them both a cup of coffee. "Sit down," she said, motioning to the table set against the big bay windows.

"I've been so worried about you," Helen said to Clancy. "Have they got any closer to finding out who killed Dex Strickland?"

Clancy shook her head. "That's why we're hoping you might recognize something in the box. It contains Lola's things."

Helen looked surprised. "Lola's? I thought all of her belongings burned in the fire."

"Not everything burned," Jake said. "Some things were saved from the fire, the rest were in this box of...keepsakes that Lola left with her sister before her death."

"This half sister you told me about who lives in Somers?" Helen poured herself a cup of coffee before joining them at the table. "A son and a half sister we knew nothing about. I sometimes wonder if I knew Lola at all."

"Her sister died in a fire early this morning," Clancy said.

"I saw something on the news, but I had no idea that it was Lola's sister," Helen said. "Oh, how awful. What was her name, Linda Grimes?"

"Glenda," Clancy corrected her. "She told us yesterday

that Dex had figured out who killed his mother. We think that person murdered Dex because of that.''

''And probably Glenda,'' Jake added.

Helen looked shocked. ''You mean, you don't think the fire was an accident?''

''No,'' Jake said.

''Well, I'll try to help in any way I can,'' Helen said.

Jake pushed the box over to her and watched as Helen riffled through the items.

She frowned. ''Why would Lola's sister have hung on to this for all these years? It doesn't seem to contain any-thing…important.'' She picked up one of the cards. ''Teddy Bear?''

''Do you have any idea who that might have been?'' Clancy asked. ''Glenda seemed to think that he was the man Lola planned to run off with the night she was killed.''

''I knew she was leaving the island, but she planned to run off with some man?'' Helen asked, sounding surprised. ''That is certainly news to me. Lola seemed to date a lot of men, but none for very long.''

''Glenda thought Lola had embezzled the money from the resort. This man might have been someone who helped her.''

''Lola?'' Helen shook her head, her look full of sympa-thy as she shifted her gaze to Jake. ''I know how badly you want to clear your father's name, but that just doesn't sound like the Lola I knew. Did this Glenda person have proof of any of this?''

Jake stared into his coffee cup, his mood as dark as Helen's coffee. ''No. That's why I was hoping you might recognize something in the box. If we could figure out who the man was—''

''I'm sorry, Jake,'' Helen said. ''Lola never mentioned him to me, and you'd think she would have.''

"For some reason she kept him a secret," Clancy said.

"You're sure she didn't…dream him up?" Helen asked. 'I mean, Lola loved acting, playing different roles. It suited her. She didn't seem happy with real life. Never satisfied with what she had, whether it was a man or a job. That's why she told me she was leaving the island. She said she needed a change." Helen took a sip of coffee. "No, if her 'Teddy Bear' existed, he wouldn't have stayed with her long. It's a shame. She was a very beautiful woman, but so…needy and dependent. That puts a lot of men off."

THE SUN HUNG HIGH in Montana's big sky as Clancy and Jake headed back to the lodge. Clancy couldn't help thinking about Helen's last remark and how lucky Helen was to have a man like Johnny. Clancy doubted Johnny could have loved her more. Just seeing that kind of love made Clancy ache inside for what she and Jake had had.

Jake said little on the boat ride back, and Clancy knew he'd hoped Helen would provide one of the missing clues. Finding the elusive Teddy Bear was proving much more difficult than Clancy had hoped. She wondered if maybe Helen was right; maybe Lola had made the man up. Hadn't even Glenda said he sounded too good to be true?

Jake brought the boat into the dock and Clancy jumped out to tie it up. She could feel Jake's frustration. It matched her own. They were no closer to finding out who had killed Dex Westfall, and her trial was coming up quickly. Without some sort of new evidence—

As Clancy bent down to secure the stern of the boat, she noticed something shiny in the water beyond the dock.

"Jake?" she said.

He joined her and squatted to look into the clear green water. "I'll take a look." He stripped off his shirt, then slipped out of his Top-Siders and reached for the zipper on his chinos.

"I'm going in with you," Clancy said, pulling her shirt over her head.

Jake stopped undressing. "You sure that's a good idea?" he asked, raising a brow. "You wouldn't purposely try to get me to break my promise?"

She mugged a face at him, slipped out of her skirt and sandals, down to her bra and panties, and dove into the water. It felt cold after the hot sun and the heat of Jake's gaze. Was that exactly what she was doing? Trying to get him to break his promise?

Jake did a shallow dive and came up next to her. They dog-paddled for a few moments just looking at each other, neither touching. His bare shoulders glistened, slick with water. They were so close she could feel his legs churning the water in front of her. It brushed her thighs, sparking a need to feel his skin against hers again. Desire flashed in his eyes as bright as the summer sun overhead. In that instant, the water no longer felt cold. Her skin ached, hot and sensitive to his gaze.

He groaned and dove into the water. She followed. Jake reached the bottom first, scooping the object into his hand. He looked over at Clancy and gave her a thumbs-up.

They burst to the surface almost in unison. Clancy watched as Jake inspected the object in his hand, then passed it to her. She stared at the silver watch for a moment, then up at Jake.

"Just as you described it," he said. "A flash of silver."

Proof that someone had tried to drown her that night. She smiled in relief and swam to the dock, hoisting herself up. Sitting on the edge of the dock, she turned the watch over in her hand. She heard Jake dive under the water and saw that he'd disappeared from sight. She looked down at the watch; something on the back caught her eye. Lettering. An inscription. She read the words in shock. Then realized Jake hadn't surfaced yet.

Getting to her feet, she stared into the clear water but couldn't see him. Where had he gone? She clutched the watch and waited for him to reappear, suddenly worried. How long could he stay under?

Just when she was about to dive in to search for him, he reappeared beside the dock.

"You scared me," she admonished.

He grinned up at her, his eyelashes jeweled with water droplets. "Sorry. I think I know where your attacker disappeared to that night." He pointed to the dock beneath her. "There're large air pockets under here between the flotations where he could have waited until we were gone."

Jake lifted himself onto the dock beside her, making her uncomfortably aware of how little they had on and just how wet and body-conforming their clothing was. She could feel Jake's gaze caress her, traveling across bare, wet skin to what was no longer hidden beneath her underwear. The air stilled around them. Time stopped.

"Dammit, Clancy, you can't do this to me."

"Do what?" she asked innocently.

He threw himself back into the water. She reached down and grabbed his hair, gently pulling him to the surface. She handed him the watch. "It's inscribed."

It seemed to take him a moment to drag his gaze from her to the watch. He flipped it over. "To Frank, love Lola," he read. His gaze flew up to Clancy's. "You have to be kidding."

JAKE CALLED TADD with the news about the watch.

"Even with the watch and the motorbike, I'm not sure

the sheriff has enough to hold Frank," Tadd said. "It would help if we had something more tangible."

Jake agreed. "Clancy and I will go over the evidence. Maybe there's something we've missed."

After he hung up, Jake dumped everything he'd collected on the Dex Strickland murder case in the middle of the kitchen table. But his attention was on Clancy. He felt a pull toward her stronger than the gravity on Jupiter.

"Where do we begin?" She leaned toward him.

He could smell her scent. It brought a rush of memory—the feel of her skin, the sound of her voice as she pressed her body to his, the look in her eyes as they made love. Damned if he couldn't still see her on the dock, wet and in that skimpy underwear. Why had he made such a foolish promise?

"Here's Dex's autopsy report," he said, trying to concentrate on the report. "This is interesting. Dex was struck from the right. That would indicate he was hit by a right-handed person."

"I'm left-handed, and the sculpture was in my left hand when I woke up. But that really doesn't prove anything, does it?"

"It helps," Jake said, flipping through the report. "If we have to go to trial, everything that puts doubt into the jurors' minds will help."

Clancy picked up a stack of photocopies of all the newspaper clippings, photos and other materials Dex had tacked to his closet wall. He saw her shudder as she sorted through them, quickly passing over an old play program from the summer Lola died. Jake recognized it. It was the play he'd taken her to the night he told her how much he loved her and that he wanted to marry her.

"You don't have to do this if you don't want to," he said. But she didn't seem to be listening.

"Look at this," she said, stepping over so he could see. It was a newspaper article. The headline read Local Woman Injured in Wreck Near Angel Point. Jake saw that it was an article about Helen Branson. The subhead read Sheriff's Wife Critical After High-Speed Rollover.

Jake read over Clancy's shoulder. Johnny Branson was driving at a high rate of speed when he lost control and rolled down an embankment. Helen was thrown from the car. She was listed in critical condition at the local hospital. Johnny was uninjured.

"It's dated the night of the resort fire," Clancy said in surprise.

The night Lola was murdered. Jake scanned the story again for the time of the accident. "It would have been just hours after the fire and Lola's murder."

Clancy looked up at him. "Dex had this tacked on his closet wall, too?"

"Johnny was the sheriff, and it was the same night as Dex's mother's death."

Clancy moved away from the table to look out into the night. "Johnny was driving the car," she said. "I didn't know that. How awful for him to know that he was responsible for Helen being in a wheelchair for the rest of her life. Why was he going so fast on that road, I wonder?"

"And what were they doing on Angel Point that time of the morning?" Jake said.

Clancy shook her head. "He was probably upset after what had happened at the resort, having to arrest one of his best friends. I guess I never realized how many lives were affected by what happened that night."

"Neither did I." Jake got up to take his empty cup to the sink. He'd been so filled with anger for so many years. He hadn't even thought about the other people who'd lost something that night. He leaned over the sink for a moment.

Like Clancy. She'd lost her family first to Alaska, then to a plane crash. Her pain had been amplified by him walking out on her. And he'd spent the last ten years in his own kind of sleepwalking. Pretending he could forget about her.

He glanced over at her, remembering the way she'd looked last night on the beach. Her eyes open. Her expression glazed. Picking up that piece of driftwood in her path and not even realizing what it was.

He felt goose bumps on his arms as a chilling thought whipped past. Had she picked up that driftwood the same way she'd picked up the murder weapon the night Dex was killed? He remembered what he'd read about the total amnesia sleepwalkers experienced from the time of falling asleep until waking. The confusion on waking.

"Clancy," he said, excited by how right this felt. "Last night on the beach when you were sleepwalking, you picked up a piece of driftwood in your path. What if that's exactly what you did the night Dex died? If that's how you ended up with the murder weapon in your hand?"

Clancy stared at him.

"Don't you see? You must have heard someone upstairs. Still asleep, you walked up there. The murder weapon was in the middle of the floor. You picked it up and went to the balcony." Jake shuddered. "The killer must still have been in the room. Clancy, that's it. You must have seen him. That's why he's after you now."

"But I can never remember anything about my sleepwalking episodes."

"The killer wouldn't know that," he pointed out. "He may be afraid that you'll remember." The thought came out of left field, fast and hard. "Oh, my God. Clancy, if I'm right and the same person killed Lola and Dex, you might have seen him *both* times." Jake slapped a hand to his forehead. "You could have seen him the night of Lola's murder when you were sleepwalking. God, Clancy, that could be what woke you up.''

"And he waited ten years to come after me?" Clancy asked in disbelief.

"No, he felt safe. Then Dex turns up, asking questions, maybe even actually knowing who the killer is. Dex could have tried to extort money from him. Or maybe just threatened to go to the cops. Remember what Kiki said about Dex being in a good mood and saying his business on the island was completed and he was leaving?" Jake stood, pacing the floor, excited by the way the pieces seemed to fit. "He thought he was getting money. And somehow the killer got him to go to your garret, then killed him and set you up."

Jake pulled off his cap and raked his fingers through his hair. "And you played right into the killer's hands, picking up the murder weapon."

"Oh, Jake, is it possible?" Clancy cried. She got up to get them more coffee, excitement in her movements.

More than possible, he thought as he watched her, his heart so full of love for her that it felt as if it would explode. And she loved him. He believed that with all his heart. Then, how could he not believe everything else she'd told him?

"I know you didn't kill Dex Strickland," Jake said, feeling a rush of emotion as he knew something else in the only place it mattered. In his heart. "And I know you didn't perjure yourself at my father's trial."

She didn't turn. Her hand clamped down on the handle of the coffeepot as if she needed support.

"I believe you, Clancy," he said.

"But?" she asked, her back still to him.

"But I believe my father, too. There's an explanation for

what you saw that night, because I know in my heart that you didn't lie.''

She turned slowly, her eyes welling with tears as she looked at him.

In two strides, he came around the table and pulled her into his arms. "Oh, Clancy," he breathed against her hair. "I love you," he said, thumbing the tears from her cheeks. "God, I would give anything to have never hurt you." He drew her closer. "I'm so sorry I didn't believe you. Can you ever forgive me?''

She drew back to look up into his face. "I love you, Jake. I've always loved you.''

"I know." He held her to him tightly, promising himself he'd never let her go again.

"Kiss me, Jake. Please. Then make love to me.''

He laughed softly. "I thought you'd never ask.''

THEY MADE LOVE in front of the fireplace. Slowly. Gently. Touching each other as if for the first time. Lovers at long last.

Later Jake cooked steaks on the barbecue and they sat on the front deck watching the sunset. Jake felt a contentment he hadn't known in years. Not since he'd left Flathead and Clancy.

He sat holding her hand, watching the last of daylight disappear behind the mountains, when he heard a sound behind them.

"Did you hear that?" Clancy asked, turning to look back into the lodge. Jake's gaze leaped to the window behind them as Clancy let out a startled cry. A figure moved through the shadows of the unlit living room, headed for the back door.

"Stay here," Jake commanded without thinking. Had he had time to think, he would have asked her, pleaded with her, begged. Because commanding Clancy had always proved a mistake. But there wasn't time to beg. Jake wasn't about to let the intruder get away. Not again.

He circled around the side of the lodge just as the figure broke into a run down the beach. Jake tore after him, stretching his legs and lungs with everything he had in him, closing the distance.

The figure headed for a rental boat pulled up on the beach on the other side of Jake's lodge. Jake knew he had to reach him first.

The moon had just started up the backside of the Mission Mountains. Dusk lay deep in the pines. Jake concentrated on only two things: the dark figure running up the beach and the shoe box tucked under the man's arm. The man raced for his life. It was a race Jake wasn't about to let him win.

Just before the thief reached the boat, Jake made a flying tackle. He caught the man by the lower legs and brought him down hard. Not hard enough, Jake thought, scrambling to his feet.

The man tried to get up. Jake put a boot toe into the man's ribs and flipped him over onto his back, noticing that he wore a dark hooded sweatshirt, the hood up, hiding his face. Next to him was a crushed shoe box. Some of Lola's keepsakes had tumbled out when he'd fallen.

Grabbing the scruff of the man's coat collar, Jake jerked him to his feet and, pulling down the hood of the sweatshirt, finally got a good look at his face. The man held no resemblance to Dex Strickland.

"Frank Ames." Jake swore and tightened his grip on the man's throat. "I ought to kill you right now with my bare hands."

Chapter Seventeen

Fear shone in Frank's eyes. "You wouldn't do that." He didn't look in the least bit convinced.

"Wanna bet?" Jake demanded. "You're the one who's been trying to kill Clancy."

Frank shook his head violently. "That's not true."

Jake shoved Frank down into the sand again. "Don't lie to me, Ames. I swear—"

"I'm telling you the truth," Frank cried, gasping for breath. "It wasn't me. Why would I want to kill Clancy?"

"That's what I want to know. We found your watch near the dock where you tried to drown her," Jake said, getting angrier by the minute.

"What watch?" Frank asked, almost sounding surprised.

"The one Lola gave you."

"Lola never gave me a watch."

Jake towered over him. "It was engraved. 'To Frank, love Lola.' Ring any bells?"

"I don't know what you're talking about."

"Are you also going to deny you were in the lodge tonight?" Jake demanded.

Frank swallowed and took a shaky breath. "Helen told me you had some of Lola's things in an old shoe box."

Jake wondered why Helen had told him that.

"I wanted to get my letters back."

"Your letters?" Jake asked. Frank couldn't be Teddy Bear.

"Personal letters."

"Love letters?" Jake demanded. "You sent Lola love letters? How did you sign them?"

Frank looked confused. It wasn't a new look for him. "I signed my name."

Not Teddy Bear.

"I want them back. They're mine."

Frank thought Lola had saved his letters? What would make him think that? Unless— "You're not trying to tell me that Lola responded to your sick fantasies."

That mean look Jake had seen many times before showed up on Frank's ugly face. He flushed with anger. "It wasn't like that. She cared about me. She talked to me when other people wouldn't. We were friends."

"Were you friends with Liz Knowles, too?" Jake demanded.

Frank frowned. "She was my waitress, that's all."

"How did she end up on your motorbike, then, Frank?"

"Maybe Liz was the one who stole it and chased your girlfriend. Did you ever think of that?"

"No." Jake figured Frank would finger anyone to save his own neck. "What possible motive would Liz have had?"

Frank shook his head. "I'm supposed to know that?"

"Look, Frank, I saw Liz on the back of your motorbike not long before her body was found in Paradise Cove," Jake told him. "Someone was driving that bike. I think it was you."

"Well, you're wrong."

Jake tried another tack. "I found a note you wrote Lola to meet you at the 'usual place.' Where was that?"

"It was just this little stand of pines," Frank mumbled. "She liked it there. Not that it's any of your business."

Jake had had about all he could stand. He moved toward Frank, determined to get the truth out of him. "Not that it's any of my business, but where did you get the money for the resort?"

Fear crossed Frank's face as he groped in the sand behind him. "I don't have to tell you nothing," he said, coming up with a hefty chunk of driftwood. He scrambled to his feet, brandishing the weapon, then turned and made a run for it.

Jake would have gone after him but Clancy grabbed his arm.

"The sheriff's on his way," she said. "Let him handle it."

Chapter Eighteen

Jake hung up the phone and pulled Clancy into his arms. "Tadd just called to say the sheriff picked up Frank Ames at the airport this morning. He was trying to make a run for it."

Clancy buried her face in his shoulder. "Then it *was* Frank?"

"He hasn't confessed, but the deputies found a mask at his cabin, and last night he was wearing a dark hooded sweatshirt."

"Mask?" Clancy asked.

"It's the kind of thing they use in the movies," he told her. "It's eerie how much it looks like Dex Strickland," Tadd said.

She stared up at him. "Frank went to the trouble of having a mask made that looked like Dex Strickland just to scare me?"

Jake tightened his grip on her. "I don't think he did it to scare you. More than likely it was to trigger your sleepwalking. Tadd agrees with me that Frank had to have been in the garret that night and saw you sleepwalking. He couldn't chance that you'd remember seeing him, not again. Nor did he need another murder on his hands. So, by triggering your sleepwalking, he could make your death look like an accident.''

''They're sure it was Frank?''

Jake had been a little surprised himself. Frank didn't seem smart—or patient enough—to use Clancy's sleepwalking to his benefit. ''With the mask, the hooded sweatshirt and his watch that we found off the dock, Tadd thinks the county can make a pretty good case against him for attempted murder,'' Jake said. ''Tadd's convinced they'll be able to tie him to Lola's murder and the others.'' He brushed a kiss into her hair. ''Do you realize what this means? You're finally safe.''

She hugged him tightly. ''I was thinking more about what it will mean for your father, Jake.''

''Yeah.'' Jake pulled back to look at her. ''I'd like to tell him about this in person.''

She nodded. ''I really need to get back to work. I might still be able to make my art show in August.''

Jake knew Clancy wanted to give him time alone with his father and he loved her for that. But it was hard to leave her, even with Frank locked up in jail. He thumbed her hair back from her forehead and planted a kiss between her eyes. ''I'll be back before you know it.'' Jake didn't tell her he had one stop to make on his way to the prison.

AFTER JAKE LEFT, Clancy poured herself a cup of coffee and went out on the deck. The sun felt warm as she leaned against the railing to stare out across the lake. The water shimmered, gold. No breeze stirred the surface. Only an occasional boat made waves that lapped softly at the shoreline. Why did she feel so antsy? The killer was behind bars. Jake loved her.

She went back into the kitchen to pour herself another cup of coffee and wandered the lodge, trying to put a finger on what was bothering her. According to Jake's theory, Lola had embezzled the money with Frank's help, Frank had found out about Teddy Bear, taken the money, killed her and burned down the resort.

But how did Clancy explain what she'd seen that night, ten years ago, when she woke up on the docks? She saw Warren Hawkins and Lola fighting and Warren push her. Jake had tried to blame it on the confusion she normally felt when she suddenly awakened in a strange place. That she hadn't really understood what she'd seen. Or had she?

She took a sip of the hot coffee and stared at the lilac bushes framing the window. Something didn't feel right. The other time Frank had come to the house, he wore a mask to make him resemble Dex Strickland. Why hadn't he last night?

Don't buy trouble, she told herself. All the evidence pointed at Frank Ames. Just as all the evidence in Dex's death had pointed to her, she reminded herself.

Not even the coffee could take away the sudden chill in the room. Clancy put down her cup. What was it that tugged at the back of her brain? The necklace. Why hadn't the rest of those tiny blue beads turned up? *Did it really matter,* she asked herself. Yes.

FRANK AMES LOOKED like a man who belonged behind bars, Jake thought as he watched the deputy bring the prisoner into the room.

"What the hell do you want?" Frank demanded when he was ushered into the small interrogation room. "You aren't going to leave me alone with this guy?" Frank asked the jailer who brought him in.

"You can always call a cop if you need one," Jake told Frank as the jailer went to stand just outside the door. "Okay, Frank, we're alone. Whatever you tell me will just be my word against yours. But I need to hear the whole story. Start with Lola and why you killed her."

Frank eyed Jake warily. "I've already told you. I loved Lola. I wouldn't have touched a hair on her head."

Jake took a seat at the far end of the table.

Frank seemed to relax a little. But he sat as far away from Jake as he could get.

"Come on, Frank," Jake cajoled. "Lola hurt you. She fell for someone else—and planned to leave the island and you to run off with him. I'll bet you wanted to kill him, too."

"There wasn't any man," Frank said adamantly. "She flirted with guys sometimes. But it didn't mean anything. I was the only one who really cared about her and she knew that."

It was all Jake could do to keep from going for Frank's throat. "We're not going to get anywhere if you keep lying to me, Frank."

"You're lying to yourself," Frank said nastily. "You want to wrap up this case, get your old man out of prison, clear your girlfriend. You want it to be me so badly that you're blind to what's right in front of your face." Frank shook his head at Jake in disgust. "What kind of killer would use his own motorbike, leave his engraved watch at the scene of the crime, hide the mask he used in his top dresser drawer? How stupid do you think I am?"

Jake decided he'd better not answer that one. Nor would he listen to that little voice at the back of his head arguing that Frank was making sense. No one was that dumb, not even Frank Ames. Maybe especially Frank Ames.

No, Jake thought, Frank was smart. He'd played it this way on purpose. Making it look too obvious.

"Who would want to frame you, Frank?"

He stared down the table at Jake. "I can think of only one person. Your father."

"My father?" What kind of bull was this?

"But since he's still in prison, someone on the outside would have to be setting me up for him," Frank said. "Maybe that explains why you've been dogging me. You're working with your old man."

Jake slammed a fist on the table, making it rattle and Frank jump. "That's a crock, Frank, and you know it. Why would my father want to frame you?"

"Where have you been, Hawkins?" Frank said, coming back like a mean, cornered snake. "You're supposed to be this amazing private eye."

He leaned toward the man, reminding himself that Tadd had gone out on a limb for him, pulling a lot of strings so he could be alone with Frank.

"Why don't you spell it out for me?" Jake said, also reminding himself he'd promised not to lay a hand on Frank, let alone give in to the urge to kick Frank's scrawny behind.

"Where do you think I got the money to buy the resort?" Frank asked in that cocky, "about to get his butt kicked" tone. "Why don't you ask your father."

"What?"

Frank shook his head, sympathetically. "I got the money from your father."

"My father didn't have any money after the fire. Especially to loan you. He fired your sorry butt."

"A loan?" Frank's laugh almost changed Jake's mind about thumping him, cops or no cops, promise or no promise.

"He didn't fire me," Frank said. "I quit after I found out what was going on. Your old man paid me to keep my mouth shut."

Jake felt like he'd been kicked in the gut. He gripped the edges of the table and bit off each word. "What did you have to keep your mouth shut about?"

Frank got up and shuffled around the table to put the most distance between them, all the time eyeing the door. "I caught him skimming the money from the businesses. He paid me to keep quiet. I invested every dime of it and waited. I told you your old man was an embezzler."

"You're lying," Jake growled.

"I've got the proof. I stole the doctored books." A smile curved Frank's thin lips. "You were right, Hawkins, Lola did play me for a fool. I thought she was in love with me and I made the mistake of telling her about your father and how he'd been skimming money from the businesses. Then I found out that she was leaving the island with some man and had told Clancy's old man about your father, his partner and friend, so Clarence Jones wouldn't think she'd been taking the money." Frank let out a bitter laugh. "So I went to the resort that night and I took the books before your father could destroy them."

Jake leaned into the table, sick at heart. His internal arguments that Frank was lying fell on deaf ears.

"So you see, Warren didn't destroy the doctored books in the fire because he couldn't find them. That's probably what he was fighting with Lola about when Clancy saw him. He must have thought she'd taken them. That's probably why he killed her. In the end, they both got what they deserved. And I got the resort. So who's the fool now, Hawkins?"

CLANCY HADN'T BEEN into the storage room in years. She waded through musty old weathered orange life jackets, past rods and reels and water skis, to the dusty boxes at the back. The one she wanted, of course, was on the top shelf.

She pulled out another box to stand on and reached up for her mother's old hatbox, remembering Lola's box of mementos. Clancy's was much the same. A box that most people would think was nothing more than junk. Little things that would remind her of summers spent on the island. With Jake.

As she stepped down she noticed that the large box she'd used for a stool held her father's yearbooks. Clancy pulled his senior yearbook from the box and carried it and the hatbox upstairs to the kitchen where there was more light.

Not ready to delve into the box and all those memories just yet, she opened her father's yearbook.

When she found her father's senior picture, her eyes filled with tears. He looked so young, she thought as she ran her fingers over his face. Oh, how she missed him. He hadn't been handsome by most standards, but he had been to her. He'd been voted class clown, she noted with a smile.

She found another photograph of her father with his two best friends, Warren Hawkins and Johnny Branson.

She looked up their senior photographs. Johnny appeared uncomfortable in an outdated brown suit and garish tie. She studied his face, remembering what her father had told her about Johnny. He'd had to go to work at a young age to help support his family and was always ready to help anyone in need. He'd been voted nicest guy in the class.

She turned a page and found Warren Hawkins. His smiling photograph was in stark contrast to Johnny's. Captain of the football team. Star quarterback. Senior class president. Voted by his classmates as most likely to succeed.

As she thumbed through the yearbook, she looked for Helen. What had her maiden name been? Clancy thought she was a couple of years younger than Johnny. She found Helen in the sophomore section. Helen Collins. Her hair, a pale blond, was long and straight. A pretty girl. No wonder

Johnny had fallen for her. Talk about contrast. Johnny had come from one of the poorer families around Kalispell; Helen from one of the richest.

Clancy started to close the book when she noticed a group photograph. The drama club. Johnny Branson would have stood out in the back row for his size alone, but no one could miss the smile on his face.

Helen Collins stood in front of Johnny in a simple shift, her hair hanging past her shoulders. She smiled into the camera. It tugged at Clancy's heart just looking at the two of them. Childhood sweethearts. They had married right out of high school.

Clancy pushed aside the yearbook and opened her treasured hatbox. Like Lola's box of keepsakes, it was filled with memories from summers of love. An odd-shaped smooth rock that Jake had picked up off the beach and handed to her. The lure she'd caught her largest fish on; Jake had netted it for her. The photo he'd taken of her holding it. Ticket stubs from movies, concerts and plays.

Clancy spotted a play program, the same one she'd seen in Dex's stuff on the back wall of his closet, she realized. Clancy remembered that play. For two reasons. It had been a special date. Jake had surprised her with dinner on the mainland and then a play at the community theater in Bigfork. It was over dinner that he'd told her he loved her and wanted to marry her.

But the play was also where she'd remembered seeing Lola wearing the bead necklace. As she'd sat next to Jake, with him holding her hand, everything about the play had been magnified. Not that she could remember the name of the play or even what it was about. But she remembered the necklace. Probably because of the tiny handmade ceramic heart. It had caught the light at the end when the cast and crew took their bows. It had stuck in her memory because she and Jake had promised their hearts to each other that night.

She opened the play program. The photographer had taken a large wide-angle shot of the cast and crew. Clancy found Lola in the front row. Her heart sank. Lola's neck was bare. Why had Clancy been so sure that's where she'd seen the necklace before?

Clancy's gaze fell on another woman in the photo. Around her neck was the tiny string of beads, the stage lights catching on the ceramic heart. Helen Branson had been wearing the necklace the night of the play. Not Lola.

JAKE DROVE INTO the state prison yard under the heat of a summer sun. His head ached. He kept telling himself he couldn't believe anything Frank said. Frank would do anything to cover his own behind. The problem was, he believed him. Hadn't Jake always prided himself on being able to tell when someone was lying? Well, he'd been wrong about Clancy. Could he be wrong about Frank, as well?

"Jake," Warren said, sounding surprised and nervous as he was ushered into the visiting room. He started toward his son but stopped as if suddenly scared. "What's wrong? Nothing's happened to Clancy—"

Jake shook his head. "The sheriff just arrested the man he believes killed Lola and Dex Strickland."

Warren slumped into the nearest chair. "Thank God they finally found the killer. Who is he?"

"Frank Ames."

Warren looked surprised. "Frank Ames?"

Maybe it was his father's look. Maybe it was realizing earlier that Clancy would never lie to him. Or maybe it was that bad feeling, thumping at the back of his brain. But he knew. "You lied to me."

Warren sat perfectly still, his gaze locked with his son's.

"It was you all along. You stole the money. And you let a slimeball like Frank Ames blackmail you."

Warren's eyes swam behind tears. "I tried to warn you. I asked you to stay out of this."

Jake felt his stomach turn to stone. "Frank thinks you're orchestrating all the evidence against him from here. He actually thought I might be a part of it."

"That's ridiculous," Warren said.

"Why, Dad? Why did you do it?"

He suddenly looked years older. "I was losing your mother, Jake. I knew she was unhappy and I thought more money would keep her. I planned to pay it all back. But then Frank found out and I found myself getting in deeper and deeper. I didn't know how to stop."

Jake swore.

"It just got so crazy after Lola was murdered. I wanted to tell the truth, but I was afraid it would make me look more guilty. Then it was too late."

"Mother knew." Her attitude toward his father suddenly made sense.

"I told her. She couldn't forgive me. It didn't matter that I did it for her. What about you, son? Can you forgive me?"

The pain was too raw right now. Jake just kept thinking about Clancy. "Clancy saw you arguing with Lola that night, just like she swore she had."

Warren nodded. "But I didn't kill Lola. I swear to you. When the fire started, I got out. I thought she was behind me. I realize now, whoever was in that adjoining room started the fire and killed Lola."

Jake stared at his father, unable to believe anything he said. A mystery person in the adjoining room. For years he'd wanted to believe that. But he hadn't believed Clancy, who'd told the truth. Now he wanted desperately to blame his father, to blame someone other than himself, something other than himself for all those years of lack of trust in the woman he loved.

"The killer is after Clancy," Jake said. He moved to the door, needing desperately to get back to Clancy. What had started as a notion, jitterbugging at the back of his mind, was now a death march. The killer was still out there.

Jake stopped at the door, all his fears pounding him like hail the size of walnuts. He thought of Clancy alone at the lodge. If Frank hadn't killed Lola— If Warren hadn't— "Who was Lola in love with?"

Warren slumped into a chair. "He wouldn't hurt Clancy."

"Are you willing to gamble Clancy's life on that? Because if you are—" Jake opened the door to leave.

"Wait."

Jake looked back at his father. He could feel time slipping away. He had to get to Clancy.

"He loved Lola," Warren said more to himself than Jake. And Jake realized his father had sat in his cell for ten years having this same argument with himself. "He couldn't have killed her."

"Who?" Jake demanded, losing his patience with this tangled web of misplaced loyalties.

"Johnny Branson."

"Johnny?" Jake cried.

"He fell head over heels for Lola. He'd never loved anyone like he loved her, but in the end he made the right decision. He was going to tell Lola that night that he couldn't leave Helen."

"Johnny was meeting Lola at the resort office?"

"He'd already been there when I found Lola," Warren said. "She was very upset, so I figured Johnny had told her. But I swear to you, she was alive when I left that room."

"How do you know Johnny wasn't still there?" Jake asked.

Warren blinked. "Johnny loved her. He's the kind of guy who wouldn't hurt a fly."

THE PHONE RANG, making Clancy jump. She glanced at the clock on the wall, surprised how long she'd been working. The rest of the morning had passed in a blur of creative expression.

Clancy stretched, content with the work she'd accomplished. It hadn't taken her long to get back into it. She'd always worked best when something was bothering her. While her fingers shaped the clay, her subconscious worked on any problem on her mind. Like the string of beads. Clancy could see where Helen might not remember a cheap bead necklace after ten years. But how had Helen's necklace ended up in Lola's keepsake box? Not that it probably mattered, she told herself as she wiped her hands and went to answer the phone. The killer had been caught. With any luck, Frank would confess and this nightmare would be behind her.

"Clancy?" Tadd asked. "Is Jake there?"

"No, he's gone to Deer Lodge to see his father. Why? Is there a problem?"

"No, I just wanted to talk to him. When do you expect him back?"

Clancy glanced at the clock on the wall. "Any time, actually. What's going on, Tadd?"

"It's Frank Ames. The sheriff had to release him for lack of evidence."

She sat down hard on the stool at her worktable. "Lack of evidence? What about the watch, the hooded sweatshirt the mask?"

"Frank had an alibi for the night you said someone tried

to drown you, Clancy. He also had an alibi during the time Lola was murdered. Everything against him is circumstantial. The sheriff couldn't hold him. Also, that watch you found off the end of the dock. It might have been ten years old, but the engraving on it wasn't, the lab says.''

Someone had planted the watch off the end of the dock? Who had even known about the scrape on her ankle? Jake. Tadd. Helen. Helen had probably told Johnny. Clancy glanced through the window at the lake shimmering under the summer sun. "When was Frank released?"

"Not long after Jake's visit this morning. I just heard about it and wanted to let you know."

Jake had gone to the jail to see Frank? "I thought you were so sure Frank was the one."

Silence. "There's been some new evidence. An eyewitness got the license plate number from a car that was seen near Glenda Grimes's just before the fire. We're waiting to get a name from the Department of Motor Vehicles. Their computer's down. I'll call you as soon as it comes in. Do you want me to send someone out there to stay with you until Jake gets back?"

Another call beeped on Clancy's line.

"No, I'm fine," Clancy said. "My aunt's coming over. That's probably her calling now."

Absently she pulled the play program out from under her sculpting tools and opened it again to the photograph, thinking about the necklace.

She clicked to the other call. "Hello?" As she answered, she pulled the photograph closer, noticing that Helen wasn't looking at the camera but off to her right. She looked upset and seemed to be glaring at—

"Clancy?" It wasn't Kiki's voice. "It's Helen, dear."

"I was just thinking about you," Clancy said, wondering if it had been ESP or just a coincidence. She looked more

closely at the photograph. Helen was definitely looking at
someone else. Clancy followed her gaze over to...Lola?
Or— Clancy blinked. Or was Helen glaring at the man
standing next to Lola? A big teddy bear of a man, Clancy
thought with a jolt. That man was Johnny Branson.

"I hate to bother you." Helen sounded upset.

"Is something wrong?" Clancy asked, her heart pounding as she stared at the photograph. Johnny Branson. Teddy
Bear?

"I was digging around and I found something I think
you should see. Can you come over?"

What had she found? Something to do with Lola's death?
Or had Helen found a receipt for the engraving of a silver
watch?

"Helen, does this have something to do with Johnny?"
she asked, voicing her worst fear.

"Yes." Helen sounded close to tears.

Clancy looked down at the play program photo. "I'll be
right over."

"Please hurry." Helen hung up.

JAKE LEFT THE PRISON and headed for the airport, his chest
aching with worry. As he drove, he dialed Clancy's number
on the cell phone. No answer. Then he tried Helen Branson.
The phone rang and rang. Jake hung up and dialed Tadd
Farnsworth's office.

"Can you get the sheriff to send a deputy to Clancy's
right away?" Jake asked.

"Clancy's?" Tadd said. "I just tried to call you to tell
you about Johnny."

"What about Johnny?" Jake asked, dread settling in his
chest.

"There's an eyewitness who saw a car parked near

Glenda Grimes's house right before the fire. When the Motor Vehicle Department ran the plates—''

"The car's registered to Johnny Branson," Jake said.

"How did you know that?"

"Johnny is Teddy Bear."

"No kidding?" Tadd sounded genuinely surprised.

And Warren had been so sure that Johnny couldn't hurt a fly. Right. "You said you tried to call me earlier."

"I talked to Clancy and warned her that Frank's been released. He had alibis for the nights in question. The sheriff couldn't hold him any longer."

Jake swore. As hard as he tried, he couldn't convince himself that Frank Ames wasn't a danger to Clancy. "Did you tell her about Johnny?"

"I hadn't received the information yet from DMV the first time I talked to her. I tried a few minutes ago, but there was no answer."

"Tadd, I'm worried about her. Something's wrong. She said she was going to spend the day in her studio."

"When I talked to her she told me her aunt was coming over," Tadd said reasonably. "In fact, she got a call from Kiki while I was on the line. Maybe the two of them are outside and can't hear the phone."

Jake wanted to believe it was that simple.

"If you're worried about Johnny Branson, the sheriff sent a deputy out to bring him in for questioning. The deputy should be there by now."

Jake tried to relax but knew he wouldn't be able to until he had Clancy safe in his arms. "I'm in Deer Lodge. I'm flying out on the first plane I can charter." Or steal. "Call me when Johnny's in custody."

Chapter Nineteen

"Helen?" Clancy called after her knock at the kitchen door went unanswered. A warm wind blew off the lake, whispering through the tops of the pines at the edge of the deck. Large white cumulus clouds scudded across a backdrop of clear blue. Clancy knocked again and tried the door. Locked. She headed up the ramp to the second level, wondering if Helen was in the pool, swimming laps. That seemed odd, considering how urgent the woman had sounded on the phone.

"Helen?" Clancy called again. The pool glistened a pretty turquoise blue, but Helen was nowhere around. A knot of worry settled in Clancy's stomach. She'd told herself all the way over that she was just jumping to conclusions. Just because it had looked like Helen was glaring at Johnny and Lola in an old photo. Just because Johnny had changed so much since Lola's death. Just because he was indeed a big teddy bear of a man. That didn't mean that he was Lola's lover. Helen could have found out something else about Johnny—

Clancy had started toward the ramp to the top deck, but stumbled to a stop as something in the crack between the boards caught her eye. She knelt. More than a dozen tiny blue beads were wedged between the wood of the deck.

Using her thumbnail, she dug one out. Her hand shook as she held it up to the light. This was a bead from the necklace. Helen's necklace. The one Dex had had the night he died.

She held the single bead in her palm, all the ramifications of finding it here battering her brain. This is where the string of beads had been broken. Dex Strickland had been here.

To see Johnny? To talk to him about Lola's murder because he was the former sheriff? Or because Dex thought that Johnny Branson had been in love with his mother and had killed her?

Clancy straightened, suddenly even more worried about Helen. What had she found out about Johnny? That he really was Teddy Bear? That he was the one who'd killed Lola? That he'd killed three more people to keep his secret?

Her steps quickened. Where *was* Johnny now? Had he returned from fishing? Clancy had ridden her mountain bike instead of coming by boat to avoid the climb up the cliffs by either the elevator or stairs. She hurried up the ramp, anxious to get to the top deck so she could see if Johnny's boat was tied at the dock.

Helen sat at the far edge of the deck, her back to Clancy, her wheelchair facing the lake. She wore her white terrycloth robe, the hood up. The wind whipped at one corner of the robe tucked around her legs.

Something about the way the woman sat made Clancy hesitate. Her shoulders were slumped forward, her head bent as if she were crying. If Clancy was right about Johnny and Lola— She tried to imagine what Helen must be feeling. Betrayed. Johnny had been her life. She must be devastated. How could a woman accept that the man she'd been married to all these years was a murderer?

"I came as quickly as I could," Clancy said as she approached Helen from behind. The woman had probably been sitting here, waiting, expecting her to arrive by boat. "Are you all right?"

When Helen didn't respond, Clancy laid a hand on her shoulder.

"Helen? It's Clancy."

Helen suddenly slumped forward in the wheelchair. Clancy rushed around to help her. "Helen," she cried as she knelt in front of her and gently pushed her back into the chair.

"Oh, my God!" Clancy threw herself backward, slamming into the deck railing. Her feet slipped out from under her and she sat hard on the deck floor at the foot of the wheelchair as a high-pitched scream shrieked from her lips.

Jake dialed Clancy's number again as he turned into the mainland marina. It was answered on the first ring.

"Kiki?" he asked. "Where's Clancy?"

"I was going to ask you the same thing," she said. "I just got here— Just a moment. Clancy left you a note. It says, 'Sorry. Helen called upset. I'm going over there. I think I know who Teddy Bear is and that Helen's figured it out, too.'"

Jake swore and hung up as he swung into a parking space beside the deputy's car. But it was the boat tied at the dock that stopped him dead.

He climbed out of the Mustang and walked down to the dock. Johnny Branson looked up from his boat and smiled.

"You must be that special fare I'm supposed to pick up," Johnny said.

Jake shook his head.

Johnny looked around and frowned. The marina parking lot was empty except for Jake's and the deputy's cars. Johnny seemed to study the cop car for a moment, then turned his attention to Jake. "That's funny," he said, still frowning. "I was supposed to meet a client here more than half an hour ago."

"Have you seen Clancy?" Jake demanded.

The older man looked surprised. "No, why? What's wrong?"

"I just got back from Deer Lodge."

Johnny's gaze dropped to his feet. "How is Warren?"

"How do you think he is?"

When Johnny raised his head, worry etched the man's thin face. Worry and a deep sadness that Jake knew only too well at this moment.

"He's the one who embezzled the money, but you knew that, didn't you?" Jake said, trying hard to hold down his anger. What had happened between two best friends that one would let the other go to prison for a murder he didn't commit?

Johnny slumped back against the side of the boat.

"You were Lola's lover. You were Teddy Bear." Jake had spent the last few hours trying to put it all together, but it still didn't fit. He told himself he was just too close to it. "You went to the resort that night to meet Lola. The two of you were taking off."

Johnny shook his head. "I went to tell her I couldn't go with her. I couldn't hurt Helen."

Jake stared at the former sheriff. At one time he'd been a big bear of a man. Now he looked frail and broken, a man worn down by secrets and sorrows. With a shock, Jake realized that Johnny Branson looked like a man who was dying. Jake knew that look; he'd just recently watched his mother die. "Cancer?"

Johnny raised his head slowly and nodded.

"How long?" Jake asked.

"I won't see fall."

Jake looked out over the lake, then back at Johnny. Jake's father was right; Johnny didn't seem like much of a killer. Nor could Jake understand why a man with only three months to live would keep trying to cover up a ten-year-old murder.

"The cops have an eyewitness who saw your car at Lola's sister's house just before Glenda Grimes was murdered and her house set on fire," Jake said. "A deputy is at your house now with a warrant for your arrest."

Johnny's gaze flicked up. He glanced toward the island, worry in his eyes. Jake followed his gaze, a thought hitting him between the eyes like a brick. A dying man *wouldn't* keep killing to protect himself. Jake felt his heart lunge in his chest. He swore and looked again at Johnny's gentle face.

"You didn't kill Lola," Jake said, the first thing he'd been truly sure of. "My God. Who told you to pick up a fishing client here?"

"I probably just got it wrong."

"Who, dammit?" Jake demanded.

"Helen said Frank Ames set it up—"

"Call her." Jake vaulted into the boat and handed Johnny the two-way radio. "Dammit, call Helen now. Clancy's on her way there. Helen phoned her and asked her to come over."

Johnny stumbled to the radio. Just as Jake had feared, Helen didn't answer.

Jake shoved Johnny aside to start up the dual engines on the large, powerful fishing boat. It would be faster than his rental boat. He only prayed they could reach the island in time.

"You don't understand," Johnny said as they sped across the water. "Helen loves me. She's always loved me. She was so pretty and popular. I was poor and a...nobody. She made me somebody, don't you see? She gave me everything. And look what I did to her.''

Jake's fears multiplied with each beat of his heart. He could see. That's what frightened him so. "You fell in love with someone else. That's not the same as murder."

Johnny's eyes clouded over. "Helen didn't know I'd changed my mind about leaving her. She didn't know."

The island grew closer, but Jake's fear grew with it.

"I was going to tell the truth," Johnny said. "Then after the accident— We were arguing. I was driving too fast. It was all my fault."

Jake could see only too clearly why Johnny had covered for Helen all these years. "She's killed three more people, Johnny. How long were you going to sit back and let her keep killing?"

He frowned. "She couldn't have killed them. How could she? A woman in a wheelchair?"

Jake had asked himself that same question. He picked up Johnny's binoculars. The home Johnny had built Helen high on the cliffs shone in the afternoon sunlight as Jake glassed it with the binoculars. The deputy's boat was at the dock. So was a bright red jet boat. "Whose jet boat is that?" Jake asked.

Johnny took the binoculars. "Frank Ames's."

Jake's heart dropped. "Maybe Helen had help." Someone like Frank Ames. Had Helen been Frank's alibi? That would explain how he'd gotten out of jail and why he was at Helen's now. To collect whatever amount she'd agreed to pay him. With a fresh rush of fear, Jake reminded himself that Helen had called Clancy to come to the house.

"Try the radio again," Jake commanded, praying that Johnny would be able to stop Helen. But who would be able to stop Frank Ames? Jake assured himself that a deputy was there—everything was fine. Except the hunch stomping at the back of his neck said everything was not fine. Not fine at all.

IN HORROR, CLANCY STARED at the face beneath the hooded robe in the wheelchair. Not Helen's face. But a man's. A man Clancy didn't recognize. Couldn't have recognized. The face purple, tongue protruding, eyes bulging. Around his neck was a white cord. The same white cord Clancy had seen Helen tie around her slim waist the day before. The cord was now taut around the strangled man's throat.

Unable to pull her gaze from his face, Clancy stumbled to her feet. The wind caught the edge of the robe and whipped it open. Clancy's heart thudded against her rib cage as she backed her way along the railing toward the house. The man wore a uniform from the local sheriff's department. Clancy's heart rate rocketed upward. His holster was empty.

"Helen!" she screamed, frantic to put distance between her and the death in the wheelchair, her brain tangled and confused. Where was Johnny? She looked over the side of the railing, down the cliff to the dock floating in the dark green of the lake below her. Two boats. Neither was Johnny's fishing boat. Two boats? Her thoughts came like bullets. A Sheriff's Department boat. But who did the other one belong to?

Clancy inched her way along the railing toward the house without consciously realizing what she was doing. Who had killed the deputy and put him in Helen's wheelchair? Where was Helen? "Helen!"

Clancy's shoulder slammed into the glass door to the living room. *Run!* The deputy was dead. Helen wasn't answering; she'd answer if she were still alive. The killer was still here. His boat was still at the dock. *Just get out of here. Get help. Don't go in the house.* She glanced toward her bike, leaning against the deck railing, but her feet seemed incapable of moving another step. She slumped against the glass door. Panic made thinking almost impossible. Where was Helen? Who else was up here?

The door began to open. Clancy felt her breath catch in her throat as she found the strength to push away from the glass. She turned, in slow motion, hoping to see Helen in her wheelchair, praying to see Helen. The sun ricocheted off the glass. Behind it nothing but darkness. The door slid open slowly. Clancy felt a scream rise in her throat.

Frank Ames stood in the doorway, smiling, his shirt soaked with blood. Clancy screamed.

Frank stumbled toward her, his face contorted in not a smile but a grimace. He tried to speak but the words came out slurred. All Clancy caught was one word, "Helen," before Frank lurched forward and fell at her feet.

Clancy would have turned and run, but she heard a faint cry for help from within the house. Helen. She slipped past Frank's lifeless body into the living room. Empty. "Helen?"

"In here," Helen called from the front part of the house.

Heart hammering, Clancy rushed into the master bedroom.

Helen lay on the floor near the bed.

"Where's Frank?" she cried as she pulled herself up to a sitting position to lean back against the foot of the unmade bed. A bloody baseball bat lay on the floor beside her.

"I think he's dead," Clancy said, rushing to her. "Are you all right?"

"He tried to strangle me," Helen said, her hands going to her throat. She jerked off the scarf that had been wrapped around her neck and cast it away from her in disgust as she reached for a smaller wheelchair near the bed.

Clancy didn't mention the deputy, strangled outside in her other wheelchair. "Here, let me help you."

"Don't worry about me," Helen snapped, shooing her away. "Call Johnny. I need Johnny."

Clancy rushed back into the living room but went to the phone instead of the radio. She punched out 911 before she realized the line was dead. As she hung up, she noticed the drawer in the desk, partially closed on a stack of papers. Unconsciously, she opened the drawer to push the papers in. Her gaze fell on the word *Sleepwalking*.

She pulled the drawer open a little farther. There were dozens of photocopies of articles about sleepwalking. One sentence, underlined in red, leaped out at her. "Sleepwalking episodes are often triggered by severe stress or trauma."

Clancy's heart thundered in her ears as something else in the drawer caught her eye. A tiny ceramic heart. The heart from the necklace.

Clancy staggered and grabbed the desk to keep from falling. Helen's necklace. It had been the clue all along. Dex had had the necklace. And the old play program. He *knew* it was Helen's. That's why he'd come here.

The two-way radio squawked. Clancy jumped.

"Helen?" Johnny's voice came over the radio. "Helen?" Desperation laced his voice. She could hear the boat's motors in the background and the sound of his boat's hull slapping the water as it crossed the lake.

"Clancy?"

A chill streaked across her skin at the sound of Jake's voice. She lunged for the radio. "Jake? Where are you?"

"We're almost there. Clancy, thank God, you're all right. Where's Helen?"

"In the bedroom. But there's a deputy here— He's dead, Jake. And Frank—" The elevator. It groaned and clanked as it climbed the cliffs. Clancy could feel the hysteria rising like lava in her throat. "Someone's coming up the elevator."

"Clancy, listen to me—" The radio crackled.

The elevator clanged to a stop. Clancy turned slowly, afraid of who she'd see in the contraption. The sun caught on the dull metal, then passed through the bars. The elevator stood empty.

"Clancy, do you hear me?" Jake yelled over the radio. "Get out of there! Helen killed Lola. Get out of there! Now!"

Clancy turned to look toward the bedroom as she set down the radio receiver. "Helen?" She moved cautiously toward the open bedroom doorway. "Helen?" A deathly quiet fell over the house. Her pulse thrummed in her ears. She fought for each breath. At the edge of the doorway, she peered around the corner into the bedroom.

Helen was gone. So was the wheelchair and the baseball bat.

Chapter Twenty

Clancy stumbled to the door and stepped gingerly over Frank. The top deck was empty except for the deputy. He sat slumped over in the wheelchair, the wind snapping the tail end of the robe. Helen was nowhere in sight, but Clancy knew she couldn't have gone far.

Cautiously, she walked to the back edge of the deck to look down past the pool and the lower deck. Her bike still leaned against the railing. If she could reach it—

She could hear Jake's words in her head saying he was on his way. He would be at the dock soon. Take the elevator down to the dock and wait for him. She turned and looked back at it still sitting empty at the edge of the deck. Then she hurried over to it and pulled open the door. She stared at the empty elevator for a moment. Why had Helen brought it up? Just to slow down Johnny and Jake? Or for another reason?

Don't get in the elevator! Clancy stumbled back, no longer sure she could trust her instincts. *Take the bike. Get to the resort and call for help.* She turned and fled, racing down the ramp past the pool. She thought she heard a noise behind her but she didn't turn. She reached the railing and grabbed her bike.

"No, Clancy," a voice behind her said calmly. "That's not the plan."

Clancy turned slowly, expecting to see Helen at the edge of the deck in her wheelchair. The last thing she expected was to see her standing with the deputy's gun pointed at Clancy's heart.

THE WIND HAD PICKED UP as they neared the island. Waves hammered the bow and spilled into the boat, drenching them both. Jake didn't slow down. A million thoughts raced around in his brain. All the things he wanted to do with Clancy when they got out of this mess. Ahead he could see the dock. They were almost there. *Hang on, Clancy,* he cried. *I'm coming!*

"YOU CAN WALK!" Clancy cried, unable to take her eyes off a Helen she'd never seen before. "You were never paralyzed!"

"I was for a while." Helen moved closer, leveling the gun at Clancy's chest. "But after a few weeks I started to get some feeling back in my legs. The doctors said I might, but Johnny worried that I never would."

"He doesn't know?"

Helen cocked an eyebrow at her that implied Clancy was smarter than to ask a silly question like that. Of course he didn't know. Helen motioned with the gun for Clancy to start moving up the ramp toward the house. "Let's go out on the deck where we can see when Jake and Johnny get here."

"You stayed in a wheelchair all these years to keep Johnny?" Clancy asked in amazement as she stood staring at Helen.

"With Johnny fishing most of the time, it wasn't hard to keep up the charade. I learned from the master," Helen

said. "I watched how Lola entrapped Johnny with her helplessness. Did he want a woman who was strong and re-
sourceful? No, he wanted one who was inept, dependent,
hopeless. Someone he'd have to spend his life's energy taking care of." Helen's gaze turned hard. "All I did was
pattern myself after Lola. She was what he wanted. So I
became her. Totally dependent on him for my very existence."

"You killed Lola!"

"I had no choice," Helen said, seeming surprised by
Clancy's reaction. "I didn't know Johnny had gone to the
resort that night to break it off with her. But it's probably
just as well. I wanted her out of our lives forever and at
any price. Unfortunately, for Lola the price was death." She
motioned for Clancy to get moving.

Clancy started up the ramp. "And Dex? Was that his
price, too?"

"He was just like his mother," Helen said. "He wanted
something that didn't belong to him. In his case, it was my
money. He thought I'd pay for his silence."

Helen shook her head as if the whole thing saddened her.
"He called to say he had something of mine. I didn't believe him at first. He said he had proof. I told him to leave
it under a bait can on the dock. Dex just figured Johnny
would pick it up for me. He couldn't know that I'd come
myself."

The message the cabin girl had taken to the dock. It had
been for Helen.

"It was a drawing of the necklace and a demand for
money," Helen said.

"How did Dex get the necklace?" Clancy asked, wondering how Helen's necklace had ended up in Lola's belongings after the fire.

"I had it on the night I went to the resort to deal with Lola. She tore it from my neck in the struggle."

That's when the clasp was broken, Clancy thought as she tried to walk more slowly, stalling for time, for Jake.

"I just assumed it had burned in the fire," Helen continued, sounding distant, as if the past no longer mattered. "The police must have found it and, thinking it was Lola's, given it to the family. It was the only proof that I'd been at the resort the night Lola was murdered."

Clancy felt a chill race across her skin and turned to look at Helen. "That night at the café. Dex saw something in the pines. It was you. Out of your wheelchair. Walking. No wonder he'd looked so frightened."

Helen smiled. "I enjoyed playing with him. Later I surprised him and his girlfriend at his cabin. I was in my wheelchair and convinced Dex he'd only imagined seeing me standing in the pines."

That would explain why Dex was killed sans underwear.

"You agreed to pay him off?" Clancy asked, remembering what Kiki had told her about Dex's mood.

Helen nodded distractedly.

"Then, how did the beads get broken at your house?" Clancy asked.

Helen looked up in surprise as if the question had pulled her from other thoughts.

"I found the beads from the necklace caught in your deck," Clancy said.

Helen smiled. "How very observant of you. Dex made me so angry, coming to the house when I told him not to. It was a good thing I'd given Johnny something to help him sleep. I grabbed the beads and..." She looked across the pool, her eyes suddenly full of tears. "The necklace broke. Johnny made it for me while we were in high school. He gave it to me the night he asked me to marry him."

Clancy thought she heard the roar of a boat on the wind. Helen must have heard it, too. She motioned with the gun for Clancy to head up the last ramp to the top deck.

Clancy felt sick inside. Jake would be here soon. But soon enough? "How did you get Dex into my garret?"

"Dex thought Lola had embezzled the money from the resort and hidden it somewhere. I just told him it was in your garret and where you kept a key, over the front door."

Jake had been right; everyone in the world knew about the key.

"And Dex believed you that *I* had the money at the lodge?"

They reached the top deck, and Clancy felt time running out as quickly as beach sand poured from between her fingers.

"Dex was like his mother. Greedy, but not particularly bright," Helen said, not unkindly. "I followed him to your lodge. I didn't know you would come sleepwalking in and pick up the sculpture I'd used to kill him. I remember your mother saying what a sound sleeper you always were. She thought that was one reason you sleepwalked."

Helen had always known about her sleepwalking. "Weren't you worried that I'd remember seeing you?" Clancy asked.

"Of course not, dear, I'd seen you sleepwalk before, the night I killed Lola. I passed you on the dock and you looked right at me."

Clancy turned to stare at her, realizing Helen had spared her that night on the dock only because Clancy had been walking in her sleep. "Then, why did you frame me with Dex's murder if you felt you had nothing to fear from me?"

"I was just buying time, dear." She frowned. "But then you came over asking about the necklace and I knew, as badly as I didn't want to, I'd have to stop you."

Clancy's eyes widened in horror as she realized this soft-spoken, caring woman she'd known most of her life had become a cold-blooded killer. "You tried to kill me." Even now, Clancy found it hard to believe.

Helen wagged her head. "It grieved me terribly, dear. You were the last person I ever wanted to hurt."

Clancy felt repulsed as she noticed the silver bracelet on Helen's slim wrist. "It wasn't a watch that scraped my ankle but your bracelet. After I told you I thought it was a watch, you planted the watch off the end of my dock to make it look like Frank Ames did it." Clancy stared at her in abhorrence. "You couldn't have been the person who ran me off the trail on the motorbike," Clancy said, thinking Helen had to have had an accomplice. Frank?

"I'm quite capable of riding a motorbike, dear," Helen said, sounding offended. "I used to be an athlete, remember?"

Yes, and Clancy had forgotten what excellent shape Helen had kept herself in all these years. She remembered seeing Helen hoist herself into the wheelchair. The woman had incredible strength for her age. And Clancy realized Helen Branson was capable of anything. Including another murder.

"Frank figured out that you were the one framing him," Clancy said.

Helen seemed not to be listening. "That young waitress saw me take Frank's bike and thought to cash in on my misfortune." Helen tsked to herself. "So unfortunate. But it doesn't matter now, does it, dear? Time has run out."

Clancy had reached the edge of the top deck. The wind whistled across the mountain, whipping her hair into her eyes. She backed the last few feet to the railing as Helen indicated her to do, intensely aware of the gun pointed at her heart, but thinking more of the cliff behind her.

"Helen, you can't expect to get away with this," Clanc
cried.

"Oh, I don't dear. I'm just cleaning up a few loose ends
Tidying up." Helen stepped around Clancy to look dow
the cliff, but the gun never wavered. "Don't do anythin
foolish, will you, dear." She smiled as she glanced up. "
always thought you and Jake Hawkins would make a fin
couple."

Clancy could hear a boat motor growing louder over th
howl of the wind. She felt tears sting her eyes.

"They're almost here. It's almost over." Helen looke
up at Clancy. "Johnny's dying of cancer. He thinks I don'
know." She smiled sadly, her eyes bright with tears. "I'
hoped for just a little more time with him."

Clancy glanced past Helen in shock. Frank Ames was n
longer sprawled in the living-room doorway. He stood be
hind Helen, blood running down into his left eye as h
reached out a hand.

JAKE WAS OUT OF THE BOAT the moment they reached th
dock. He didn't bother with the elevator but took the stair
two at a time. Below him Johnny stumbled from the boa
Jake heard him try the elevator. It groaned but didn't move
Helen had locked it on top to slow them down. Behind him
he heard Johnny running up the stairs. Jake ran faster.

HELEN SMILED AS SHE SAW the startled expression o
Clancy's face. "You really don't think that old ploy is go
ing to work, do you, dear? I'm suppose to see that look o
your face and then turn around so you can jump me an
take the gun away. Really, Clancy, I thought you were mor
intelligent than that."

Frank laid a hand on Helen's shoulder. Surprise, the
fright, registered in her eyes. She started to wheel around

Clancy lunged for the gun and, grabbing Helen's wrist, ought to wrestle the pistol away. Helen swung her body to atch Frank in the face with her elbow; he fell backward, itting the deck hard. The gun went off, the shot echoing cross the deck.

AKE HAD NEARED THE TOP of the stairs when he heard the hot. His heart in his throat, he drew his .38 from the holster t his ribs and bounded up the steps, fear racing him up the st few.

Clancy still wrestled with Helen for the pistol, but her oncentration broke when she spotted Jake. Helen wrenched e gun from Clancy's grasp and was raising the barrel to oint it at Clancy when his foot came down on the last step.

"Drop it!" he yelled over the wind, ready to fire if Helen esitated for an instant.

The gun dropped from Helen's hand and hit the deck ith a thud.

Jake rushed over to scoop it up. Then pulled Clancy to im. "Are you all right?" His heart slammed against his bs, making each breath a labor.

She nodded.

Helen smiled as she saw Johnny lumber up the last of e stairs. She ran to him. He took her in his arms and held er, seeming only mildly surprised that she could walk. ke looked into the big man's face and saw the pain. And e silent plea. "Let me take her in."

Jake nodded.

"It's all over, Helen," he said to his wife, hugging her him.

She nodded and turned to look back at Jake and Clancy. Yes," she said. "It's all over."

"Shall we take the elevator down?" Johnny asked Helen.

She looked up at him, her face full of love. "Yes. That'
exactly what I thought we'd do."

They walked arm in arm to the elevator.

"Jake," Clancy cried softly. "No, you can't let them—'

Jake pulled her closer. "Let them go, Clancy," he whis
pered.

Johnny helped Helen into the elevator and stepped i
after her, closing the door behind them. He turned to loo
at Jake, tears in his eyes. Then he pushed the button. Th
elevator dropped like a rock.

Epilogue

The wind whipped Clancy's hair as she watched the Galveston skyline grow smaller behind the boat. She brushed her hair back and breathed in the smell of the gulf, letting it fill her lungs as she looked at her husband.

Jake stood on the bridge of the thirty-six-foot trawler steering them toward the endless horizon, his Astros baseball cap cocked back, his tanned hands strong and sure on the wheel.

Her husband, she thought, and smiled as she joined him.

"What are you smiling about, Mrs. Hawkins?" Jake asked as he pulled her closer.

She liked the sound of that, loved the feel of him. "You," she answered. For so long, Clancy thought she'd never smile again.

The days after Helen and Johnny's deaths had been as dark as the days after the resort fire and the loss of her parents. But unlike then, Jake helped her through those early summer days, piecing together what had started ten years before and finally ended on the Bransons' deck.

Some of the answers died with Helen and Johnny. Others were locked in Clancy's subconscious. Had she really walked along the cliffs all the way to Helen's in her sleep to return with a single blue bead, not once, but twice? Had part of her known all along it was Helen? Is that why she'd continued to walk down the beach each night?

Whatever the reason, the sleepwalking had stopped as abruptly as it had started. She knew that as long as she could curl up with Jake each night, she would have no reason to walk anywhere in her sleep again.

Frank had lived and become a hero, taking credit for saving Clancy's life, although Clancy knew now that Helen had never intended to harm her or Jake at the end. But Frank seemed happier than he had in years. Maybe he'd finally gotten rid of that chip on his shoulder. Or maybe he'd just finally laid Lola's ghost to rest.

With Tadd's help, Warren Hawkins's case was reopened. He got out of prison in time for their wedding and stood next to his son as Jake promised to love, honor and cherish.

Their lives had been different as they'd left Hawk Island. Like Johnny, she and Jake had once seen the world in blacks and whites, rights and wrongs. Now they could see the grays.

It had been Jake's idea to marry as soon as possible. "Life is too short," he'd said. "We've already lost enough time. Let's not lose any more."

"Aunt Kiki isn't going to like it," Clancy had pointed out.

"Oh, you might be surprised. I think I finally figured out why she hired me to investigate your case."

Kiki had cried at the wedding, then presented them with the thirty-six-foot trawler. "Go see the world, and when you get back, I'll have the nursery ready at the lodge." Clancy had assured her that wouldn't be necessary. Not yet, anyway.

Clancy snuggled against her husband and looked back to see the Galveston skyline disappear behind them. When she turned back, Jake was gazing down at her as if just looking at her brought him joy.

"Did I ever tell you about these hunches that I sometimes get?" Jake asked.

She shook her head and grinned up at him. "I don't believe you ever have."

He rubbed at the back of his neck. "How do you feel about twins?"

"Twins?" Clancy cried.

"Twin boys. Born nine months from now."

She laughed. "You really don't put any stock in these hunches of yours, do you?"

"Nah," he said as he put the boat on automatic pilot and led her down to their cabin. "None at all."

Romance, cowboys and
small-town living and loving…
The town of Glory, Alberta, has it all!

Bestselling author

JUDITH BOWEN

brings you a brand-new story in
her popular Men of Glory miniseries!

WEST OF GLORY

Burned-out reporter Daisy Sutherland returns home
to recuperate from the pressures of the big city…
but soon finds herself working with handsome rancher
Ben Goodstriker to solve a local mystery.

Look for WEST OF GLORY, in stores August 2003.

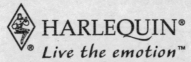

Visit us at www.eHarlequin.com

PHWOG

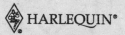

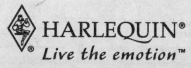

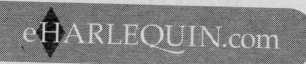

HARLEQUIN BLAZE COVER MODEL SEARCH CONTEST 3569 OFFICIAL RULES
NO PURCHASE NECESSARY TO ENTER

1. To enter, submit two (2) 4" x 6" photographs of a boyfriend or spouse (who must be 18 years of age or older) taken no later than three (3) months from the time of entry: a close-up, waist up, shirtless photograph; and a fully clothed, full-length photograph, then, tell us, in 100 words or fewer, why he should be a Harlequin Blaze cover model and how he is romantic. Your complete "entry" must include: (i) your essay, (ii) the Official Entry Form and Publicity Release Form printed below completed and signed by you (as "Entrant"), (iii) the photographs (with your hand-written name, address and phone number, and your model's name, address and phone number on the back of each photograph), and (iv) the Publicity Release Form and Photograph Representation Form printed below completed and signed by your model (as "Model"), and should be sent via first-class mail to either: Harlequin Blaze Cover Model Search Contest 3569, P.O. Box 9069, Buffalo, NY, 14269-9069, or Harlequin Blaze Cover Model Search Contest 3569, P.O. Box 637, Fort Erie, Ontario L2A 5X3. All submissions must be in English and be received no later than September 30, 2003. Limit: one entry per person, household or organization. **Purchase or acceptance of a product offer does not improve your chances of winning.** All entry requirements must be strictly adhered to for eligibility and to ensure fairness among entries.

2. Ten (10) Finalist submissions (photographs and essays) will be selected by a panel of judges consisting of members of the Harlequin editorial, marketing and public relations staff, as well as a representative from Elite Model Management (Toronto) Inc., based on the following criteria:

Aptness/Appropriateness of submitted photographs for a Harlequin Blaze cover—70%
Originality of Essay—20%
Sincerity of Essay—10%

In the event of a tie, duplicate finalists will be selected. The photographs submitted by finalists will be posted on the Harlequin website no later than November 15, 2003 (at www.blazecovermodel.com), and viewers may vote, in rank order, on their favorite(s) to assist in the panel of judges' final determination of the Grand Prize and Runner-up winning entries based on the above judging criteria. All decisions of the judges are final.

3. All entries become the property of Harlequin Enterprises Ltd. and none will be returned. Any entry may be used for future promotional purposes. Elite Model Management (Toronto) Inc. and/or its partners, subsidiaries and affiliates operating as "Elite Model Management" will have access to all entries including all personal information, and may contact any Entrant and/or Model in its sole discretion for their own business purposes. Harlequin and Elite Model Management (Toronto) Inc. are separate entities with no legal association or partnership whatsoever having no power to bind or obligate the other or create any expressed or implied obligation or responsibility on behalf of the other, such that Harlequin shall not be responsible in any way for any acts or omissions of Elite Model Management (Toronto) Inc. or its partners, subsidiaries and affiliates in connection with the Contest or otherwise and Elite Model Management shall not be responsible in any way for any acts or omissions of Harlequin or its partners, subsidiaries and affiliates in connection with the contest or otherwise.

4. All Entrants and Models must be residents of the U.S. or Canada, be 18 years of age or older, and have no prior criminal convictions. The contest is not open to any Model that is a professional model and/or actor in any capacity at the time of the entry. Contest void wherever prohibited by law; all applicable laws and regulations apply. Any litigation within the Province of Quebec regarding the conduct or organization of a publicity contest may be submitted to the Régie des alcools, des courses et des jeux for a ruling, and any litigation regarding the awarding of a prize may be submitted to the Régie only for the purpose of helping the parties reach a settlement. Employees and immediate family members of Harlequin Enterprises Ltd., D.L. Blair, Inc., Elite Model Management (Toronto) Inc. and their parents, affiliates, subsidiaries and all other agencies, entities and persons connected with the use, marketing or conduct of this Contest are not eligible to enter. Acceptance of any prize offered constitutes permission to use Entrants' and Models' names, essay submissions, photographs or other likenesses for the purposes of advertising, trade, publication and promotion on behalf of Harlequin Enterprises Ltd., its parent, affiliates, subsidiaries, assigns and other authorized entities involved in the judging and promotion of the contest without further compensation to any Entrant or Model, unless prohibited by law.

5. Finalists will be determined no later than October 30, 2003. Prize Winners will be determined no later than January 31, 2004. Grand Prize Winners (consisting of winning Entrant and Model) will be required to sign and return Affidavit of Eligibility/Release of Liability and Model Release forms within thirty (30) days of notification. Non-compliance with this requirement and within the specified time period will result in disqualification and an alternate will be selected. Any prize notification returned as undeliverable will result in the awarding of the prize to an alternate set of winners. All travelers (or parent/legal guardian of a minor) must execute the Affidavit of Eligibility/Release of Liability prior to ticketing and must possess required travel documents (e.g. valid photo ID) where applicable. Travel dates specified by Sponsor but no later than May 30, 2004.

6. Prizes: One (1) Grand Prize—the opportunity for the Model to appear on the cover of a paperback book from the Harlequin Blaze series, and a 3 day/2 night trip for two (Entrant and Model) to New York, NY for the photo shoot of Model which includes round-trip coach air transportation from the commercial airport nearest the winning Entrant's home to New York, NY, (or, in lieu of air transportation, $100 cash payable to Entrant and Model, if the winning Entrant's home is within 250 miles of New York, NY), hotel accommodations (double occupancy) at the Plaza Hotel and $500 cash spending money payable to Entrant and Model, for a romantic dinner for two (approximate prize value: $200). Prizes are valued in U.S. currency. Prizes consist of only those items listed as part of the prize. No substitution of prize(s) permitted to winners. All prizes are awarded jointly to the Entrant and Model of the winning entries, and are not severable - prizes and obligations may not be assigned or transferred. Any change to the Entrant and/or Model of the winning entries will result in disqualification and an alternate will be selected. Taxes on prize are the sole responsibility of winners. Harlequin all expenses and/or items not specifically described as part of the prize are the sole responsibility of winners. Harlequin Enterprises Ltd. and D.L. Blair, Inc., their parents, affiliates, and subsidiaries are not responsible for errors in printing of Contest entries and/or game pieces. No responsibility is assumed for lost, stolen, late, illegible, incomplete, inaccurate, non-delivered, postage due or misdirected mail or entries. In the event of printing or other errors which may result in unintended prize values or duplication of prizes, all affected game pieces or entries shall be null and void.

7. Winners will be notified by mail. For winners' list (available after March 31, 2004), send a self-addressed, stamped envelope to: Harlequin Blaze Cover Model Search Contest 3569 Winners, P.O. Box 4200, Blair, NE 68009-4200, or refer to the Harlequin website (at www.blazecovermodel.com).

Contest sponsored by Harlequin Enterprises Ltd., P.O. Box 9042, Buffalo, NY 14269-9042.

HBCVRMODEL